Diamonds of August

Barbara Capell

Copyright 2020 Barbara Capell

All rights reserved.

Names, characters, locations and incidents portrayed in this book are creations of the author's imagination and are totally fiction. Any resemblance to actual events, locations, organizations, or persons, living or dead is entirely coincidental and beyond the intent of author or publisher.

Any unauthorized reproduction or distribution of this copyrighted work is illegal. No part of this book may be scanned, uploaded or distributed be the Internet or other means without permission of the Barbara Capell is prohibited.

Published in the United States of America

Copyright 2020 by Barbara Capell

ISBN: 9798615792878

Dedication

A very special thanks to Vicki Caine who guided me and never gave up.
Even though they are gone the women who saw in me what I didn't.
Elnora King, Rose Wolk and Betty Jarman

Chapter One

Summer 2014, Martha's Vineyard, Massachusetts

Claire, chilled by the afternoon breeze, stood cocooned in Jeff's arms. Droplets of ocean water beaded on his hair and reflected the setting sun. They moved as one performing a private dance with the sea while the tide shifted white sand beneath their feet. He rested his chin on her head. She nestled against the nape of his neck inhaling his musk. His afternoon beard brushed against her cheek and his lips kissed her forehead then the tip of her nose before he found her lips. Soft butterfly-wing kisses warmed her.

She looked into his eyes. Eyes filled with desire. A desire she wanted. A desire she deserved. A desire she thought lost to her forever.

She concentrated on his mouth as he whispered, "Stay with me, Claire."

"If only I could."

"I love you," he said against her lips.

She kissed him back, letting all her inhibitions dissolve. He held her tight and she let his hands explore her. She shivered as his fingers ran up her sides, igniting a fire low in her core.

"Claire!"

Her name drifted over the dunes.

She jolted from Jeff's embrace. She squinted into the sun but couldn't identify the figure stumbling toward her. The voice though …

"Claire."

Her limbs froze as her mind raced. How did her husband, who should be two hours and a ferry ride away, get here? To this private cove?

Huntington Lake, California, ten months earlier.

"Star light, star bright," Claire whispered to the moonless sky. "Make my …"

Claire Flannigan Richter believed in magic, plain and simple. She believed in the magic of leprechauns whose stories were dutifully delivered by her ever-so-Irish father. The wee people, as he liked to call them, were not only responsible for pots of gold but for diamonds and gemstones buried beneath the earth's crust. A vision she'd witnessed every year since turning five, watching the shooting stars in the sky—scattering diamonds.

Mark, her husband of twenty-eight years, didn't believe. There was a scientific explanation. They could never agree on the mystery of the sky but they both saw the beauty and shared the predictable and magical night with their children. Claire infused them with myth while Mark instructed them about cosmic events.

Every year their three, now adult, children, wished upon a star for their mother and reveled in the Irish beauty, and for their father discussed the facts about the Perseid Meteor Shower.

Colleen, Sean, and Mark were already around the campfire drinking hot cocoa and eating burnt marshmallows.

In the hammock, hung between two large sugar pines, Katie, her nineteen-year-old, snuggled with her newest flame, Peter.

"Wow," Peter said.

"Shush," Katie whispered as she put two fingers to Peter's lips.

"I've never seen this many shooting stars." Peter let Katie's fingers slip into his mouth. He sucked them, casting suggestive eyes on Claire's daughter.

Claire opened her mouth to demand they stop. Instead, she sighed and cast her eyes to the night sky. "I wish Katie would find a better boyfriend," she said softly to no one.

Katie scrambled out of the hammock then turned toward Peter. "We've been watching the falling stars for as long as I can remember. Mom used to tell us stories about leprechauns tossing diamonds to earth."

"I thought leprechauns had rainbows and pots of gold," Peter said.

A united moan filled the air. Their Flanagan blood rose to the challenge.

"Now you've done it," Mark said as he turned to Peter. "In reality, it's nothing more than a meteor shower. It happens every mid-August when Earth passes through the Swift Tuttle debris field."

"I prefer to see them as diamonds," Claire said.

"And we all humor her," Sean added, putting an arm around his mother.

One by one they gave up the night vigil and headed into the cabin until only Claire remained.

She wrapped her arms around her knees and watched the diamonds adorn the inky sky as she embraced the melancholy that seemed to chase her everywhere these days.

Close to dawn, Claire let the chill chase her inside. She slipped on her flannel gown and into her half of the bed, the sheets cold as she inched toward Mark. He stirred. She moved closer.

"Cold feet," he mumbled as he turned from her, pulling the down comforter tighter around himself.

Claire removed her feet but rolled against his back. Mark's gray sweatshirt smelled of Downy and smoke. A richness of memories rushed over her. She reached over his semi-curled body and whispered, "Wanna?" letting her hand stroke his shoulder, then down his back to cup his butt.

He scooted closer to his edge of the bed. "I'm trying to sleep."

Claire sighed and turned away to the warmth of her flannel gown and the embrace of the sheets. When was the last they'd made love? Easily six months. It had to be a Sunday afternoon because that was when Mark liked to have sex. She closed her eyes to summon the feelings, the smells, the sounds of that last afternoon. Was a mocking bird laughing or the jasmine blooming?

If she'd known it was going to be the last time, she would have memorized it all.

Chapter Two

Mark woke to the silence of the cabin. He sat up and listened for the chaos of family.

Nothing.

He must have missed breakfast and the good-byes. Why hadn't Claire awakened him to tell the kids bye and to drive safely and to call or text when they got home?

So, she waved the kids off and just left for her morning walk? He ran a hand over his stubbled chin.

They needed to talk, and the knowledge and dread kept him awake most of the night. An early outing would have been the ideal time. Hardness formed in his stomach. There was no good time to tell her. He should have said something six weeks ago when the issue first came up. He should have told her before they came up to the cabin. He should have done it when she roused him last night.

He'd had a dozen opportunities.

Lying on his back, he stared at a stain on the ceiling. He should paint it next year. He really should have painted it this summer, but with all the trouble at the winery he hadn't been able to make it up to the cabin as much as he wanted.

He couldn't fall back to sleep, but the bed seemed to have a magnetic pull on him. The last month, while Claire was up here, his new boss told him, Ahwahnee, the large winery he worked for, was reorganizing and his position would be eliminated. They offered Mark a transfer to Boston to lead the Public Relations section. Mark didn't want the "promotion."

He was an enologist, for God's sake, not a wine peddler. He rolled over and heaved a sigh. He wanted to promote and develop his own award-winning, rich, fruity wine from the vines he imported from Spain and South Africa. They already showed some promise. Last year, with a small harvest, he had enough at crush to run a limited production. It sold well, even won first place at the California Culinary Expo.

Mark lived for Rainbow's End, the vineyard he and Claire bought in the seventies, when the Paso Robles Hills were beginning to be competitive with the Napa Valley wineries.

He purchased the land just east of Shandon, eighteen months after he and Claire were married. His seventy acres, neatly planted against the foothills, became visible just as you dropped over the last of the Coastal Range from the Central Valley.

He pulled himself up and sat on the side of the bed. The old metal wind-up clock read nine-thirty, late for him. He liked to be up and out by daybreak. He looked again at the gray and perhaps moldy spot, appearing more like an alien wood-eating fungus. Maybe he'd paint it today.

He heaved a sigh. On second thought…why start a project he wasn't sure he could finish? They were leaving soon.

He liked knowing the end of a project before he started. Perhaps that's what was eating at him. He hadn't planned to move cross-country at fifty-seven and start over. His life was right where he wanted it and with the kids gone, Claire would be around more for him.

When he met Claire, he knew his future was tied to California. She was a beautiful young woman with wild auburn hair and flashing blue eyes. She beguiled him with made-up Irish stories. He'd given up trying to make them logical. He fell in love with her, elaborate fantasies and all.

He gazed at the ceiling again. The moldy stain seemed to grow even while he watched. The circle darkened, foamed, and grew into flesh-eating mold. He rubbed his arm, glanced at it to be sure nothing had sprouted there. No flesh eating bacteria, just bit of surface damage.

Damn that ceiling spot. Why did he care? But if he left the job to a handyman, the guy'd probably screw it up.

There was a correct way to do everything, so there must be a correct way to tell Claire he'd be fired if he didn't take the position in Boston. She would understand. He needed to stay employed three more years, and a job in this economy a blessing. By then he would be fully vested in the benefit package, Katie would be done with school, the second acreage producing, and he would retire. They could make it. He—

they—just needed to hang on a few more years. Claire would understand.

He hated getting old. He hadn't felt old until the younger, aggressive, new graduates were hired. And it wasn't their brains he feared competing with.

Chapter Three

"I'm back," Claire announced as she bounded up the porch steps and through the front door. "Mark? Where are you?" Her walk after waving goodbye to the kids had been a little longer than usual, but she'd needed the extra thinking time. Now she felt ready to face the journey home.

"In the bedroom."

"What are you doing?" she asked, surprised to find Mark on a ladder chipping away a part of the ceiling.

"Fixing this stain I didn't notice until this morning." His brow furrowed, as he scraped at a spot like it was the vector for Downy Mildew in all California vineyards.

"How long do you think it'll take?"

"Almost done. I'll paint the ceiling next year. Just want to do some prevention."

"Okay. I'll start packing."

She dragged their suitcases out to the porch for Mark to load in the back of the van, then busied herself with the rest of the tasks needed to close up the cabin for the fall.

Each chore included a memory. Turning off the water heaters reminded her of the ski trip they had to boil water over the fireplace for baths. Opening the taps after she'd turned off the water reminded her of the year she'd missed draining a pipe and they'd come back in the spring to a flooded bathroom. The floor was still a bit warped in there. Some people might sand it down, make it all perfect. She treasured the imperfections. It proved real people lived and loved here.

What did Mark think about while he prepared to leave? For her, every dish, every windowsill, every crack in the tile reminded Claire of times gone by. In the mountain cabin the kids stayed babies, her parents were physically active, Mark remained passionately young. Years of good memories and dreams soaked the half-hewn logs that made up the walls. On the bedroom doorframe, each child's age and height remained recorded, including her and her brothers'.

"Ready?" Mark called.

"Yeah," she responded.

He'd already be in the front seat, adjusting the mirrors, fiddling with the radio dial and drumming his fingers on the steering wheel.

They backed out of the gravel driveway, onto the mountain road. The car stirred the dust as they started the drive. They always stopped halfway and spent the night at Claire's childhood home.

Mark liked the routine. Claire loved the ritual.

He looked at his watch. "Four thirty-eight," he announced. "We should be in Fresno by six-fifteen."

The access road to the main highway was slow with large potholes making the ride bumpy, requiring Claire to hang onto the grab bar above the door. Once they reached the highway they turned right and headed down the mountain. It was thirty miles into Shaver, the lake below Huntington, and the switch-backed road remained dangerous.

Claire opened the window, drinking in the last remnants of the sweet balsam smell. Trees cast shadows, with flashes of sun peeking through. Equal parts of sadness and excitement filled her. Sad to say good-bye to the lake but excited to learn if she would get the full-time position to oversee the development of the day care component at the Women's Center where she worked.

She'd written the grant last year and learned mid-summer it was funded. She applied for the position and was confident she'd get the director job. Mark and the kids no longer needed her at home full time, and the extra money wouldn't hurt. Down deep she bubbled with pride. She hadn't shared the news with Mark, waiting until it became a real offer.

When Claire saw Shaver Lake off in the distance, she exhaled with relief. The hard part of the trip was behind them. She studied Mark's face. It had creased like fine, tanned leather into a sun-etched carving. His sharp blue eyes sunk deeper than usual though. A knot formed in her stomach. He hadn't slept well last night. "Want me to drive?"

"No."

"You look...tired." She paused. "You okay?"

"Yeah." Mark's fingers gripped the steering wheel. "Claire, we need to talk."

She twisted in her seat belt and waited for him to speak. "Any sentence that starts with those words rarely ends well."

"I'm being transferred to Boston."

Claire's stomach lurched, her breath escaped. She needed air. "I don't understand. What? Why?"

"I've tried to tell you about all the problems at work,"

His jaw clenched. Claire examined his set chin and closed her eyes. He wasn't in a discussion mood.

Her mind reeled. "Mark, back up." Her back stiffened. "Tell me what you're talking about." She searched her memory for any hint of this. No. None. She was sure.

Mark's eyes stayed fixed on the road. "I've been telling you things are bad at the winery, with all the re-organization last spring," he said. "I thought I could keep my position, but apparently, I can quit or move."

"Bad, yes. Boston, no. Start from the beginning. Tell me what happened."

He glanced toward her for a brief second then focused back on the road. His lips were moving but Claire couldn't hear him.

"Pull over. I'm going to be sick." She clapped a hand over her mouth.

He took the next turnout, crossing in front of an oncoming car.

"Shit, Mark! You damn near got us killed."

Mark braked to a stop and Claire bolted from the front seat to the boulder barrier at the side of the road. She bent at the waist, grabbed her knees and gagged.

Mark climbed out of the car. "You don't get car sick."

Bile burned her throat. Claire staggered to the nearest rock. Her head throbbed. She closed her eyes against the sun.

"You okay?" Mark asked.

"A little dizzy."

He handed her a towel from the back of the car. Claire wiped the dampness off her upper lip and breathed deeper. The scent of the manzanita bushes rose to meet her. She gazed out over the cliff. The San Joaquin Valley lay below. It was one of the few views of her birthplace unobstructed by trees. The irrigated farmland looked like a patchwork quilt of varying shades of green. Did Mark really expect her to leave this for Boston?

"I don't understand what happened."

Mark was done talking, but she was screaming on the inside. She wanted her new job, not a move. Not now.

It was finally *her* turn.

Until now, their life had been about supporting Mark, about his career goals, about nurturing the kids. She'd been a good daughter, a good mother, a fine friend, but now...now she needed life to be about *her*. She wanted this new opportunity at work, to see the day care center through the first few years.

She raised a shaky hand to swipe at her mouth. Why hadn't she said something sooner about the possibility of her promotion? She and Mark were living together, sharing the same house but no longer telling each other what was important in their lives.

"We need to talk about what I want to do." Claire sat on a boulder, let her head drop.

"What you want to do?" He sounded doubtful, like she'd suggested a theatre company in the barn at the winery.

"About what we're going to do," she amended while looking out and letting the toe of her shoe inch over the edge. She sighed. If only a solution would drop from the sky. "I have a job, too." She folded her arms over her chest. "Can't we talk about my thoughts, my feelings? My position in this?"

"We can talk all you want, but the facts remain the same." He lowered his chin, met her gaze and spoke levelly. "I need the job, Claire, and the job is in Boston."

He kicked at a rock. Claire watched it tumble away, out of his path, leaving a dust trail that wisped away in the breeze. And she felt just like that rock, a pebble to be kicked away.

She ignored the hand he offered and strode past him to the car. She closed her door, buckled her seat belt.

A part of her spirit was left on that boulder at the mile-high turnout on Highway 180.

Chapter Four

Mark concentrated on the twisted, heavily traveled highway. One miscalculation and he might be in a head-on collision with some inexperienced mountain driver. He tried to force the image of Claire, sick on the side of the road, out of his mind, but it replayed like a movie.

They had been over rougher roads and she never got carsick. They had been over rougher times in their marriage and survived. For the first time, he worried they faced a challenge he might not be able to fix.

What was different this time? Claire hadn't lived outside of California but in the past, she would have viewed this as an adventure. They always set a goal and achieved it. Together.

The vineyard, their vineyard, produced some of the finest grapes and last year, with Claire's insistence, the wine Mark blended became a winner at the state fair. He would have waited another year or two before risking an entry. Not Claire, always the one forging ahead and willing to take the chance. She stood behind him, supporting his dreams.

The last time he saw Claire carsick was when she was expecting Katie and for a moment he wondered if Claire might be pregnant. They were both too old for that, besides they hadn't had sex in months. That was something else falling apart. He'd lost his drive along with his power. Claire didn't seem to notice. Should they talk about it? He wasn't comfortable talking about sex. It should just happen, like waking up or yawning.

He looked over at her and decided not to bring it up now. She sat straight, motionless and silent in her seat. In less than an hour, they'd be at her parents. They couldn't spend the time there not speaking.

He wanted to break the silence, but how?

She would eventually see Boston was their only choice.

Claire loved her father, and he worshiped his daughter.

Mark hadn't always loved his father-in-law. Their relationship started out strained since Mark wasn't the man Paddy thought his daughter should marry. Paddy told long Irish stories that rarely had any basis in reality.

Paddy refused to figure out the simple things around the house that needed to be done and that is where Mark shined. So they learned to respect each other's skills. Over time the respect slipped toward love.

Claire's mother remained more a mystery. She, in contrast to Paddy, spoke softly and rarely to Mark. She wore red lipstick on her permanent smile. She raised three children, Claire being the youngest and only girl. Mother and daughter were close, and they talked without speaking, as if they read each other's mind.

Mark loved to watch them in the kitchen. He and Paddy would sit at the table, sipping a brandy, while Claire and Alma silently washed dishes.

"You okay, Claire?" he finally mustered.

"Fine." She stared out the passenger window.

"Do we need to stop again?"

"No."

She didn't look his way, but he studied her reflection in the window. This would not blow over within the next hour.

They were out of the foothills now with the remainder of the road straight and long.

Claire ground her teeth, afraid of what might pour out of her if she opened her mouth. She didn't look at Mark. Instead she concentrated on the passing landscape.

A thousand arguments ran through her head. She carried on both sides of the conversation, without including him. The first part of the trip, from the turn out to the rolling hills, was the furious part. *Again, another decision without including me.*

Her anger flared so intensely it frightened her. She wanted to release the words that screamed in her head. This insult became one more piece of kindling to add to the flames she suppressed.

Missed birthdays.

Forgotten anniversaries.

Comments about her age, the gray in her hair, the new wrinkles.

Dogs he found and brought home to dig in her garden. And on and on.

Some wounds were big, some so small, even she resisted believing they still bothered her.

But now she held onto every offense as the voice in her head raged on, pouring more fuel on the fire with each passing mile.

Her contribution was no longer needed. She twisted her wedding band. Mark should be concerned, treating her as a partner in their future. Instead he examined options and presented them as solutions and conclusions and never considered any alternatives.

After a faltered attempt at marriage counseling, she became more comfortable living a parallel life. What they did together centered on the family. They shared a love of good food and wine and on Sunday afternoons they would share the intimacy of the bed, but now even that connection had disappeared.

What still held her to Mark? With a sigh she slipped the ring past her knuckle and quickly slid it back into place.

She wanted a marriage like her parents, one the heavens envied. On their anniversary, her father gave her mother a rose for each year of their marriage. Mom made Dad's favorite meal, corned beef and cabbage, and served it on the Wedgewood plates she inherited from his mother.

Mark never wasted money on flowers that would die. Instead he purchased bare root roses in December, on sale. He could have added a diamond to her ring on their twenty-fifth, three years ago, but instead he bought a new water pump. He purchased the second vineyard four years ago and had all the negotiations done before he told her. How could he put them in further in debt without consulting her? She could have refused to sign the mortgage papers. The mortgage added more fuel to the fire of wrongs. The second vineyard was a good purchase, but again without consulting her.

As the litany of offenses mounted, Claire cried in her heart below the rage. She understood her hurt. She understood her anger. She didn't understand the lingering fear.

Chapter Five

"There's Dad watering his lawn," Mark said as he turned into Claire parent's home. "I wonder why he still uses the hose. I put in sprinklers for him two summers ago."

"Are they broken?" Claire asked.

"Shouldn't be." Mark opened the window. "I bet he messed with the timer again." Mark muttered. He waved at his father-in-law. "What are you doing?"

"Watering, Goof Ball, can't you see what I'm doing?"

Long ago Mark learned to play and tease with his father-in-law. In the early years, Paddy constantly played tricks on Mark. He had been raised to respect his elders and Paddy's love of life and play took a while to get used to.

He made everyone laugh with endless jokes and pranks. Mark wished sometimes that he could be more like the stocky, ruddy-skinned man. In contrast to Mark's angular features, Paddy was a study in roundness. At only five foot eight he was a bald, aging elf. His girth ample and often his belt would rise and fall as he laughed.

"Why hand watering?"

"Some damn fool put in a crappy sprinkling system," Paddy said. He crimped the hose, "Alma and I thought you got lost."

Wiping her hands on a green kitchen towel, Alma stood on the raised cement porch.

"Finally, I was beginning to worry," Alma said as Mark closed the car door and climbed the step.

"Hi, Mother Flanagan," Mark said as he kissed her cheek.

"Hi, Mom," Claire added.

Alma pushed a stubborn lock of hair away from Claire's face then kissed and hugged her tightly.

"I just made potato salad and set out some cold cuts. It's too hot to cook these days."

Mother and daughter walked arm in arm into the house, chattering about the heat, talking in soft voices about siblings, pansies in flower pots, a new porch swing and of course potato salad.

Mark joined Paddy while they rolled the hose in a serpent-like coil. Both men worked together like men do. Side-by-side. Mark liked doing things with his father-in-law, they made sense to him, nothing like he and Claire trying to work on a project.

Once, when they planned to paint the kitchen, Claire wanted to spend hours discussing which color on the wall made her feel best. Was it a cheerful wake-up-yellow or Celadon? A color didn't have feelings. But, oh no, Claire had to have a shade of yellow that said, "This is morning and welcome to me." He was not about to go to Home Depot and ask the paint guy for that. He asked for yellow. He would stick with Paddy and other men who understood yellow, broken pipes, and neatly curled hoses.

Before Mark knew it, he had eaten his fill of sliced turkey, potato salad, fresh melon and berries. Claire was still not her bubbly self but at least she was talking. She and her mother discussed the upcoming Labor Day party. They talked menus and memories. Mark listened with contentment. A full belly, good people, and his wife making future plans, all a man could ask. Perhaps the fight was over.

It was time for him and Paddy to share a brandy and good cigar.

"Open the windows, Patrick," Alma directed her husband. "If you insist on smoking those stinky things in my kitchen, then open the windows."

Mark chuckled. "Alma, you say that every time he lights up."

"And you'd think he would learn to open the windows after all these years," she finished.

They clipped the tip of the cigar, dipped it in the brandy snifter, licked the sides and flicked the special cigar lighting torch. Mark really didn't like the taste of the cigar, but he enjoyed the manly ritual. He followed Paddy's lead. He swirled the brandy, sniffed it, tipped the crystal bowl, so the rim rested on the bridge of his nose and sipped the first of the warm liquid.

When Alma put the last dish in the cupboard, she announced it was time for a game of Scrabble. Mark really didn't want to play but again it was what you did after dinner in the Flanagan house. He would have rather taken a walk or watched the news. Claire, clever, always went for the triple word boxes. Mark was happy if he found a single word in the jumble of letters lined up on the worn wooden ledge in front of him. How many times had that box been opened, the pieces dumped, turned face down on the table?

They played well into the night, Claire laughing when she challenged her father's spelling of chignon. He swore it was with a *sh*. The Oxford English Dictionary was called for.

The two volumes of the OED rested on an old maple telephone stand alongside a desk lamp and magnifying glass. It became the ultimate referee in a competitive game.

"You made it up," he accused.

The beginning of a giggle erupted from Claire, as she squinted looking for the word, handing the magnifying glass to her father.

"Look for yourself."

Her father teased her like only a father can. Alma bragged about her daughter taking after her side of the family. Paddy, looking closely at the page, to save dignity said, "Must be the Irish spelling."

"Right," Claire said. "Irish spell it with 'sh'? Then why does the dictionary say French origin with a Latin root?"

"Damn book was written by a Brit," he said.

They loved each other. Mark sensed it in their play. Claire's eyes danced. Her hair, still a shade of red, flew wildly around her face. She kept it cut shorter, but the natural curl would never lay flat against her head.

"Is that a word?" Mark asked trying to join in.

Claire looked right past him. "Look it up," she said pushing the magnifying glass across the table toward him.

The game dragged on well past Mark's bedtime, and Claire didn't let up with the snide, side comments. Ranking this as one of the worst games he had ever played, and he played a lot of bad games. Claire even challenged her father. That was rare, and she sent him repeatedly to the dictionary. Her bad humor spilt over, and he was no longer her only target.

Looking at his watch Mark announced, "Time for this old soldier to hit the sack."

"Me too," said Paddy. "Got to wake this useless son-in-law up early so he can fix the sprinklers." Bowing at the waist, he said, "Good night fine ladies," before disappearing up the stairs.

Claire stayed in the kitchen with her mother putting the Scrabble game away.

"Should I put the kettle on for a spot of tea?" Alma asked, stretching an old rubber band around the frail cardboard game box.

"That would be nice."

The offer of tea at 11:30 at night meant her mother sensed something was wrong.

"Pull up a chair and talk," Alma finally said.

"I don't know, Mom." Claire fingered the groves of the table.

"Just talk, say whatever, and a story will come."

All the Flanagan children solved their problems at the round oak table while Mom served tea. She never asked questions. Mom would sit, pour tea, stir in a sweet lump and listen. If it were a big problem, she would take one of the square lumps of sugar in her teeth and suck the tea through it. Claire drank her tea without adornment unless with Mom. The mixture in the cup would be a beige swirl against ecru china. Her granny's old Dalton teapot was a healing vessel. Claire stared at the crackled glaze and viewed each slightly stained line as a sorrow absorbed. The teapot became a vessel of continuity and history.

As the tea poured out, Claire poured out her woes. The mantel clock in the living room chimed, 2:30. The evening breeze lifted the sheers that hung in the windows. They looked like a floating angel wanting to join in. The delicious, perfumed night jasmine growing along the fence blended with the roses her father grew. In this spot, with scents of her past swirling around and Mom's Jergen-lathered hands, healing began.

With the teapot empty, Alma reached over and touched her daughter's arm. "Claire, what happened to the girl who loved life and saw adventure around every corner?"

"I don't know." Claire ran a finger around the cup rim.

"Find her." Alma rose from the table, took the pot to the sink, softly rinsed it and discarded the dregs of leaves along with the sorrows of the evening. Once clean, she placed the pot on the corner shelf.

"Remember dear, where you came from and cherish it. Grow from it. Pass it on."

"Good night, Mommy." Claire rose and kissed her mother on the cheek. Alma embraced her daughter. Claire went to her childhood room and crawled into the empty twin bed across from Mark.

Filled with the strength of her mother's love, Claire fell asleep. She dreamt of stars falling. She was little and stood alone, staring up into the star-dense sweep of the Milky Way.

"I see sparkles, Daddy," Claire said pointing her finger skyward.

"Those are leprechauns' diamonds and they are there just for you," Paddy said as he picked her up, giving her a tight hug. "Look." He pointed to the eastern sky. "They just threw one to you. Can you catch it?"

She held out both hands and then giggled back into her father's arms. Paddy rocked her until she fell asleep then carried her to bed. He tucked her in, kissed her forehead and whispered, "No need to be scared. Your daddy is always here to protect you."

Chapter Six

Claire woke to the noise of men talking and digging outside her bedroom window. She blinked at the unfamiliar wallpaper and rosebud dotted valence over the window.

Oh, right. She was in her childhood home, between sheets that held the fragrance of the sun. She stole a glance at the alarm clock. 6:25. Grabbing the pillow, she buried her head seeking more of the safety of her old bed.

"Get me a shovel," Mark hollered.

"You got one right there," Paddy answered.

"I need one with a point to break through this hard pan."

By the sound of clinking mugs in the kitchen, Claire knew her mother would be pouring coffee for the men from the old Farberware percolator.

When Mom headed down the two steps, the first always creaked, to the service porch past the washer and dryer, where she would rest the cups long enough to open the back door.

Memorized from childhood, Claire listened to the sounds of this house awakening.

"Morning, men," her mom called. "I brought you both coffee."

It wasn't fair to lie in bed while Mom made breakfast, and Claire reluctantly threw the covers back and quickly dressed in shorts and tank top.

"I'm up, Mom," she called from the door.

"Good. I can use your help."

Her mother, like the old Farberware coffee pot, remained a remnant of the fifties. Mom, in contrast to Claire, had already done her make-up, donned a cotton shift and happily made the men in her life breakfast.

"Should I set the table inside or out?" Claire asked as she joined her mother in the kitchen.

"Inside. Your brother Paul will be stopping by, so set a plate for him."

Paul, two years older than Claire, often stopped by for breakfast. He had taken over the insurance company when Dad retired, and her brother kept their father posted on what was happening. Dad liked hearing the latest gossip and Paul liked getting breakfast.

"Got some waffles for the laborers?" Paddy asked leading the men in.

Paul walked past his mother, kissed her on the cheek, and grabbed for a piece of bacon off the platter she held.

"Paulie!" Mom reprimanded.

Automatically taking their childhood seats, with Mark taking Mike's unused chair, they chatted noisily, about the day's events, people Claire barely remembered and the comings and goings of all their children.

"So, what's new at the winery?" Paul asked Mark.

"Not good," Mark answered.

Paul put his mug down and looked at his brother-in-law. "Tell me more."

"Well, the new management is of the opinion I should take a promotion and work with the marketing team in Boston."

"And?"

"I accepted it."

Claire felt the waffle go dry in her mouth as he continued. "It's a good raise. I only have three years until I can retire with full benefits. I figure Claire and I can do anything for that long." Claire saw him glance her way.

He accepted it? When? Was she losing her mind or memory? He told her family before he told her. Nice. He knew she wouldn't chew him out in front of everyone. But just wait.

"You going to get a job in Boston, Sissy?" Paul asked after swallowing.

There was no question in anyone's mind, except Claire's, that she would be moving with Mark.

"I don't know," she answered.

"Well, she won't have to," Mark said.

Claire's jaw tightened at the thought it appeared Mark alone decided she didn't need to work. "Just what will I do?" she demanded.

"Whatever you like," he said.

She turned to Mark and stared him down. *I want to stay here.* The silence at the table hung as thick as Paddy's brogue until Alma asked Claire to help with the dishes.

Claire, with a bit of attitude, cleared the table, while the men fled the scene to finish the sprinklers.

Close to eleven, Claire announced it was time to head home. Home where she thought she would be spending the rest of her life.

It was ninety-three miles to Shandon. The road and rest stops scored in her mind like an old song. Claire had done this trip so many times: the ranch to Mom and Dad's, then up the highway to the mountain retreat, back down the hill to the house on Clay, then past cotton fields and rolling hills to the ranch. Her parents secure in the middle, like a fulcrum, of a well-traveled highway. Yes, they were the balance she sought.

Mark in his driving mode, eyes fixed, teeth clenched, ears listening to the hum of the engine, said nothing. She thought about talking to him but decided against it. She would choose what she wanted to do, alone. She realized she still hadn't let Mark know about her job offer. She should have said something, like he had, in front of the family.

Mark broke the silence. "Penny for your thoughts?"

"Just thinking about how many times we've traveled this road."

"Claire?"

"Yeah?"

"Tell me what's wrong," he asked. Then, as if he had been reading her mind, "Are you coming to Boston?"

"You should have asked me sooner…" She drew a breath. "I should've been part of the decision."

"What difference would that make? It's out of my hands."

"I could go to work full time, and you could work the vineyard and let Jessie go."

"That won't work." He declared it and put the period at the end of the thought when he jutted his chin.

"I haven't told you, yet, but my grant was funded, and I've been offered the job as director of the child-care center." She exhaled slowly and continued, "It would be full time and I would be making a good salary."

"We can't survive the next three years on your salary if I wasn't working."

"You could work the vineyard."

"I can't make the second vineyard grow any faster and it's at least two years from being enough for us to live off." Frustration escalated in his voice. "Besides we need my retirement. I don't want to lose that after all this time."

Claire closed her eyes against the facts he insisted on enumerating.

Mark continued, "Don't ask me to throw it away."

Her brief fantasy Mark would embrace the idea of her getting the promotion and being the main income, sucked out his open window.

"I just don't know if I can go," she finally said.

"You can do whatever you decide to do."

"I am not sure I *want* to," she corrected. "I want to run the Child Care Project." After a long pause, she muttered, "I have dreams, too."

Her body a whirlwind of emotions, she looked ahead. They passed the first set of hills outside Kettleman City. Sunburned grass laid on both sides of the flat and straight road. Gusts of wind blew up dirt devils that whirled randomly. She saw one off in the distance and watched it slowly gaining speed as it headed her way, crossing the two-lane highway just in front of her. As a little girl she imagined them as wind ghosts and wished she could spin as fast.

"Mark?"

"What?"

"I need some time to absorb all this. I need to figure out what I am going to do with my clients."

The dust ghost caught her in its vortex, and she was spinning too fast.

Chapter Seven

After a long, hot, drive they arrived home in a cloud of silence. Turning onto the hardened dirt road leading up the hill to the 1930s farmhouse they had refurbished, her shoulders relaxed, and her neck finally eased. Soon Mark's dog, Bear, ran to greet them.

They drove slowly past the first few acres of vines, green with hope, past the shed that housed the tractors and equipment, then past the newer, simpler stucco house of the foreman, Jessie. He waved as they passed.

"Hola, Boss!" Jessie called.

"Hola, Amigo," Mark yelled back.

Claire saw Marta, Jessie's wife, standing at the kitchen window. They waved at each other. Jessie and Marta had come to work for Mark twenty-two years ago and somewhere along the way they had become family. The men shared a love of the fertile land they understood. Marta found out she was pregnant with her first and only child, Cecilia, two months after Claire discovered she was pregnant with Katie.

"I'll be up with the mail later," Jessie called after their car.

Mark flashed him a thumbs-up and continued to the last of the incline toward the garage. Bear now ran alongside them, barking and shaking his plumed tail. He was a mutt of unknown origin. His face and body had a hint of shepherd, but the tail was that of a Golden Retriever. Not an especially good-looking dog in Claire's opinion, and the fact that he still growled at her didn't improve their relationship. Katie had found him alongside the road, hit by a car, leaving him with a deformed left leg. She soon lost interest in the daily healing of the dog but Mark didn't.

Mark reached for the garage opener. He slid the car in and set the hand brake.

"Home," he announced.

She just gave him a side-glance. As Mark lifted the hatch to the back of the SUV, Claire unlocked the side door. She stepped up into the service porch and smelled lemon-oiled wood, Tide-laundered clothes and a hint of nutmeg. Her house always had a hint of nutmeg that she couldn't find.

She put her purse down on the kitchen counter and looked around, making sure everything was still in place. Of course it was just as she left it. She glanced over her shoulder at Mark behind her, hauling a cardboard box of supplies.

"In the kitchen?" he asked as he set it down.

"Yeah." She started to unpack and put the contents in their proper places.

Mark was out the side door and back before she really began.

"You want the suitcases in the bedroom or the laundry?"

"Laundry," she replied.

Then from the open door he yelled, "What about the box of pinecones?"

"Leave them in the garage."

"What?"

"I said leave them in the garage," she yelled back.

"Where?"

Claire breathed deep. "In the garage, Mark."

"Where in the garage?"

By now Mark was in the kitchen with the box of pinecones Claire had gathered to use for Christmas decorations.

"Just put them down."

He slammed them on the counter top.

She fumed as he kept marching in and out, dropping boxes off, pulling rags from under the sink, filling buckets with warm water to clean his car and in general getting in her way.

It all happened in the flash of a moment.

Claire had just picked up the can of Yuban dark roast coffee when Bear ran past her, making her drop the can. Fine coffee grounds sailed through the air and landed on the floor. She backed into Mark who passed with a full bucket of water. In slow motion, waterfalls of soapy water arched out of the bucket to mix with the fine ground beans.

Claire's cat chose that moment to sashay into the room. Bear gave chase and when he hit the water, slid across the adobe-tiled floor. In his scramble to keep the cat in sight, he churned the water, soap, and coffee into a lathery mess.

"Shit!" Claire screamed.

"Bear! Stop," a drenched Mark commanded.

But by now the dog had tracked soap and coffee into the den. Pooh Cat jumped on the windowsill while Bear returned obediently to his master, wet tail wagging, shaking water on the walls.

"Mark," Claire yelled at the top of her lungs as Mark led Bear to the back door.

"Why are you yelling at me?" Mark hollered back.

"It's your dog and you left the door open."

"So? It isn't my fault the dog decided to chase your stupid cat."

"Whose fault is it?"

"No one's, Claire. It's nobody's fault. It just happened." Mark grabbed a towel from the kitchen drawer and wiped himself before throwing it on the floor to soak up some of the mess.

"Don't use my good kitchen towels on the floor."

"Damn it, Claire."

"Damn it nothing. Pay attention, will you? You have royally messed this place up." Words flew faster than she could control. Her face burned with anger.

"What should I use?"

"Grab some rags from the garage."

"And open the back door again? Are you sure I won't let the dog back in? Are you sure I'm capable of getting the right rags for Your Highness?" The words were spoken in an overly controlled tone as Mark stood, hands in the air, not moving toward the door.

"Stop it, Mark."

"Stop what? Cleaning up? Unpacking? Living? What, exactly, should I stop, Claire?"

Claire drew a deep breath. Tears formed in the corner of her eyes. She pushed past Mark, stomping out to the garage. She returned with an armful of the old T-shirts she called floor rags. She tossed them, with exaggerated motion, to the floor.

"Do you want my help or not?" Mark asked, hands now on hips.

"Help? No, Mark, I want you to leave."

"Leave?"

"This mess is all your fault. I'm sick and tired of having to clean up your messes. Just leave me alone. Get out of my kitchen. Get out of my house. Go to Boston and do whatever you want. I'm staying here. I've made up my mind."

"Grow up, Claire."

Hot anger burned her throat. She was an adult too. *He* messed up the house. *He* messed up their life. She didn't need any of this. She was hardly breathing as she tried to regain control. Tears threatened to roll down her dry cheeks. She wanted to be left alone. She wanted to hurt him. For the first time in their marriage, she really wanted him to leave.

"Claire, you're a fucking mess."

That was it. Mark never cussed. Now she had his attention and he wouldn't ignore her or pretend that it was okay. Now, for sure he knew his decision to move wasn't what she wanted.

"Fucking?" Claire felt the *f* sound strangely cross her lips, and it actually felt right. It felt good. Liberating. "Don't you ever use that word in this house," she said with force, "do you hear me?"

"I, and half the world, hear you, Claire."

"Well then let them hear this—" Her voice cracked. "You've fucked up my life."

"I thought we were not to use that word in our house," he said in a measured voice.

"Get it right for a change, Mark. *You* are not to use that word in my house."

"Your house?"

"Yes."

"And where do I live?"

"Boston, I guess."

"Are we fighting about Boston or coffee?"

"We're fighting about my right to decide where I live."

As the dammed-up tears exploded from her, the sound of the old diesel pickup heading up the drive reached her, and she didn't care. It was Jessie, of course, coming to check the vines before dark and drop off the mail. Mark turned toward the window.

"Here comes Jessie," Mark said with irritating calmness.

"I hear. I'm not deaf."

"Get the mail."

"You get the mail," she said with her back to him. "Just leave and take that damned dog with you."

Mark headed to the bedroom.

"The side door is open," she called out the window as both Jessie and Marta got out of the truck. Claire wiped away the tears and put on her game face.

"Careful, we had a bit of an accident," she said as they looked down at the brown wet mess on the floor and tracked into the den.

"Oh my," said Marta. "What happened?"

"Long story, but Bear, the cat, a bucket of water and a can of coffee all collided." The edited short version all she wanted to share.

Jessie smiled big and almost laughed till Marta gave him a stare that warned him not to.

"Where is Mr. Mark?" he asked.

"Changing. He was at the epicenter of the explosion. You're just in time to rescue him and the dog by taking them out to walk the vines." Claire tried to lighten the atmosphere still hanging in the room.

Jessie placed the mail on the still dry oak table. Marta had already started moving the floor rags with her feet, cleaning a path. She carried a basket of fresh fruit that she set on the same table.

"I'll help you clean up," she offered.

About then Mark came down the hall tucking a clean white t-shirt into his old faded Levi's. He half bowed to Marta and took Jessie's hand in his. "Good to see you both."

"You men leave. Claire and I will clean this up. Men are useless in the kitchen," Marta said. "Better in the yard."

Claire saw Mark look over his shoulder at her.

"Go." Marta grabbed a roll of paper towels and started wiping the counter muddle into a pile. "We'll get this."

"You don't have to help, Marta," Claire said.

But Marta had already gathered the wet rags into a bucket, rinsing them.

"What a mess," Marta whispered softly as both women bent on their knees to get a better angle on the job ahead.

Marta whispered in soft song-like tones. Asking how was the vacation? How were the kids? What were they doing? Who were they dating? Claire automatically answered. Not really listening nor correctly responding. Finally, they finished the cleanup and with one-sided questions about Claire's summer exhausted.

"Did I tell you that Cece was accepted to medical school?" Marta asked.

"Really?"

"Imagine, my baby a doctor," Marta said, her tone infused with pride.

Imagine indeed. Katie wasn't even ready to graduate. Cecilia finished college in three years and accepted to medical school. Claire and Marta sat for a moment looking at each other, then Claire continued listening to Marta's joy, sharing her pride in Cecelia, wondering if she'd failed Katie.

Chapter Eight

Monday morning, Claire felt like sprinting into her small office at the Women's Center, even though she'd hardly slept the night before.

After sitting at her desk, she riffled through the stack of pink memos while her computer booted up. Most of the notes were generated by the long weekend staff and only one really needed her immediate attention. In front of her lay the official job offer with a red *Sign Here* sticky.

She read it. Then read it again. After picking up her pen, she poised it over the signature line while last night's fight replayed in her head. With a shaking hand, she made a paper-denting C.

The office door opened. "Miss Claire, Miss Val says to meet her for lunch," Mary, her secretary, announced.

Mary, one of Claire's first clients, came to the shelter late one night with a broken nose and two black eyes, all the result of not having her husband's dinner on the table when he came home from a night of drinking. Despite her Master's in Social Work, Claire had not been prepared for such violence, or the hopelessness many of the victims faced.

She placed the pen on the veneer desk top.

"Thank you, Mary. Did she say where?"

"Downtown Diner." Mary laughed. "Someday you ladies are going somewhere else but, in the meantime, she'll meet you there."

The morning passed quickly with phone calls to be returned and emails responded to until finally Claire pushed past the noontime patrons into the diner. Val would have secured a booth already.

Sure enough, she waved from a spot along the wall. "Glad you're back," Val said as Claire slipped on to the bench seat.

"Good to be back...I think."

Val, still studying the list of lunch options, peered over her glasses. "You think?"

"Long story. Let's order first."

Both Claire and Val put the menu down and looked toward the approaching waitress bringing them water.

"You girls ready?"

Val answered for both of them. "We'll each have a side salad and share an order of chili fries with extra cheese—" She glanced at Claire — "and two of your thickest chocolate shakes."

"Now, spill." Val reached for her water. "If this is about the job offer on your desk, I already know about it. It's been the office buzz for a week."

"Sorta." Claire looked at Val and wondered how much she could tell her best friend and co-worker. "The short story is Mark announced, and I mean *announced*, he's taking a position in Boston."

Val put her glass down, splashing a bit of the water onto the faux wood grain. "What?"

Claire made a *shushing* motion and nodded. "He's been told that to keep his job with Ahwahnee, he must take a position in Boston."

Val shook her head. Her mouth fell open and her hand reached out for Claire. "Continue."

"It's complicated, and I'm still trying to put it all together myself." Claire picked at an overdone fry. "Apparently while I was at the cabin the last two weeks, Mark's boss made it clear that they need—" Claire made air quotes. "—no, insist on him moving to Boston to head up the promotion department. Honest, Val, I haven't been told the whole story. I'm learning more every day."

"Tell me what you do know or suspect."

"Not much. Mark and I are hardly talking yet it has consumed the last two days. The facts are simple. Mark didn't take the position of CEO last year, so the winery hired a guy from Washington. My suspicion is Mark is in the way, and the workers still look to him for direction."

"Is that enough to send him to Boston? Isn't there a role for Mark here?"

"I thought so. But I don't really understand what happens at the winery, so who knows how Mark came across. He can be opinionated." Claire reached across her delivered food order for her shake and took a long pull on the straw. "Once he refused to use what he considered inferior grapes, and the corporate people had to come out to settle it."

"I forgot that, but didn't the bosses back him?"

"Yeah, but Mark's name was mud for a few years. He had to prove he could be a team player."

Val nodded, chewing a bite of salad. "That isn't his best trait."

Claire barely touched her half of the fries while she unraveled the story of the "Announcement," as she labeled it. Val sat, ate slowly, and listened. Claire talked on and on.

Val finally grabbed Claire's hand and stopped her. "This is a lot deeper than not telling you about a job. And you know it." Val paused then... "So...what do *you* want?"

As soon as Val asked, the whirlwind in Claire's head stopped. The fight wasn't about just Boston or coffee. What did she want?

She set down her fork, folded her hands behind her plate, and spoke slowly. "I want Mark to respect me, to treat me like an equal, to talk and laugh with me. I want a marriage like Mom's. For him to just once, put my desires before his. I want the man I thought I married."

Val's face filled with sympathy.

Claire shook her head. "I've been empty for a while now, and I had hoped the new project would make me feel ..." She hesitated "... happy, like I was doing something. Or at least fulfilled? Is that too much to ask? Nothing makes me happy anymore. I thought after the kids left, Mark and I would find what we used to have. Instead..." Her voice trailed off.

"Instead what?"

"I don't know him anymore. He's drifting away."

"Are you sure he's the one drifting?" Val asked.

Irritation rose in Claire's chest. "Whose side are you on?"

"It's not about sides. It's about what's happening. Mark has always been a predictable, driven man."

Claire shrugged. Predictable, yes that was one word to describe Mark. He was always a man who made a decision and moved on it. Why did it bother her now?

The tears welled up again. "What should I do?"

Val leaned closer, pierced Claire with her clear gaze. "No one can answer that for you, Claire. I think you're angry with Mark and probably have been for a while. In some way he's disappointed you. But only you know how," Val looked down then continued "and remember when you start deconstructing a marriage, well, lots of old rotten wood is found."

Claire forced a smile. "I hate when you use metaphors."

The waitress passed and asked if they wanted dessert. They declined, and she left the bill on the table's edge.

"I'm around. I'll listen. But this is something you have to work out. I can't imagine you guys separating." After a pause in which they both dug through their wallets for cash to leave with a generous tip, Val leaned toward Claire. "Do you think Mark would consider marriage counseling?"

They looked at each other. Then at the same moment both shook their heads, and said aloud, "Men!"

Claire finished her day at the office, the conversation with Val nagging at her. Claire wasn't ready to make a final decision on which fork in the road to take. The unknown and uncertain road to Boston or the one that would keep her nestled deep into the coastal hills she loved.

On the way home, as she passed the cattle grazing at the brown stubbled hills, Claire decided she needed a *Pros and Cons* list about the move.

Pros: They had twenty-eight years of marriage. You didn't throw that away. He was taking the transfer with the plan to come back in three years when he retired. It wasn't forever. Boston. She'd always wanted to visit the east coast.

She slowed to make the turn up their driveway.

Cons: This was supposed to be her time, her turn. Her job. Could she walk away from it? The kids and her parents were in California.

By the time she opened the garage door, tears were falling, and she knew she would be moving with Mark to Boston. They had been together all this time, and when she saw it through Mark's eyes, he was right. There was little to be gained by her staying and his going.

She swiped at her eyes and blew her nose. She had one condition. If she was going, she wanted them to work on their relationship.

Claire startled when she saw Mark sitting at the kitchen table with a cup of coffee.

"Why aren't you in the field?" she asked.

"Waiting for you, Claire."

"Let me put my things down and get a cup."

She placed her purse and briefcase on the floor, walked over to the pot on the counter, and poured the strong coffee into a thick mug. After sipping a taste, she added milk from the carton Mark had left out.

Placing her hands protectively around the cup of fortification she asked, "What?"

"Because of our argument, I talked to Martin and indeed they want me to go to Boston."

"Done deal?"

"I have to give them an answer by the end of the week," he answered, eyes downcast.

"What are you going to say?"

"What can I say?" He looked at her, brows raised, as if she might have a magical answer.

She drew a deep breath, letting the oxygen steady her voice. "It's too late for us to have a reasonable discussion. Too much has been said. I'm hurt. I'm angry...about a lot of things."

"Look, you know I'm not good at all this emotional stuff. Tell me what to do and I'll do it."

She shook her head. "That's not fair," she said. "I don't want to just tell you what to do. That's not the kind of relationship I want."

"If you want to talk about fair, we can list a bunch of 'not fair' on both sides." He looked right at her and his voice took on an edge. "I can't win." Again, he paused. "You accuse me of making the decisions? Someone has to." He put his coffee cup down. "You want to talk an issue to death, but never make the decision because it might not be right."

Claire reeled back. "It's not that simple."

Before she could say anything more, he leaned forward on the table, his face less than three feet from hers. He continued, "What does it take to make you happy? Do you even have an idea?"

Claire saw his anger and felt her body shrink. She squeezed the mug tighter. She sat straighter and fixed her eyes on his. "Mark, if I agree to move, will you agree to work on our marriage?" Her voice didn't waiver. "We need counseling. Our communication sucks. Our marriage is in trouble."

Mark hung his head. "Whatever it takes," he said barely above a whisper.

"I want you to understand, I'm still hurt you didn't talk to me, you didn't include me in the decision. You aren't treating me like a partner. You're treating me like an employee you direct." She wrapped her arms around her midsection. "I don't want to give up my job. I would rather take a leave if I can arrange it. I want you to promise me this will only be for three years." She negotiated on the spot. "Then we'll come back here, and I can work full time."

"What if Katie is still in school?" he asked as he slid back into his chair.

"Then she'll have to pay for it, Mark."

"I'm not sure I'll be fully vested so I can't promise we can come home any sooner."

"Then you can work part-time for a few years while I work full time. There are all kinds of solutions."

The silence stretched between them.

They sat drinking coffee that soured in her stomach till the sun set behind the hills.

"Did Katie call you about her tuition payment?" he asked.

They talked about nothing of substance in short, non-threatening sentences.

Finally, Claire got up and went to the refrigerator to start dinner, the critical issues sinking, like the sun, below the surface of their emotions.

"Will you pick some vegetables from the garden?" she asked as if they hadn't just survived a crisis.

"It's dark," Mark said.

She looked at him over the refrigerator door. "Take the flashlight. You can feel if the tomatoes are ripe."

Mark grabbed the flashlight that sat on the bookcase, headed out the back door and walked the fifty feet to the house garden. She followed the bobbing beam. He returned with squash, tomatoes, an eggplant, two fresh carrots, a handful of snow peas and some fresh basil. He handed the basket of odd ingredients to Claire. She cleaned, chopped and made a fresh pasta primavera.

Without her direction, Mark opened a bottle of Merlot and set the table.

They ate as if everything might be all right.

Chapter Nine

The days following came and went, spiced with bursts of energy followed by long hours of punishing silence.

Mark methodically arranged for the move, and Claire reluctantly trained her replacement. The Labor Day picnic brought the extended family together and Claire hung red, white and blue banners, like she did every year. They ate a variety of cold cuts, cheeses, layered cakes and of course personally selected wines. Cousins brought cousins current with their changing lives.

For one sunny afternoon and sunset, Claire pretended nothing would change, even though of course it would.

The Labor Day brunch the next morning was reserved for a private good-bye for her, Mark, and their kids. Claire dwelled on them as she dressed, wondering what she would miss during the next three years.

Colleen and Sean spent the night in their old bedrooms down the hall across from Claire and Mark. Katie and Peter stayed at a local hotel in Paso Robles. Allowing Claire to believe they had separate rooms.

Claire took a last look in the mirror. She pulled the wrinkles around her eyes back and had a flash of her younger, less-stressed self. Removing her fingers allowed the lifelines, as her mother called them, to return. Claire picked up the burnt orange lipstick. She had worn since turning forty and dashed it on her, now thinner, lips and promised herself a makeover when she got to Boston. A new look for a new home and a new stage of life seemed like the least she was due.

In the kitchen, she started a pot of coffee and waited for the aroma to wake the rest of the family. Colleen was first into the kitchen. "I'm off for a morning run." She grabbed an apple and dashed out.

Mark and Sean wandered down a few minutes later, poured themselves coffee and settled at the patio table. Claire watched them reading the Sunday paper, occasionally pointing out something of interest to the other.

With a frittata and yeasty pecan rolls in the oven, she headed out the back door to join the men.

Sean handed her the book section of the Chronicle and she sat for a few glorious, sun-drenched minutes, before the oven timer went off. The smell of melted butter and sugar flavored the air as she returned to the kitchen. She heard Katie with Peter coming in the back door.

"I hope your Mom is in a better mood," Peter said in a low voice.

"Oh, forget Mom. She gets like that."

Hearing Katie's comment, Claire slammed the frittata on the counter, chipping one of the tiles. She didn't want Peter here to begin with and worse, who gave him permission to evaluate her? "My mood is fine," she snapped.

At least Peter had the sense to look abashed and avoid her gaze.

"Sorry, Mom." Katie gave her a quick hug. "I just know you're not happy about this move and it shows."

Claire forced a smile. "Grab some plates and let's have a quiet brunch and send your father off to Boston with our blessing." And pretend that we're all in agreement with the choices he made, Katie made, and she'd made. "Carry the fruit bowls, will you, Peter?"

Peter and Katie chattered their way out. Claire took a deep breath to calm herself. She wanted a nice day. She wanted to leave with no bitterness. They wouldn't all be together again until Christmas.

She walked toward the patio with the frittata in hand. The Richter family marked all occasions with food and wine. Warm rolls, savory frittatas, fresh field fruit and hearty wines cemented this family.

As she joined them at the table, she smiled and passed the bowl and platters around. She looked at Colleen, who sipped her orange juice. She turned out to be the perfect blend of her and Mark, and Claire sensed a twinge of guilt when she remembered how she feared if she could love her first born.

Sean had grown into a self-confident young man and he talked at length with his sister about his upcoming bar exams.

Claire knew he would do well. Like his father, he was determined, and goal driven.

Katie spent her meal describing all the dishes to Peter. Just like at the cabin, he seemed to be lost in the tradition of family. What did his family celebrate, laugh or cry about, or bond over?

"When do you plan to leave, Dad?" Colleen asked.

"I have my car packed with what I'll need, your mother will ship what's left and then fly out."

Sean turned toward her. "When is that, Mom?"

"Not sure. I have stuff at work I need to complete before I go." Because she had to wait and make sure his dad was happy there before she packed up her life and moved it across the continent. "At least a month. Maybe six weeks."

Mark raised his eyebrows at the time frame. "Didn't you tell work already?" Mark helped himself to two pecan rolls.

"I've told them but haven't put in a formal written notice." She paused and scanned the faces looking back at her. "I'll do it soon." She lowered her head and studied her plate.

"Sean," Mark asked, "are you sure you can stay here for a while?"

"Yeah, I'll be working for a small firm in Atascadero and studying. I'm fine as long as I don't have to work the fields."

"I can still hope you will." Mark looked at him. "If this law thing doesn't work, you can always come back here."

"I sure hope the law thing works out because if we depend on me running a vineyard, we'll go hungry."

"And thirsty," added Colleen. Everyone chuckled.

"No worries about the vineyard, Jessie is more than capable. He'll keep me informed. Your job is to feed Bear," Mark said as he passed a piece of bacon to the dog.

Claire watched, listened. Why couldn't she be the one to stay?

Claire took her time cleaning up that evening. Peter, Katie, and Colleen had left for their apartments, and Sean was in his old room. Around nine, after sweeping all the floors and putting the dishes from the washer back in the cupboard, she brewed a cup of chamomile tea. On impulse, she brewed a second and took both to the bedroom where Mark was sitting up in bed working on a list.

"Can't sleep?"

"Just thinking about all I have to do tomorrow." He flipped through the pages of a yellow legal pad.

She put the cup of tea on the bedside table. "The car is already packed. There shouldn't be much for you to do."

He reached for the tea and sipped, grimaced, blew across the top and put it back on the coaster. "I need to meet with Jessie one more time to make sure he understands to hire additional laborers and not try to do all the work himself."

"He's been hiring the seasonal help for years."

Mark sighed. "Yeah, I guess he doesn't need me."

Claire softened a bit. "We all need you."

"You know what I mean." He looked down at the list neatly printed on the tablet.

Claire changed into her gown and got into bed. She sat against propped pillows, looked at Mark, "Are you okay?"

"I am," he answered. "I'm just getting too old to drive cross country and you know I don't do well alone."

She patted his hand. "What time are you leaving tomorrow?"

"Early. Should I wake you?"

"Of course," she said. "Will you want breakfast?"

"Was thinking of leaving around four and getting breakfast in Barstow."

"I'll get up and make you a thermos."

She slipped under the covers, rearranged her pillows and waited. Soon, he got up gathered both teacups, took them to the kitchen, then returned to their bed. He adjusted his body and settled in for sleep. Claire anticipated his next move. She edged closer while she waited for his gentle caress on her thigh, a kiss on her lip.

Instead, a soft snore reached her.

She sighed.

So much for some farewell sex, a lingering goodbye to remember. So much for his touch bringing her comfort.

Settling for his hand resting on hers, she dreamt of the past.

Mark woke before dawn with Claire sleeping curled on her side. Out of habit he slipped on a brown plaid flannel shirt, jeans and his work boots. He looked at her snuggled, childlike, under the blankets. Her hair mussed on the pillow.

If only she would ride with him. He swallowed a lump of need.

In the kitchen, he fixed his own coffee. He liked it black, strong and hot. Bear wagged his tail at the patio door and Mark wondered if the dog stood there all night waiting for him. Bear had a house Mark had built for him, but the dog preferred sleeping and waiting on the woven raffia welcome mat. On their few really cold nights, Mark pulled one of his old sweatshirts from the closet and covered Bear. Would anyone think to do that come December? Would the dog even still be around when Mark returned? Bear, like the rest of them, wasn't as young as he used to be.

Mark drank his coffee while Bear sat rigid, begging for bits of cheese. The coffee steamed aroma in the morning cold. On the days Mark took the pick-up out to the fields, he would have a thermos on the seat beside him and Bear would jump in, knowing they had work to do. Mark rested his hand on the dog's head and fingered his ears. Bear's fur was coarse, but the ears were velvet.

"No fields today, buddy." Mark handed him the last piece of cheese. "Don't tell anyone I'm feeding you the Havarti." The dog's dark eyes promised he would keep the secret. "I'm going to miss my morning coffees, but you already sense that, don't you?"

The dog seemed to nod.

Mark sighed. "Come on Bear, time to pack up and leave."

The dog looked toward the pickup but obediently followed Mark to the back door and stood, cocked his head waiting for further instructions.

Mark waited until Claire joined him in the kitchen. They shared one last cup of coffee and she promised to join him in Boston soon.

He drove down the driveway, watching Claire's silhouette in the rearview mirror, trying to shake the feeling he was leaving more than a few vines and a house for just a few months. Because they'd be back, and everything would be the same.

It had to be.

Chapter Ten

Clair packed for her move to Boston and realized this had been her home for over twenty-six years. There wasn't a part of this house that didn't have her energy, her heart, her soul.

She's the one who scrubbed the terracotta tiles and re-grouted them on her hands and knees, the one who carefully picked out the furniture and set it in the perfect place for viewing the morning birds or the evening sunset. Mark was about as much a part of the surroundings as the overstuffed armchair he fell asleep in every night.

She hoped she'd packed all she'd need. She stood in the living room, turning slowly, examining the walls, the shelves, everything she was leaving behind.

Maybe she should take their wedding picture—the one of them gazing at each other. Although...odd, she'd never noticed before. Her younger self looked up at Mark with love in her eyes, while his expression held something closer to...panic.

She lifted the portrait from the wall, but it left a noticeable faded outline and an empty space. Fine. Since this was going to be a temporary move, she would leave it. Along with the other memories.

A *beep-beep* sounded from outside where Sean waited in the car to take her to the airport. It was time.

She turned off the ceiling fan. Out of habit, she folded the dishrag in half and hung it over the faucet.

She picked up her tote bag, squared her shoulders, and prepared to enter the next phase of her and Mark's life. And determined to make their marriage work.

"Come on, Mom, I hate the drive and don't want to be late for your plane," Sean called from the car.

"We have plenty of time." She inserted her key to lock the dead bolt.

"You have security to deal with and LAX is the worst."

"We have six hours. Relax."

"Six hours to drive over two hundred miles, find parking, and check you in."

"I'm ready," she said with a catch in her throat as she closed the car door.

She half listened as Sean talked about his firm's latest case using terms like *amicus curiae* and *sua sponte*. How bright he was and how amazing that she gave birth to him.

Twenty-something years ago, it was a Saturday in March when the poppies were in bloom, Mark came home and announced he found a house. She had been looking for a house in the city of Paso Robles to rent or, if the price was right, buy. Mark hadn't been looking. With Colleen, a toddler, and Claire discovering she was pregnant, the apartment they were living in would be too small.

"You did what?" she asked.

"I found a house. It's perfect for us so I made an offer."

"What?" He couldn't be serious. He bought a house without taking her to see it? What if she hated it? What did he know about an efficient kitchen? About a laundry room with a toddler and an infant?

"I found a great place. Come and see."

So she stuffed her doubts into her gut and rode in Mark's black '72 Ford pickup to see the "great place." She remembered fastening Colleen in a car seat and lap belting herself in. The shocks on the truck never gave a smooth ride, but it seemed as if Mark was going out of his way to find every back road. Then, with little warning, he headed up a dirt drive.

"There it is," he announced as they rounded the last bend. He waved a hand, spokesmodel-style.

Claire looked out the dust-covered windshield and saw atop a rise a rundown ranch-style house. He put the vehicle in first gear and drove slowly, leaving pillows of dust clouds following.

Claire wasn't as impressed as Mark. She saw a dirty place that needed lots of work. Mark came to her side, helped her from the cab and talked with an infectious enthusiasm. She let Colleen down who ran toward the front steps and clumsily tried climbing them. Mark scooped his daughter into his arms, pulled Claire close and talked about the future vines this property would support. He told his dreams to grow the finest grapes this area could produce. How working at Ahwahnee would provide enough income until the acreage could support them. Then they would retire and work the land together with their children.

Almost against her will, Claire found herself as in love with the potential as she was with Mark. His vision of their future became hers. She remembered them standing there for a long time talking about the family they wanted to raise, the security he wanted to give her, and how he wanted to make all her dreams come true.

That night they made love and held each other. Together they could do anything, achieve it all, and conquer the world. Their little family unit had found the place to grow. That night, held tightly in Mark's arms, the reality of the work ahead was lost to the power of love. That night, he was her dream.

Those warm memories felt like the only fuel moving her to Boston.

"Mom, are you listening?"

Claire turned from the past. "What?"

"We're an hour out. Do you want to stop and get a sandwich?"

Claire didn't want a sandwich or coffee or anything except for this trip—hell, the next three years—to be over and the car heading north instead of south. "I guess we should stop before we hit the Los Angeles traffic," she finally said.

Sean, the embodiment of the future continued. "Bet you're looking forward to seeing Dad."

Amazing what the kids assumed. Sean didn't have a clue she might not be eager to fly three thousand miles to a new house, a new life, and an old cracked marriage. She and Mark were fixtures in the kids' lives and as supposedly as perfect as the pictures that hung on the wall.

Instead, Claire saw the sun fading behind the eclipse of her life.

She insisted Sean drop her at the curb check-in, which allowed only a fast hug and much too short a farewell. She would have almost six-hour flight to miss him, miss his sisters, and watch California shrink away from her window seat.

All too soon she heard the stewardess announce the landing instructions. Claire tightened her seat belt and closed the paperback she'd impulsively purchased at the newsstand. In the billowy clouds, suspended above reality, she could believe life might be different.

Early in their marriage, she set up candlelit dinners with soft music. Mark usually came in tired but played the game and awkwardly danced her around the kitchen. Soon, however, when the children grew older and had more needs, they gave it up, instead attending school dances as chaperones. Perhaps it wasn't too late. They were alone and starting over.

Mark had called the week before and told her all about the new Boston house, a condo overlooking a harbor. Soon she would see it with her own eyes.

A new addition to the houses in her life. First of course, her parents', the house filled with security. Then the apartment she and Mark first lived in, the tiny one filled with promise. That's where they dreamt and planned for the future.

Then she and Mark bought the ranch house and moved to Paso Robles and built their lives. Like the vineyards that surrounded the house, the family matured within adobe walls stained with the emotional patina of a growing family. She never imagined she would live elsewhere.

The plane bounced as it met the runway.

Mark stood next to the carousel that would spit out her luggage. He looked good, his sandy-brown hair still as thick as when she met him. She wanted to run to him, hoping he would pull her close and swing her around. Except they were in an airport and Mark wouldn't do that.

He noticed her and while waving her closer, his smile owned his face.

She picked up her pace. She had missed him, she really had. As she drew close, her steps faltered. Maybe he hadn't missed her the same way. Maybe he'd decided he was okay alone after all. But now she was at his side and he kissed her cheek.

He took her bag and looked at her. His deep-set, blue eyes still stirred her. "Good flight?"

She gave a nod. "I read most of the way."

"Hungry?"

"Not really, maybe a smoothie."

"Damn it's good to see you," he said without warning.

Heat unfurled low in her abdomen. He did have feelings. "I missed you," she replied. Claire kissed him on the chin, still surprised by the revelation. He was the person who knew her the best, who watched her grow into a woman while he became a man. They'd each affected the path the other took.

"Those yours?" Mark asked. He released her and pointed to the black bags with the orange tags.

"Yeah."

Before she knew it, they were wheeling the bags out to a parking garage. Mark talked non-stop about the job and Boston. The food was good, the job hard, the condo okay, and the city full of noise. Claire discovered the ride to the house was a blur of honking horns, sirens, and flashing lights. Mark missed turns, cussed at other drivers, pointed out buildings and landmarks then abruptly turned into a dark underground garage. He parked the SUV in a small slot that appeared too narrow for anything but a smart car.

Claire followed Mark as he pulled both bags behind him. They silently entered the elevator, and she found herself standing close to him. She smelled his aftershave and upon closer inspection realized he must have shaved before picking her up. She smiled to herself. It felt like a date. The doors opened on the eighteenth floor to a hallway with four inner doors, identified with brass letters. Mark put his key in 18-C.

They stepped into a small entryway with hooks for hats and coats, the hardwood floor scuffed from years of wear.

"This way," Mark directed as he left the suitcases resting against the wall.

She followed him around the corner and found the kitchen. The sink, small counter, and dishwasher were on one wall. Less than an arms-length away, on the opposite wall stood the fridge and stove. Cabinets hung from the ceiling on both sides. The galley was long, narrow and windowless. Mark turned on the overhead fluorescent light as Claire opened one of the cabinets. It was full of white dishes and un-patterned glassware.

"It's very efficient," Mark said. She couldn't tell if his voice held hope she'd agree or dread she'd hate it. Maybe a bit of both.

The north archway opened to a dining room with a small balcony beyond double sliding glass doors. The walls were white, the table chrome and glass with white muslin covered chairs. The view was of a fountain below and another high-rise across the courtyard. There wasn't even a picture on the wall. The dining nook was open to a room that ran the width of the apartment. She walked past furniture, a couch and two armchairs covered in the same material as the dining chairs, to stare out the bay window that overlooked the harbor. In the distance, past the moon-reflected water, she saw the lights of the airport. On the wall opposite the window were several shelves. The owners left some books, and Claire fingered them, hunting for familiar titles. But these were all Reader's Digest Condensed Books, chosen for the colors of their bindings, not their contents.

Claire missed the colors of home, the rich brown dirt, the green soft carpet of lawn and the fluttering of leaves on vines as the night breeze teased them, exposing deep purple grapes.

"Over here is the bedroom."

Claire followed Mark to the last room in this square place. It was large with a nice sized en-suite bathroom. The king-sized bed was covered in a white duvet.

"For a year or so, it will be fine." At the end of the one-year lease they had signed, maybe they could find something a bit bigger with a lawn. "Do you think we can get planter boxes for the deck and plant some herbs? I could make pesto …"

She stood at the bedroom window looking into the distance. Mark walked up behind her. "I'll look for some this weekend. We can try to grow here, but remember the weather is against us."

She leaned back against him, hunting for his strength, yearning for it. As she felt his breath against her neck, an old desire rose in her. She turned to him, lifted her head and kissed him. Relaxing into him.

He kissed her back. "I'll get your bag if you want to shower and clean up," he said as he released her.

"The small black one," she directed, "and a shower sounds nice."

It seemed strange to step into a new shower. Where was her favorite soap, her washcloth or the back brush? She fumbled with the faucet, at first turning it too far to the right and the water was cold, then over-compensated to the left and almost scalded herself. She closed her eyes, letting the water spray her face. She shuddered as she first heard then felt Mark join her.

"Let me wash your back," he said. He spoke softly, invitingly, in a voice reminiscent of their youth. Her body responded. How soothing to have him lather her back with the soft terry cloth. He turned her to let the water rinse the suds off. She was happy that her body, although much older than the last time they showered together, was in decent shape. Again he kissed her, and she sensed his hunger.

Warmed by the shower and encouraged by his kisses, she stepped out. Mark picked up an over-sized white towel and dried her before drying himself.

"Come to bed," he said.

Tonight, she didn't fear he would turn from her and be too tired. Tonight, the first night in this strange bed, in this strange house, in the strange city, promised to be a renewal of what they once had.

Tonight, she would not have to ask if he loved her.

Tonight, he showed her.

She fell asleep with him curled around her. Cradled and protected.

Chapter Eleven

Morning sun woke Claire to the familiar smell of Mark. She reached for him, but only his imprint on the pillow remained. Her still naked body shivered as she recalled last night.

When she finally located the clock on the nightstand, it was almost eleven. How had she slept so late. Forcing her feet to the floor, she acknowledged it was time to start a new life.

After a fast shower, with memories revived, she quickly pulled on jeans, and a cotton shirt. The room remained as plain as she remembered. No color fairy came in the night and danced subtle hues on the walls. White, not even a pretty white, but a flat, dull white, like the envelopes she sent mail in. She would have to find some pillows, rugs, plants, and something magenta. Yes, something the color of a California sunset.

Claire hunted for coffee but didn't find a pot or grounds. A new coffee maker was added to her list of things she would need.

Mark had told her the neighborhood had lots of little shops and bakeries. No time like the present, she thought, tying her old Nike walking shoes. Her cell phone rang.

"Hello."

"Claire, it's Mark."

"Hi, and thanks for last night." She hugged herself as she said it.

"Ahhhh," Mark hesitated. Claire knew he didn't like to share intimacies out loud and especially on cell phones. "It was fun," he finally said.

Fun. It was more than fun. It is the start of our new life.

"I'll make this fast. I thought you might want to know where the grocery store is." His voice turned all business.

"How about the nearest coffee shop?"

"On the corner," he answered.

"Which corner?"

"The doorman is Donald and he knows where everything is. Just ask. You'll like him."

At the moment, Claire loved anyone who pointed her to the nearest source of caffeine. "Okay," she said, "what do you want for dinner and when do you think you'll be home?" She could be practical. After all, there was time for romance later.

"Not till after seven. Sorry. I promise to give you the Boston tour on Saturday."

"It's okay. I plan to walk around a bit. I figure I can't get that lost and now that you told me Donald knows everything, I'm fine."

"Okay. See you tonight."

"Hey, Mark." She ran a finger around her lips.

"What?"

"In case I haven't said it. I love you." It wasn't all that hard to say. She tried to remember when she last said it and it saddened her to realize—too long ago. Claire told her kids every time she saw them, and always kissed her parents good-bye with a quick, "Love ya." She even told the cat. Right then and there she made the decision to say "I love you" to Mark every day.

"What did you say?" he asked.

"I love you."

"Yes, the wine was outstanding last night."

Let's have wine, their secret code when either of them wanted sex.

She smile as the call ended and found the keys, and the local map Mark left on the counter top and headed out. When she entered the lobby, a man dressed in a brown uniform was on the sidewalk helping a loud woman wearing a too short and too tight skirt into a limo. Once she was on her way, he came inside and greeted Claire.

"Good afternoon, Ms. Richter." She'd expected a Latino accent but instead a very British tone met her ears.

"You must be Donald," she said, extending her hand. "I'm Claire. My husband, Mark, told me you might direct me to the nearest coffee shop and closest grocery store."

"Yes, indeed." He pulled out a clean sheet of writing paper and drew some lines. "We are here and if you walk four blocks to the east" — he looked up and pointed out the right side of the door— "there is a local coffee house, The Daily Grind. May I recommend the scones?"

Claire watched as he marked a C where coffee would be. "As for groceries, most people here order them from the delivery service. I will be glad to give you that number. In the meantime, there is a small family-owned store on the corner of India Row and Sixth." He marked that with a G, and it appeared to be about six blocks beyond the coffee shop.

Claire waved a good-bye and headed in search of strong, black caffeine. Tonight, she would talk Mark into going out for dinner, and tomorrow she would tackle a grocery store. Ordinarily she planned her meals around what was ripe in the garden and the idea of ordering groceries she hadn't personally touched was beyond her.

Indeed, The Daily Grind was exactly where Donald said it would be. Cozy colorful chairs, set in groups of four or six, made the place quaint and inviting. She saw a group of middle-aged women sitting in the corner. They were leaning into each other, talking feverishly, occasionally reaching across to touch one or the other.

Claire's heart ached for Val. She wanted to tell her friend about last night. She might not tell all, but that things looked promising. Her girlfriend, not her mother, knew the intimacies of Claire's life. For one brief moment, while looking at a newspaper-hidden man, she felt sorry for men. Who did they talk to? Then she felt a small sorrow for herself. She missed

Val. Claire ordered her coffee to go and reached for her iPhone. She hit Val's picture and it rang into her friend's voice mail.

"Hey, kiddo, it's me, just letting you know I'm here. I'm safe. I found a coffee shop, and I already miss you." She shut her phone and checked the time. It already re-calculated to Eastern Standard Time and read 12:25. So 9:25 in Paso Robles. Val would, of course, be at work and probably seeing her first client of the day.

Holding the extra sleeved paper cup, Claire exited back to the street for further discovery. The harbor—the same one she saw from her condo window—lapped at the breaker wall. Tall buildings and overhead crisscrossing tracks were on the left. Steel wheels chattered and shrieked as they traveled to places unknown. A fresh breeze had to sneak past too many buildings, signs, and smells in such a small space. On docks, men sold fish. Gulls cried overhead circling for scraps. Garlic browned in olive oil mixed with diesel exhaust.

She missed open fields and the smell of rich fertile dirt.

Claire spent the afternoon unpacking her suitcases. At first, she felt strange opening drawers and closets but soon arranged them to her liking and began making friends with the condo. Around six, she set out the cold cuts she'd picked up at the store. She found the music Mark brought with him and immediately sought out four jazz CDs and loaded the player. Checking her watch, she had just enough time for a fast shower.

Finally, after the sun died hours earlier, after the candles burned to the bottom, after she ate her fill, Claire heard keys in the front door. She took a fast look at the clock on the wall. It was past nine.

"I'm home," he called.

Claire sat in the chair and didn't reply. Disappointment paralyzed her.

Mark turned on the light. "What's this?" he asked.

"I planned dinner." Her voice stayed steady and flat, but her fury burned under her skin.

Claire stood and started picking up the platters, walking each one purposely to the kitchen.

"I thought you said you would be home for dinner at seven." On the ranch things were predictable and if he was late, she had lots to distract her.

"I had a late meeting, and we ordered in."

"And you forgot to call?"

"I left a message on the machine."

Claire reached for her cell phone and didn't see any message.

"I called the house and left it on the recorder." He pointed to a white phone with the blinking red light hanging on the dining room wall.

Claire never noticed or heard it and now she felt stupid. Of course, Mark would have called. He was Mark.

"I'm sorry," she said out of habit. She didn't feel it. Instead she remembered all the times he didn't show up because of work. All the times he fell asleep in the recliner while she waited for him in bed. All the times she tried to bring romance back and he didn't get it.

"It was a long day. Any of that wine left?" Mark had already moved on. As usual.

He poured a glass and added some to hers. They sat quietly listening to music. When Claire saw Mark's, eyes closing, she retreated to her new empty bed.

Mark sat on the sofa tapping the side of his glass in cadence to the crying saxophone of Coltrane. His memory went back to an old hi-fi playing forty-five RPM vinyl records in his parents' living room.

Dad, a massive man, sat close to Mark's mother on a green floral couch. Mark would fall asleep to their soft voices. On occasion, they noticed him. Dad would pick him up and the three of them danced. The outside world saw his parents as the hard working, hardheaded immigrants on the old Doyle Dairy.

Mark sipped and as the jazz, wine, and twilight sleep combined, memories came. It didn't matter how old or accomplished he became, when Monk, Coltrane, Fitzgerald or Davis played, he was a small boy again. Tonight, a fifty-seven-year-old body housed a fourteen-year-old.

When Mark was twelve, his father borrowed money to expand the dairy. The drought that year hit a lot of farmers hard and their family became one of many casualties. The bank extended the loan for a few months, but it was too late to save the dairy.

When Mark turned fourteen, he watched others pick and choose from their possessions. The John Deere was bought, for half its value, by a neighbor. Most of the equipment went to small farmers in the state. A large conglomerate purchased the house and land. From their headquarters in New York they offered to hire his father to manage the place.

Mark had little memories of his dad that year, only the one. On a hot, humid August day, with flies clinging to the screen door, he heard his mother. "Mark, it's past seven and your father isn't in from the field, go find him."

Mark, only fifteen, was allowed to drive on the property. He loved climbing in the old Ford and smelling the years of dust and dirt it stored. The engine started with a backfire and Mark put it in first gear. There was an art to driving stick, a skill passed from father to son. One foot let out the clutch as the other pressed the gas and the truck bucked forward.

He slowly drove along the farm road, searching for Dad's tractor. When he saw it in the alfalfa field, he honked the horn, but the tractor didn't move.

Mark didn't remember finding his father slumped over the steering wheel, he never remembered pulling his father to the pickup or driving him back to his mother.

He did remember her screams. Could still hear them echo in his dreams.

They buried Dad three days later. Mark's mother claimed, "He died of a broken heart."

Mark never heard music in the house again. It was when the music stopped that the reality of a life without both parents set in. He became the man of the house. His mother retreated into memories of earlier times, leaving Mark to take care of the day-to-day chores. She listened to the radio occasionally but never again played the records. Never again two-stepped around the living room. Never again let herself believe everything would be okay.

One night, Mark could never remember exactly when, he woke to Mom crying. In years past, when he woke in the night, he would fall back to sleep listening to the lullaby of his parents talking. But that night, hearing his mother's soft sobs, he lay under the cotton quilt until his own tears coursed down his temples.

He got up and found his mother sitting in bed. Letters and cards she had kept in a shoebox in the bottom drawer of her dresser were scattered around her.

"What are you doing up?" she asked.

"I can't sleep."

He remembered her saying, "I can't stop crying."

More tears fell and joined his mother's as they stained the letters. She rescued the notes and cards and clutched them to her chest.

She turned still-wet eyes to Mark. "Babies and women cry. You are the man of the house and men don't cry. Go back to bed."

He obeyed, choking on his tears. He learned to hide them. In his family, public displays of affection marked weakness. Unfortunately, private moments after the age of fifteen seemed to be out of the question as well.

He always woke at this point. The end of his childhood drifted away as the start of his adulthood loomed to meet him.

He stood, stretched, and turned off the CD player.

He had no more idea what to do about Claire now than he'd known how to comfort his mother back then.

Chapter Twelve

Over the following weeks, Claire found herself going to The Daily Grind each morning. She began to recognize some of the regular patrons.

In the afternoons, she busied herself decorating, exploring, and organizing. Little changed between her and Mark. Regular calls to Val kept her posted on the modifications at the Women's Center. Claire's project came to fruition without her. It was both sweet and hurtful to learn Mary, her secretary, held the position of Coordinator. At least the job for lead therapist was still open, and, if things in Boston got unbearable, Claire would return and apply. She comforted herself with that thought. She had an escape plan.

Mark and the marriage were once her passion. She wanted to please him, make him proud of her, raise their children, and live in bliss. Wasn't that what happened in the stories of her childhood? Except life wasn't a fairytale. Mark wasn't Prince Charming. Even if she once thought he was her knight in shining armor.

As she sipped her morning coffee, nestled into a blue chair at the Daily Grind, Claire drifted into the memory of first meeting him.

In her rush to get to Biology she left her lights on and by the time the lab ended, her battery was dead. Fresno State University was over ten miles from her dad's fixing hands. Then out of nowhere, Mark appeared with a set of cables.

"Looks like you might need these," he said with wide grin.

"I guess." She shook her head ruefully.

He opened the hood, attached one end to the battery of her old Plymouth then drove his dusty, dented, red pickup across from hers. In minutes her motor turned over.

"You probably left your lights on. Lots of people forget to turn them off in the fog," he said, while efficiently coiling the cables he placed neatly in the bed of the truck.

"How much do I owe you?" she remembered asking.

"There's no charge for saving damsels in distress. Just part of the service I offer." Claire swore he winked at her, but maybe he only squinted.

A week later she saw him on campus. He leaned against the trunk of a Valley Oak, reading a Chemistry book.

"Save any distressed damsels lately?" she asked.

He looked up. "I've retired from killing dragons and slaying monsters or even starting broken chariots."

Clever. He looked older and a bit thin for her liking, but under his blue denim shirt she saw a muscular build.

"Can I buy you a coke, a coffee, or something as a thank you?"

"I could use a coffee. These formulas are driving me crazy."

He ordered a glass of milk, she got a lemonade.

"Do you have a major?" she asked.

"Agriculture," he said.

"Interesting." She smiled out of politeness.

He wiped the milk from his lip, using the back of his hand. Claire handed him a napkin from the dispenser on the table. He folded it into a square and put it down.

Then, without her invitation, he launched into a soapbox speech about the land in California versus the soil in Wisconsin. He talked about milk production, fertilizer, the pros and cons of using growth hormones for greater production.

Claire, bored after two minutes, smiled, nodded, and stifled a yawn.

At the start of the new semester, she found him sitting in the last chair of her women's study class. It was one of the required courses and the few men who couldn't find an alternative sat together with the appearance of camaraderie. Claire waved and took a seat far from his. After class, he tried walking her to her next class. He was bashful, quiet and polite.

Over the semester, he opened up about himself and Claire listened. For almost a year there was nothing romantic, they were pals. She helped him pass classes, and he would hang pictures in her dorm room.

In late March, when the valley came alive with wildflowers and all the fruit trees bloomed, he asked her on a picnic in the almond orchard. His romantic side emerged. They drove down a dirt road among the trees. They lasted ten seconds before the mighty Ag king realized that, of course, the blooms were being pollinated by swarms of bees. With only one stinger in her upper arm, they took the picnic to the safety of campus grass.

"Nice try," she remembered saying.

This morning, with her coffee almost gone, she didn't imagine Mark even trying to be romantic anymore and old memories weren't enough.

After ordering a refill, she settled in her chair again and opened a pamphlet that originally hung on the coffee shop bulletin board. An invitation to join a book group caught her eye. The book being discussed was one of her favorites, *The Grapes of Wrath*.

Hmm. She rubbed a finger along the middle of her chin. That would be something she could do. She'd meet new people and maybe they would help her adjust to Boston.

Except...with a sigh, she leaned back in her chair. It was her old and familiar pattern. Rather than fight with Mark, she'd seek out a distraction.

After he bought the second twenty acres, she went back to school. She always found something to do alone. In the early years, she tried telling him how she felt when he independently made decisions, she should have a say in. But when he repeatedly made decisions without telling her, she'd devised her own defense system.

Claire always chose activities that excluded him rather than face him with her anger. It wasn't even anger as much as frustration.

This time she would deal with him, she really would. Soon. But in the meantime, she opened her mapApp to find the nearest bookstore. She had to purchase a new copy of the Steinbeck classic so she could escape with Jed and his family on their journey from the Dust Bowl to the promised land of California.

Or was she the only one who thought of California that way?

Katie called at the end of the week. Peter and I want to come to Boston to visit."

"When?" Claire aske. What she wanted to ask was why. "Don't you have classes?"

"Yeah, but ..." Katie hesitated.

"But what?"

"Well, we thought it would be fun to get away for a long weekend. Besides I've never been to Boston."

Katie assumed Mark would pick up the tab. Claire's stomach tightened. She didn't need Katie here. Not yet.

"Don't you think Thanksgiving would be a better time?"

"We're going hiking in Yosemite with friends then."

"Katie, stop and think a minute. Yosemite in November is really cold for hiking. Why don't you and your friends go hiking now or in a couple of weeks and then come to Boston later?"

Claire heard only silence on the other end of the phone. So, either Katie was considering her request or — more likely — pouting. Katie rarely got told no.

"Mom, please."

Something in her voice triggered Claire's *mama alarm*. The tone in Katie's *please* sounded needy. And Katie rarely needed her mother.

"Is everything okay?" Claire asked.

Katie quickly answered, "Yeah, of course. So, what do you think?"

Claire chewed her lower lip for a quick second, considering. "Let me talk to Dad and in the meantime why don't you see if you can change the plans to Yosemite." She paused. "Deal?"

"Okay."

Claire then asked about her professors, roommates, and the weather. "Have you made new friends in your classes?" A frisson of surprise sparked down Claire's spine when Katie, the social butterfly, said she hadn't. That was odd. By this week in the semester, Katie was usually bubbling over with tales of dorm pranks, study group dynamics, and complaints about the cafeteria's limited seating options for her social circle.

"And what about you, Mom?"

"Not yet, it's harder to meet people at my age."

They said good-bye and Claire returned the phone to the cradle then stared at if for a minute. If only she were closer to Katie, she'd be able to figure out what exactly was going on. And even better, maybe she'd understand why they had to be on opposite sides of the country. Was it really all about retirement benefits?

As Claire gazed at the phone, she recalled Katie's birth as if it was last week, not nineteen years ago. Even now, she remembered Katie moving inside her, a sweet presence. When did it change? When did they first start fighting?

It evolved slowly, over time, over issues, over independence. Claire wanted her daughter to be a fairy princess, and Katie wanted to be a Ninja Warrior.

Katie adored her father and everything he did. She loved the fields, often begging for tractor rides, and he was putty for her molding.

Yet today—Claire patted her warm chest, fought the smile erupting—Katie needed her mother.

When Mark came home, only an hour later than planned, Claire shared the call with him. She plated some cheese and cracker while he poured two glasses of wine.

"She just misses us," he said, flopping on the couch and toeing off his shoes.

Claire shook her head. "No, something's wrong."

"You're too suspicious. She just wants to see how we're doing and where we are."

"Maybe."

"Come sit next to me." He patted the cushion.

She moved to the empty spot on the couch, plopped down, and pulled her feet under her.

He picked up the remote control to the CD player and restarted the blues. They sat there, a peaceful, pleasant harmony, listening to Miles perform a private concert.

Claire's memories floated back to younger, sweeter days with Mark. It had been a long time since they sat, just the two of them, on a couch drinking in the excitement of music and wine. Perhaps things *would* be different in Boston. Bumpy, yes, but they'd find what they lost in raising children, pursuing careers, and praying for good crops.

"Mark?" she whispered.

"Yeah."

"What are you thinking about?"

"Nothing. Listening to the music."

"What do you think about us?"

"What is there to think about?"

"Well, what are we going to do here?"

He drew a sharp breath. "I am going to work and you, Claire, are going to be the lady of the house."

"I might get bored."

"Nah, you'll love it."

"I hope so." She pulled back from him and looked into his eyes. "What's up with Katie?"

He shrugged. "Nothing."

"Maybe...do you like Peter?"

"I don't know Peter."

"I just have this...uneasiness that he isn't good. I don't trust him. It's a gut feeling."

He closed his eyes. "Don't spoil the music with feelings. Okay?"

"Okay." She curled against him. Mark liked silence, and this was a chance to be close to him so she wouldn't ruin the opportunity.

He offered her a sip of his wine. "This is a new label we picked up. Do you like it?"

"It's okay." She returned the glass to him. "Do you love me?"

"What?"

"Do you love me?" she repeated.

"Of course, I do."

"What do you love the most about me?"

He kissed the top of her head. "I love that you like to sit quietly and listen to jazz." She sighed and allowed him to pull her close.

Mark shook his head. They were sitting, having a nice evening, listening to some good music, drinking okay wine, and Claire wanted to know if he loved her?

Of course he loved her.

He was working his ass off for her and the kids. If he didn't love her, why would he come to Boston and leave his vineyard?

He did that for her. So they could have a secure future. He would never leave her like his father left his mother, penniless, in debt with a kid to raise and educate. Real love was about providing.

Claire still had that silly romantic thing about running in fields and into each other's arms. All he wanted was for her to be next to him, to sit, listen and enjoy.

"Ready for bed?" he asked.

"I guess." She looked at her watch. "It's only 7:30 California time."

"I need to get to bed. I get up at five and like to stop at the gym." He continued talking while rising from the couch. "If I'm not walking the fields, I should walk the treadmill."

"Good thinking. Go ahead to bed. I'll clean the dishes and see if I can get the dishwasher working. It stopped mid-load this morning."

"Let me look at it."

In just a few minutes Mark discovered a loose wire and reattached it. "Should be fine." He stood, washed his hands at the sink, and reached for a towel.

"And that is what I love about you. You can fix anything." She gave him one of her dazzling smiles before she resumed filling the dishwasher.

"Finish up and join me in bed." He grabbed her elbow, so she'd look at him. He gave her a wink. It had never been easy for him to initiate sex, but his body responded to her praise, which had been rare lately.

Later, from the bedroom, he listened to her opening cupboards, searching for something, maybe tea or cookies.

What kind of cookies did she like? He used to know… She often got up in the middle of the night in search of a snack. In the first part of their marriage he wondered why. Later, it was just a habit. He would hear milk being poured. Sometimes she talked to the cat and poured her some as well, followed by the crackle of the cookie wrapper and then silence.

He missed the nighttime lullaby his wife's feet sang on the ranch house tile floor. Then she would crawl into bed, icy toes searching for a warm spot, sigh deep, turn on her side and breathe slowly.

Oh, how he had missed her.

Hunger gnawed at Claire's belly and she couldn't locate the right snack in the kitchen. She picked up a box of crackers, kicked off her shoes and looked around. This was like staying in a hotel, you knew everything was there, but not where it should be. Or rather she wasn't where she should be.

Picking up the remote to the television, she turned on the late news with a host she didn't know. Clicking thru the channels, she found nothing familiar.

Nothing to take her mind off Katie. What did Katie want? How could Mark sleep when three thousand miles away his daughter was in trouble? Well, maybe not trouble, but something was wrong. She knew it. Claire turned to the window and prayed, asking for protection for her babies. *Better yet, watch over me.*

Claire still believed in prayer.

It was the one thing she brought from California.

Chapter Thirteen

As Claire predicted, Katie did as Katie wanted.

Mark called and said Katie's plane had landed. They would be home within the hour. Claire, who'd made semi-peace with the condo's small kitchen, stirred the marinara sauce. At least it smelled like home. She pulled a large pot from under the counter and filled it with water. After setting it on the fire to boil, she measured the pasta as her Italian neighbor taught her. In a thick accent, Mrs. Capelluppo told Claire that a proper amount of pasta per person could be measured by circling it with your thumb and index finger. It worked for Claire. Besides she loved the sensation of the dry, straight rods in her hands.

Spaghetti with marinara sauce smothered in fresh shredded Asiago cheese was Katie's favorite. Claire finished setting the table while letting the small apartment fill with steam and welcoming aromas. As she heard the key in the lock, she drained the noodles.

"Yummers," Katie yelled from the door.

"Your favorite, I hope you brought your appetite."

"Of course," Katie said.

"Hello," Peter said.

Claire stiffened. She had momentarily forgotten about Peter. She'd been angry when Mark called Katie and offered to pay for both tickets. They exchanged words, but Claire decided to pick her battles and wait for the bigger war looming on the horizon.

"I hope you like pasta," Katie said to Peter.

"I eat anything as long as it doesn't eat me first."

Katie laughed at his joke.

Claire didn't.

Mark hung coats and placed suitcases in the front closet that had been cleared for this occasion.

Claire listened as he showed the layout of the apartment and then offered them sodas. Mark poured a glass of Chianti and brought it to Claire. She exchanged the platter of pasta for the glass. He invited the kids to the table. Peter pulled out the chair for Claire, then for Katie. Claire eyed him with suspicion. Why couldn't she accept he was just a nice kid? Perhaps because he was having sex with her daughter. Claire shook the thought from her head.

Dinner was full of rich stories told between bites of hot comfort food. Claire listened hard to figure out what brought Katie here, now.

Then it dawned on her. Katie hadn't mentioned school.

"Anyone for dessert?" Claire asked.

"Spumoni?" Katie begged in a wishful voice.

"Nothing less."

"What's spumoni?" asked Peter.

"Only my favorite ice cream," Katie said. She put on an exaggerated pout and then gave Peter a big grin. "You should remember." Katie kissed him on the cheek. "Just in case...we ever have a fight, all is forgiven over spumoni."

Claire returned to the table with the carton of hand-packed frozen goodness, four bowls and a scoop.

"How's school?" she asked as she delivered the first serving.

"Fine," answered Peter.

Claire looked over at Katie who hadn't answered. "Katie?"

"I thought we might talk after dinner."

Claire put the bowl down a bit harder than she planned. "Dinner is over. How is school, Katie?"

Katie let her spoon pierce the roundness of the ice cream but didn't look at her mother. "Mom, I'm not in school. I dropped my classes."

Claire sat in her chair, letting drips of melted cream run down her arm. "Excuse me?" She looked at Katie looking at her bowl. "Did you just say you aren't in school?" Please, dear God.

Katie put down her spoon. "I decided it was better if I went to work and helped Peter finish his degree."

Claire looked at Mark who seemed as surprised as she. His brows nearly met his hairline.

"You did what, and why?" Mark asked.

"I'm going to help Peter finish his degree. Then we'll work on mine. Sorta like you and Mom."

"I had my undergraduate degree when Dad and I got married," Claire said. "Your dad had his degree...*and* a job."

"You know what I mean. You went back to school after Sean."

"For a master's. I wouldn't have dropped out of school, and I certainly wouldn't have let my parents pay a semester's tuition and *then* drop out. What are you thinking?"

"Peter doesn't have the money and he could only get enough to pay for tuition on the student loan. We still have books, rent, and food."

Claire's voice rose. "Please tell me you are only *thinking* about this." Spumoni melted in front of her. Mark sat with his spoon still suspended halfway to his mouth.

"Mom, you don't understand—"

Claire cut her short. "I understand that you just threw away eighteen thousand of our dollars and ruined your life."

"Ruined my life?" Katie shoved her bowl aside. "Please, Mother, isn't that a bit dramatic?"

Claire fought for self-control while her biceps tightened. She looked across the table. She wanted to shake her daughter. "Mark, what do you have to say?"

Mark did not respond.

"Tell her how disappointed you are in her," Claire continued to fill the silence.

"Claire, I can tell her my opinion. You don't need to tell me what to say."

Claire recoiled as if he'd slapped her. So that was the way it was. He could never be mad at "his" Katie.

Mark spoke, still looking at Claire. "Katie, this has taken both me and your mother by surprise. We're disappointed in your decision and concerned."

Concerned? No. Try pissed...furious...*scared*. Without an education, Katie's future was dependent on Peter's success or failure. Until someone else came along and he dumped Katie for someone younger or with perkier boobs or with more money. Claire had seen it happen to more than a few of her friends.

"Daddy, I wanted to call and tell you but thought it was better if I did it in person. Peter and I talked about this a long time. And the tuition money isn't thrown away. I was able to get some of it refunded and we're using it for Peter's books and some living expenses." Katie had the gall to look pleased, as if they should be proud of her ingenuity. Claire swallowed the bile that rose in her throat.

Katie continued as if everything she said made perfect sense. "When Peter's done and working, he'll support me while I finish."

Peter's lips turned up in a thin smile. He reached for Katie's knee and placed his hand there.

Stop touching my daughter. Red hot anger burned Claire's cheeks.

"Mark." Claire narrowed her eyes. "I am not only *concerned*, as you put it, I am furious."

"I understand, Claire, but what is done is done."

Indeed, it was done! Defeat weighed Claire's shoulders. Katie had been making decisions her whole life without consulting her mother. From which Skechers she wanted to wear in middle school, to sneaking out in high school for a Korn concert, and now Peter and dropping out.

Katie rose, pulled on Peter's hand. Peter stood next to her, placed an arm around her shoulder. Katie's voice cracked. "I can't take this." She stomped her foot. "I'm an adult and you are treating me like a four-year-old." She turned to Peter. "Come on, let's take a walk, and let my mother calm down."

Peter followed Katie. The door slammed with a dull thud when they left.

Claire sat. She wanted to yell, but with Katie gone the only person to yell at sat across from her, looking like he'd been stunned with a Taser.

Without talking, Claire cleared bowls of melted ice cream from the table. She drew water and rinsed dishes and slammed them into the dishwasher.

When she returned, Mark no longer sat in the dining nook. She found him in the living room gathering the kids' luggage. He looked up and said, "I texted Katie. I told her I thought she should spend the night at a hotel."

Claire nodded in agreement.

Mark continued, "I told her to meet me downstairs, and I'll bring their suitcases." He walked past Claire. "I've gotten them a room near the airport. I'll be back in about an hour."

When he was at the door, he paused. "Claire, go on to bed and get some sleep."

Instead of going to bed, as instructed, Claire did what she often did when upset. She vacuumed. A mindless task, with repetitive movement, and loud noise, often quieted the screams within.

Before Mark returned, she also bleached the kitchen floor and dismantled the stove for a scouring. *If my house gets cleaned, I can clean my mind enough to solve the problems.*

Mark returned mid-oven ritual. "Cleaning the oven at this hour?"

"You should know me by now." Claire glanced at Mark, his face empty of all emotion. "I'm almost done," she said as she took the scouring pad to an invisible spot. "Go on to bed, and I'll be there shortly."

When Claire looked up, he was already gone. She finished, carried the trash to the garbage-chute in the hall, and dropped in the remains of the dinner. With her surroundings clean, she stepped in the shower, hoping to rinse away the despair that seemed to cling to her closer than spider mites on their cabernet grapes.

Finally, in bed, Claire couldn't sleep. She tossed and turned and then tossed some more.

Mark's stillness and even breaths irritated her. She envied Mark sleeping when she couldn't. How could he sleep when their daughter had chosen to drop out of school and pin her future on this...this *user*?

Katie and Mark had no idea how hard life could be for a woman without an education. What kind of job was she going to get? Flipping burgers? How many textbooks would that buy?

Claire was the one who took on the responsibility of the children's schooling. She did homework with them and volunteered in the classroom. The hours researching what colleges they applied to fell on her shoulders.

If they failed, she failed.

Finally, she couldn't stand another minute of Mark's snuffling snores and she poked him.

"Wake up."

He shifted. "Wh—huh. Why?"

"Let's talk."

"About?"

"Katie."

"Let's talk in the morning." Mark rolled on his side and hit his pillow with a closed fist.

"No, now."

His voice muffled by the pillow, Mark said, "It's too late. Katie has already dropped her classes, and we have to adjust."

"Adjust? *We* should adjust?"

Mark sat up. "We don't have a choice. She is her own person. She's already done it. Do I think it's good? No, but there isn't anything we can do."

"Mark, this is a big mistake. She's ruining her life for this boy."

"We don't know that."

"I know it." Claire rose to the challenge in his voice. "You have to say something to her. She'll listen to you."

"I'm not going to say anything. She has a right to make her own choices and mistakes. Our job is to be here if she needs us."

"I can't stand to see her hurting herself this way. I'm going to tell her that we won't support this and unless she goes back to school, we won't talk to her."

"Don't be silly. You can't cut her out of your life."

Hurt and frustration jumbled in her chest until she had to swallow them to speak. "Silly, is that the word you used? I'm not being silly. I'm a mother who knows more than her daughter. I wouldn't have let her play with fire when she was small, why should I let her hurt herself now? Where did I go wrong?" Tears stung Claire's eyes.

"You're being overdramatic. Again. Please go to sleep, Claire. I'm sure things will look better in the morning."

"I can't." She looked at Mark, just a shadow in the dark. "How can you?"

"I don't know why you can't, or I can." Mark slid flat under the blanket. "Claire, at her age we both made mistakes that probably kept our mothers up at night." He closed his eyes. "We turned out okay."

She sat the rest of the night watching Mark sleep.

Chapter Fourteen

By the first week of November the leaves changed from green to brilliant reds, yellows and oranges and fell, littering the sidewalks and lawns of Boston.

Katie left for her new life with Peter two weeks ago and along with the first freeze turning the leaves, came a freeze between Claire and Mark. Their marriage, like the mighty oaks, now lay dormant and with each passing day the good memories of their happiness fell to earth.

The East Coast Fall everyone raved about didn't impress Claire. It was too showy. She missed California's more subtle color changes. In November the vines, absent their purple fruit, turned a soft yellow with orange tinted leaves. The hills were painted warm against the green of the winter grass.

Claire discovered The Daily Grind acted as an information center. An assortment of advertisements hung on the bulletin board. There were local poetry readings held on the first Monday of the month at the downtown library. Parenting classes were offered on Wednesdays at the YWCA. Toys for Tots could be dropped off in the basket below the rows of Dark Roasted Sumatra Decaffeinated beans. She memorized the number and information about the book group, picked up her cell phone and called.

With directions from Martha, the lady on the church phone, Claire found the entrance to the subway, the Bostonians called the 'T.' After she took a seat, looked around. She studied signs diagramming the stops of the green line, the red line, and the orange line. It made sense and seemed simple. In black, readable letters were the names of the stops.

The rocking of the train helped her indulge in her favorite pastime—making up stories about the people she saw. Daydreaming was underrated. The nuns at her grade school led her to believe it was a sin, instead she found it a great escape.

Three seats in front of her sat a gray-haired man in a blue pin-striped suit who read a stapled stack of papers. His tan leather briefcase cried of money. Boring, not like the sandy-haired man next to him, reading the Globe. He, she decided, was on his way to meet a lover for lunch. What could she learn from his shoes? She bent over to see, but her view was blocked by that brief case. She tried peering around it, but the train slowed, and her stop was next. Finally, he shifted his feet enough to expose expensive Italian leather loafers. She smiled. Just as she guessed.

Exiting the train, she glanced at her scribbled note. According to the directions, she should be able to see the church from the platform. Picking up her pace and clutching her scarf, she lowered her head against the wind and marched uphill toward the steeple in the sky.

The Congregational Church, a traditional gray, was an impressive turn of the century attempt at gothic architecture. She entered the door at the top of the steps and found herself in the main part of the church, full of aged, Murphy-oiled pews. There were no people reading, praying or meditating.

Alone in the darkness, she startled when she heard footsteps on the tile-slab floor. The ribbons of light, filtered by the stained-glass window, danced prisms of color on...hmmm...none other than loafer man.

"Are you here for the book group?" he asked, brows raised over green eyes.

"Yes."

He had lost the tie some place between the train and the church.

"We meet in the basement. Follow me." He gestured toward the back of the church and she followed.

"By the way, I'm Jeff Wentworth, and welcome to our group. Martha said someone new might join us." His voice was strong, cultured, and definitely Bostonian.

"I—I'm Claire," she said.

He pointed to a side door that opened to a cacophony of sounds and light. She followed him down the stairs into a basement filled with people gathered around a table laden with coffee and cookies. She hadn't expected such a large crowd. The book groups she knew were small and mostly women. She learned later the group began as a lunchtime literary discussion made up of men. Over the years, it moved to the basement of the church and opened to all.

Claire felt a bit lost, but before the aloneness took grip, someone with a look of authority called the cookie eaters to a long table. Jeff turned to Claire and offered her the empty chair next to him. Turning to the group, he said, "This is Claire. I found her upstairs."

They all smiled and introduced themselves. Martha, like Claire suspected over the phone, was a sweet gray-haired, bun-wearing woman. Very efficient in appearance, and Claire knew she gave good directions.

"Claire grew up in California and is familiar with the area Steinbeck writes about," Martha announced.

They all shifted to look at Claire as if she might have known John himself. Her cheeks warmed.

"Of course, I've read *The Grapes of Wrath,* but I'm not sure I have a better understanding of it than any of you."

Yet she discovered, even those who'd traveled in California, few had explored the Central Valley. She found herself talking about the land that both she and Steinbeck loved. How the core and strength of the people she called neighbors, were etched out of a dry, blown away land. How they brought a culture of survival and respected the earth and its bounty. Talking about her part of California brought her back to life. She felt welcomed, embraced by the warmth of the group and loneliness slipped away like Bear sneaking off with a rib bone.

At some point, loafer Jeff rested his arm on the back of her chair, as if they were old friends.

The people ranged in age from the young mother of two Joan, to the eighty-three-year-old Henry, who tried his pickup line on all the females. Claire took an instant liking to most. There was cynical Joe, who commented negatively on everything said. According to him, a retired English professor from Harvard, his was the last word on literature. The group politely gave him that.

But the star of the show was Agnes. She was a short, full figured, brassy blonde with unabashedly black roots. It appeared everyone knew her. She even seemed familiar to Claire, who was certain they'd never met because she would remember Agnes. She spent most of the evening tugging on her too-tight skirt that kept riding up. Her blouse also appeared to be one size too small, the fabric straining at the buttons while ample breasts rested on the table like two bold exclamation points

Agnes talked loudly, laughed easy, and charmed all with her blue eyes and southern drawl, calling everyone, "Honey," "Sweetie," or "Love." Claire usually found it irritating if people didn't remember names, but Agnes made it sound warm-hearted and natural.

By the time the meeting ended, it was dark outside. She followed her new friends through the side door. The cold air bit her nose and she sucked in a breath before she buttoned her heavy coat and pulled mittens from the pocket. She sensed someone behind her. Jeff. Would they share the same train for the ride home?

"Nice group," she said, as he stepped to her side.

He nodded. "Most of us have been together for years. Some come and go with the winters, but the core has been here forever."

"Nice," she said again. Brilliant.

"See you in two weeks?"

"You bet."

"Good." He flashed a grin before sprinting toward the parking lot where a young woman in a Mercedes waved at him.

Claire thought she knew the way back to the 'T' but soon found herself lost. The map was little help since she really didn't have a good idea where she was. Finally, she spotted a newsstand and asked the man behind the counter where she might catch the Green Line. He pointed, and she obediently followed the tip of his finger, walking on and on. But really, how far should she trust a man who only grunted and gestured?

Finally, the iron archway that guarded the stairwell to Copley Plaza Center station came into view. She heard the train, took the stairs two at a time, and squeezed onboard.

She gave a sigh of relief and settled into a seat.

The first stop went by and a prickle rose on the back of her neck. She didn't recognize the name.

Three stops later and she didn't know any of them.

Something was wrong. Drowning in a sudden tidal wave of panic, she admonished herself to stay calm. *Breathe.* She would not, would *not* cry.

This was a nightmare. Should she just ride to the end then wait until it returned to Copley and start over? But what if it didn't turn back? What if she got off and there was no other train for the night?

Claire looked at her watch. Five forty-five. She nodded and squared her shoulders. There would be more trains since they woke her in the night. Since she had cashed a check for groceries that morning, she could get off and catch a taxi. Simple.

Waiting until the train pulled out of the tunnel, she got off at the first above ground exit she came to. Weeks ago, she realized Boston was great for taxis. Mark complained that with all the good public transportation, it was a waste of money to use them. But she felt safer being lost with a local, and no matter what the cost, she would get home.

Once in the back seat of the White Ajax taxi, and safely on the route home, a deep pang of longing clutched her heart. It wasn't India Row Claire wanted to go to, but home to the vineyard and the night jasmine. Settling in the back seat of the cab and letting the driver deal with the gridlock of rush hour, tears welled.

The safe basement filled with warm smiles became only a memory.

Mark paced the floor. The note on the brown grocery bag said only Claire was at a book group in Newton. Why Newton? She could have found a local place to read.

The clock on the stove read 7:15. She should have been home by now.

The note said she would bring dinner. Hopefully sushi from the place across the street. If the window in the apartment faced the street, he could see if she was there.

Out of habit, he opened the refrigerator and stared inside. The light welcomed him but there was nothing to satisfy his hunger. Or his emptiness.

Claire hadn't taken to weekly grocery shopping here. Instead she seemed to pick up just enough for their daily sustenance. So no more leftovers in pink Tupperware containers. No more cutting a hunk of pepper jack cheese for a before dinner snack. No more gazing into a full refrigerator and feeling the satisfaction of knowing his family was well taken care of.

He let the door close with a soft *snick* as the rubber gasket sucked fast and turned back to the kitchen and dining nook.

Where was Claire?

The table where he found the note was littered with unpaid bills, notes to herself, advertisements, paper clips, an empty paper coffee cup and a half-eaten peanut butter sandwich. All evidence Claire had been there and in the middle of something when she decided to go to a book group.

How did she get anything done? He'd told her a million times, she should make a list daily and then check things off as they were accomplished. She insisted she didn't have time to make a list.

His anxiety grew as he shuffled through the untidy remains as if he might find her hidden there, or at least a clue as to exactly where she went. He went back to the kitchen and now the clock read 7:25. At 8:00 he would call the police. He opened the fridge again, the light blinded him for an instant, then he heard the keys in the front lock.

"Where have you been?" he barked, striding to the small foyer.

"At the book group. Didn't you get my note?" She shrugged out of her coat, hung it on a hook.

"Well, I had to dig through this mess, but yes."

"Sorry."

He turned from her and flipped on the fluorescent light in the kitchen. "So what'd you bring for dinner?"

"I forgot to get something."

He spun to face her. "Forgot?"

"Sorry."

The relief he'd felt seconds ago bubbled into irritation. "Sorry doesn't cut it, Claire. What the hell is going on with you?" he blasted, louder than he intended.

She rubbed her forehead. "I got lost on the 'T' and had to take a cab home. I spent the money, but honestly I just forgot about eating."

"Didn't you take a map?"

"Mark, except the first day here to find the coffee shop, I haven't used a map in years. I had my phone and the transit app, but I got on the wrong train and was lost. It's confusing."

"Not if you pay attention."

She gave him a look he recognized as *back up or else*.

She broke the silence. "Are you hungry?"

"Starved and there's nothing to eat."

While he tried to figure out how she'd gotten lost on a train and why it was so overwhelming, she took out a skillet and melted butter. She produced a can of crabmeat and four eggs that must have been hidden in the previously empty refrigerator. She deftly made an omelet with fresh mushrooms, crab, and cheese, all things that magically appeared for her and hid from him.

He didn't mean to make her mad, but damn it all he was tired of her silently blaming him for the move to Boston. And the blame wasn't always silent, but since the Katie incident they hardly talked at all.

All Claire wanted to talk about was Katie and the move, but why? It didn't do any good. Nothing ever changed. She could ask about him and his job and his pressures, about his asshole boss. But she didn't.

At night he would wake to her crying. She was lonely. He got it. But there was no need to be this upset about a move.

If she was so concerned with feelings, why didn't she ask about his—what's happening at work—He felt the pressure to make it all come together. They used to be able to talk to each other, but since arriving in Boston all they did was exchange information on brown grocery bags. Claire slipped away, and he had no way of pulling her back. He shoved a hand through his hair, drew a breath.

"How was the group?" he asked.

"Okay," she replied, pulling two plates from the cupboard.

"Anyone or anything interesting happen in your day?" he asked. Maybe they could still find something to talk about.

"No one to speak of." She placed a plate of eggs on the only clean spot on the table. Mark reached for a soda in the refrigerator then popped the top. The fizzing sound filled the silence. He gestured to Claire, asking with his eyes if she wanted one.

She shook her head, reaching instead for the remnants in the coffee cup.

"Want me to nuke that?"

"I don't mind it cold."

They sat in silence, eating eggs and hard rolls Claire produced from the white bakery bag on the table.

He reached for her hand. "Look, I'm sorry I was so grumpy when you came in. I was worried."

"It's okay." She twined her fingers through his.

"So, tell me about your new group."

Claire didn't really want to tell him about the group, but she was certain he didn't want to listen, again, about the mix up on the train. He wouldn't understand the fear of being lost nor that a woman becomes more aware how vulnerable she is to the violence of a big city, more so than a man. She wanted him to gather her in his arms and tell her it would be okay, and he would make sure, he would keep her safe. She wanted him to assure her they could go back to the farmhouse in the vineyard and all would be right again.

Instead she told him about the book they discussed, and he pretended to listen. Their words dangled in the air over Boston Bay, waiting for clarity in the hostile winds of the Atlantic breeze.

Chapter Fifteen

At five in the morning, Mark parked his car in the downtown, underground parking lot where he rented a heated space for more than seemed reasonable. He turned off the motor and classic music he now listened to, rather than the farm report, opened the door, stepped out, and took in a deep breath of cold, city air. He walked two blocks to the gym at a brisk pace, trying to escape the freezing wind.

He'd learned, over time, to like the pre-dawn hour. As a child, his father woke him to help with the milking before school. He shared that precious time with his often-quiet father and the bellowing cows. His father talked to each one as he began the milking. After he died, Mark did the job alone. He and the herd missed the man with the reassuring touch and comforting voice.

In the Navy, the cows were replaced by the piercing blast of the base horn and the yelling of the sergeant. In Paso

Robles, a rooster crowing woke him and called him to the vineyard.

Somewhere, Mark couldn't pinpoint the day, he realized he loved the routine. It became a habit and a challenge to find the moments of quiet and cherish them.

In Boston, it was the buzz of the alarm clock. After a few weeks of waking and not doing something physical, he joined the gym. With trains running, buses releasing air brakes, and endless cars honking, he listened carefully for what nature sounds were present. A bird talking to her chicks, or a breeze picking up a piece of litter for flight. These were the closest raw earth sounds he found.

"Towel, Mr. Richter?" the attendant asked.

Mark handed him his membership card. "Thanks."

"You're late today but I'm sure your treadmill is still free. Have a good workout."

Tired of fighting with Claire, worrying about her last night exhausted him, and he hadn't sleep well.

He changed into workout clothes in the florescent-lit locker room. He'd begun to recognize a core of middle-aged regulars who silently acknowledged each other. Some read while they worked out. Others wore headphones to block the constant chatter flowing from the overhead television. Mark walked for forty-five minutes on one of fifteen treadmills lined up against the gray back wall. A green computer screen displayed simulated trails over phantom hills. For three quarters of an hour, Mark pretended he was home walking the hardened dirt paths of his rolling vineyards. On rare mornings, he imagined the sensation of damp fog wetting his face and hunted for the weight of his favorite shovel on his shoulder.

With corporate meetings every Monday, he dressed watching the clock so he wouldn't be late. Endless discussions of how to sell the wine—wine he hadn't tasted, hadn't cellared, hadn't aged and barreled and bottled—was the topic of most of the meetings. These were foreign grapes, without the character he knew. The consumer market here preferred French blends and looked down on *California wine*—said with a note of disdain. A large part of Mark's job was educating the Ahwahnee sales force about domestic alternatives. Mark tasted the top ten selling imported wines and matched them to California and Pacific Northwest vintners.

He left his tie hanging open around his neck while he walked the short distance to his office building. Outside the double glass doors, he tied a Windsor knot, put on his game face, and prepared for corporate warfare.

"Morning, Lynn," he greeted his assistant.

"Morning, sir, the meeting is in the north conference room. I have it set up for you. I put the file on your desk and made copies for everyone. You're ready to go."

"Thank you," he said.

"Anything else?" she asked.

"Is Taggart in?"

"He called this morning and his plane from New York is late." Lynn handed over a pink phone message.

That threw a wrench in Mark's plans for the day. He'd intended to spend most of the meeting letting Ralph Taggart tell how he sold an inferior wine to a mass distributor. Ralph was a great talker and enjoyed letting everyone know about his triumphs. Mark liked him personally, but he often glossed over the facts. Still, he could sell grape juice or vinegar with the same enthusiasm. Mark hoped to upgrade the quality in the future, but in the meantime, the sales team could use some of Taggart's skills. Now Mark had to rethink the meeting agenda.

Mark stopped at the coffee station and poured a cup, thinking furiously. "Lynn, did we get that proposal back from Healthy Growers?"

"I filed it. Want me dig it up?"

"Please," he said, as he stirred in powdered creamer. "That went way wrong. I think I'll have the staff review what we did and then discuss what we should have done."

"You'll need eight copies. It'll take me ten minutes, but I'll bring them in."

"Thanks. And add the projections of our resources in Chicago."

The Healthy Growers proposal kept the team silent while they read.

Mark saw the problem right off. This was a store that prided itself on its healthy, organic approach to life. It catered to a loyal upper middle-class shopper, the thirty to mid-fifty-year-olds who would rather spend their dollars on sushi than tuna in a can. Their mistake had been not emphasizing the small local vineyards Ahwahnee owned. Some even grew the crops pesticide-free. Stores like Healthy Growers, although national, sold themselves as the neighborhood store, peddling local fruits, vegetables, and meats.

The team found other missteps in the proposal.

One of the younger men, the type Mark once feared, listed in his analysis, a winery in each of the store locations. Quite by accident, he even listed Rainbow's End in Paso Robles. Without Daniel knowing it, he burned himself into Mark's memory.

As they left the meeting room, Mark slowed to allow Daniel to catch up.

"Why did you think of looking into local wineries?" Mark asked.

"In my MBA program, I did some marketing strategies for Ahwahnee." Daniel stopped. "They didn't actually know I did, but we had to turn in a mock presentation on a real company."

Mark studied Daniel. He appeared no older than his own son, the model employee Ahwahnee sought, the sort hired to replace the old regime, like him. Mark didn't want to like Daniel, yet he felt drawn to him. He had youth's energy, new ideas, and willingness to take a risk, all traits Mark now realized he'd abandoned for security.

"An MBA?" Mark asked. "From where?"

"I went to Wharton in Philadelphia, sir."

Mark blinked at the respect in the kid's voice. Manners, it seemed, still did exist. This young man was a contrast to Peter.

Mark shook off thoughts of Peter and the trouble he caused and turned back to Daniel.

"Wharton. That's a top program. I'm impressed."

Before moving to Boston, Mark hadn't heard of Wharton or any other MBA program or how they ranked. In California, people were judged on their ability, rather than where they went to school. Or at least he'd thought so.

"I learned a lot, sir, but it never can compare to life experience."

"Well, I have lots of that." Some days Mark felt every bit of it. "I'm impressed with your work. How did you know about Rainbow's End, in Paso Robles?"

"It's one of Ahwahnee's suppliers. A small, privately owned vineyard in California, somewhere on the central coast."

Mark interrupted him, "Coastal hills, close to Paso Robles and only fifteen miles from the main Ahwahnee winery I transferred from."

"You know the area?"

"Very well." Mark studied Daniel to see if he gave any hints he was already aware of that and was "sucking up" to the boss. But did it matter if he was? Mark continued, "Actually, Rainbow's End is my vineyard."

Daniel looked surprised. "Didn't know that. At Wharton I dated a girl from Cal Poly, and she raved about the pinot. She brought a bottle back after spring break and I liked it." The words rushed out of Daniel.

They had stopped at the juncture of two hallways in front of Lynn's desk. She interrupted the conversation saying Taggart was waiting in Mark's office.

"I need to meet with Ralph, but would you like to put together another proposal of how we can work with Healthy Growers? Your initial work is good. Take the suggestions made by the rest of the team and incorporate them. Get it to me by Friday. Can you do that?"

Mark picked up a business card from Lynn's desk and wrote his home number on the back. "This is all my contact numbers. Call any time you a question." He handed the card to Daniel who put it in his top pocket. "And sometime perhaps I can introduce you to some other California wines."

Chapter Sixteen

Nightmares of underground tunnels going nowhere and without an escape kept waking Claire. She turned over, groaned, hugged her pillow but finally gave into the eastern rising sun. Mark left earlier. He, of course, made enough noise to wake her while he gathered his stuff for the gym. Mark started each day with vigor and slipped into silence at sunset. She preferred to creep up on the day slowly, surprise it, and then conquer it.

Instinctively she knew caffeine would help. Mark used to make the coffee before she woke. She missed his grinding the beans, the smell of the dark roast, and the final hiss of brewing. The pot here was a percolator that noisily bubbled and left grounds floating in her mug. She'd made peace with most of the kitchen utensils, but not that damn coffee pot.

The Daily Grind was her solution. The walk was pleasant enough, short enough and with reward enough to do it and call it exercise enough to order a muffin.

The days had changed from pleasant fall breezes with rustling leaves to a biting wind and drizzly rain that chilled her to the bone. She learned mittens were warmer than gloves, you didn't wear scarves for decoration and hats with earflaps weren't funny.

Along with her extra-large-café-au-lait, Claire purchased the San Francisco Chronicle to see what was happening on the West Coast. She sat in the same corner, next to the window facing the street, so she could soak in as much sun as possible. A previous customer usually left a copy of the New York Times folded open to the crossword puzzle. Claire liked to fill in the boxes he—she was sure it was a man—left blank.

The book group had indeed lifted her spirits. It and The Daily Grind might be sufficient to make this temporary stay doable. Oh, and of course, the secret word-lover. She ran into other readers, who seemed buried in private gardens fenced off by the bindings of a good book. She became the woman hidden behind the pages of The Chronicle or bent over the maze of The Times.

"Good Morning," the barista sang out. "What can I make for you?"

"The largest café-au-lait and ..." Claire hesitated. The double chocolate brownie looked good, but the calorie count on the display label warned her to order the bran muffin.

The girl marked a cup sleeve, and without making eye contact, held out her hand for the money. Claire handed her five dollars and efficiently dropped the change in the tip-box.

Her chair in the corner was vacant and indeed the paper had been left folded open to the puzzle page. Sipping her coffee, and picking at her muffin, she tried to think of a knot whose fourth letter was G

"Howdee," spoken with the emphasis on the second part, came booming from the counter, caused Claire to look up. Agnes from the book group scrutinized the bakery display case.

"And a How Dee to you," the girl behind the counter said.

Then with a Texas wave to all the clerks, Agnes said, "How y'all today?"

A few answered. Others gave a thumbs up. Soon Agnes balanced a plate of cookies and a tall drink and headed right for Claire's table.

"Hi." Claire smiled and waved weakly as other customers lifted their heads momentarily to see who or maybe what, invaded the silence.

Agnes wasn't tall, maybe hitting five feet four inches, but she had a huge presence. She wore red stirrup pants and an oversized sweater with the state of Texas appliquéd in gold across her ample bosom. The state bounced north and south as Agnes walked in red alligator cowboy boots toward the empty chair.

"Care if I join you?"

"Please." Claire pushed the paper aside to make room. But please lower your voice, she thought. She could do without everyone looking their way.

"So, love, did you get the book for next month?" Agnes drawled.

"Yes. I've read several reviews in The Times about it. *Life of Pi* sounds interesting. I can't figure out how a boy and a tiger on a life raft can co-exist, but…" She let her voice trail off.

"Well, it keeps coming up as a 'must read' and won several international book awards."

They smiled, recognizing in the other a kindred soul. They settled into a nice discussion of books they'd both read. Agnes, it turned out, was an avid reader of all that was on the bestseller list. Engrossed in conversation, they didn't notice Jeff enter the coffee shop.

He walked behind Agnes, touched her shoulder and made her jump. Claire looked up and stared at him.

"Damn it, Jeff, you could give a girl a heart attack," Agnes said as she swatted him on the butt with the back of her hand.

"Didn't know you had a heart." He laughed. Without invitation, he pulled a chair from another table and joined them.

"What're you doin' in town?"

"Do I have to tell you everything, Aggie?" He waggled his eyebrows at her.

"Hell, yes!"

"I wanted to buy the book and thought I might stop over and see Dad."

Claire noticed his green eyes sparkled, and who could ignore the deep dimples that creased his cheeks.

"You're Claire, right?" he asked as he turned toward her.

"Yes." She certainly remembered his name but apparently she hadn't made much of an impression on him.

"May I join you ladies?"

"Looks like you already have," Agnes answered.

"Let me get my coffee." He pushed away from the table. From the counter, he asked if they wanted anything. When they refused, he turned back and ordered a tall black for himself.

Agnes leaned forward as if to whisper something secretive to Claire. Instead in a voice audible enough for Jeff to hear she said, "Nice ass on that man."

He turned and gave Agnes a big wink. Claire blushed, fearing her thoughts could be read.

When Jeff returned, coffee in hand, he noticed the crossword puzzle.

"Chignon," he said pointing to the last open space.

Claire looked at him. Of course. How could she forget the Scrabble word she and Paddy had fought over just a few short weeks ago? The day Mark announced they'd be moving to Boston. The day that forever altered her future.

"Sorry. I did the puzzle this morning, and it stumped me for a bit." Then to Agnes he asked, "You coming to the Bakerman party?"

"Big Jim wouldn't miss it."

"How is Jim?"

Claire looked back and forth trying to follow the conversation. She assumed Big Jim was Agnes' husband.

"The same ole devil."

"He's a good man." Jeff curled his hands around the mug. "Keep him happy."

"Happy!" Agnes puffed up, drawing in a deep breath. "That man couldn't be any happier. I meet his *every* need." She punched Jeff's arm. "Git my drift?"

Claire noticed his hands with the manicured nails. So different from Mark's. This loafer-wearing man with soft hands intrigued her.

Jeff hung his head, shook it and laughed. Then turned to Claire. "You met Big Jim?"

Claire shook her head, "No."

"Jim and Aggie are a team. Been together how long?"

"Forty-two wonderful years, barely kids when we met in Austin."

"You married, Claire?"

"Yes." She almost added for twenty-eight wonderful years, but she didn't.

Chapter Seventeen

Claire returned to The Daily Grind every day at the same time. Some days she ran into Agnes in the building lobby. She lived on the top floor, which explained why she seemed familiar at the book group. They'd had some near meetings in the lobby. According to doorman Donald Agnes and Jim owned the "whole" floor and had converted it into a very nice place.

Donald became Claire's source for information. He really did know most everything. He definitely knew everybody in the building and would dole out interesting tidbits in exchange for a rather large piece of apple pie. It turned out that it didn't need to be apple, any pie would do.

"You off to coffee, Madam Claire?"

"I am indeed, Donald. Should I get my umbrella?"

"Not going to rain. The bursitis acts up when it is. I'd be quite stiff if it were planning on raining. No rain, but you'd best bundle up."

"I'm not used to this cold."

"It isn't cold, yet."

She huffed a breath. "Thanks, Donald." What was she going to do when it got what Boston labeled *cold*?

Claire heard the elevator open. She turned to see a bundle of white fur emerge.

"Mornin', Madam Agnes," Donald said.

"Good morning, Donald. How's your son?"

"Doing better. Thank you for asking. My wife took him to the doctor you recommended, and he had pneumonia. He's much healthier."

Agnes pulled on mittens and turned to Claire. "You going for coffee, Claire?"

"Of course."

"Well, button up and let's go. I need a cigarette and I don't want Donald telling Jim I smoke." Agnes winked at Donald.

He buzzed open the front door and off they went. They weren't half a block from the building when Agnes lit a cigarette and offered one to Claire.

"I don't smoke."

"Nor do I," she exhaled with the smoke.

They both laughed.

Claire learned over the last couple of weeks there was a quieter side to Agnes, a person full of kindness who, like a fairy godmother with a wand, scattered good deeds on unsuspecting recipients. Once, it was rumored, she left a fifty-dollar bill in the tip box at the Daily Grind for the clerk whose purse had been stolen that morning.

"Ready for the book group?" she asked between puffs.

Claire couldn't see much of Agnes's face above the fur collar and below the fur hat. She answered the cloud above a cartoon.

"I'm ready. I hope I don't get lost this time."

"Come with us. Jeff is picking me up."

"I couldn't," she answered too fast.

"Oh hell, he won't care."

Claire considered. The prospect of being safely taken to the group was awfully appealing. "What time? And where should I meet you?"

"In the lobby at 11:30. Don't eat. We'll stop on the way and get a sandwich."

"Deal."

They walked on talking about nothing of importance.

Claire checked the lobby clock. She was early. She often waited for Agnes who ran late.

Claire's time in Boston felt like a big waiting game. She waited for Agnes, for Mark, for the seasons. And she waited to return home to California.

Pacing in front of the elevators, she kept checking the time. Adjusting and readjusting the scarf hanging around her neck, a bubble of excitement brewing just below her skin. She'd been looking forward to book group. *The Life of Pi* was really good. But, she admitted to herself, her nervousness wasn't about the book.

The elevator doors opened, and Agnes exploded into the lobby, wearing a turban and matching neon pink raincoat.

"Expecting rain?" Claire asked.

"Never can be sure, Boston rains when it wants. We should be having snow any day."

Claire turned to Donald who touched his hip and shook his head, no.

"I've never lived where it snows," Claire said.

"Neither had I till we moved here. It hails in Texas. Big ole hail balls. Saw one kill a cow once."

Claire laughed. Agnes loved to exaggerate. Claire doubted that a hailstone ever killed a cow.

They both turned to the door when a car honked from the curb. Jeff waved. Donald buzzed them out.

Agnes got in the front seat as Claire slid in behind her. The heater was on full blast and she loosened the scarf around her neck and shoved the mittens in her purse. Not only were they warmer, they were easier than gloves to take on and off.

"How ya doin', dahlin?" Agnes drawled as Jeff leaned over, allowing her to kiss his cheek.

"I'm fine." He returned to his position behind the wheel, put the car in gear, and headed out into the traffic circle Claire still found confusing. He negotiated the streets with familiarity and ease.

He and Agnes talked. Claire watched their banter more than listened to it. They had the ease of two old friends. She overheard them talking about a girl named Emily, and surmised it was a daughter. She took a second look at Jeff's ring finger. No wedding band, but then Mark didn't wear one either. He lost his their first year of marriage. For safety reasons he learned to remove it while working around equipment and one day just forgot to put it back on. She twisted the band around her finger. It was tighter than she remembered.

"Did Anne show up at Emily's wedding?" Agnes asked.

"Oh, yeah. With her new live-in. She got drunk and started spouting off all the old shit," Jeff said.

"What did you do?"

"I stepped outside, and she followed. Screaming and yelling I never sent any money, that I destroyed her life, turned Emily against her."

"I'm sorry. I thought she was over it. Didn't she go into rehab?"

"I heard that too." Jeff's voice took an edgy tone. "That's why Emily thought it would be safe to invite Anne. The new boyfriend tried to calm her." Jeff turned momentarily to Agnes. "Eventually he apologized to Emily then forcibly stuffed Anne in the car and left."

"I guess the clinic didn't work."

"It's her pattern. She gets out of control. Her Daddy or I pay for a detox program. She swears she's fine and then within eighteen months is back on the bottle or pills. I don't know what else to do."

Looking into the rear-view mirror, Claire saw sadness roll over Jeff's face.

"I don't care what she says about me, but it kills me for our daughter. She'd been to Aspen to visit her mother and Anne was sober. Emily so wanted her at the wedding."

"Is Emily still mad at you?"

"Nah. We had a rough time of it a couple years back, but Brad, the guy she married, helped her see her mom has an illness. He's a good guy, I couldn't have asked for a better son-in-law."

"Sounds like he is." Agnes turned to the back seat. "Claire, you have any kids?"

"Three, two girls and a boy."

"How old?" Jeff asked.

"Oldest daughter twenty-eight, son twenty-seven, and Katie is almost twenty going on fourteen."

"I haven't been blessed." Agnes offered without being asked. "So, I just love hearing about everyone else's. I like being the Auntie."

"And a damn good Auntie you are," Jeff said as he patted Agnes's knee.

"Your kids all in school?" Jeff asked Claire.

"Colleen is a teacher and Sean a new attorney. Katie is a third-year student at Davis." *At least she was.*

"Are they coming for Thanksgiving?" Agnes asked.

Claire couldn't yet admit Katie had dropped out of school to live with her boyfriend. She twisted the wedding band again. The skin under the ring itched.

Agnes' voice penetrated her thoughts. "Where did you go, girl? I asked if your kids are coming for Thanksgiving."

"No, for Christmas, unless we go home."

"Then join us at the club," Agnes said as she turned to Jeff. "Don't you think she should?"

"Yeah, join us. We're a strange group of people and if you can stand the two of us then come to the club for Thanksgiving. Bring your husband."

"I'll check with Mark."

Claire knew Mark hadn't made any plans. But how he would fit in with this group? He hated big parties. He preferred small intimate dinners where he was well acquainted with everyone. He always had a strategy—let her deal with Thanksgiving dinner.

"Oh, join us," Agnes pleaded. "The club puts on a big feast. Usually the men go early and watch some silly ball game in the bar till we women arrive and drag their sorry asses to the tables. Afterwards, to make us feel better, they dance with us."

"Don't believe everything this Texan says, not all of us men gather in the bar." Jeff made a face at Agnes before he paused then asked, "What's your husband's name? What does he do?"

"Mark. He works in marketing for Ahwahnee Winery. He's really a farmer, which is what he likes the most. We have a little vineyard in the foothills of California." She nervously continued, "We're here for a couple of years then we'll go back." She said it in a rushed way and added, "Then we'll live off our small vineyard." She smiled at the thought.

Jeff pulled the car into the church parking lot and claimed a stall near the back entrance.

"Let me buy you girls a sandwich," Jeff said as he opened their doors.

Claire fell in behind Agnes and Jeff as they headed with purpose across the lot to a small storefront deli. She saw no clues it was a restaurant. As they stepped through the door, the smells of vinegar-soaked pickles and garlic-laced salads filled the air. The ethnic foods here were different than those in California. She ordered pastrami on rye with hot mustard. To her delight it came with homemade coleslaw.

They sat at a small chrome-gray table in the back.

"So, what kind of law does your son practice?" Jeff asked between bites of his oversized hot dog smothered in sauerkraut.

"Sean?" Claire answered somewhat surprised.

"I'm a lawyer, and I remember you said your son is."

"Oh yeah, he wants to practice water law."

"That's interesting. I bet it is a hot topic in California."

"It is. He likes it. What kind of law do you practice?"

"Corporate. I went in with my father. He had a well-established practice. And I being the good son ..." he hesitated, "... actually his only son, I joined him."

"Good son, my ass," Agnes interjected, wiping mustard from her lips.

Jeff shrugged. "Okay. I joined my father's practice to irritate him."

"Closer to the truth."

"Isn't your father proud of you?" Claire asked.

"He was proud I graduated third in my class from Harvard. He was proud I joined the firm. He wasn't happy I went to Stanford Law instead of accepting Harvard. We don't agree on politics. I'm a liberal, and he isn't."

Claire assumed there was much more to the father-son relationship. Her counselor training wanted more.

"Is your father still alive?" Claire asked.

"Yes, he suffers from Alzheimer's. Actually, senility has improved our relationship."

Her heart tightened at the thought of her own father. She couldn't imagine him senile.

Jeff continued, "My mom was younger, but she died five years ago. I still miss her."

"So do I," added Agnes.

"You knew his folks?" Did everyone know everybody? Or was it only these two who talk as if she should?

"Everyone knew his folks. His mother threw the best parties." Agnes looked at Jeff and smiled softly.

Claire studied Jeff's eyes. A dark brown ringed the green iris. They invited her in yet held her back.

Chapter Eighteen

The *Life of Pi*, November's book, divided readers. The ones who liked it talked, and those who didn't complained about the symbolism and the book needing fewer pages.

Agnes stood and placed one hand over her breast. "When no one believed the boy's story, I damn near cried." She dabbed at an emerging tear. Agnes always joked and now, a vulnerable side? What was her story? Everyone had one. Somewhere a tiger stalks through lives, something we feared, yet accepted.

"We all rewrite our history. When we do, we are the hero, the knower, the prophet," said Jeff.

Am I the hero, knower, and prophet of my story, or a victim and denier and stuck?

Glen, the young paraplegic, agreed. "If I lived every moment of my life from the confines of my disability, I would give up. Instead, I dream and make my dreams part of my every day."

"How about you?" Jeff asked, directing his question to Claire.

"Unfortunately, I'm a realist. I used to see the cup half full, but lately I've been concentrating on the half empty."

"Why?" Glen asked.

"Not sure." She searched her mind for a reason. Finding none, she shrugged. "Sometimes I'm lost." *And there's a Bengal tiger in my raft.*

She looked up and caught Jeff studying her face. She smiled to mask her insecurities.

The coffee poured, the cookies eaten, the discussion ended. One by one, members gathered their belongings, said their good-byes and headed to wherever they called home. Soon only Agnes, Claire, Jeff, and Glen remained, and the men were absorbed in conversation.

"Give me a minute, ladies," Jeff called.

Claire saw Jeff hand Glen a business card. They shook hands, clasping a little longer than strangers do. Glen spun on his wheels, waved good-bye to Agnes and Claire, and rolled out the back door and down the ramp.

"Looked heavy," Agnes said as Jeff joined them.

"Yeah ..." He paused and adjusted his coat. "Glen's company passed him over for a promotion. It would have meant a move uptown, and he's pretty sure it's because the building isn't accessible. Sounds like discrimination to me, so I offered to look into it."

"Dayum," Agnes drawled. "He's been with them for so long. I thought he was one of their best designers."

"He's worked for them for thirteen years. Even after the accident, he was promoted several times. Next to make partner, but it would have meant the move and renovations to the main office."

"Shit, they're a damn building design firm. Give me a Texas break." Agnes jutted her chin. "Can they do that?"

Claire loved how the Texan came out in Agnes, especially when she cursed. "How long has he been in the chair?" Claire asked.

Jeff looked at Agnes. "Six years?"

"Almost seven," she corrected.

"It isn't my business, but what happened?" Claire waited for a story she was certain Agnes would embellish.

"He'd just run out to buy milk at the neighborhood store late one Sunday night. Horrendous car accident, his minivan slammed into a pole by another vehicle. Glen spent two weeks in a coma, and when he woke up, they sent him to Spaulding for rehab. After six months, he went back to work. His wife supported every step along the way."

"Wife?" She didn't know why she was surprised. She would've probably stayed with Mark and he was so responsible, he would have stayed with her. "Are they still married?"

Both Agnes and Jeff replied, "Yes."

Before anyone could say more, Agnes's phone rang.

"Hello," Agnes raised her voice. "Where are you? Okay. See you there." She closed her screen and shoved it in her pocket.

"That was Big Jim. He's in Newton and said he would come by and take me to dinner." She paused then asked, "Wanna join us?"

"Can't," Jeff said.

"I shouldn't." Claire added, "Mark gets nervous when I don't show up on time." She shuddered at the memory of being lost and Mark's reaction.

"You need a ride?" Jeff asked Agnes.

"No. I'll meet him at the deli." Agnes headed off.

"Afraid to be alone with me?" Jeff winked at Claire.

"Should I be?"

"Yes," yelled Agnes over her shoulder. "Be afraid. Very afraid."

Jeff waved her off as he opened the car door for Claire. Maybe she should have been afraid. Not of Jeff but of her own vulnerability. They settled in the car, this time with Claire in the front passenger seat. Jeff turned toward her and smiled. She fought the sudden urge to touch his dimple, to run a finger down his cheek to his chin.

She cleared her throat and folded her hands. "It's very kind of you to give me a ride."

As he pulled into evening traffic, he asked, "Tell me something about you."

"Like what?" She was usually the one asking open ended questions. Should she tell him how much she missed home, or how age had taken her by surprise?

"Well, do you work?"

It had been a while since someone asked about her about a job. Agnes hadn't. Then again, she hadn't asked Agnes. "I'm a licensed Social Worker and in California worked with battered women."

"That was hard, I bet."

"In a way, yes, but also rewarding when I helped change a woman's life. As soon as I think I've heard it all, a woman comes in with a story that blows me away. I love the challenge and the uniqueness of each case." She hesitated and stared out the window as a slow bubble of loss floated around her. She missed her clients, the office, and Val. *I miss the old me.*

"Where do you go when you get silent?"

She jolted back to the front seat of Jeff's car shook her head, shook away the Sirens calling her home. "Nowhere special, just remembering my co-worker and wondering how she's doing."

"You looked...sad."

"I miss working. It gave me some self-worth."

"Why not work here? We have battered women."

"My license isn't good here. I could volunteer but it really takes time to know the community. I thought I would offer to do some work with the church but haven't found one I like."

"What faith are you?"

"Catholic, and the priest at the local parish appears to be a bit heavy on sin." She remembered her discomfort at part of his sermon three weeks ago. "I like my priest to be into grace and forgiveness."

"Don't you guys go to confession for that?" Jeff asked, not looking at her while navigating a left turn.

"Not like we used to. We have the option of confession now. Things have changed. We even eat meat on Fridays."

"No! Not meat on Friday." He chuckled. "As a kid, I loved to eat Friday night dinner at the neighbor's because Billy's mom made the best macaroni and cheese."

"Well, nowadays you wouldn't be guaranteed mac-n-cheese or even fish sticks. More likely a delivered pizza on a Friday night."

"Ah crap. The simple joys of life thrown out the window."

They laughed, bantered comfortably, and before long drove into the circle of the condo.

"Thanks for the ride," she said as she opened her own door.

"No problem. Hey, if you're bored, would you be interested in helping me with the research for Glen's case?" He leaned across the seat to look at her, brows raised. With hope?

Don't be ridiculous, she told herself. He was simply being kind to a bored and lonely friend. "Maybe. I'm not sure how much help I can be."

"Well, I know laws. I'm not sure how to find out what Glen needs to make this job accessible to him."

"Ask him."

He shook his head. "I'm not good at getting that kind of information from people. Agnes blows me away with what she learns about strangers."

"I'm no Agnes."

He chuckled. "Thank God."

She considered a moment. "I do know how to gather information in a professional way. One of my strengths at the center was interviewing," she said.

"Think about it. It wouldn't take a lot of your time. There is a little money in it. I'm doing it pro-bono, but it might be fun."

She nodded. "Okay then. See you." She waved over her shoulder as Donald buzzed her in.

Claire decided to call Val as soon as she got upstairs. She already knew she would work with Jeff, but the excitement she felt also raised some alarm. In the quiet of the sterile condo, Claire dialed the Women's Center.

Mary answered.

"Mary, it's me, Claire. Is Val in?" Claire immediately envisioned the lobby of the center with its stained couches and worn rug. She could see Mary sitting behind the old oak desk piled high with papers.

Claire looked around the neat white living room. She'd planned to buy pillows, bright sun yellow, a few deep grass green, and rich earth brown to make this place warmer. She shivered in the cold of Boston. Pillows. Warm pillows. First thing tomorrow.

"Hi, Miss Claire. Val is in and finishing with a client. We miss you. How are you?" Mary spoke fast.

"I'm fine, Mary. How are you?"

"Real good. I graduate in December, and I met a new guy."

Oh yes. The days Mary stood in Claire's doorway talking about each new man. Claire envisioned herself standing in Val's doorway, announcing she met someone.

"Val is free. I'll let her know you're on the phone."

Claire quickly added, "Congratulations on the new man."

"Thanks. I'll keep you posted."

The phone, put on hold, went to a country rendition of "Only the Lonely." Claire laughed remembering how much she hated the canned music of the center.

"Claire?"

"Who else would call you in the middle of the day and stay on the phone listening to that horrid music?"

"If I knew it was you, I would have ordered in jazz."

After bringing each other current with family, Claire shared she was still working hard at finding her way in Boston.

"So, tell me about this 'maybe' job," Val said.

"I think it might be fun, I need to do something."

"Hmmmm."

"Hmmmm, what?" Claire asked.

"Why debate it? If you want to work, then work. What's the hesitation?"

"Mark won't approve."

"Mark never wanted you to work, and it didn't stop you before. Why this time?"

Claire paused before answering, "I don't know."

Mark wasn't thrilled when she was offered the part time job at the church's counseling center. He objected when she had evening meetings and she expected him to watch the children. She planned her life around his and the children's schedule.

So, what was stopping her now? No kids. No schedule to work around. Mark probably wouldn't even notice.

"Look, Claire, you've always needed something more than kids, home, and Mark. I do my job because I like knowing I'm capable of taking care of myself. You work because …?"

"To be needed," she answered fast, without thinking.

"Good, being needed is okay," Val answered in her professional voice.

Mark once needed her. She remembered late nights in bed sharing their days. He listened to all the stories about the kids. She helped him with job choices and they both wanted the vines and small boutique winery. When did they stop talking, stop sharing?

She missed the intimacy of pre-sleep chatting.

Before Claire saw him, she heard Mark's key in the door. She said a quick goodbye to Val and met him in the kitchen. Before leaving for book group, she'd put a roast in the slow cooker, so she didn't repeat forgetting to bring dinner home.

"Mmmm. Something smells good," he said as he rounded the corner.

"Roast." She spooned out potatoes and carrots. "How was work?" She tossed salad greens in olive oil and balsamic vinegar.

Mark put the platter of meat and potatoes on the table and waited for Claire to bring the salad. They sat across from each other filling their plates.

"Work was the same." He lifted his forkful of meat, but before eating he asked, "Did you go out today?"

"Book group and I met a young man who's losing his job. I might work with his attorney to see if there is a discrimination case."

Mark stabbed a cherry tomato and, with seeds on his lips, asked, "What are you talking about?"

While they ate, Claire told him about Glen, his wheelchair, and his non-promotion. She talked about Jeff and how he asked her to help with the case.

"Is he going to pay you?" Mark asked while buttering a third piece of French bread.

"Not much, but I wouldn't do it for the money."

"Then why do it?"

She suppressed the impatience she knew colored her tone. "For something to do."

"I thought you would love doing nothing. Lots of women would kill to be in your position."

He still didn't get it. She sighed and put down her fork. "I'm not lots of women."

He shrugged. "Do what you want. You do anyway."

"I wanted to stay in Paso Robles." Her throat closed, holding back irritation.

He stopped chomping his bread and looked at her like she'd declared herself at war with the pope over visiting hours at the Sistine Chapel. "You didn't have to come."

Claire pushed away from the table. Anger flowed from her like water over a broken levee. "I don't remember being asked. My memory is you announced we were moving." She gathered the plates. "Don't try to rewrite history."

"Calm down," he said.

"Calm down? Why? So you can make more announcements that complicate my life?"

He blinked rapidly. "Does this mean you're leaving?"

Her shoulders sagged. "No, Mark, I'm not leaving." Then she added, "Yet."

"What does that mean?"

She breathed deep and said, "It means I'm taking the job if it's still available and I'm working on making myself happy." She turned her back and walked to the kitchen. At the doorway, she turned half way. "Because I sure can't seem to please you."

Mark blanched, his shoulders slumped, the tips of his ears turned red. She had hurt him. Her levee broke and she couldn't pretend things were okay or going to improve.

"Is there more?" he asked.

"You want it all now?"

"Go ahead. I might as well hear it." Sarcasm colored his voice.

She leaned against the door, folded her arms. Considered if he meant it. "Fine then. I'm still pissed about Katie. You always take her side. You think it's okay she dropped out of school and moved in with Peter?"

"Stop." He stood. On the ranch he would have stormed out the back door and cooled off in the vineyard. She would have slammed the side door and taken a hoe to the vegetable garden and demolished the weeds. Here they had no place to run.

He looked around, as if lost, bewildered. Finally, he settled on glaring at her ankles. "Do you really believe I'd choose Katie over you? I don't. But I don't think fighting with her will help. It didn't in the past." He sighed. "I'm just as upset as you, but one of us had to stay calm. I thought it best to just get her out of here."

"I'm scared for her. Hell, I'm scared for us."

"I've done my best." Mark walked into the living room.

So, he was done. He wasn't willing to show his feelings. Again.

She turned to the sink and attacked the dishes.

Chapter Nineteen

Jeff, unable to sleep, cursed the cold of the bedroom. Getting up and turning on the heat felt like surrendering early to winter.

"Screw it," he said aloud to the dark as he threw off the down comforter. His finger stabbed the pad until the numbers climbed past seventy and he waited for the register to click on. On his way back to bed he grabbed the white socks he'd shed earlier and hadn't put in the laundry basket.

"It's going to be a long winter." He jumped back in bed and pulled the socks on and then the comforter. "Better."

Talking out loud to himself. Man, he needed to find someone to talk to. He might be certifiable.

The smell of vented heat rose as he relaxed. What he wouldn't give to turn to a lover and cuddle next to her for warmth, waking her slightly, then slipping into a comforted slumber.

Amy would have spent the night if he'd asked. Except he didn't want Amy. Or any of the women he seemed to be attracting.

He hadn't fallen asleep with a woman in his arms in years. That wasn't to say he hadn't had many women in his bed. When Emily, his adult daughter, lived at home, he wouldn't have girlfriends over. Emily eventually figured out when Nanny spent the night, Daddy didn't come home. Father and daughter never really talked about it, but she would give him a morning glare.

On sleepless nights like this, he often went to her room and watched her sleep. He never realized how much he could love one person. Since the divorce from Anne, he vowed to provide the best of everything, including himself, to Emily. He could never give Anne what she needed, but she gave him more than he deserved in their daughter.

He hugged his pillow. Why did he keep women at arms' distance? What was he looking for? He kept attracting superficial women who were into status. Repeats of Anne.

They grew up in the same neighborhood, went away to private boarding schools, played tennis at the same country clubs and were worlds apart.

Jeff had gone off to Stanford while Anne stayed and attended Smith. Her earned degree in Art History helped her grow into a decent impressionist.

Jeff loved his California years of radical thinking. Stanford had a more sedate coming of age than say, Berkeley, but it was a political hot bed with their own core of free thinkers. He returned to Boston with a different social conscience. He wanted to be part of the new. It wasn't that easy hailing from one of the established families. So, he joined his father's law firm and slowly took on cases that changed laws. His father objected at first until he realized his son was acquiring a name for himself and headed for politics.

It seemed only natural he and Anne started dating, she beautiful and full of talent, he, handsome and full of promise.

The room warmed but sleep evaded. He tossed and turned. At almost 4:00, it would be 1:00 in the afternoon in Paris. He got up and made a cup of instant in the microwave and called Emily.

He listened while the automatic connection hummed and beeped till finally, "Bon Jour."

"Um, it's me, Dad."

"Daddy."

He smiled at her affectionate tone. "Glad you still speak English. I'd hate to have to go back to school to learn French."

They talked for a bit with Jeff bringing her up to date on all the local gossip, and she told him her adventures, and about life with her new husband.

"Still not sleeping I see," she said.

"Nah, too cold. I just got up and made a cup of coffee."

"Real or that jar stuff?"

"Oh, you coffee snob," he teased back

"Anyone ever tell you coffee when you can't sleep doesn't help?"

"I'm not ready for warm milk."

"It's cold here as well. I had to learn how to work the European heating system. I miss my old room."

"Come home."

"So, I can drink bad coffee with you in the middle of the night?"

"If you were here, I'd make hot chocolate."

"You do make a mean hot chocolate with canned cream."

"Coming home for Christmas?"

"Yep. We don't get Thanksgiving here and since I can't find a turkey, I might have to stuff a goose."

"Poor goose."

Then without warning the conversation changed.

"Mom called last week," she said.

"Oh?" Then as an afterthought, "How is she?"

"Not good. I can tell when she's using. She talked on and on then got silent. She passed out. Her new friend came on and hung up the phone."

"I'm sorry."

"There's a part of me that still wants to save her, Dad."

"I know, princess. There's a part of me that still believes we can."

"But we can't," she finished the sentence.

"Want me to check up on her and get back to you?"

"Not really. Did Mom always drink and use?"

"She didn't drink at all when she was pregnant."

"I never asked, Dad, but why did she start?"

Jeff inhaled deeply and curled his toes in his socks. "I'm not sure. It became a problem after your birth. I mean she always had a glass of wine or a gin and tonic at the club but never really got more than a little tipsy."

Jeff remembered so many things and tried to sort which ones he wanted to tell his daughter. This topic, like his dates, was taboo, but now she was asking.

"I guess it started around the time her art show failed."

"I vaguely remember Mom painting."

"She was pretty good and had planned on making it a career." He leaned back against the chair. "She gained some weight with you and a doctor prescribed diet pills. Another doctor prescribed sleeping pills."

"That wouldn't happen in this day and age."

"Maybe not." Jeff tried to pick his words carefully, after all Anne was Emily's mother. "All along she drank, too."

"Did you try to stop her?"

"I was busy with the law practice and thought that she was exhausted from caring for you. That's when we hired a nanny. I thought if your mother could get some rest, she could get back to painting. And she did for a bit. She had a gallery show, but it was a major failure." Jeff shook his head at the nasty comments of her so-called "friends." "The critics were hard on her, calling her a 'rich kid with a new paint set.'"

"Wow, that is harsh."

"After that, she stopped painting. You must have been about three. She hung out at the club more and more with other wives. I didn't think much of it since our mothers had been part of the club social set."

"I vaguely remember. Mom was still painting some, wasn't she?"

"A little. More and more she was getting drunk and attacking life with her brush."

"Something happened though, when I was about five?"

Jeff knew exactly the day she was asking about. Why had he waited until now to tell her? So far away, he couldn't touch or comfort her. But she asked and deserved the answer. He took a long sip of lukewarm coffee.

"It was a Thursday. I got a call from the nanny. She needed me to come home because your mother was crying and screaming and tearing up canvasses." The nanny talked about a knife and Emily crying, but he'd better not share all the details. "I came home and she was out of control. Nanny grabbed you and ran. I tried talking to your mother, but she wasn't making sense."

"Did Nanny take me to Grandfather's?"

"Yeah. And your grandfather came over as soon as he heard what was happening. He's the one who got your mom to the hospital. That's when I found out how big the problem was."

Jeff still felt guilty for not realizing earlier. When he thought back on it, there were all kinds of signs he'd ignored.

"Something else happened that night. I can't remember what," she said softly.

"You got spanked. You had never been, even when your mother was the worst, she never hit you. She might forget to feed you, but she never once laid a hand on you. The nanny helped with that. That night when we all came back from the hospital you were crying for your mother and wouldn't stop. Crying so hard you threw up. Then your grandfather, in his frustration, picked you up and spanked your bottom telling you—"

"That he would give me something to cry about," she finished the sentence.

"Yes."

"Then you hit Grandfather, didn't you?"

"I broke his nose. There was blood everywhere. Not my proudest moment."

"It all makes sense now. You and Grandfather's distance—his blaming you for mom's illness."

"None of it makes sense, baby. It was a big mess. He was your mother's father and just as scared as I. I vowed to never let anything happen to you again."

There was silence for a moment.

"You fulfilled that promise," Emily said.

Warmth filled his chest. He had. She grew up well adjusted. Normal. Happy, even.

"How many times did Mom go through rehab?"

"I'm not sure. I paid for three stints. The first was back then. I went to the groups with her. I thought we could save our marriage. She blamed me as part of the problem and maybe I was. I wasn't there for her. I couldn't make her happy."

"Not your job to make another happy," Emily reminded him.

Well aware of that, he still felt he'd failed as a husband. Was that why he was cold at night? He'd failed and no matter how much he understood about the illness of addiction, somewhere deep inside, he knew he'd failed.

"How come so silent, Dad?"

"Just wishing you were here."

"We'll see you for Christmas."

"Can't wait."

"Hey, Dad."

"What?"

"Thanks. Thanks for everything."

He heard her blow a kiss and hang up.

He rinsed his coffee mug and went to bed.

The room finally grew warm.

Chapter Twenty

At a conference, in the early years of her career, Claire learned to journal. It was a sporadic habit she turned to whenever she felt at odds with the world.

Tonight, she decided to immerse herself and write herself steady. She let the new leather cover fall open for her late-night entry. A mirrored reflection of her inner self spilled across four pages. The black ink flowed thick with anger then tear-stained with hurt. It had been her tradition to always end an entry with some conclusion. Then in clear, deliberate printing she read her own suggestion: *Wake each morning with a new goal and let go of what isn't. I'm excited and a bit scared taking this new job. I live for a challenge and this might be a good one.*

Jeff dropped off a copy of the American Disabilities Act. Claire turned her dining table into a makeshift desk. She spent a few days going through the documents, spreading them out the length of the table and using the chairs as temporary folder holders.

The messy visual of work and accomplishment made her smile each time she walked into the small eating nook.

She still had coffee daily with Agnes, and when the bold Texan heard about Glen's situation, she offered to get a congressman involved. The sheer number of people Agnes knew was impressive enough, never mind who they actually were. Movers and shakers, politicians, businesspeople, Hollywood folks and fashionistas. If Agnes didn't know them personally, she knew someone who did.

This morning as Claire waited for Agnes in the lobby, Donald handed Claire another manila envelope. She weighed the heft then slipped a finger under the seal to peer in. This document appeared to be additional and more specific information on accessibility regarding work environments. Highlighted portions needed answers she was expected to obtain from Glen.

"Hey, dahlin'," she heard behind her.

"Agnes. You about scared the poo out of me."

"Shit, hon. I about scared the *shit* out of you. Don't be afraid to say it." Agnes launched a monologue about Pooh being a bear while putting on her gloves and adding several expletives Claire ignored.

"You're in rare form this morning," Claire finally broke in.

"I'll be better as soon as I get a smoke."

Donald reached under his desk and handed Agnes a pack of unfiltered Camels then held the door open for them.

Agnes pulled a cigarette from the pack using her lips and carefully, while not removing the gloves, lit it with the disposable lighter. She inhaled dramatically, held it and slowly exhaled.

"Dayum, that's good."

Claire coughed and waved the smoke away from her face.

"Sorry, dahlin'. What's in the envelope?"

"More cases and interpretations of the accessibility of the ADA from Jeff."

"More likely from his secretary." Agnes dismissed her with a wave. "Read it yet?"

Claire riffled through the stack. "It's forty-four pages."

"Let's look at it when we get inside." Agnes talked around the cigarette balanced between her lips. "I like legal documents. They're bullshit. Us Texans know a cow patty when we see one."

The cold chased them to the Daily Grind where Agnes stamped out the last of her cigarette on the curb. "Damn laws. Soon we won't be able to smoke outdoors. Second hand smoke will kill some endangered species."

They walked inside and to the counter where the barista efficiently took their orders. Nodding to some of the regulars they passed, they found their table in the corner. After settling, Claire cleared a space and they read, turning pages when the other indicated.

Claire finally leaned back in her chair and looked at Agnes. "I'm not sure, but two of the cases sound like Glen's."

"One of 'em, the judge ruled in favor of the client and the other in favor of the employer."

"I guess Jeff wants me to find the things Glen has in common with the winning client," Claire said.

Agnes pressed two fingers on her lip as if she were still smoking. "You think?"

Stuffing the pages back in the envelope, Claire laughed. "You're still in a great mood."

"Just ignore me. Shall we get a refill and head back?"

"Yeah, I'm meeting Glen at Jeff's office this afternoon." She stood. "And it looks like I have some re-reading to do."

As they walked home it dawned on Claire she hadn't asked if Agnes had a degree or even went to college. As a matter of fact, she recently learned Agnes would be turning sixty-five this year, when one of the group members asked if she was going to be signing up for Social Security.

Claire glanced at Agnes strolling next to her. The other woman smiled as if listening to a private joke. "Did you work?" Claire finally asked. "I mean, outside the home?"

Agnes's brow furrowed for a moment. "I was a nurse. That's how I met Big Jim. He fell from a horse and came into the emergency department with his shoulder dislocated." Agnes smiled. "Never saw a man cry as much as he did." She winked around a soft giggle. "Told him to buck up and be thankful. If he were the horse, we would've had to shoot him, and if he didn't stop caterwauling, I might shoot him anyway." Agnes broke into a full laugh. "He said he thought people cared more about the horse. I reminded him that was Texas."

Claire couldn't help but laugh too.

Agnes seemed to take that as encouragement to continue. "So, I shot his ass full of Demerol and the doc pulled his arm back into the socket. Mean procedure but the only way to do it." Out of nowhere a cigarette appeared. "When he was coming down from the Demerol, he was one happy camper and asked me out." She blew smoke in the air. "I worked for many years. Even worked here in Boston at Mass General, then retired when I was fifty."

"Do you miss it?"

She waggled her head, considering. "Yes and no. It was hard work, and I came home bone tired—no pun intended—every night. I developed a little cancer and quit work to take care of my health."

Claire's heart stuttered. "Cancer?"

Agnes gave one quick nod. "Yeah. Cured."

"And you still smoke?"

"That's why Big Jim doesn't approve." Agnes flicked the remains of the half-smoked cigarette into the street. "But, hell, I'm down to two cigarettes a day."

Claire fought the sudden urge to take the cigarettes and throw them all down the gutter. Instead she smiled, put a hand on Agnes' shoulder and gave her friend a quick squeeze.

That afternoon Claire took a cab to Jeff's office.

"I'm Ms. Richter and I have an appointment with Mr. Wentworth."

The perky thirty-something receptionist held up a finger indicating Claire should wait a moment while she dialed an extension.

"A Ms. Richter is here to see you," she said into the mouthpiece, then turned to Claire. "He'll be right with you."

Claire looked around the well-appointed office, rich in mahogany and cushioned chairs, very different than the thrown together miss-matched donated furniture of her old office. It resembled someone's living room more than a waiting room. The pictures on the walls were prints of Audubon birds. She studied the detail of an American Flamingo-Phoenicopterus, subtitled *Old Male* when she realized Jeff had entered the room.

"Great. You found us."

"At least the cab did." She smiled and looked back at the picture to hide the uptick in her pulse.

"I call him Gus," he said, pointing to the flamingo. "And there's Lou." He pointed to a Blue Heron. "As a kid, when I had to wait for my dad, I would stare at these pictures and name them. Over here is Dad." He walked toward a picture of a buzzard. "It's a California Vulture or Condor. He was one of the last Dad bought. I left for Stanford and found it ironic. So, I named him Senior."

Claire chuckled and took a long look at the bird. "He looks worried."

"He does?" Jeff slanted his head sideways. "I always thought he looked menacing." He shrugged. "Let's go in the conference room." Jeff pointed to a windowed room with a large glass table and comfortable black leather chairs arranged around it. At one end, a pile of books with colored Post-it notes sticking out all over waited.

"I've pulled some rulings from current hearings. We have a good case here, actually pretty straightforward from my point of view." He pulled out an arm chair so Claire could sit. "We need to document Glen's employment history from day one with the company. See if there's any change in how he was treated after the accident." Jeff took the chair next to hers, pulled it close until his elbow skimmed hers. She ignored the heat that raced up her arm. "It would be helpful to see if coworkers were promoted above or around him. I've subpoenaed his personnel file. That should give us a lot of information."

Jeff's aftershave, a musky scent, tickled Claire's nose. *Stop.* She had to pay attention to what he was saying and doing, not how he smelled. Jeff listed questions on a yellow pad. He wrote in square letters and put bullet notations before some of the notes.

He looked up, met her gaze. She stifled the involuntary shudder. At least she thought so. "Your job is to listen carefully to what Glen says and get a good handle on his medical needs."

Jeff circled one line. "We need names of coworkers who may have been given positions Glen was eligible for, then pull those employee records or get them to testify."

Jeff slipped into lawyer mode and talked fast and factual. All business. He was no longer book-group-Jeff who named birds.

She studied him. Dressed in black slacks with a matching leather belt and shining black, tassel-less loafers, he also wore a white pressed shirt, cuff links and a charcoal and red geometric tie. He belonged in this office.

"I'd like you to read some of these opinions and see if they make sense to you. See if they help us," he said.

She dragged her attention from him and back to the list. "I'm not sure I know what an opinion is, much less if it helps with our case."

He flashed her a quick smile. "Sorry. I get into lawyer shorthand and lose people. Let me try this. How about you read some of the cases I've tabbed and then you tell me if they sound anything like what we're doing with Glen."

She nodded. "I can do that."

"I never doubted it." His beam made her stomach do a flip and she dragged her gaze away from his.

She looked at the pile of books and forced herself to think about where in that condo she was going to stack them. Mark already groused about the papers she spread on the dining table. Also, how was she going to drag them home?

Then, as if he read her mind, Jeff said, "You could work out of this office. If it makes it easier. Plus, we can use Carol for some of your secretarial needs."

Flustered—did he really have ESP?—Claire looked around. The heavy furniture contrasted to her simple, scarred, pine desk back in Paso Robles. His coordinating attire, probably from Barneys, belonged here. Her wool skirt and bulky sweater bought at Marshalls, clearly didn't.

"My dad's secretary's old office is empty, and you could set up there. It has a telephone, Wi-Fi, a computer station, and desk. Not much but a place to spread things."

Jeff leaned into the hall, asked Carol to come in. "Claire will be working in Dad's secretary's office and will need to have it set up with supplies. Will you take care of that?"

"Not a problem. I'll clean it up a bit," Carol answered.

Jeff looked at Claire as he led her to the new office. "I don't really understand Glen's medical condition and how it impacts his work. I imagine he has some special needs besides the wheelchair. It would be helpful if you could find those things out for me. I've never been good at asking personal questions."

She flushed. "I *am* good at that. You teach me briefs, I'll teach you to interview."

They smiled at each other for a long moment. A tingling sensation began below her diaphragm and spread up her chest, to her neck, until she finally had to look away.

He opened a door behind the desk she hadn't noticed on a side wall to a small office with large windows. The smell of old polish and forgotten dust made the office more inviting, but that was probably just to her.

She leaned against the sill below the window while they talked in general terms about disabilities until Carol knocked at the open door.

"I'm sorry. Glen Peters is on the phone. He says his wheelchair lift is stuck and can't make it in tonight." Carol relayed the message with a quizzical look.

Jeff scratched his neck. "I wonder how often that happens?"

Claire took the opportunity to check her watch. It was past four and she should be heading home and getting things ready for dinner.

Jeff must have noticed her gesture. "It's getting late," he said.

She nodded. "I need to get home."

"Can I have Carol call for a cab or are you using the T?"

"I'll figure out the T. A cab will get expensive."

"It's easy," Jeff handed her the yellow pad with the list.

She started for the door, but he grabbed her elbow and looked at her. "Are you joining us for Thanksgiving at the club?"

Claire startled. She'd forgotten Agnes's invitation for Thanksgiving. It hadn't dawned on her Jeff would be there as well. She hadn't even mentioned it to Mark.

She swallowed. "I'll talk to Agnes."

"I'm sure they'll give you a ride," Jeff said.

"Ahh...yes...see you." She was flustered and hoped it didn't show because she wanted to appear in control. And she so clearly wasn't.

She gathered her purse and coat and fled.

She took the T home, smiling the whole way, confident she wouldn't get lost. Not again. She knew who she was maybe, now. And where she was going.

After all, she had a job. She had an office. She had a purpose.

Claire unlocked her front door, then inhaled sharply to find Mark in the kitchen opening a bottle of wine.

"Want a glass?" He held out the one he already filled.

"Thanks." She looked at her watch. It was only six and lately he wasn't home until seven, "You're home early—everything okay?"

"Things slow down the closer we get to the holidays. Our big marketing push is done. Now we wait for the post-holiday sales to see if we were successful."

"Did you eat?" she asked, taking the wine glass with a shaky hand. Him being home early… She wanted to be hopeful, but …

"Nope." He poured a second glass of wine.

"What would you like?" She opened the refrigerator.

"Too drained to think about food," he replied. "Just this glass of wine and maybe some cheese and crackers."

Claire turned to take a good look at him. *Mark turned down food?*

He'd lost some weight but more startling…he'd lost his farmer's tan. She always associated his brown skin with health. Now, he was pale. Dark circles under his eyes. She shook her head. Some caring wife she was. So preoccupied with herself, she didn't notice her own husband's health? She could do better. She would do better.

She pulled a brick of cheddar and a round of brie from the refrigerator and put them on a plate. Stepping around Mark, she opened the opposite cabinet and brought down a box of water crackers. After adding some grapes, and prosciutto she had a makeshift charcuterie board. "Will this do?"

Mark nodded and picked up the two wine glasses then followed her to the living room. They sat on the sofa and picked at what was now called dinner.

"You're still going to the gym?" she asked.

"Yeah." Mark spread a chunk of brie on the round cracker. "I met a guy, named Jim... Adams, I think... who lives somewhere in this condo or the one next door. We made plans to meet up early and play some handball."

"When did you learn to play?"

"Didn't. How hard can it be? You hit a ball with your hand, and—according to Jim—duck when the other guy hits the ball back." Mark half smiled at Claire. "He said he would teach me."

"Smart ass." She smiled back. This is how they once were, happy and teasing. "Did you say Jim Adams? And you think he lives in this building?"

"Might. I really don't remember. We didn't exchange numbers or invite each other for a dinner date. We're guys. I said I lived in a condo on the waterfront. He said he did too." Mark pointed out the window. "There are only three." He handed her a brie-lathered cracker. "We should've had French bread with this. Why do you ask about Jim?"

"You remember my friend Agnes?" She took the cracker.

His brows rose. "Your walking partner? Is that Agnes?"

"I think her husband is Jim. Her last name is Adams and they live on the top floor."

"Ahhhh, our first Boston couple," he said as he toasted his almost-empty glass. "I'm going to change and uncork a new bottle. You'll have more, won't you?"

"Deal. And check if we have any chocolate bars," she said.

She smiled as she leaned back into the couch cushion. It would be nice to see Mark in jeans again. He rarely wore them anymore. She'd never again complain about the worn denims with permanently mud-stained knees.

Oh, and yes, by the way, she had a great day, too, thanks for asking. She had a job and an office. There were pictures of birds framed on the walls. Oh yeah, she had a secretary.

She got up and chose a Miles Davis CD, Mark's favorite, then hit *Play*.

Mark's aftershave announced his arrival as he entered the living room wearing casual jeans and a blue T-shirt. He carried a new bottle of wine and a package of dark chocolate she'd bought on one of her walks.

Mark handed her a square of chocolate and poured more wine. "You know what this plate needed?"

"Besides French bread?"

"Fresh tomatoes. They aren't the same here."

She leaned back into the couch. "Ugh. Don't start. I miss my garden."

"I miss my vines." He dusted make believe dirt from his pants. They both chuckled.

Claire ran a finger around her glass rim. This would probably ruin their congenial evening, but she needed to give Agnes an answer. "Since you mentioned Jim, um...Agnes invited us for Thanksgiving dinner at their club."

"When?"

Claire sighed. "On Thanksgiving Day, two weeks from now."

"I know when Thanksgiving is. When did they invite us?"

"A couple of days ago. I didn't think it was a real invitation at the time, but she asked again today." That might be a white lie, but he didn't need to know it was Jeff who reminded her.

Mark shook his head, winced. "I don't like crowds. Can't we just stay home and watch football?"

"We could, but I want to go." *Besides this isn't home.*

"Go without me."

Her jaw clenched. "Come on. You'll meet my friends and maybe it's the same Jim."

Mark stared into his wine glass. "Claire...I don't like fancy things."

Claire took a deep breath, expelled it past the irritation. "That's ridiculous. You work for a high-end wine supplier. You deal with 'fancy' people and things for a living. I'll talk to Agnes tomorrow and find out if your Jim Adams is her Jim. If it is, we're going."

Chapter Twenty-One

Disoriented, Claire struggled to the surface of sleep, rolled against Mark. "I need to get up and start the rolls. Mom wants us at the house by three."

"What time is it?" he asked with a yawn.

"Early." Claire turned to get up. "Go ahead and sleep a bit longer. I need to start the rolls. I'll bring your coffee in here."

"We're in Boston. We're not going to your Mom's." He put his hands behind his head. "I'll take the coffee though."

Claire expelled a breath and threw herself against her pillow. She blinked and the dim bay lights came into focus. "Compromise?"

"Okay."

"I sleep for another ten minutes, and you go for a walk and bring back coffee."

"Not much of a compromise. I'll let you sleep and make the coffee." Mark laughed as he got up and went to the kitchen.

Claire rolled over and made a mental note to call her mother at noon. Mom always made sausage dressing the night before Thanksgiving, filling the house with the first hints of sage overtaking the clove aroma of baked pumpkin pie.

Thanksgiving morning, the Flannigan family always ate a breakfast of cinnamon toast and cold milk while Mom opened and closed the oven, sucking up pan drippings with a plastic baster then squirting them over the turkey.

Occasionally an errant drip would spit steam from the oven floor. "Be careful, love," Paddy would say. "That's the good stuff you're losing."

After breakfast, Dad took them to church. Saint Helen's held their annual food drive on Thanksgiving Day. Claire's family arrived with large bags of canned food for the poor. Mom always added a ten-pound bag of sugar. "Everyone needs a little something sweet," she would say. One year, Claire slipped in a new jar of cinnamon she bought with her allowance.

The females of the parish didn't show up, this was the Father's Club project. The women were brilliant to have the men and children gone while they prepared their own homes. By noon when they returned to Alma, the table would have been set with all the special china and silver.

After the kids grew up Alma just made the turkey and the rest of the family brought the "fixings." Claire had a window of time when the turkey was roasting, and the table set. She would call then, and maybe, just maybe, she'd inhale a breath of the joy she missed.

She heard Mark in the kitchen making coffee. He brought two cups into the bedroom. Her coffee was in one of the new white cups on a saucer. In his other hand, he carried the chipped oversized mug from home. She pulled herself up against the headboard and waited. How many years had she watched him drink from that brown pottery mug? She remembered when they found two matching mugs at an art fair in the late eighties. One lost the fragile handle and sat for years on her desk as a pencil holder. She missed the oddest things.

"Morning," she offered.

Mark handed her a cup and the newspaper. "I kept Sports." He climbed in on his side of the bed and opened his section with a rattle.

"I talked to Agnes and she'll meet us downstairs around three."

"For what?" he asked absently not looking up from the latest football scores. Claire opened her mouth to say something about his memory and then decided to let it slide.

"For the afternoon at their club. Cocktails from noon on. Dinner is served at five. Then dancing." Claire took a sip of her coffee. "Should be fun." Mark said nothing so she continued, "I thought I would call Mom just before we leave. It'll be before everyone shows up, and she has a few minutes to talk.

"I promised Katie we would call when they were all there," Mark said.

"Call again when we get home, they'll still be there and groggy from the turkey." Claire put her mug on the bedside table.

"I think we should call during dinner." He turned a page.

"Mark. Stop it." Claire squared her shoulders and faced him.

"Stop what? Caring about my family?"

"Our family," she corrected.

He folded the newspaper carefully, making sure the pages all matched at the edges, then putting it down, he looked at her. "I don't want to go."

"I get it and I want to."

"So, if Claire wants to do it, we do it?"

She stared at him. How could he say that? She didn't want to be here and yet she was. She was doing her best, just trying to make *here* livable.

Her hands trembled so she folded them. She inhaled, afraid to be firm and push him into a corner, but knowing this was one of those moments that mattered. She slowly said, "Mark, I haven't asked for much. Please do this for me."

He looked away, fastening his gaze back to the newspaper. "I won't go in their car. We'll take ours. I want to be home before nine. I need some rest, not to be spending my four days off with strangers."

Several quick retorts floated up from Claire's throat. Thankfully her filter stopped her from spitting them out. She had, after all, won. They were going.

"I can get directions."

"I can get it off my phone, but it's better if we arrive with someone who's a member, so ask if we can follow them."

Claire saw he was thinking again. A potential battle averted, and, on some days, it would be called a victory.

"Can I get you anything? I'm getting up," Claire asked.

"I want to sit and read. I haven't had a day of silence since I moved here. I want to sit and do nothing," he said as he picked up the rest of newspaper she left behind.

"You rest. I have work to do." She inhaled and rubbed the back of her neck. The breakfast she'd promised to prepare sounded like a chore now instead of a holiday treat.

Mark moved to the living room recliner where he half read, half slept. Claire left him alone until noon. She made a tomato basil soup and served it with a baguette.

She called her mom exactly at one o'clock and indeed Dad was still out, and the rest of the family hadn't arrived. She grinned, hearing her mother talk about the size of the turkey, the difficulty of getting it browned on the outside and still remain moist. Nothing changed, except she wasn't there so they had to buy rolls for dinner. Claire held a hand to her heart. How like her mother to let her know she would be missed.

A little after two, Claire said, "Mark, time to dress. Could you wear your blue suit?"

"I'm wearing the brown," he said.

Damn, she hated that suit. It was the color of dirt and he wore dirt every day. She drew a deep breath, counted to twenty. "Okay, whatever," she said instead.

She picked a black pencil skirt with a coral silk blouse, and black four-inch heels. She let her curls fall naturally.

"You look nice," Mark offered. "I don't think I've seen that outfit."

"Oh, thanks, it's old. I just never had much use for it in California."

They both grabbed coats and mittens on the way out and found Agnes pacing in the lobby.

"Big Jim is in the car already," she said.

"It's just three," Mark mumbled, without introducing himself.

"Oh, I know. BJ's always early. I'm Agnes." She offered her hand.

"This is my husband, Mark," Claire announced quickly, to head off Mark finding a reason to bolt and be all self-righteous about not going.

A minute later they followed the BMW out of the garage and, armed with Agnes's cell phone number, they were off. The music on the radio played oldies. Mark kept changing the channel, a habit that made Claire's fingers twitch and tap, but she forced herself to look out the window at the newly fallen snow. Patches of snow melted into strange shapes with mud edges.

"I guess we're here," Mark broke into her thoughts, as they turned into a winding drive.

Claire glimpsed a massive shingled building up ahead. "It's just like I pictured. Like the hotel in the movie *Holiday Inn*. I expect to see Bing Crosby come around the corner and greet us." He sounded annoyed with her excitement, but she didn't care. If she couldn't be home serving homemade rolls and eating Aunt Vivian's string bean casserole, then why not have a movie Thanksgiving?

Mark pulled in alongside the BMW. He opened Claire's door and offered her a hand.

"Claire, Mark, this here is my Big Jim," Agnes said. Claire saw pride and ownership in Agnes as she leaned on his arm.

Mark extended his right hand and nodded. "We've actually met at the gym. I think we've been assigned to play handball together."

Jim smiled big and double grasped Mark's hand. "Glad you joined us."

He turned to Claire. "So, you're the Claire my little Aggie talks about?" Jim said without a hint of drawl.

Claire felt her face burn, the curse of the redhead. The man wasn't tall, possibly five ten but surely not six feet. He had short gray curly hair, a little mustache, and a huge smile. He wore black slacks and a gray sports jacket that made his blue eyes pop.

Claire, checking for boots, looked for a hint of his Texas roots. "Hello," she finally mustered. "I expected a big cowboy in a ten-gallon hat."

"I am a native-born Bostonian, but if you marry Agnes, you're a Texan by association."

They entered the foyer of the old renovated clubhouse. It was a great combination of old on the outside and fresh on the inside with new paint and modern murals.

They checked their coats at the booth and started toward the bar.

"What are you drinking?" Jim asked.

Mark answered, "I'll have a scotch and water."

"I'll have a beer," added Agnes.

"And you, my dear?" Jim asked turning toward Claire.

She hadn't thought about a drink. It had been so long since she ordered a cocktail. "I'll have a martini, shaken not stirred." Claire had never had a martini, but this place looked like a martini kind of place so, why not?

Before long they were introduced to couples as they greeted Agnes. Claire would never remember them all and soon gave up trying. Half of them Agnes didn't even introduce but called them all "honey." Mark shook hands and smiled in a bashful, boyish way. The women seemed to all know each other or about each other. They talked in fast short sentences only hinting to who they were in life.

Jim soon returned followed by a waiter with drinks. He suggested they find their table and settle down for the evening.

Agnes wore a fitted red velvet dress which hung below her knees, revealing nice legs. Instead of her usual boots, she had on a fine pair of silk low-heeled pumps. Her dress had a deep V-neck accented by a lovely ruby pendant that floated in the fullness of her cleavage. Claire became aware of her lack of jewelry as she met each new couple. Her simple gold wedding band with the quarter-carat diamond in the matching ring could not compete with the sparkles lighting this room.

Tables were set with crystal and fine china. She sat between Jim and Mark. The rest of the table guests started filling in. With each additional couple, and they were all coupled, she and Mark were introduced.

Next to Agnes sat a professor from Harvard named Frank who taught environmental law and his much younger wife, Andrea. She was into herb gardening. Next to them sat a couple about her age. John did something with computers. She practiced law with a large firm. Marla, the attorney, a substantially built woman, appeared not to approve of cute, tiny, bubbly Andrea. It didn't help that John seemed taken with her. Bunny, wearing a strapless cocktail dress, and a frown, sat next to an empty seat. Her red, perfectly manicured, nails kept clasping and unclasping her small Kate Spade clutch.

"Where is that man of yours?" Agnes finally yelled down the table.

"Who knows," Bunny answered. She sounded as if she didn't care, but her frequent glances at the entry gave her away.

"I bet he stopped to see his father," John offered, obviously trying to cover for his friend.

"Oh, yeah, a tough year without his dad here," said Agnes.

Bunny just shrugged and picked at an invisible thread on the purse. Marla passed her the basket of bread, as if the carbs could absorb any problem. Chatter consumed the table and Claire, sipping her martini, felt a tad of a buzz. The drink burned a bit on the way down. Best not to order another.

The waiter came to the table carrying a tray of small individual pumpkins filled with a thick orange soup. It looked and smelled luscious. When she turned from her soup, she saw Jeff slip silently into the empty seat. So, he was the late guest.

He winked at her.

She looked away, trying to not notice, willing her pulse to slow. Did he really just wink? At her? How could he, his date next to him, her husband next to her? The flush returned, but she could blame it on the martini.

Claire paid turned her attention to Agnes's story.

When the last of the bread passed, she saw Jeff looking at her again.

Her breath caught chest and her heart pounded *th thum th thum* against her rib cage.

Chapter Twenty-Two

In the almost thirty years Mark knew Claire, he never saw her drink a martini. He watched her play with the olive on a stick, talking freely with the other guests, ignoring him. The memory of a time she taught the kids to put olives on their fingers flickered through his mind. Back then simple things made her laugh. Today with the green olive, she'd become someone he didn't know. Her laugh, nervous and shallow, with a superficial cheerfulness others thought real, had him shaking his head.

"I took the privilege of pre-ordering the wine for tonight," announced Jim as he waved a hand toward the waiter. "I discovered it at a meeting in San Diego and bought a case. It's from a small vineyard north of Santa Barbara."

"Which vineyard?" asked Claire.

"I don't remember. Rainbow something, I think."

"Rainbow's End?"

"That's it." Jim hesitated. "Are you familiar with it?"

Mark lifted his eyes and glanced at Claire. She reached under the table and put a hand on his knee and laughed, like she used to. Heat rose in his chest.

"That's our wine," she said.

Jim turned his view from Claire to Mark, who now leaned back in his chair with a proud smile. As the sommelier approached carrying two uncorked bottles in an ice bucket, Mark stood. "Do you mind?" he asked as he reached for one of the bottles.

After a nod from Big Jim, the steward pulled a bottle from the ice, wrapped the bottom in a white table napkin and handed it to Mark.

Mark motioned the waiter off and poured. Forget country clubs, handball, stock markets. Wine? This, he knew. As he moved around the table, he talked about the process of turning grape to nectar.

The questions never stopped once people found out he was an enologist. Some wanted to know about the process, some wanted advice on which wines to serve with what, some wanted to impress him with their palate. The herbalist inquired if it was without pesticides. Her partner asked about investing in wine, and Mark, his stomach finally not churning, talked easily with the strangers.

He noticed Claire watching him and this time her smile didn't seem false. He smiled back at her, and for just one instant they were the old Claire and Mark.

Bunny—funny name for an adult—leaned her chin on her poised hands and, winking, asked, "So, you grew the grapes in this bottle?"

"Planted them, grew them, picked them, blended them, bottled them and now poured them for you." Mark winked back.

Bunny turned away from Jeff and smiled brightly at Mark. Jeff excused himself from the table. He headed to the bar, leaving a full plate of food.

Mark felt Jim's hand on his arm and turned to give his host his full attention. "I must say, this is a small world," Jim said.

"It is. And the vineyard is way north of Santa Barbara, in the Paso Robles area. It's a very young area for grapes, compared to the Napa Valley, but we're producing some fine blends."

"So I've heard," Jim said, as he drained the last of his glass.

"We're a small producer with a limited run of this wine. I'd hoped to spend the next few years nurturing another fifty acres. Instead, the company I work for transferred me here."

"You don't just farm?"

Mark shook his head. "I am an enologist by degree. I work for Ahwahnee Wines. I'm in Boston to work with their marketing department."

The meal continued. Agnes entertained the table with tall tales of over-sized turkeys in Texas. The laughter was contagious.

Bunny, minus Jeff, tried to join in the conversation with Jim and Mark, then withdrew when the discussion turned to chemistry.

Mark and Jim remained engrossed talking about the business end versus the physical logistics of wine production.

"I love the creation of wine, not the selling of already existing labels," Mark said.

"That shows. Of course, unless you know the other part, you end up drinking a lot your own wine," Jim countered.

Dinner and individual conversations ended when the live band struck up *In the Mood*. Several couples headed for the dance floor, others gathered their possessions and left. Agnes pulled a tube of bright red lipstick from her purse and made a production of applying a new layer. Looking into the small mirror attached, she took the napkin and removed a smear on her teeth. She offered the mirror to Claire. "Need to freshen up?"

Claire raised her hand. "I'm okay, besides red isn't my color."

Mark looked at Claire and then at his watch, his way of signaling her it was time to go. She turned away from him and accepted a dance from the professor.

Soon Mark found himself at the table alone with the herbalist. She watched her husband as he danced with Claire. Her eyes followed him. Mark glanced over and saw him moving Claire easily across the dance floor. Mark always meant to learn to dance. It was one of the things Claire used to ask him to do—go to lessons together. But there had never been time. He flashed back to a younger Claire dancing with the children, doing the boogie to *Elmo's Rock* and singing all the words to *It's Not Easy Being Green*. Hair would be flying wild, his house full of laughter, and his grapes like his family, thriving.

He stood and waved his hand to Claire and mouthed, "Time to go, we have to call the kids."

Claire gave him a look and a head shake. Probably reminding him of the long nights that had been hers since moving to Boston. But she excused herself from the group, kissed Agnes on both cheeks and gave Jim a quick air kiss. They waved to the others as she gathered her purse and took Mark's arm.

They drove home in silence, but as soon as they were inside the condo, Mark again checked his watch. Seven here, meant four in Alma's kitchen. "They should be getting ready to sit down."

"Yeah, Dad likes to have the turkey carved by four fifteen and the cranberries passed by four-twenty." Claire hung her purse on a hook.

"I'll call." He reached for the computer, prepared to open Skype.

"Why don't we wait 'til dinner's over?"

He paused, fingers hovering over the keyboard. "I don't want to miss anyone."

"We won't. We'll catch them as they're finishing."

He faced her, furrowed his brow. "I don't get it, Claire. I thought you'd be missing them so much you would want to call and see them this morning, this afternoon, now, and later."

Claire faced him. "Miss them? I miss them all so much. I miss them and everything about my old life." With tears in her eyes, she glared at him. "I would do anything to not be here." She swept her hand around the room. "But here is where I am." She gulped air. "I miss them so much, I hurt. But you know what I miss the most? I miss you." She jutted her chin. "You're the one here, and I miss you."

She stalked to their bedroom, closed the door with a soft click.

He stared after her, blinking. What just happened? How did they go from calling their family on Thanksgiving to a fight about moving to Boston? Again.

After a few minutes, he knocked, spoke in a low voice. "We'll call in an hour."

Chapter Twenty-Three

Three weeks passed, trees with lights went up all over the city. Claire and Mark would be going home soon. Anticipation made her nearly giddy. She sang to herself as she cleared her desktop. "Over the river and through the woods, to Paso Robles and the ranch we go." Files into the drawers. Pens and highlighters back to their holders.

She sighed and leaned back in her desk chair with her coffee cup, then glanced out the high-rise window, where the time and temperature—10:45 a.m. and 33 degrees—blinked on the bank's digital sign down the street. A shiver ran down her spine. She never dreamed she'd live in a place so cold that holding a steaming mug wasn't enough to warm her.

"Ms. Richter," the intercom squawked, "a Mr. Glen Peters is here. He said you're expecting him."

Returning the half empty cup, like a paperweight, to the desk, she pushed the button and said, "Show him in." She rose, straightened her skirt, brushed invisible crumbs from her blouse, and opened the door for Glen who wheeled in.

"Wow!"

"Wow, what?" She brushed her lips. Did she have a coffee mustache?

"Wow, don't you look all professional," he said.

"Oh, that's right." She laughed. "I guess you've only seen me at the group in jeans. Surprise, I own a dress."

She watched the expression on Glen's face as he wheeled to the chair in front of her desk and, without asking permission, smoothly moved it aside. How many times a day did he move something out of his way? How often did he have to change things, shuffle them around? How often did he have to adapt to the world?

She was very aware of her own legs now as she moved easily to sit behind the desk. "First off, what is discussed in this room will stay here and is between us. Later, with your permission, we'll decide, together, what to make public. I am a Social Worker, licensed in California but not registered here. I will be gathering information for a lawsuit you are pursuing with this firm. If you are at any time uncomfortable with the questions, you don't need to respond." She looked at him, grinned.

"Whoa, breathe." He laughed.

"I'm sorry." She chuckled, too. "Years of training. But you need to be aware I will be asking tough questions." She used to tell Val it was the desk and pantyhose that spawned her professional personality.

"I know," Glen's lips thinned. "I broke my back, but my heart has been broken more by others' insensitivity. Thank you for telling me ahead of time you may trigger some emotions."

She met his gaze squarely and gave one nod. "Well then, let's begin. Full name?"

"Glen Howard Peters."

"Education?"

"I have a Master's in Architecture from Cornell. I graduated in 2000."

Claire made notes and then looked up. "That was the easy part. Now hang on as we get into your work history, but instead of me asking questions, why don't you summarize how you came to work for Cole, Roberts, and Wright."

Leaning forward in his chair a bit, he took a deep breath. "I first worked for them in Ithaca. I was accepted at Cornell right out of high school."

"Did you know then you wanted to be an architect?"

"I wanted to design and build from the time I got my first set of Legos." His smile owned his face. "My dad died when I was little, and I spent summers with my uncle. He had a farm upstate. Uncle Bernie was Dad's older brother and loved to paint. He gave me a drafting table when I was nine. He showed me how to draw in charcoal. I think he wanted me to be an artist like him." He waved his hand in a dismissive gesture. "But I wasn't interested in the pasture or the animals or even the people. All I drew was buildings." Glen turned his chair a bit sideways and leaned his forearm on Claire's desk. "I would see the barn and sketch it from every angle. Summer after summer I would draw the barn over and over again. Then one time, Uncle Bern said to draw a new barn...the one in my head. I did."

"What a great story," Claire interrupted.

"So, when I got accepted to Cornell, I knew what I wanted. I wanted to design barns into homes. They offered me a decent scholarship. If I wanted to date or put gas in my car, I had to get a part time job. Ithaca is a small town and there was only one architectural firm." He pulled his arm back to the chair. "So, I walked in and asked if they could use a part-timer. When they stopped laughing, they told me the only position open was in filing. I told them besides being a good draftsman, I knew my alphabet. I got the job. It grew. They found additional hours for me. I think Mr. Wright created work. He treated me like a son."

Claire acknowledged the sadness in Glen's voice. "Where is he now?"

Glen looked at her with an undeniable tear on his cheek. "He passed two weeks after my accident. I couldn't even get to his funeral. I was in the Intensive Care Unit still ..."

Claire handed Glen a tissue.

"Thanks. So, I started with them while I was in college. Then I needed an internship and Mr. Wright arranged for me to come and work with the main firm here in Boston." Glen pressed his hands on his knees. "He even found me a place to live. I learned so much though it was a faster pace here. The people more formal, but they loved my work, and I loved the city. I met my wife that summer." Claire saw his face soften and a small set of dimples she'd never seen formed.

"Your wife's name?" she interrupted.

"Marina. She was...I mean still is a nurse."

"You met her at Cole?"

"No, she's from Cuba and lived with a cousin. We met at a dance. The prettiest woman there, and I figured I didn't have a chance. After a drink—" He smiled showing perfect teeth—"Okay, more than one, I had the nerve to talk to her. We started taking long weekend walks. We rode bikes and rented boats on the Charles. She was easy to be with. When it was time for me to go back to Ithaca, I couldn't leave her here. So, we moved in together. She hated the small town, and when I graduated, we moved back."

"You've worked for them since?"

"Since 1997 and then for the Boston office since 2001."

"Good." Claire remembered to look at Glen instead of making notes. "Now, did you ever have problems with the company prior to your accident in 2011?"

"No. I was on the fast track as they say, promoted every year, good reviews, and brought in new clients. I became known for my barn conversions. Big business here—buy a failing farm and convert the barn into a house."

She tapped her lips. "I wasn't aware of that."

"Yeah. I loved it. The summer before my injury, Marina and I went to New Hampshire to find our own barn to convert. We had three kids and wanted to expose them to the simple beauty of country life I grew up with. I anticipated full partnership the following year since I had my own client base. Our life was ideal. Then the accident …"

Claire put down the pen. She wouldn't need to take notes about the accident because it wasn't important to the case, but it was to Glen. To him, it was a life-altering event and he needed to tell it.

On a Sunday night, he drove to the corner all-night market to buy milk for the next morning's breakfast when a man coming home from the local pub ran a red light and forced Glen's minivan into a light post. The impact threw him forward with such force, his back broke at the L-5. There was no pain, he said, and only later he realized that wasn't good. A wedge of the vertebra lodged itself into the fragile spinal cord.

"The good news," he said, "is that I didn't lose the use of my hands and arms. I didn't suffer any brain damage. I would be, after a time, able to go back to work."

Glen leaned forward and placed his hands on the desk between him and Claire. "It took me a while to get over it. The anger and all. You know the stuff—" he waved an arm in the air— "about life not being fair?"

"You seem to have adjusted."

"I've accommodated. Thanks a lot to Marina. She's been matter of fact about it. At first, I didn't see myself as a man, but we even worked that out."

Claire noticed him grin a bit, and she smiled back. "Good for you."

"I wasn't upset the first year I didn't get a promotion. After all they needed to know I could do my job. Then the following year I started asking. They started avoiding me. Then others were being promoted around me. I asked again about my position with the company."

"About two years ago?" Claire wrote without looking up.

"A little over that, but close."

"Did you ever ask in writing?"

"I did, last spring. Here's a copy of the letter." He handed her a paper dated May.

"Did they respond?"

He handed her another paper on Cole, Roberts, and Wright letterhead.

"They said they had no positions open at that time. But they did promote James Butler, a man hired three years after me with half the client load. I bring in about half a million dollars in billable hours, and he barely bills two hundred thousand."

"You're positive of those numbers?"

"I have a copy of the financials, but don't ask how I got them." He pulled more papers from a manila envelope.

"That's between you and Jeff," Claire said, cutting her hand through the air.

Glen slid the stack back into the envelope.

"Why do you think James was promoted over you?"

"According to Mrs. Wright, who in a weepy moment talked, the company thinks I don't represent them."

Claire blinked in confusion. "Explain that."

"The way I understood her, it isn't about my ability, but a wheelchair isn't their image. They don't want to attract a crippled clientele."

"They used that word?"

"No. I'm sure they used a politically correct term like handicapped or disabled." He shrugged. "Physically challenged. But it is the old attitude. At first, I thought she was wrong. They're a business firm and business is the bottom line. But then I was excluded from the after-work weekly beer at the local pub. When I asked a friend why, he said, 'because the bar is in the basement.'"

Their book group met in a basement. "Isn't there an alternate way in?" she asked.

"There is. I showed up. You should have seen the faces." He laughed. "I realized my friends no longer knew how to talk to me. They saw me as...less. Like somehow, I no longer wanted to talk sports because I couldn't play. I didn't play before but still talked about the Celtics. I finally put two and two together and got mad when I realized I was being ignored. Or worse, pitied."

Glen stopped talking. Claire noticed he'd gone somewhere deep, and those emotions welled in his eyes. "You see, Claire, I'm the only one who's earned the right to feel sorry for me." Claire picked up her pen and opened her mouth to ask more about how that made him feel. But a vein pulsed in Glen's jaw and he stared out the window.

She closed the file folder and capped her pen. "I think that's enough for today. We'll finish after the holidays."

After walking Glen to the elevator, Claire stood and stared at the blinking time and temperature sign again. It didn't seem possible, but in the last hour, it had gotten even colder.

Inside as well as out.

Chapter Twenty-Four

The rest of the day passed without interruption. When Claire looked at the clock, it was already past six and she'd promised Mark she'd be home early. She picked up the phone and dialed.

"Claire, where are you?"

"I'm getting ready to leave the office." She slipped Glen's file into the desk drawer.

"It's snowing hard and all the trains will be crowded. I came home at three to avoid the blizzard."

She hadn't noticed the snow, but when she looked out the window, big white flakes fell silently to the ground. "I'll call a cab."

"Why are you so late?"

"Just got absorbed in this case. I didn't notice the time."

"Or the blizzard?"

"I guess not."

"Well, be safe and get home. It looks like a strong front."

"Are you planning on going in tomorrow?" If he wasn't, that would be a first.

"Of course, but I told the staff to take the day off."

"We'll talk when I get home. In the meantime, let me shut down my computer. I'll call a taxi."

She hung up the phone abruptly, then remembered she'd sworn to end every call with "I love you," and she hadn't. What if on the way home she was hit by a drunk driver and left a paraplegic?

Halfway to the door she turned back and grabbed the case notes. Mark grew up in Wisconsin, and he might be right about this storm. But she wouldn't tell him that. No, she could be as withholding as he.

When did this war begin? When would it end?

With her head and hands full she headed to the lobby when she saw Jeff's office door still open. It needed to be shut for her to set the alarm. She put everything on the corner of Carol's desk. Jeff's lights were out, so it surprised her when she saw him sitting in the dark as he looked out at the lit town square down below.

"I'm sorry, I'm leaving and wanted to set the alarm. I thought you left?"

He turned to her and from the street lights outside she saw tears on Jeff's cheek.

She took a step forward. "You okay?"

"Yeah." He swiped his face with his fingertips.

Instinctively she searched her pocket for a tissue. Two crying men in one day? What were the odds?

"I just hung up from talking to my father. He didn't know me. He asked if I knew his son. I told him I am your son. He got angry and said I couldn't be." Jeff sat for a second then shook his head. "Dementia sucks."

"It's a hard one."

"Do you see that decorated tree down in the courtyard?" He nodded toward the window.

"I do." She followed his gaze.

"My grandfather planted it, and every year when the staff decorated it my father would tear up. I didn't understand until tonight." He stood, faced the view. "You don't cry for what you lose but for what you never had. My father is dying and so is the dream of the father I'd hoped for. I'm fifty-eight and still want a dad. Pretty sad, isn't it?"

She took a step to be at his side. "Do you have brothers or sisters?"

"No, and there is no Jeffrey Andrew Wentworth the third. I have a daughter and perhaps she will finally improve the character of this line." He glanced at a photograph framed in silver on a nearby credenza. "She's already an improvement over me."

"You didn't improve it?"

He looked back at Claire. "Who knows? I did my best."

"Perhaps your father did his best."

Jeff looked at her but said nothing.

"I'm sorry about your father. Agnes once said we had to look at the opposite of our perception to truly understand another's."

A smile crept into the corner of his eye. "Agnes." He shook his head. "She would find beauty in the worm eating the last apple in the orchard."

"And she'd probably give him the apple to make sure he didn't starve next winter," Claire added. "Do you have any good memories at all? Any you can share with him?"

"Maybe." He shrugged. "If by good you mean times when he wasn't working, or distracted, or yelling, there might be one or two."

They stood in the dark for a bit longer, not talking.

Claire had thought she understood silence. The angry silence when another word spoken would be dangerous. Joyful silence like at the birth of your child. Comfortable silence when communication with the other person doesn't require words. Or the silence of a miracle and more importantly the empty silence when no one heard your heart crying. But this was an anticipatory, shivery silence. She wanted to learn more about this man who cried.

Lights twinkled through the snow flakes. The white blew thick and piles drifted against immovable objects, yet the lights on the tree fought through and kept shining. She put a hand on Jeff's shoulder. His muscles relaxed, and slowly she removed it.

"This is a Nor'easter and these storms are rough. Let me give you a ride home. I have four-wheel drive," he said.

"Jeff, you have improved the bloodline."

He picked up his coat and scarf, met her eyes with a rueful half-smile. "I can only hope."

On the drive home, he talked about Christmas and Claire listened. He planned to fly to Paris then he and Emily and Brad were going skiing in Austria.

What a difference between the son with a tear on his cheek, and the father who couldn't wait to be with his daughter, shushing down a slope.

Claire looked out the tinted passenger window as cars crawled recently plowed streets where banks grew on the sides. Tonight, there were no loud horns honking, no pedestrians who dashed in and out of traffic. The rules changed with the weather.

Jeff talked softly, hesitantly, while listening to the traffic report. He leaned forward on the steering wheel, peering through the ever-shrinking circle the windshield wipers fought to keep clear.

"We call this a whiteout because if you're on a country road or highway the snow blows uninterrupted making it impossible to see in front of you. Lots of pileups happen. If you don't mind, I need to pay attention to the road reports."

She nodded and stared ahead. Mark had been right about the storm. She glanced at Jeff. Both hands on the wheel, his eyes scanned right and left. This was a man in charge, a man with all tears gone.

Jeff's confidence and the warm leather seat eased her tight muscles and a memory tiptoed into her heart. The only time Mark cried. At Katie's birth, one tear fell from his cheek onto hers, a tear bonding father to daughter which so often still excluded mother.

Chapter Twenty-Five

Thanksgiving and the first Boston snowstorm were a mere memory when Claire sat next to Mark as they flew home to celebrate Christmas in California.

Mark usually read when they flew but for some reason he wanted to chat and kept interrupting her mental preparations for the events ahead. He had a list of things he needed to do, all pertaining to the vineyard, and didn't seem to even consider she might need him to help with the holiday arrangements.

In frustration, she pulled out a yellow tablet and started a grocery list, only occasionally nodding at Mark's verbal worries. Long ago she learned to plan around him, being sure to always have it appear as if he were the center of it all. Once upon a time, she'd liked being his supporting cast.

Jessie picked them up at the airport and when the car tires finally crunched the gravel road, the warmth of familiarity wrapped around her. Everything lay where it belonged. The sun broke through the morning fog and lit the dampened, still green leaves in luminescent crystals. She even saw a few hangers-on in the vegetable garden and couldn't wait to taste the freshness of California again.

The aroma of ground and brewing coffee met her as she opened the side door. "Hey," she called into the rooms, "anyone here to greet the parents?"

Soon, Sean and Colleen came from the den and hugs abounded. How wonderful to hug her children while the house hugged her. Sitting around the kitchen table, they gobbled adventures of the past three months like a box of succulent chocolate.

Claire's heart overflowed with thanks as she looked at Mark beaming while Sean told him about the bar exams, and Colleen described a rather naughty, trick playing, adolescent in her class. *I'm so proud, look at the family Mark and I created and nurtured*. The Flanagan flare for storytelling, along with the Richter sense of right made interesting people.

Sean ordered pizza and over slices Claire reminded everyone what needed to be done. They still had to find a tree, not artificial, the lights untangled, the garland unfurled and with every yet-to-be-unpacked ornament—a memory.

Tomorrow Sean and Mark would find the perfect tree while Claire and Colleen stalked the aisles for the ingredients for Claire's traditional, and much loved, holiday menu. Tonight, was set aside for beer, olive pizza, and reconnecting.

Christmas Eve, the Richter family, in order to secure their usual pew, arrived early for Midnight Mass at St. Patrick's. Since Claire joined the parish, she claimed the eighth row on the left side, directly in front of the pulpit. She enjoyed Father McGoldrick's animated hand gestures while he read the sermon.

Poinsettias and winter-smelling pines adorned the altar and the lights in the church were dimmed as parishioners filed in, the elderly still genuflecting and crossing themselves before settling. Claire identified with these people. They were her neighbors, friends, and clients. It didn't seem like she had been gone months, but only missed a few Sundays.

After service, the family drove home to a prepared platter of cold cuts and Peter, Katie, Alma and Paddy. Mark, coming from a German background grew up with gift opening on Christmas Eve. Claire's family kept the night before the eventful day for the religious celebration and made the children wait, ever so impatiently, until morning. The Flanagan-Richter compromise allowed each to pick one gift from under the tree which they tore into while munching on sandwiches. The "Santa" gifts were saved for Christmas morning.

"Open mine," called Sean.

"Oh, Sean you always want them to open yours first," whined Katie.

"Okay. Open Katie's. See if I care," Sean said.

Claire had made a personal decision, a long time ago, not to show favorites and to always open Mark's gift first. This year, like others, she hunted for the one gift wrapped in brown paper with a red ribbon. Even Mark had some traditions.

"I'll open this one. I wonder who it's from?"

"Yeah, like we don't already know." Sean shot a toothy grin his father's direction.

"This is so small. I wonder what it can be," Claire said. Being the right size, probably his yearly gift of perfume.

"I'm sure it's the new Viking stove you've been hinting about," said Alma.

The contagious laughter rippled among them while she unwrapped. Peeling back the brown paper, a blue velvet box appeared.

Slowly lifting the hinged lid, she gasped. A small gold cluster of grapes on a fine chain rested on a velvet background.

"I know you miss the vineyard and thought you might wear a bit of it each day," Mark said.

Speechless, she stared at the necklace while her fingers stroked the fine gold links. She smiled at him, and for a moment, they connected as he smiled back. She got up and hugged Mark, hunting for that old, lost flame. He patted her shoulders, turned his face so she kissed his cheek. So instead of igniting a fire, she settled for familiar comfort. Again.

Still. He gave her something not perfume. Something of home. Something that showed he did pay attention.

A seed of hope sprouted a root in her heart. Maybe their marriage wasn't beyond saving.

The kids dug under the tree, shaking packages, trying to guess the contents. Indoor pine trees brought out the childlike behavior in all of them. It was a season of happiness. Then she noticed Katie sitting with Bear next to her. She didn't dig, tease, or complain. Claire chewed the inside of her cheek. Was Katie silently peaceful, brooding, or in some blossoming stage of trouble?

"Katie," Claire finally said, "open the present from your grandfather. You'll like it."

Claire had been informed Paddy's gift this year would be Katie's first piece of Waterford. Claire's father always loved how Katie, as a small child, let the sun make rainbows dance on the table while holding her glass to the window. He'd called all excited and told Claire he wanted to start Katie's collection for "her hope chest."

Katie sighed and looked disinterestedly under the tree for the box that bore the tag from her grandparents. After finding it, she opened it, and smiled a flat thanks for the gift. What was wrong with her? Claire read the disappointment on the face of her father.

"You're welcome, darlin'," he said.

Claire ached for him and regretted her own sometimes inadvertent comments to her parents. She saw only his pureness and Katie's apathy. She wanted to shake her daughter, yell at her to *wake up*. Yet she could do nothing, trapped between two generations and two worlds. She couldn't fix anything. She walked to her father and laid a kiss on his balding head.

"I love them, Daddy," she whispered.

"She will also," he said confidently.

Mark started to open Colleen's gift. First, he shook it, then lifted it as if weighing it, and finally smelled the red-wrapped package. "I give," he said as he untied the white ribbon.

"Remember, Dad, it's the sentiment...not the cost of the gift."

"Well, I know for sure it isn't my usual book. Way too light." Mark carefully lifted a piece of tape.

"Just rip the paper," Sean said.

"I may need it for another gift in the future," Mark replied.

"As if you've ever wrapped a present in your life," Colleen ribbed.

When he lifted the lid, a gray scarf lay inside.

"It is the first thing I've made." Colleen reached over and pulled the scarf from the box and held it up for all to see. "It has a few mistakes but according to my teacher, it's, 'not bad.'"

"I love it." He draped the scarf around his neck. "I sure can use this."

Alma walked over and examined the work. "Colleen, this is great. I want one."

"You never know what Santa has for you." Colleen winked.

Sean reached for his gift. "Clearly a book," he said.

"Guess which one on your list of twenty?" Katie asked.

Peter shook the gift he had been given, reluctant to join in the ritual by offering any comment.

Claire sat and observed. A Norman Rockwell moment, but she felt like the one who didn't fit. She had changed.

Boston changed her. Age changed her. Life moved on around her. In the middle of the biggest compromise of her life, this time had she given too much of herself away?

"Let me help you clean," Alma said, picking up dishes.

"Leave them, Mom," Claire said. "I've got this. You and Dad goT."

"Can I help?" Colleen asked as she gathered discarded wrappings.

"That's my job," Mark said. "Why don't you, Katie, and Peter head on over to your place?"

Peter offered Katie a hand and pulled her to stand. "What time do you want us tomorrow?" she asked.

"About nine-thirty. That okay with everyone?" Claire looked around the room, most nodded yes.

"I want to take a run tomorrow." Sean grinned. "Anyone care to join me at seven?"

He had no takers, so headed to his old bedroom.

"You know you can leave those 'till morning," Mark said.

"And you know I hate waking to dirty dishes." She carried the stack to the kitchen.

Mark followed. "I'll straighten up the living room and meet you in bed." He pulled a garbage bag from under the sink and headed back to the living room.

The back door opened and closed and re-opened. The trash wasn't only picked up but disposed of. Mark rarely did a job half way.

She filled the dishwasher, put away the leftovers, wiped down the counter top, expecting Mark to be in bed, probably snoring by now.

Looking out the window above the sink, she watched the marine fog roll over the hill, slowly blanketing the vines.

Claire liked the titillation of the mist on her skin and decided to grab one last cup of tea to drink on the porch and soak in the atmosphere of home. Warm on the inside, cool and damp on the outside, yet so familiar, she relaxed under the disappearing moon.

Her cell phone chirped jolting her back to reality. Who would be calling at that hour? Probably one of the kids left something behind.

Checking the darkened screen, she read a 617-area code. Clearing the haze from her head, she recognized Jeff's number. Why would he be calling? It was five thirty a.m. in Boston.

Hesitantly she answered. "Jeff?"

"Claire," he said in a soft voice. "I didn't expect you to answer. It must be the middle of the night for you."

Her shoulders relaxed at the sound of his voice. "Why call if you didn't expect me to pick up?" She laughed.

"Thought I would get your voice mail, and I'd leave you a morning wish."

"Should I hang up?"

"No." He paused. "Merry Christmas."

"And to you as well. I thought you'd be in Paris."

"Truth is I'm heading to visit my father and spend the day with him, then my flight out is tomorrow. And ..."

"And?"

"And thanks to you, I'm going to focus on the old good memories."

She laughed softly. "There you go, pal. Throw out lots of times and keep going until you find something he responds to. Pretend it was yesterday and enjoy what he still has in the old memory bank." She waited for Jeff to say something and when he didn't, she continued. "Do you remember a particular song he liked around Christmas?"

"Funny, I hadn't thought of Christmas music, and it's everywhere."

"Often music triggers old memories."

"Dad used to play a Harry Bellefonte Christmas album, over and over again. One year I hid it so I wouldn't have to hear it again." Jeff's memory made him sound like a young, naughty kid. "I still have it, and I think I know where it is."

"Great, now you have to find an old-fashioned stereo," she said.

"No worries. Dad still has the old turntable and speakers."

She heard shuffling across wood floors. Claire imagined him getting out of bed and dressing. Did men all dress the same? Like Mark, first boxers, jeans left unzipped, then socks before finding a shirt and tucking it into the waistband.

"I need to get going," Jeff said. "Again, Merry Christmas, I'm glad I know you."

"Thanks," she whispered as she sat staring at the vanishing screen and waiting for the foggy ghost memories to blanket her.

Chapter Twenty-Six

Claire woke early to start the coffee and pecan rolls her family loved to wake up to. Opening the front door for the newspaper, she paused on the porch, raised her face to the sun as it chased the hazy remnants of the night, and sighed with contentment. The musky smell of dampness on vines evaporated as the sun rose. The view from the front of her house always made her smile. Rows of vines slopped gently down the hill to the road. Their home, built in the thirties, sat on the crest of the property with newly pruned vineyard surrounding it.

When they moved in so long ago, it was a fixer-upper and she didn't know if Mark had the skills. He couldn't stop talking about all the possibilities the land held for them. As she toured the worn floors, she saw an old building with one outdated bathroom and two small bedrooms. Not enough space for a growing family. Today, after years of remodeling, adding rooms and updating bathrooms, then filling it with prized possessions and memories, she barely remembered the dread.

Then was a time of future and endless belief in Mark. He was ambitious, and the world was his to conquer. Now, especially with the move to Boston, he seemed to be settling.

She tucked a wisp of hair behind her ear. She wasn't ready to settle. And the old Mark wouldn't have accepted the transfer.

Mark, wearing a faded flannel shirt, appeared halfway down one of the rows heading her way. He waved. She waved back. How many times had she stood at this door and watched her husband walk, always with a hoe or shovel over his shoulder, toward home? A much younger and happier Mark flickered across her memory. Her heart clutched. How she missed that man. She missed him following her into the kitchen and then sitting at the table to remove his boots and talk about the growth of the grapes.

Today, although smiling, he walked slower, more reverently. He looked older. The years were creeping up on them both. When did it happen? Even the land couldn't stop ageing. Somehow, she'd believed it could.

"Do I smell pecan rolls?" Mark climbed the porch steps, kissed her cheek.

"Would it be Christmas without them?" She handed him the newspaper.

"I thought I stopped the paper," he said as he took it.

"Guess not."

Mark kicked against the top step, knocking caked mud from his boots and headed into the foyer where he sat and removed them. "I forgot how dirty they get," he said while he inspected them and eventually put them outside the door. The timer buzzed and Claire moved quickly past Mark to the kitchen. "Hot rolls," she called over her shoulder.

"And fresh coffee?" Mark rounded the doorway into the kitchen. "What time is everyone showing up?"

Claire turned the sugary, cinnamon covered yeast rolls onto the Christmas tray she inherited from her grandmother. "Mom, Dad, and kids should be here within the hour. I heard Sean go out earlier and assume he'll be back soon."

Mark reached and picked up a pecan that fell on the counter and put it in his mouth.

"Careful," Claire warned. "They're hot and you'll burn your tongue." She turned and poured two mugs of coffee, handed one to Mark.

Mark's eyes were fixated on the rolls. "Want me to serve you?" Claire asked.

He smiled and leaned against the island, coffee in one hand and reached for the offered pecan roll with the other. "Mind if I take this to the den?"

Claire waved him off, and he left her standing alone. When did he become so formal, he asked permission to leave her presence?

Slowly guests arrived, full of excitement and expectation. They laughed at each other's jokes, shared memories of Christmases past, and filled the house with the patina of family.

Claire wanted the clock to stop ticking so the time filled with love would last forever. She didn't have the power to hold back the future. Babies grew into teens, teens to young adults, the adults to the elderly and the elderly to heaven. But not today. Today, everyone and everything was in their God-appointed place and time and she was here to savor every moment.

Chapter Twenty-Seven

"Sorry I'm late," Claire said to Jeff as she entered the office.

He looked at her and waved a dismissive hand. "I figure you got shut out of Boston because of the huge storm."

"Exactly," she said, shaking fresh snow off her jacket.

"Hopefully you were still at home and not re-routed someplace." He smiled, dimpling his cheeks.

"Stuck in Los Angeles," she said. "At least we could get a room and …" She blushed. "Dare I say we spent the day drinking wine by a pool."

"Oh yeah, rub it in."

Claire hung her head then looked up and smiled. "I really enjoyed being home." She took a step away, stopped, then turned back to Jeff. "I forgot to ask. Did you have a good time in Paris?"

"I did. Now, get to work," he said in a teasing tone. "We've got a case to win."

Claire busied herself at her desk, a small forty-eight inches of space all her own. The pencils were where she left them, the papers neatly piled in an organization she created, and the chair adjusted to her leg length. She gave a crisp nod.

The latest report from the investigator Jeff hired had the employee pay records of the people on the same level as Glen. She began to draft a chart of the pay increase and advancements. Although time consuming, in the end, she had a colored display of salary growth compared to years of employment and gross income earned for the corporation. She did this for six of Glen's contemporaries. She laid them over each other creating a revealing graph of discrimination.

She breathed out an audible, "Yeah!"

"Yeah?" Jeff asked from her doorway. "What?"

She startled, then recovered. "Look at this." She pointed to the red, blue, green, purple and black lines.

"This black line is Glen's employment and salary history. You can see he was clearly on the rise until the year of the accident. You would expect to see a year of a dip, then resume. Instead, it plateaus. Yet if you check the number of his clients, the money they generate, you can see growth. But here's the real interesting thing." She glanced up to be sure Jeff was tracking with her. "Look how the raises and promotions for the other employees in the company are so clear. More clients equals more promotion equals more money."

Jeff folded his arms across his chest and nodded. "Now, I have to figure out how to enter this into evidence."

"Is that a problem?"

"Might be. Depends on the judge and what he or she will allow."

"At least we know that indeed this is based on the disability," she said, thumping down her marker.

"Sorry, Claire, but us knowing it doesn't prove it to a court."

"Allow me one day of believing the virtuous shall be victorious." She sighed and leaned back in her chair.

Jeff laughed. "Okay, you believer in good and evil, but in the meantime how about lunch?"

Claire looked at her watch. "Oh dear, it's mid-afternoon. That's why I'm starved."

"You know you did a pretty amazing job. Don't you?"

Claire opened her mouth to say it was nothing. Instead she said, "Thank you."

Mark liked a lot of what she did. He liked how she raised the kids, how she baked bread, how she cared for him. Jeff praised her for her mind, and it had been a long time since a man said something so meaningful to her.

His eyes settled on her. If she didn't know better, she'd say she saw a smoldering longing. Something she hadn't seen in Mark's eyes in years.

She turned from Jeff and grabbed her jacket. Talk about imagining things.

They went to lunch in the basement cafeteria, a glorified break room with about a dozen aqua and chrome square tables. Each had salt, pepper, napkins, and sugar and four plastic gray chairs. Vending machines lined one wall of the windowless room. The coffee urn dispensed stale coffee, drinkable if you added enough milk. It was where you ate when time mattered, or it was too cold outside to stroll to the deli.

They picked at ham and cheese sandwiches and tore open bags of corn chips. She felt acutely aware of Jeff's presence, like he was a magnet and her nerve endings were iron filings.

Jeff put his spoon down, folded his arms over his chest, leaned back in his chair. "Claire, did anyone ever tell you that when you get excited, your eyes are crystal blue?"

She sensed the blush coming. It always started just below her collarbone and crept up into her cheeks. She wished she could stop it, but the more she tried the hotter she became.

"You also blush." He laughed.

She lowered her head, shielding her face.

He reached across the table and lifted her chin.

"You amaze me. Do you know you are a beautiful woman?"

She started to remove his hand from her chin, but her fingers lingered longer than she intended. She liked the sensation of his hands on her face, close to her lips. Another time and place she might just let her lips kiss his hand. Instead, after a long moment, she pulled away from him. Pushed her hair back, tried to look casual.

"Thank you," she finally managed. "I haven't been told that in a long time."

He sounded doubtful. "Your husband must tell you."

A canyon of silence between them echoed in her ears. Her face apparently said it all.

"His mistake," Jeff said as he stood to clear their empty paper plates.

Claire rose, refilled her coffee cup, added the cream, put a lid on it, and started for the door. Her thoughts raced ahead of her. A man, not her husband, touched her today. He hadn't only touched her face but touched a part of her soul she'd thought dead, but found, thankfully, had only been asleep.

She walked faster back to the office than she wanted.

Like in her late teens, desire danced like an unrestrained lightning storm within her.

The adult part of her remained in control.

The teen part yearned to rebel.

Chapter Twenty-Eight

As winter took grip, Mark and Claire settled into parallel lives. He remained busy with work and she warmed under Jeff's attention.

Mark and Claire talked in short spurts without any real communication or connection. They ate together. He fell asleep watching the news. She read poetry into the night. She no longer had the energy or desire to pull his feelings from him.

"What are you guys doing for Valentine's Day?" Agnes asked between puffs of her half-smoked cigarette as they strode down the sidewalk one bitterly cold morning.

"What?" Claire blinked. The question seemed out of left field. She and Jeff weren't Valentines.

"What are you and Mark doing for your Valentine's Day?" Agnes repeated.

Oh, right. Mark. Claire pulled the hood of her down jacket tighter around her head. "Nothing, haven't even thought about it." She shoved her mittened hands deep into the pockets of the coat. "Why is it so cold today?"

"The wind." Agnes gestured at Claire. "You need a parka with a below-zero rating."

"Coats have a temperature rating?"

Agnes nodded. "Don't worry. I have an extra that'll fit you. I'll drop it off." Agnes inhaled deeply. "Big Jim and I always celebrate," she exhaled. "It's my favorite holiday. My honey proposed on Valentine Day. Sent me a dozen red roses every hour and at five o'clock, he picked me up at the hospital carrying one red rose with a three-carat diamond tied to it."

"He proposed to you in the lobby of the hospital?"

"Actually, the emergency waiting room." Agnes chuckled. "And the patients clapped."

"Well, Mark sort of just announced we would get married." There was no engagement. Just the small diamond and matching gold bands they bought the week before the wedding. "I'm afraid to ask, but what do you have planned?"

"I rented a limo and will pick BJ up at work and take him to the theater. I have tickets for the Yo-Yo Ma concert."

The abundance of cultural opportunities in Boston still amazed Claire. She hadn't yet been to any of the symphony offerings. "That sounds like a nice evening," she said.

"You aren't all here today are you?" Agnes shook her head.

"Things on my mind. Plus, this winter stuff is getting to me. At home, we'd be starting to see the green of spring."

"Most of the locals head for Florida or the Bahamas by the end of February."

"You and Jim stay?"

"I kinda like the winter. The first couple of years we flew back to Texas, but now I have the book group, the club, and Jim isn't big on travel."

Claire grew colder, both inside and out.

She liked her morning walk with Agnes. It propelled Claire out of bed and helped her learn to cope with the harshness of winter. The bonus being Agnes, who had a depth that didn't surface until you got to know her. Now Claire understood why people liked her. Agnes laughed a lot and looked at life through positive eyes. She kept up a conversation whether Claire felt like talking or not. This morning Claire wanted Agnes to talk so she could space out.

"I want to do something to shock Big Jim," Agnes said. "I think I'll wear just my fur and nothing else."

"Say that again," Claire asked, not believing she heard correctly.

"What do you think Big Jim will do if I'm naked in the limo? A bottle of champagne chilled, have on great boots and the fox fur …"

Claire didn't believe her ears. "Stop," she said, and Agnes stood still. "You would not have on anything under the coat?"

"Yeah. You've never done that?"

"No."

"Well, you should try it. I did it several years ago, and I thought Big Jim was going to swallow his front teeth," she drawled.

"I don't own a fur." Claire shook her head. "You are too much." With that she opened the door to the coffee shop, ordered for both of them, and then greeted the customers she'd met through Agnes.

Claire chuckled, still having visions of an oversized Agnes wrapped in an expensive fox coat.

Mark was cold. He'd known February in Boston would naturally be cold, but the reality was much worse than what he'd expected. He'd thought he could handle it.

He grew up on the vast cold plains, and he remembered the wood burning stove heating their entire home. Now, looking back, he realized a good amount of winter was spent keeping the house warm. His father, and later himself, would be up before dawn laying a fire in the kitchen stove. A cast iron kettle sat on it steaming the room. He still remembered the odd aroma of heated iron. That, along with the smell of bacon frying, woke him in the winter.

At night, he crawled into bed under the handcrafted, feather-filled, quilt to fall asleep. His door open to keep his room warm. His father, who often fell asleep in the rocking chair, must have stoked the fire sometime during the night. Mark never woke. His world was snug under the hand stitched cover.

This morning he would have done anything for one of those covers. Did Claire notice he turned the heat up so when she woke, the condo was warm. She never said anything about it, but then he never asked.

"Good Morning, Mr. Richter," Daniel called from across the break room.

"Morning," Mark replied.

"Did the snow slow you down?"

Mark shook his head. "Just not a good morning." He poured a cup of coffee. Time to get son with the cold day and get his work done. Mark sipped his coffee, then noticed Daniel's lips were stained red. A tray of red frosted, heart shaped cookies sat next to the coffee pot.

"Who brought in the cookies?" He handed Daniel a napkin. "You might want to get rid of the extra frosting before we head up to see the boss."

Daniel took the napkin and dabbed at his face. "I made them."

"You bake?"

"Learned in college. A woman loves a man who cooks more than looks good."

"A man of many skills," Mark said sarcastically.

"Hey, the women were impressed." He grinned. "What are you doing for the wife today?"

"Claire? We don't exchange gifts."

"You don't? No dinner? No card? Flowers? Nothing?" Daniel threw the napkin in the wastebasket. "How long have you been married?"

"Twenty-eight years."

"And no gifts?"

"Claire is practical. Roses cost too much, and she doesn't wear the jewelry she has. We go to dinner a lot so why go out when the service is going to be bad?"

"I thought all women liked something on Valentine's Day. I know mine does."

"Well, I like cookies," Mark said as he grabbed one with his coffee.

When Claire got to the office, the thought of Agnes in a fur clouded Claire's mind. Where did she come up with those ideas?

Claire didn't notice a bud vase on her desk at first. When she did, she didn't know what to do with it. A simple heart shaped vase held three white roses. There was a small card tied to a white ribbon. She read and reread the inside: *Happy Valentine's Day! Jeff*

What would Jeff do if she showed up dressed in fur in a limo? Heat crept up her cheeks and she kept her face away from the door so no one would see her blush and guess her thoughts about her boss and friend.

Chapter Twenty-Nine

Daily now, Claire had lunch with Jeff, and on some days lunch lasted until dinner.

On the surface, their discussion was about the case, his father, her life in California or as simple as which wine to order with dinner. Underneath, she found herself more and more attracted to him.

Jeff encouraged her to talk about herself. His attention to details reminded her of her father who never failed to notice the smallest change her mother made. Jeff noticed when she trimmed her hair. Not Mark. Over time, Jeff offered her a hand out of the car, held her jacket for her or lent his arm while they navigated the icy walks. All that became natural.

They won the first round of Glen's trial in the courtroom, proving they had enough evidence to take the case to a jury. The preparation required more of Claire's time and she willingly agreed to extend her working hours. She came home often just in time to throw food on the table. She could have gone to work earlier but that would have meant giving up coffee and Agnes.

She rode the T home most nights, watching the neighborhoods fly by. They once looked all the same but now she could tell them apart, they had their own characteristics.

This time of year, early March, back home, the grass would be a deep emerald green. Here, things were a dirty white. The snow melted slowly, exposing spots of frozen earth.

"Winter isn't over yet," Agnes warned as they dodged slushy puddles on the way to The Daily Grind one morning. "We might have a warm day or two then get hit with a Nor'easter burying us."

Along with the daily weather report, the walks, the smokes, and coffee, Agnes gave abundant and unsolicited advice.

"Rachel's is having a big sale," Agnes continued. "You need a suit if you're going to court."

"I'm not going to court." Claire shivered despite the down jacket Agnes had loaned her.

Agnes stopped, put a hand on one generous hip. "You mean to say you've worked this long on the case and aren't going to go and see the end?"

"I'll have to ask Jeff if I can go." Claire shrugged, tugged Agnes to resume their walk to warmth and caffeine.

"Sugar, don't ask. Just buy a suit and go."

"Mark," Claire called from the door. "Sorry I'm late."

Mark was on the phone and held a finger to his lips.

Claire mouthed, "Okay, I'll start dinner," and went to the kitchen.

She listened to Mark's end of the conversation. Work or personal?

"Okay… Are you sure?" Followed by a long silence. "But you're sure? What? When?" Again silence then, "Yeah, I'll tell Mom," followed by the sound of the phone falling back into the cradle.

"Who was that, and just what do you need to tell Mom?" Claire asked, putting a plate of sliced tomatoes on the table. When she looked at Mark's face, he was ashen, and his eyes were tearing.

Her heart stopped. He never cried. "Mark, who was that? Has something happened to one of the kids?"

"That was Katie. Sit down, Claire."

"Just tell me what happened. Did Peter leave? I knew it! She has bad judgment in men."

"Claire, stop and listen. Sit down."

"I don't want to sit." She paced. "Just tell me. What happened?"

"That was Katie on the phone."

"You said that," she snapped.

Mark hesitated, looked skyward. "It seems she's pregnant."

Claire stopped and whirled to face him. "Pregnant? Is she sure?"

"She says yes. She took a test, and it was positive. She's scheduled to see the campus doctor tomorrow."

"How did that happen?" Claire asked as she scrambled for a chair to sink in.

Mark just blinked at her with a blank face. Of course, she knew how it happened. She really wanted to ask why Katie hadn't used protection.

Claire's mind swam with thoughts "What's she going to do?" Emotions churned in Claire's chest, tumbling too quickly for her to sort through them, to identify them.

"Have a baby. I guess."

"I wonder?"

Mark moved to the table, pulled out a chair and sat opposite Claire. "You wonder? She'll marry Peter and have the baby. What else can she do?"

"She has lots of choices."

"Katie is a good girl. She'll marry Peter. We might have to help out a bit, but they'll do fine."

"Mark."

He looked up. "This isn't our problem."

"We are family, Claire."

"She's an adult."

"She is your daughter. She is carrying your grandchild."

"She's too young. She needs to finish school. Having a kid now will ruin her life," Claire said, without thinking.

"And did Colleen ruin your life, Claire?" Mark strode to the front door.

"Where are you going?" she asked.

"Out," he said and then added, "Get a reality check, Claire. Your magical way of looking at things won't change this."

Her breath left with Mark.

The one thing they'd agreed to never talk about again came back to haunt her. What was it that Father O'Malley had said...the sins of the father?

But in this case, it was the sins of the mother.

Claire sat frozen in the chair, only her survival instinct continued to breathe, to pump her blood.

The sun set and still she didn't move.

Her life lumped in her stomach. Time took on a new dimension. There was no yesterday, today, or tomorrow it was all in Now.

Like a black and white film, memories played across her eyes.

Claire assured Mark it was probably the stress of exam week, but she feared the worst. She missed her period. Her breasts were tender to his touch and in the morning the smell of coffee made her sick. When she missed her second period, she went to Planned Parenthood and took the test that confirmed the pregnancy. They gave her the option of termination. She took the information to Mark.

She was the Catholic, but he was the one who was horrified by the thought of an abortion. He announced they would get married. They would go to Reno and have a Justice of the Peace officiate the ceremony. Then they would tell their parents. Mark handled it so matter-of-factly. It wasn't a romantic invitation to elope down a ladder, run to Reno, get married and surprise the world with their secret love. It was more an escape to cover their secret sin.

"Do you want to get married?" she remembered asking.

"Sure. Don't you?" he replied.

"Yes."

It wasn't exactly the proposal Claire dreamed about, but then getting pregnant wasn't in her original dreams. She'd been careful, gone to Planned Parenthood and been fitted with a diaphragm. How did it happen? When? Why? The questions were as current today as they were then.

"We can leave after classes Friday. I'll call in sick for work Saturday," Mark said.

Claire remembered fingering the glossy pamphlet in her fingers, dog-earing the corners. "Are you sure?"

"We probably would have gotten married next year anyway. We just moved the date up."

That *Probably* still sat crossway, like a fishbone, in her throat, but they married that weekend. They told her parents on Sunday. Mark called his mother and promised to bring his new bride for a visit in the summer.

In her fourth month, they drove to Wisconsin. They called it a honeymoon. Claire started wearing Mark's shirts sometime around Dakota. His mother's eyesight was failing, or she was so self-absorbed she didn't notice. Three weeks later when they returned it was clear to Claire's family why they married, yet no one vocalized the obvious.

Claire and Mark never talked about the beginning; they just went forward. The early years were full of spontaneous lovemaking, long walks, and shared plans for a future and few arguments. She couldn't remember any real fights. They just sort of grew apart. Mark got busy with his work. It consumed him. Just like her with the kids, then her own work.

Mark stalked down the street. He couldn't believe Claire. She didn't remember how alone and isolated she felt when she found out she was pregnant.

All this time together and he thought the kids made her happy. Now she acted like they ruined her life. Having children altered *his* life, not hers. He was the one who always did what was best for "the family." Long ago he gave up any dreams of moving back to Wisconsin because Claire wouldn't.

He went into a bar and ordered a beer. He, who never drank alone, needed a beer. He sat there and the darkness of the room felt like a cellar. The beer was a cold draft, cool against his dry throat. He wanted to yell at Claire. He hated when his father yelled at his mother and Mark swore he would never do that. Instead he walked away.

Of course Peter would marry Katie. That's what a decent man did, take responsibility. He and Claire would have to help out financially. It wouldn't be as hard for Katie as it had been for them. Claire might have to watch the child once they returned to California. He remembered her in the days when the kids were small. She smiled more then. A grandchild would give her life meaning.

She'd come around. She'd love having a baby in the family again.

Claire didn't notice Mark come in until he turned the lights on, and she blinked back to now.

"Where'd you go?" she asked.

"Had a beer."

"Oh." She stood to finish setting dinner on the table. The food was cold, but neither commented on it.

"Katie should come here so we all can talk," Mark said.

"She'll have a break soon."

"I'll call her tomorrow and send some money. I'm sure she could use it," he said between bites of dry roast beef.

"Remember, Mark, this is her choice. We can't make decisions for her."

"She's family. We'll do what is right."

Claire forced a smile. "We always do."

Or at least he did.

Chapter Thirty

The next day, Mark called Katie.

"Katie?" The conversation started out stilted.

"What, Dad?" Her voice was flat, like she expected a scolding.

"Your mom and I would like for you to come here for Easter."

"Why?" Now she turned suspicious.

"Just to talk. I'll book you a ticket."

"How about Peter?"

Mark hesitated. He wasn't sure what to say. After all, Peter was now very involved in the family. Like it or not.

"Yes, he should come." He made the decision and would live with the fallout. There wasn't an easy solution. From now on, Peter was a part of their collective history and, at the very least, the father of his grandchild. "I'll get two tickets."

"Thanks, Daddy. We'll come in two weeks, at break."

"You might get married while you're here" he said. "I'd like to be there when you do."

Katie didn't respond. He waited. She might tell him they were already married, like he and Claire had done.

"Well...we aren't sure we're getting married."

He blinked. "What?"

"We aren't sure marriage is for us."

"But...what about the baby?" he asked.

"Dad, we can have the baby and live together. Lots of people do."

Mark heard a catch in her voice. He knew her well enough to know there was more to the story. He wanted to learn it all so there would be no surprises when they were here, and then with Claire. He didn't like surprises, especially if they involved him resolving them. He used one of Claire's old tricks. "Katie, what aren't you telling me?"

"What do you mean?"

How many times he'd sat as an observer to conversations between mother and daughter. He searched his memory for the next line in this play of inquiry.

"I mean I feel ..." *That* was the word he'd heard... "you aren't telling me everything."

"You sound just like Mom."

"I know but tell me what's going on. I won't judge. Just tell me. We've had a good relationship and never kept secrets from each other."

He heard her open a door and assumed she went out on her balcony. Cars rushed by in the background and wind chimes echoed in the breeze. Then the soft voice of his daughter who was crying.

"It's like this, Daddy. Peter wants me to get an abortion. He says a baby isn't in his plans right now. Well, it wasn't in my plans either, but I can't do it. I know some consider it's only a bunch of cells, but not to me. It's a life."

Mark listened. He didn't know what to say. Of course, he thought about Colleen and was glad he and Claire hadn't terminated. He was glad they got married. He wanted to tell his daughter so many things, but he shouldn't. He shook his head. Disappointment in Peter filled his chest.

"Dad, talk to me."

Mark took a deep breath and said the only thing that came to his mind. "I love you Katie." Then after a few seconds, "Why don't you come alone? We can talk better."

Maybe it was selfish on his part, but he needed for Katie to be able share without worrying about what Peter might say or think or overhear.

All he told Claire later was Katie would be in Boston for Easter.

Chapter Thirty-One

"What're y'all doing for Easter?" Agnes asked.

"What?" Claire's thoughts were consumed with her daughter.

"Where's your head been, girl? For two weeks now you haven't listened to a word I've said. We walk, I smoke, we have coffee, I talk, and you walk around in a daze."

"I'm sorry. Things on my mind."

"That's pretty obvious. You going to tell me, or do I have to crack the bullwhip to get it out of you?"

"No whip, but I'll let you buy the coffee." Claire wasn't sure she wanted to tell Agnes the whole story about Katie, but then Claire hadn't talked to anyone, including Mark, about it.

After they had their drinks and were settled in their chairs, Agnes gave Claire a raised brow look.

Claire drew a deep breath. "Katie's coming tomorrow."

"Oh, darlin' that's grand. To spend Easter?" Agnes gushed.

"Sort of."

Agnes leaned forward and placed a hand on Claire's arm. "You don't sound excited. What's up?"

The warm coffee worked like truth serum.

"It's complicated." Then she cried.

She hated crying, especially when she didn't know why. Was she sad because her daughter would live a repeat of Claire's life and always question whether she married for love or because she had to, or be angry Claire failed her in some way?

Tears ran down Claire's cheeks and she couldn't stop them. She fumbled for a napkin, but the only one close was under Agnes's spoon. She reached for it anyway and caught the errant tear as it was about to drop from her chin. She held her head up straight and blurted out, "She's coming because she's pregnant and wants to talk."

Agnes leaned back in her chair and exhaled with a whoosh. "Oh, thank God. I thought she had cancer or something. A baby. How wonderful."

"Wonderful?" Claire's tears stopped mid-cheek.

"Well, love, it sure could be worse. A baby *is* wonderful."

"But...but she's not married. She hasn't finished school. She's too young. They don't have jobs."

"All that's true, but it's a *baby*." Agnes smiled looking like she just received the word of the Annunciation. "Is she going to marry this boy? What's his name?"

"Peter. I don't like him. She probably will marry him for that reason alone," Claire said, trying to add a soft laugh.

"What's Mark's reaction to this?"

"We aren't talking about it. Or much of anything these days." Claire blotted her cheeks.

"Problems at home?" Agnes's expression changed from smiling to serious.

"Not really." Claire shrugged. "We just don't talk about things. Mark's attitude is 'we just keep moving forward.' Sometimes he has blinders on. Like a horse, he can only move ahead and doesn't get distracted to the right or left. I, on the other hand, see all the possible problems that could, maybe, perhaps, cross my path. I want to have a plan for each and every one of those possibilities." She stopped talking for a moment, drank a long sip from her cup, then continued. "I'm not sure who has the better life skills."

"Ever think you both may have them?"

How could they both be right when they were so opposite? "Are you sure you aren't the therapist?" Claire asked with a small smile.

"No degrees, but lots of living," Agnes offered.

"Best degree I know."

They finished their coffee. Agnes declared herself an unofficial auntie and planned on spoiling the baby with gifts.

While at Jeff's office, Claire didn't think about Katie or herself. It was a place where the work directed the mood of the day and absorbed time. She started dressing more businesslike, wearing tailored skirts and button-down blouses with either a jacket or sweater. She felt more a part of Jeff's business and on occasions part, of his life.

She discovered her background in Social Work not only a benefit to the clients but also a tool to better understand Jeff. He shared personal facts about his life and how it complicated his relationship with his father. She encouraged Jeff to keep trying. He, unlike Mark, listened as a willing and eager student.

One lunch Jeff told about how his mother and he were often left alone for days when his father would be off on a business trip. His mother needed him and treated him like an adult, often taking him as her dinner partner at the club or "date" to the movies. It wasn't until high school, when the other boys teased him, he realized how different his life was from theirs.

He began to resent his father. After Jeff's marriage failed, the nails in the coffin were driven. He already worked in the same office, but he and his father had separate practices. It was about three years ago, just after his mother died, he noticed his father's faculties slipping.

"Some days he would show up at work wearing his pajama top as a shirt," Jeff told her. "Then one day Phyllis took me aside and said my father needed a bath." Jeff's lips tightened into a thin line. "I was embarrassed. Not only for my father, but that I hadn't been close enough to him to notice. Then I realized I'd become the parent."

Jeff's tender smile betrayed the otherwise somber moment. "It was Agnes," he said. "She took me for dinner one night after book group and told me to grow up."

Claire remembered how he looked at her while he told the story. Pools of unshed tears—saved for years—forming in his eyes.

"She said, 'Your father is slipping away. Has been for years. Your mother used to cover for him.'" Jeff brushed a potential tear from his cheek. "Agnes told me how Mom finished sentences for him when they were out. How she laid his clothes out daily and checked to see if he matched before he left for work. How she would always cue him to the name of who was talking." Jeff shook his head. "I hadn't noticed any of it. I was consumed with my own life."

He told Claire he moved to a house closer to his father and had breakfast with him every morning. For a long time, Jeff kept his father coming to work. Phyllis gave him the same work to do, and he never figured it out. The hardest day was when Jeff moved him into the Alzheimer home.

Claire never tired of hearing Jeff talk. She wanted to know more and more. She drank him up. He would talk to her while holding her hand. At first the uncomfortable soon became the natural.

What would her life have been like with a man as open as Jeff?

"Hey Claire, what's happening for Easter at your house?" Jeff asked on his way past her desk.

"Not much. My daughter is visiting." She didn't want to tell him why. "We'll find a midnight mass and celebrate. I'm not hiding eggs or anything." She laughed.

"I wanted to see if you'd like to come out to the Vineyard for the weekend."

Claire always hesitated when a local referred to Martha's Vineyard as the Vineyard. After all, a vineyard is where you grow grapes. The most she figured that grew on Martha's Vineyard were blueberries and compounds to house the rich and famous. She hadn't been, yet, but both Agnes and Jeff owned houses there. They both talked about Claire joining them as if once invited, you couldn't refuse.

"Well, maybe for Memorial Day weekend. Why don't you plan on joining us? Agnes has a big party that opens the season, and I know she would love for you to be there."

"If I'm invited," she answered.

Chapter Thirty-Two

A bit after seven, Claire heard Jeff close his office door. She planned to work late. Mark would pick Katie up at the airport and then they would meet at the apartment around eleven. She could get in another couple of hours before heading out and have nothing on her desk for the weekend.

She rubbed her eyes as she looked at the screen searching through Supreme Court decisions on The American Disability Act, passed in 1998. In the interpretations is where a law had teeth, so she hunted for similar cases that would help Glen's case. Jeff thought the company would settle once they saw the downside of going to court. Claire wasn't so sure. People could be stubborn and after all, management couldn't afford to open the door for future lawsuits. The laws were vaguely written so it could include a variety of disabilities. Absorbed in her work, she didn't notice Jeff standing in the doorway. He cleared his throat.

She looked up and hid the uptick of her pulse with a quick swallow. "I thought you left," she said.

"I did, but I saw you were still here, so I came back to see if you wanted some dinner."

Claire had grabbed a scone earlier, and her fridge at home held a plate of cheese and meats set up for visiting later with Katie. Yet her stomach growled as she noticed his double-dimpled smile.

"I don't have time for dinner," she said.

"I thought you might say that, so I brought dinner in for us. Come see."

"See?" she managed to say as she rose from her desk.

Jeff bowed at the waist and dramatically pointed his arm toward an array of paper cartons with chopsticks poking out arranged on the lobby side table which usually held a selection of magazines.

"I picked up Chinese," he said as he escorted her to the couch.

Claire opened her mouth to speak but nothing came out.

Before the danger warnings could win, she sat. Jeff poured white wine into a paper cup.

"Not fluted," he said.

She accepted the cup, sipped, to allow herself time to think. "I'm a bit hungry, but I need to leave soon. My daughter is arriving and will be at the house before I get there." Her legs going so weak, she couldn't have run from this moment if she wanted. And she didn't want to. A small voice told her to leave, but she swallowed it with the wine. It went down easier than she expected.

Jeff handed her a box of ginger cashew chicken.

She savored every morsel and his attention.

"A penny for your thoughts," he said.

She breathed deep. "Thinking how kind you are."

"Me? Please. It's you who gives. You're always listening to my complaints. This is the least I could do." He took a pork dumpling out of the box presenting it to her lips. She opened her mouth and took a bite.

His fingers rested on her cheek. She flashed to the day in the cafeteria he brushed her hair back. She swallowed the dumpling and started to pull from him when he leaned over. His hand moved to the back of her head blocking her retreat. He sat next to her and now she sensed how close. His warm hand cradled her head and his massaging fingers drew her nearer. With his breath against her lips, she exhaled a sigh of surrender.

He was going to kiss her and wasn't going to rush into it. She looked into his eye and caught the scent of Jovan aftershave mingled with his own masculine perfume that defined Jeff. Then she tasted the ginger of the chicken on his lips.

Softly he kissed her, his fingers slipping to the nape of her neck. A quiver of excitement ran the length of her body. His lips didn't leave her but parted slightly and kissed her again. Her hands went to his cheek, outlining his dimple.

He pulled away, but held her eyes, smiling all the time.

"I have wanted that for a long time, Claire," he whispered.

She lowered her eyes, wanting to suspend time and linger. The excitement of a new, fresh start brewed in her. Words failed her. Instead, she allowed her lips to reply.

She kissed him, letting him know her desire and Jeff responded.

When he reached for the top button of her blouse, her cell phone rang. She darted to retrieve it. It's glowing blue screen calling her back to reality.

Mark. She tried to compose herself.

"Hello," Claire said, striving to sound casual rather than annoyed.

"Hey, Katie's plane landed early, and we're on our way home," he announced cheerfully. "Claire? You there?"

"I'm here."

"Well, come home. We'll meet you at the apartment. See ya in fifteen." He always ended calls that way—see ya.

She clicked the phone off and turned back to Jeff.

"It's later than I thought. I need to head home. Thanks for the dinner." Her voice cracked.

He held her gaze steadily. "I hope we continue this soon."

All the way to the condo she forced herself to think through the swirling confusion. Her heart and body threw off sparks when Jeff was near. Sometimes she worried she might spontaneously combust.

But what about Mark, her head reasoned? They had a family, a shared past, a *marriage*, for God's sake. She'd be a fool to risk any of that.

By the time Claire parked the car, she resolved to do nothing. She would go forward and take care of the business waiting for her in the living room. She dropped her head to the steering wheel, sighed deeply. What she wouldn't give for an evening with her mother, the old teapot, and some wisdom. In the elevator, Claire tapped her toe. When did she and Katie start fighting?

Forever ago...it was a part of who they were. Claire would offer her daughter a doll to play with and pig-tailed Katie would throw it across the room.

It was the silly battles Claire remembered, the ones without a winner.

She wanted to stop fighting, but their war had a life all its own. If she could just hold her daughter close, maybe the ice around their hearts would melt. But that only happened in the movies. And her life wasn't even G-rated any more.

The elevator dinged and the doors opened. An older woman carrying a dog stepped on and smiled at Claire.

Maybe...maybe she should tell Katie how she'd dealt with an unplanned pregnancy. But no. That wasn't fair to the others involved. There were too many people who'd kept their family secret. A silent bond forged with her parents, siblings, friends. And Mark.

So many secrets. And they grew heavier each day.

With Jeff, she could start all over, no secrets. She and Jeff would drive to work daily, solve problems for clients, and then spend hours talking. They would go to dinner, and she would order warm potato cheese soup with crusty French bread. As she dipped her crust in the soup, they would laugh about shared intimacies. Jeff would pour her wine, remove the errant curl from her forehead and rush her away to bed.

Oh, the bed part excited her. He'd be both tender and rough, kissing her to arousal, owning her thru climax, and holding her until morning.

Then guilt swept over her. How stupid. She didn't know if Jeff wanted her. She only knew she wanted him. The elevator's cheerful ding reminded her she had a different life, a different reality, and it waited for her.

"Have a nice day," the woman with the dog called after her as Claire stepped out of the elevator.

"Too late," Claire murmured, but she waved a hand in acknowledgment.

When she opened the door to the condo, the place she still didn't call home, three of them sat at the cold glass table. She kissed Mark on the cheek, nodded toward an expectedto Peter, and held her arms out to her daughter. Katie stood and walked into her embrace. A first step toward peace? Maybe. Whatever it meant, she'd take it.

As they sat around the table and talked, Claire did her best to listen and not judge. That's what she'd wanted from her parents and what happened years ago was still as fresh as the current news. Claire remembered the priest saying in confession she was forgiven. She assumed he meant the mistakes of her past no longer mattered. But they did. They came back to haunt her in the pain on her daughter's face and the sadness aching under her heart.

Claire let Mark lead the conversation. He and Katie talked in non-argumentative ways.

Peter remained vocal—he didn't want a child. Mark stated he thought every child needed a father. He stressed the word "needed."

Claire stayed calm and asked her daughter to return to school—in order to support her baby.

The evening ranged from controlled tension, to fear, anger, and eventually silent acceptance.

Claire accepted Katie's decision to have the baby, regardless of Peter's input.

Concern, worry, and experience crawled into bed with Claire and Mark and didn't let them sleep.

What needed to be said had been said and this time there were no secrets.

Chapter Thirty-Three

Monday morning, with Agnes still away for the weekend, Claire skipped coffee and took the train to work early. As it click-clacked away from downtown toward Newton, she reviewed the last three days.

The weekend went better than she'd dared hope. Katie, perhaps due to morning sickness, rested and didn't fight Claire's attempts to mother her. Katie ate the soda crackers and drank the warm tea Claire placed on the nightstand. Peter went on long walks by himself. Mark read in the living room and ran errands. If Katie said she felt like ice cream, Mark returned with four flavors.

Claire's nerves jangled as the train screeched, like fingernails on a blackboard, around a curve. That's what Peter was, a nerve-wracking irritant.

"Mind if I take this seat?" a tall man in a suit asked.

Claire picked up her book from the empty space.

He sat and opened the newspaper to the financial page. Claire stared out the window and watched him in the reflection, his face imposed upon the buildings they passed. He belonged here.

What would her life have been like if she attended an East Coast school? She might have gone on for a doctorate in counseling and opened a private practice. Random unconnected thoughts, like the flickering lights of the train, flashed before her. *What part of my life would I change if I could?*

"Damn," the man said.

"Excuse me?"

"Sorry, I didn't mean to say that out loud." He turned red.

She smiled. "Not a problem, something bad?"

"Not really," he started. "I intended to buy a stock last Friday and didn't get around to it. Today it split and I could have made a lot of money."

"So, you only lost something you didn't already have."

"Good way to put it." He turned slightly to look at her. "I hate when life interferes with potential."

"Don't we all." Claire wasn't thinking about her financial portfolio, rather her life-folio.

"Sometimes we should act on our instincts," he said, as he stood to exit the train.

Wise man. There was no going back to repair the past, only forward into the future.

As she entered the office, she saw Jeff behind his desk. After dropping off her coat and purse, she made her way to the break room.

"You're early," Jeff said, leaning in the doorway.

Claire stood next to the coffee station and prepared a cup of tea. "No Agnes this morning," she said. Dipping the tea bag up and down, she watched until the water turned a deep cinnamon brown. Then on impulse, "Hey, you want to get drinks after work?" Her blood raced and her heart pounded. Surely he noticed the flush creeping up her neck.

"Love to," he said. "How about McGinnis's down the street? I need to see a client but can be there by five."

After work, she stood at an entrance to a blackened bar window, uncertain what awaited her. Up until now Jeff had been a nice fantasy—one she used as a salve for boredom.

In eighteen days, she would be turning fifty and she wasn't willing to settle for...for what? She had been unhappy for so long it began to smother all the days of laughter. She remembered warm days on beaches, her younger, firmer body absorbing the sun while she watched small children play in the sand. She had plans and dreams in those days. She wanted that energy back.

Moving to Boston was supposed to be a new start for her and Mark. Instead it became a clarification of how far apart they had grown.

Claire looked around, checking if she spotted anyone she knew. Guilt clung to her, choking like a too small sweater. She'd lied to Mark, telling him she was going to shop after work.

Shuffling her thoughts, she decided she didn't have to go inside. She'd tell Jeff she had to leave. She'd have one drink and then leave right after. But a part of her knew...if she opened the door, she would stay as long as he allowed.

Oh hell, just open it.

Mark unlocked the condo door and entered the quiet unit. Why did Claire have to go shopping after work? She had all day to do that, and she knew he wanted her home when he arrived. That job of hers was stupid. He made enough money for them both. He'd lived for years with her making the kids a priority, so why couldn't it be about him now?

He opened the white box of Chinese he picked up on the way home. Cold. He hated microwaved food. He hated eating alone even more. Taking the tepid Mongolian beef, he sat in front of the television.

Pushing the buttons on the remote didn't turn it on. The batteries must be dead. Frustration overtook him and he got up and started hunting through drawers for AA batteries. He tried to remember where they were in this house. On the ranch, they were in the kitchen drawer next to the den door. Claire bought them by the packs from the discount store. She had all the sizes. But here, he couldn't find any.

Nothing was right.

No one was where they belonged.

Claire noticed Jeff sitting in a booth at the back of the room, chatting with a young waitress who twirled a lock of hair around a finger and threw her head back as she giggled.

Claire straightened the wrinkles in her skirt, inhaled deeply. Now was a fine time to think about it, but should she have gotten some injections or something in the crow's feet around her eyes?

"Hi," she said and gave the girl a dismissive look. At least she hoped it was dismissive.

"What can Samantha bring you?" Jeff stood, kissed her cheek.

"I'll have a margarita." She sat, settled herself and her purse on the bench seat.

Glancing around the room she became acutely aware of her age. The bar was full of middle-aged men with much younger women. Some were dressed in business attire, others in cocktail dresses, but none were over the age of thirty. They all had long flowing hair they fingered while they talked. She was out of place in her tailored, brown tweed skirt and sweater.

"How's your father?" She opened with a safe subject.

Jeff went on for some time about the newest crisis at the care facility. How his father wanted to be home. Jeff continued on and on, like Claire knew all the characters he was talking about. She only half listened. Instead, she watched him talk. His face intrigued her. The movement of his brows as he weaved through the events of his father's life knitted the worry he talked about.

She thought about taking him in her arms to comfort him. It would be natural for her to pull him close to soothe his mood.

Thoughts of Mark and how he behaved when his mother died intruded. She'd been ill, and Claire kept encouraging him to go back to Wisconsin to see her before it was too late. When he finally did make the trip, it was to bury her. Claire went with him and attempted to hold him and tell him all would be okay, but Mark wanted to be alone. She couldn't comfort a man who didn't share his grief.

Jeff leaned across the table and took her hands. "Thanks for listening."

"I care about what's happening." His hands were softer than Mark's.

"You're the rare person. Most don't. Sometimes I wish my daughter was here. She makes me laugh. She's a lot like you."

Claire's brow furrowed and she glanced away. She didn't want to be compared to his daughter, or his mother. She wanted him to look at her like he looked at the waitress.

"How are your kids doing?" he asked as he released her hands.

"They're fine." She didn't want to talk or think about Katie, who should be finishing school and instead had attached herself to a man without ambition.

Claire finished her drink, savoring the time.

"Let's go for a walk," Jeff said as he laid two twenties on the tray.

"Shall we wait for change?"

"Call it a random act of kindness. The kid is probably in school and can use the extra for books."

If Samantha was a single mother, like Katie might end up, she'd need the extra for diapers. How would Katie make ends meet?

Fiddle dee was what Scarlet O'Hara would say. She'd worry about that tomorrow.

"What did you say?" Jeff asked as he settled her coat on her.

Claire hadn't realized she'd said it out loud. "I just said fiddle dee. Something Scarlet would say."

Jeff laughed. "And what are we fiddle deeeing?"

"Life."

"You amaze me. Out of nowhere you come up with Scarlet. Shall we pull the curtains down and dress you for the part? Shall I play Rhett?"

"Well, frankly, Jeff, I don't give a damn."

"Wait, isn't that my line?"

"Maybe we should re-read the book."

They laughed as they walked down the path along the Charles. The sun and time slipped into the river and rushed by. Walking on a birch-covered path along a river with her real-life Rhett Butler filled her with heat and she sneaked a glance at him.

Then he, Jeff—or was it Rhett?—stopped and took her in his arms. He kissed her on the forehead before letting his lips touch hers.

She kissed him back. The anticipated surge of desire made her flush. When had Mark last kissed her like that? Had he ever? Surely, he had. But the years of knowing each other took the surprise out of kissing.

Jeff took her head, cupped it in his hands, and kissed her softly with exploratory lips. The kisses traveled down her neck and then her shoulder tops waiting for her to respond. Taking a deep breath, he stopped and pulled her close, held and rocked her. Their bodies pressing against each other, she felt his excitement slip against the surface of hers.

Her phone rang. She fumbled in her pockets to find it.

"Hello." Breathless, she tried to not sound annoyed.

"Claire. Mark."

Of course. "What's up?" she asked. What time was it? How long had she and Jeff been walking?

"I assume you're heading home soon since the stores are closed."

Claire took a fast glance at the time on the phone screen, almost nine.

"Yes, I'm getting the train now."

"Well, we're out of batteries and the remote doesn't work. Could you stop at the corner store and pick some up?"

"You called because we don't have batteries."

"Yeah, is it a problem?"

She made no effort to hide the frustration in her voice when she said, "No, I'll stop and get them."

"Good, we need AA. Might want to pick up some triples too. I'll change all the batteries in the clocks while I'm at it."

"Anything else?"

"Could you pick up something to eat? I didn't have much for dinner." Claire swore she could hear him whine.

"Sure. See you soon."

She hit the red end button.

"Your husband?"

"Yeah. He wants me to pick up batteries for the clocks."

"Well, his timing couldn't have been better." Jeff laughed.

"No kidding, but I do need to head home."

They were near the T when he asked, "Want me to give you a ride?"

"No, I'm okay. If I know Mark, he'll be waiting at the other end."

Jeff leaned down and kissed her good night. But this kiss had no passion.

Mark hung up. He heard irritation in Claire's voice. Why should she be irritated? After all, she was out, and the store was next to the T station. It wasn't out of her way to stop and get batteries. They had cell phones to eliminate extra trips.

The phone rang. Probably Claire calling back to see what exactly he wanted for a snack. He imagined the fast food places near the station. He'd tell her to pick up some croissants from the bakery at the end of the strip mall. They made great brie and spinach ones that would be just right with a glass of white wine.

"Hello."

"Hi, Mark. This is Jim."

"Jim?" he asked, trying to remove the bakery from his mind.

"Jim Adams, Agnes's husband."

"Oh hi, Jim, what's up?"

"Remember how much I liked that wine we had at Thanksgiving?"

"The pinot?"

"The one you said you helped develop."

"My wine." Mark corrected him but wasn't sure Jim heard.

"I want to get a case of it and can't find it. Was wondering if you could help me?"

"Well, it was a limited production, but I have a couple of cases in my cellar at home and would be willing to share. When do you need them?"

"I want to take them out to Martha's Vineyard for the summer so in the next two months if possible."

Claire walked in but he continued with Jim. "Shouldn't be a problem. I'll get my son to send it." He waved.

"Thanks. Tell me how much."

"Don't worry. I'll let you know when it's here." He was anxious to get off the phone and talk to Claire, but she left the plastic bag on the table and headed to the bathroom.

He hung up and followed her.

"No shopping bags?" he asked as she undressed.

"Nothing good."

He leaned against the door jamb and watched her. He'd watched her undress many times. There was a time when it excited him. Now it just amazed him that she did it the same way, again and again, in layers. First her shoes, then her blouse, then her skirt and each piece hung up or put in the laundry before the next piece was removed.

"I'm going to shower. Your batteries are on the table."

"Did you get us a snack?"

"Some cheese croissants."

"Great," he said as he turned to leave. It *was* great she knew what he would want. That is what a long marriage was about.

He decided to forgive her for not being home earlier.

Claire, tired to the core, let the warm water wash over her newly discovered self. Did Mark notice any difference?

Chapter Thirty-Four

Claire jerked awake, gasping for air. What a crazy dream. In one scene, Jeff held her tight and kissed every inch of her. In the next, she and Mark walked hand in hand in the vineyard. When she came to the end of a row of vines, she froze, Mark on one side of the grapes and Jeff on the other. Jeff held out his hand inviting her, Mark stood motionless waiting. Mark, clear and in focus stood for all she knew. No surprises. Jeff appeared like a spirit—nothing about him known, nothing safe. She felt her body turn to Jeff, but her feet, planted firmly in the soil of home, didn't move.

Rubbing the remnants of sleep from her eyes, Mark's soft, even snores irritated her. Long ago, she'd learned to sleep through his snoring. Tonight, she couldn't ignore it or perhaps she couldn't sleep for fear the dream would return and provide an answer. Worse yet, there might not be one. She turned and watched Mark sleep. When did he change? When didn't she? Or was it the other way around?

Each of his labored inhales brought back good memories of their young marriage. With each exhale, the memories evaporated into the black of night. Which was stronger, the inhale or the exhale? No longer equal.

The digital clock's bright red numbers blinked letting her know there had been an electrical blip she'd slept through. She leaned over Mark, who never went digital, and lifted his wrist to check his trusty wind-up. She sighed and dropped back to the pillow. It was too early to get up for the day and too late to fall back to sleep.

Some of her best worrying occurred between three and four in the morning and tonight that ritual followed her to Boston. At home, she would walk out to the patio and count the stars. She forced herself out of bed and opened the blinds to an overcast night.

Sleep became a desire rather than a reality. Claire reassured herself she did what she could for Katie—she had opened a door for communication. The last part of their visit, although tense, ended peacefully. Both mother and daughter used restraint and called an unspoken truce. Mark and she rarely talked about Katie's future because Mark pushed for marriage and Claire prayed they wouldn't. It would be hard enough for Katie to care for a baby and Claire feared Peter, who didn't want it, would only add to her daughter's burden.

Claire knew women who went back to school after a child entered the picture, but she also was aware of the women who couldn't overcome the anchor of a husband who felt forced into marriage.

Was Mark an anchor? If not, why did she wake shaking in the night? Was she his anchor or responsibility? She'd worked with lots of women whose marriages didn't make it when they married "for the child." Were she and Mark the exception? Would Katie be?

Claire fingered the wand on the blinds, twisting it open and closed. Each time she opened them she searched to find a star breaking through the clouds.

Jeff crept into her head again. He opened a world of challenge. Glen's company had offered a monetary settlement, but Glen and Jeff, and she, in a smaller way, continued to fight for the reinstatement of Glen's job with the proper promotions. Claire's time at the office would be coming to an end soon. Knowing all along it wasn't a forever job didn't diminish its value. Maybe it helped the time pass faster.

Now, in the predawn stillness, Claire's thoughts flitted to the ranch. She'd loved spring in the coastal hills. How she wanted to be there and how she hated missing the new growth unfurling on the vines. Would this new Claire, the Boston Claire, could she ever find the peace those tender green leaves once provided? She couldn't remember the smell of the earth.

She let the blinds fall close and moved down the hall.

The kiss floated back. The kiss she tried to remove from memory. The kiss so real, it woke her in the night. How could she continue to deny Jeff moved her in ways Mark had forgotten?

No longer able to sleep with her own deception, she took her secret to the kitchen for hot tea. Not finding the strong leaves of Mom's blend, Claire brewed the self-healing orange spice tea of her college dorm years. Those were the days, when every breath was filled with expectation, life full of endless choices, and the years she still slept at night.

Someone or something could make sense of this dilemma, perhaps a therapist. Why did she doubt her own skills? She was good at helping others so how did she help herself at three in the morning?

In a few hours Agnes, who returned late last night, would meet her for their walk and Claire debated sharing...or should she wait until later and call Val? No. She shook her head. She wouldn't involve either.

As a little girl, Claire imagined she'd grow up, get married, have children and be happy ever after, because for every overworked, misunderstood girl there was a prince. Like believing on falling stars, Claire wanted to believe in "the" prince. There were never two princes in the stories. Only one perfect, right prince per girl, and for the first time in their marriage it wasn't Mark.

As the clock ticked closer to dawn, and the tea grew cold, Claire stayed confused and lonely. Not one man met her needs, at least not the man who slept in the other room. She wondered if Jeff was awake. Maybe she could call him and meet him for breakfast. But she didn't have a good lie prepared to give Mark.

How easy it had become to lie.

The second cup of tea suggested she should start listing reasons to be alone. Or if not alone, then with Jeff.

What was her justification for an affair? The simple, "I want it," wasn't a good enough reason. Perhaps just let it happen and pretend it wasn't a choice. Some of the women at the center said they got swept away with emotion, and the next thing they knew, they were in the arms of a lover.

She tsked. Claire wasn't the swept away kind. Even if with Jeff she felt out of control.

The future would change, and if Mark wanted to sleep through her life, and Katie didn't care about the outcome of hers, Claire could step over the line. Forget waiting for the elusive star of happiness.

Chapter Thirty-Five

A week later, Claire opened the condo's front door and entered.

"Claire?" Mark called from the living room.

"Yeah," she answered. Who else would he expect to walk in the front door? She hung up her jacket.

Since the winery's office faced the route of the Boston Marathon, they'd closed for the day. The closure had caught Mark off guard. In Paso Robles he would have a list of projects, things to catch up at the ranch.

"Did you want something?" she asked, moving to the living room doorway.

"Where were you?" He looked up from the newspaper.

"Walking with Agnes. Remember I do that every day."

"I didn't know that."

She'd been walking with Agnes for months. How could he not know? "It would help if you listened when I told you things." She took a deep breath. "Remember I have book group this afternoon."

"Are you going?"

"Of course."

"I thought you might stay home."

"And do what?" She had no plans to stay home and sit and watch him watch television. Since the court case went to Settlement, she didn't really have a reason to go to the office every day and Jeff would be at book group. Part of her hoped Jeff would take on another case he needed her help with.

"Oh, by the way," Mark said. "Katie called while you were out."

"What time?" Claire asked, moving to the kitchen.

"About an hour ago."

Claire looked at her watch. That would have been only eight-thirty which meant Katie called at five-thirty California time. "What did she want?"

"I don't know. I told her you were out."

"Did it sound like something might be wrong? I'm surprised she was up so early."

"Didn't sound important, but you're right, early for Katie." Mark joined Claire in the kitchen then stared in the refrigerator.

"Did she sound upset?"

"Nope, just said she wanted to talk to you." Still fixated by the fridge light, he didn't look at her. "What's for lunch?"

"I don't know. It's only nine-thirty. As a rule, I eat lunch out or make a tuna fish sandwich. Am I supposed to call her or is she going to call me?"

"She didn't say. I don't see any tuna fixed. Where is it?"

Claire reached into the cupboard and pulled down a can. "Here," she said as she went toward the phone in the bedroom. She knew Katie's number by heart and dialed. Peter answered.

"Katie called," she said not bothering with introducing herself. A boy living with her daughter better recognize the mother's voice.

"She's asleep," he said.

"Wake her. I'll be out later." Claire nervously picked at a piece of lint on the edge of the bedspread.

"When did she call?" Peter asked with an edge in his voice.

Claire had had it with Peter and also wasn't pleased with the man in the kitchen who mixed tuna and mayonnaise so loudly it could be heard in the next county.

"Her father said she called so wake her." She made it a command rather than a request.

"Okay." He sounded blasé. It might be nothing, but Claire's gut told her something was wrong. "Mark," she yelled, "if you chip my bowl by banging the spoon on the side, you'll have hell to pay."

"Dad cooking?" Katie's voice lacked her usual vibrancy.

"Your father is home for the day and hunting for lunch at nine-thirty. You called?"

"Yeah."

"What's up?" Claire heard Peter grumbling in the background.

"I can't talk."

"Damn it, Katie, you call at the break of dawn California time and now tell me you can't talk." What was going on? "Can you listen while I ask questions?"

"Yeah."

"Something wrong with you or the baby?"

"Nothing wrong with the baby." Katie dramatically paused.

"Are you sick?"

"No. I'm fine. How about I call you later on your cell?"

"As long as you assure me, you're okay." As long as she knew Katie wasn't dying, she could wait to find out anything else. How bad could it be?

"I just need your help, Mom," Katie whispered.

If it were financial, she would have asked Mark. Katie rarely needed her mother's advice.

"Okay. Call whenever you're alone and I'll make myself available." Claire hung up and went to check the damage in the kitchen.

Mark, still mixing the tuna, looked up. "What did Katie want?"

"I don't know yet. Peter was there and she couldn't talk. I guess it has something to do with him. He sounded pretty flat when he answered the phone."

"Did you try to engage him?"

Claire gave Mark a hard are-you-serious look and said, "I was nice."

"You don't like him, and I'm sure he knows it."

"I don't have to like him," she said, handing Mark a cloth to wipe the smeared mayonnaise from the counter.

"You could try to be nice to him."

"Why?"

"Because our daughter loves him."

Claire sighed. She loved how Mark accepted things and kept them simple. She also hated it. He could ignore a person's bad characteristics and suppress his own opinion about them. Claire believed Mark thought Peter wasn't treating his daughter right. Mark wanted to take Peter out to the woodshed and give him a little two-by-four education about marrying the mother of his child. Yet Mark remained polite, engaged Peter in conversations, and stood up for him when Claire criticized him.

Claire, on the other hand, relied on her instincts, and Peter made her skin crawl.

"I just don't like him," she said.

"You didn't want one?" Mark held up his sandwich.

"Not at ten in the morning."

"So, what are we going to do today?"

"I'm going to the book group at four." She paused. "Do you want to do something?"

"I don't know. What do you do during the day?"

Claire couldn't even begin to answer. She cooked. She cleaned. She read. She walked. She ironed on some days. She talked on the phone. She met with friends. She had been working. Her days were full but to break a day down and tell Mark what she did made them sound simple and unexciting.

"Why don't you walk down to where the marathon is going to pass? That's what most of Boston is doing today." She handed him the condo newsletter she'd tacked on the corkboard. "Then when you're bored, stop by the used bookstore next to the coffee shop and search the racks for something to read." She washed the dishes and inspected her bowl for chips. "On the way home, stop and pick up sushi for dinner. I should be here about seven."

"I might go for a walk. That sounds good."

He grabbed his jacket and Claire went to take a shower.

As she dried her hair, her phone chirped. She ran to catch it before it went to voice mail.

"Hello," she said a bit loudly, tightening a towel around herself.

"You sound like you're out of breath," Katie said.

"I just left the shower and was drying my hair." Claire wiped her ear dry and put the towel down. "I ran to get the phone. I left it in the kitchen."

"But you're okay?"

"I'm fine, just worried about you," Claire sat on the kitchen chair. "Why did you call this morning?"

Katie hesitated before answering. "It really wasn't anything. Peter and I had a little fight that's all."

"It must have been a rather big fight if you were up so early and an even bigger fight if you called me."

"It's just we don't fight much, or at least we didn't."

Claire heard sadness in her daughter's voice. The therapist in her knew she should let Katie take her time to reveal the story, but the mother in her found patience a wasted trait and pressed on. "What did you fight about?"

The hard part of waiting for a person to answer is the silence while they decide how much they want to tell. Claire gnawed the inside of her cheek as seconds hung, like heavy braided rugs on the line, between them.

"I don't know what happened, really I don't," Katie said.

"Just tell me what you remember."

"Peter has been under stress with mid-terms and the baby."

"Okay." Claire moved to the chair in the living room since this might be a long story. Usually, the worse the fight, the longer and more painful the story.

"Last night he said he wanted to go out for a beer with the guys." She spoke slowly and haltingly as if getting the events in the correct order would be important. "And I said go, but be home early."

"And that was a problem?" Claire picked at an invisible thread on the towel.

"Everything I say is a problem. He says I'm controlling him." Katie drew a deep breath and rushed the words out. "He says he didn't want a baby, he doesn't even know if he loved me. He said he wanted to leave and forget he ever met me."

Claire knew all too well the mixed emotions that surfaced when you find out you're pregnant and have another person you're responsible for. "And you, Katie, how are you?"

When Claire was first pregnant, she was mixed about it. Part of her was excited, part angry, part scared. The hormones—they played havoc—one moment happy, the next crying for no reason.

"I don't know, but I'm not blaming him for our getting pregnant. It wasn't my fault either. If he wants to be mad — blame the condom company."

Claire squirmed. She didn't want to know actual details. Some things should be kept from parents. And children, for that matter.

"Anyway, he left and stayed out until four in the morning. He came home drunk. Said he fell asleep at a friend's house. When I asked whose house, he wouldn't say."

An empty feeling crept into the pit of Claire's stomach. "Then what?"

"Mom, I can't remember all I said or what he said but we were yelling so loud the neighbor called the cops."

Claire sat up straight and stiff in the chair. "Cops? Sounds like it must have been a loud fight." Claire and Mark never fought like that. They had a more passive way of hurting each other.

"The cops insisted I go to the emergency room They kept asking me if he hit me."

Claire shot to her feet. "What? Why did they think that? Tell me the truth."

"I told them. I — I fell against the side of the nightstand and sprained my wrist." Katie took in a breath. "I went to emergency for an X-Rays and I was given a splint."

A sprained wrist? Was that the truth or was there more? "Katie." Claire fought to keep her voice calm and dispassionate. "Did Peter push you? Is that why you fell?"

"Mom, he didn't mean to. I questioned him about where he was and with who. I started to accuse him of being with another woman. I threatened him, and he just tried to hold me until I cooled down. It was an accident." Sour bile filled Claire's mouth. So many times, she'd heard the same story from her clients. It was an accident. He didn't mean it. *I caused it.* This was worse than she'd thought. How did she keep Katie talking? She had to listen and not confront her. Katie said pushed. Go with that. Claire gritted her teeth and drew in a breath, forcing herself to speak calmly.

"Look, Katie, you may need a 'time-out' from Peter. I want you to call someone and spend the day with him or her. It is never okay for a man to hit or push a woman. *Never.* Understand?"

"I'm okay, Mom. He's sorry and promised it will never happen again."

"How can you be sure of that? I don't only worry about you and the baby's physical well-being, but the controlling and verbal abuse. Your body can heal, but once words are said, they last. Please. Consider my advice and find a girlfriend to spend the day with." *Go to the center*, Claire pleaded internally. What else could she say? "Call Val, she's a safe person to talk to. She'll protect you and tell you what to do." Claire felt sweat build under her arms. "I know it's hard to share with your mother, but find someone who listens and understands."

"Really, Mom, I'm fine. It was an accident. I was just confused this morning when I called. I thought you might overreact, so I hesitated even telling you when you called back, but I knew you would keep pushing until I told you about the accident."

Claire glanced at the clock. Should she book a flight home? She could be there, or at least in California, by tonight.

"Look, Mom, I need to do some grocery shopping and I'll talk to you later. Please don't worry. I'm okay."

Her daughter was not okay. But calling was the first step toward an open relationship.

"Okay, Katie, I'll let you go. Call anytime. I'll keep my phone with me. If you need me to come home, I will. If you need to come here...come."

"Thanks, Mom."

Claire held onto the phone, unable to loosen her fingers. She would have to tell Mark. But...how?

Chapter Thirty-Six

Her phone rang. Claire, her thoughts still in California, jumped. "Hello? Katie?"

"Where are you?" an unfamiliar male voice asked.

"Who is this?"

"Jeff."

She shook her head, exhaled. "Sorry, didn't recognize your voice."

"We were going to meet at three for drinks before book group. Are you sick? You don't sound like yourself."

"I'm okay." Claire straightened in her chair and ran a hand through her hair, as if Jeff could see her. "I ..." She hesitated and tried to think about what she wanted to tell him. "I had an upsetting call from my daughter, and lost track of time."

"Anything serious?"

"I guess." No guessing about it. Katie didn't realize how once pushed, slapped or hit—a boundary crossed—opened the door for more.

"Can I help?"

"No. This is something I have to take care of …" She hesitated again. "If she'll let me."

"Sounds like you need to talk. I can ditch group and come into the city if you want."

Claire didn't want anyone at the moment. The heaviness in her stomach reminded her she still needed to tell Mark.

"Thanks," she said. "Maybe later, but tonight I need to be home."

"Okay," he said. "Don't hesitate to call if I can help. I'm here for you."

"Again, thanks." Having someone, even if only on the phone, reminded her she wasn't alone. "I'm sorry I didn't call to cancel. I'll talk to you later." She hung up and held the phone close while she waited for Mark.

Mark enjoyed the day more than he expected. It would have been fun to share it with Claire. The marathon, massive with observers eating picnics, turned out to be *the* thing to do in Boston. He imagined Claire making comments about the runners in their shorts. She used to make him laugh all the time with stories she made up about people she didn't know.

After the marathon, he explored old bookstores. The books smelled of mildew and salt and housed hidden treasures. Mark bought two for his collection. One, a turn of the century chemistry book with a section on brewing. The other took him on an adventure to the northern part of their home state. The maps alone were priceless, and once he held the book in his hands, he couldn't send it back to the shelf. He would take it to California and let its dry air breathe new life into it.

They both cost more than they would have if he had found them in a garage sale, but less than if discovered on the West Coast. In the early years of their marriage, weekends were spent at garage sales, flea markets, and when they had a bit of extra money, at an antique store.

Claire refused to pay full price for anything she could buy used. When she found nursery furniture at the church fundraiser, he had to bring it home and then unload the pieces of what became a crib. Strange, how those memories were so recent. Was the crib still in the barn? Maybe Katie would want it for her baby. He could teach Peter how to refinish it. Maybe over the fumes of varnish, like men, Mark could tell him how important a father is to a child.

He sensed Claire, rather than saw her, when he opened the door.

"Thought you'd still be at group," he said.

"I should be."

"Well, I'm glad you're home. I have dinner. Want me to set the table?"

She turned toward him, tears on her face. Putting the bag down, he walked toward her. "Are you okay?"

"We have to talk." She took a deep breath. "I spoke with Katie and things aren't right."

Mark was more than aware of that.

Claire suggested they open the bottle of wine, which he did. He poured two glasses, handed her one and motioned for her to sit next to him. She instead stayed in the chair across from his, pain etched in the corners of her eyes.

"What's this all about?" he asked, foreboding curling inside his chest.

"Katie had an accident ..." she said, her voice almost inaudible.

"She okay?" he asked.

Claire shook her head. "She sprained her wrist and is in a splint, but didn't break it. She'll be okay."

His neck tightened. "What happened? A car accident?"

"A little more complicated. Peter pushed her, and she fell."

"What?" Fury rushed over him as he rose and paced the room. "What?" He couldn't think of anything else to say. Anger blocked his ears, and he only heard his heart pounding. "What?" He asked again hoping she would say something else. "He hit her?" His voice echoed and bounced between the poundings in his ears.

"Pushed, I said pushed."

"Pushed." He said the word loud enough to vibrate out. "Excuse me." Louder, he spoke again. "Pushed? Pushed her hard enough to break her wrist?" His fists clenched and arms tensed, he hunted for Peter who he wanted to punch into a wall. Blood pounded in his ears until he had to sit, afraid he might pass out otherwise. "Peter hit Katie? Are you sure?"

"Calm down, Mark. I said Katie called and said Peter *pushed* her. Pushed not hit."

"I'll kill him." It came out as a primitive cry. Somewhere in him a vengeful monster grew. Mark hunted for control. He again paced the room. Guilt fueled the burning fire within him. How could he be thousands of miles from his baby?

"Calm down, Mark."

"I'm calm. What do you want me to do?"

"There isn't anything we can do at this point except be here for her."

"Call her and tell her to come here," he demanded

"I offered her a ticket. I offered to go there. She wants us to back off."

"Then why did she call?"

"I think she called when Peter left, but she had second thoughts when he returned."

Mark halted abruptly and pivoted toward Claire. "She let him come back?"

Claire shrugged. "That's the pattern. Lots of women think it won't happen again. The boyfriend is sorry and promises …"

"Claire!" Mark yelled. "This is Katie. Not one of your clients. I don't want to know what others do." He wanted to wrap his arms and hold Katie, like he did when she was little. He wanted to protect her from monsters. "Claire, it's simple. We're the parents. We tell her to leave him. We tell her to come here. If she isn't going to come here, then you go there. We can't just sit here and do nothing."

"I wish it was that simple," Claire looked at him. "Until Katie wants help, or admits there is a problem, there is little we can do."

Mark's muscles twitched, now weak from holding back his anger. Adrenaline drained as reason returned. He needed to be calm and find a way to make everything right again. Because he would make everything right again.

Chapter Thirty-Seven

As any concerned mother would, Claire kept in touch with Katie who assured her everything was great.

Claire didn't believe it but over the next two weeks she lessened her calls to every other day. Mark asked daily for an update and vacillated between rage and pretending it didn't happen. Like the green sprigs of grass fighting through the melting snow, they both wanted to believe Katie's version of the story.

Claire may have overreacted, Katie pointed out.

Mark buried himself at work.

Thinking about Jeff, the finished job, Agnes, and book group helped. Spring, being a season of hope, she moved forward, accepting the harshness of the past winter.

Jeff's attention during long lunches became more frequent. Claire tried to keep the relationship from going too far. In her mind she justified the touching, hand holding, flirting, and the occasional kiss as okay as long as she didn't sleep with him. The teeter-totter of proper and desired behavior balanced on a moving moral fulcrum. She convinced herself she could keep her fantasy life with Jeff and her real-life crumbling marriage in balance.

The morning walks with Agnes were predictable when the weather wasn't. Claire dressed for the walk in a light jacket after seeing the sun bright against the window, however, the bone-chilling cold and Agnes's cigarette made white puffs in the air.

"So, do you think you and Mark will be joining us?" Agnes asked.

"Sorry, I missed the question."

"Where is your mind? The Vineyard. Are you and Mark coming?"

"Did I know?" Claire asked.

"I guess Mark forgot to tell you Jim invited you folks to the island for the Memorial weekend."

"I guess he did." Since the news about Katie, Mark wasn't sharing much. He was depressed. She got it. What about her own helplessness? She was supposed to be an expert, and she didn't have the answer. She could advise a client, but until the victim wanted to change—things wouldn't. Couldn't he see she hurt as much as he did? Not only did she hurt, she'd failed. Was he punishing her by not telling her that her friend invited them someplace? What else had he hidden from her?

"Mark's been busy with work. He has a big deadline and stays at the office. What are the plans? I'll see if we're available." It would be nice to be away from the condo.

"Simple. We have a big picnic on the beach every year and wondered if you folks would join us. It's a bunch of us from the book group plus some other 'outlanders.'"

"Outlanders?"

"That's what the locals call us who own summer homes on the island."

"Clever." *I'm an outlander.*

"It's supposed to be an insult." Agnes exhaled a huge amount of smoke, hitting Claire smack dab in the face.

"I got it." Claire coughed.

"What's the matter with you?"

"Nothing, just your smoke in my throat. Haven't you read the Surgeon General's warning on the side of the package?"

"I'm not talking about my second-hand smoke killing you. I want to know what's going on with you and Mark, and yes, I'm aware this will kill me." Agnes held the cigarette to the sky. "I could also get hit by that car," she said, pointing the smoke toward a passing taxi.

"Didn't know we were down to two choices." Stopping at the crosswalk, the silence between them hung as choking as Agnes's smoke.

"So, are you going to tell me what's up?" Agnes asked.

"Nothing."

"Don't bullshit a bullshitter. We've been walking this route for seven months now and by the time we hit the light we've solved a world crisis, trashed a politician, critiqued a dress choice, or laughed till we damn near peed our pants. You're miles from here."

Claire rounded her shoulders like an adolescent being brought to task by an over vigilant parent. How could she tell Agnes? She gave up a good job to be here with a husband who saw the world in black and white. She questioned if they loved each other enough to survive his silence.

"I can't put it in words. Everything is wrong. I have a pregnant daughter. Her boyfriend beats her. I'm here. My husband is miserable. I'm miserable. I can't fix it." Claire slowed to breathe. "All I want is happiness and if not that, peace." *Oh yeah and let me add an affair.*

Agnes's hands dug into Claire's arm. "Look at me," Agnes demanded. "I asked you what is happening to you. I know all the stuff happening in your life. Yeah, it's shitty. Why are you so miserable you can't deal with it? It has nothing to do with being here. We all have a plate of worms to eat at times, but we get over it. Action, my dear young one, is the answer. Not wallowing in self-pity."

Chastised, Claire noticed Agnes had a determination in her eyes as her fingernails sunk in. Unblinking while she stared into Claire's teary eyes, demanding she pay attention. Well aware Agnes cared for her, Claire couldn't put words to the emptiness she felt when she inhaled the pain.

She sobbed.

Agnes removed her grip, reached into her pocket and handed Claire a tissue. "Buck up, girl," she said, as she more lovingly embraced her.

Claire couldn't stop. At first, the tears were of frustration. She wept for the failure she owned. She wanted everyone to be happy again and for life to go back to the time when it was, and back seemed to be a lifetime ago.

Chapter Thirty-Eight

After talking to Sean in Paso Robles, Mark enjoyed the quiet of the spring evening. He wanted to thank his son for stepping up and taking care of the ranch but didn't know how. Sean said Jessie taught him a lot about how much work was required growing the perfect grape. If only Katie would go to the homestead where Sean could protect her.

Satisfaction and gratitude, for Sean, for the ranch, for Jessie, washed over Mark. He leaned back in his chair and listened to the news.

He heard Claire in the bathroom. He hadn't heard her come in.

"Claire?" he called.

"What?"

"When did you get home?"

"Been here a while, but you were sleeping in your chair."

"I wasn't sleeping."

She walked toward him, a face towel still in her hands. "Then you were snoring for no reason."

"Are you sure?" He sat up, looked out the window. The last he remembered the sun had been casting shadows on the bay. Now it was dark.

"I'm sure."

Mark relaxed back into his chair. His body, as drained as his mind, felt out of place here. At home, after work he would have spent another two or three hours in the field or on the books. Here he woke early, exercised in an indoor gym, worked eight to nine hours under fluorescent artificial lighting, and came home to a late dinner and sleep. His biological clock liked the rhythm of the sun on the left side of continent.

"Did we have dinner, and I missed it?" he asked.

"I haven't eaten. Want leftovers?"

"That works." They had avoided each other and those few words were the most they exchanged. He didn't want any more fighting and lately no matter what he said ticked her off. He didn't chance asking what leftovers there were, but hoped some of the scalloped potatoes remained. He didn't see them on the table. Claire shopped at the corner grocer where everything was "healthy" and served in little brown boxes. He wanted fat, cheese, and flavor. He wanted seasonal vegetables, and fresh, overly sweet tree fruit.

"Any of the scallops left?" he asked.

"I tossed them. You should watch your cholesterol."

Mark stifled a sigh. He never worried about his cholesterol. Claire dieted if she gained five pounds and imposed a diet on him. He picked at the cold salmon and some pickled beets.

"I talked to Sean today," he said between bites, "and he said things are greening up."

"How is he?"

"Fine. He said the vines look good this year. Budding up. We need to water because of the drought. Looks like the price should be reasonable."

"Did he say anything about his job?"

"Just it was good." Mark picked up a spear of limp asparagus.

"Has he seen Colleen?" she asked.

"Didn't say."

Claire sent him one of her disapproving looks. He wasn't sure if it was because he put the weak asparagus back in the box or because he hadn't asked about Colleen.

"Colleen thought she would spend her break at the house. Maybe give it a little extra cleaning, and I wondered if she did." Claire inspected the asparagus box and closed it.

"Is Katie joining them?" The whole family loved spring and the beauty of the hills covered in wildflowers. Even if he and Claire couldn't be there, the others should still enjoy it.

"I haven't talked to Katie in a week, but the last she told me she wasn't planning on going to the ranch. She said something about visiting my folks. But I don't know if she did."

Mark's brow furrowed and his fork paused on the way to his mouth. He thought Claire talked to Katie daily. How would they know if she needed them? He depended on Claire to be the conduit of information. "When did you last talk to her?"

Claire stood and started clearing the table. "Ten days ago."

"Leave the salad. I'll finish it." Even though wilted, he hated to see it thrown out. "How is she?"

"Fine," Claire said.

"Did you tell her she could come here or go to the ranch?"

Claire dumped the soggy salad remains on his plate over the only fresh roll. "I did," she said. "It led to a lecture on minding my own business and my telling her she was my business, to her slamming the phone in my ear. I'm waiting for an apology."

"You think she owes you an apology?"

"Well, I certainly don't owe her one."

"You know she can be stubborn," he said, hoping to placate her.

"So?" Claire leaned against the counter, folded her arms.

"Maybe you should call is all I'm saying."

"Since you have all the answers of how to handle this, why don't you call?"

She returned the ice cream container, the one he thought was dessert, back to the freezer and slammed the door.

"I'm not good at talking about all this," he said. "You know that."

"Neither am I. And she isn't talking at all. Which she got from you."

Talk about a blow below the belt. He didn't respond because he didn't want to fight. Claire called him passive-aggressive. He never understood passive being wrong. If he said what he wanted, she would just shoot him down.

"Fine. I'll call her. What should I say? Does she know I know about Peter pushing her? About her wrist? Do Colleen and Sean know?"

Claire sat, rubbed the back of her neck. "I haven't told the other kids. I guess I should have, but I'm not sure how they'll handle it. In truth, they have enough on their plates. Katie isn't their problem."

"They do know she's pregnant, don't they?"

Mark felt Claire's burning stare. "I told them. I also told them they should wait to say anything to her until she tells them. Sean had all kinds of legal advice about her protecting the rights of her unborn child, on how to collect child support, and how to make Peter responsible. Colleen offered to help any way she could."

Mark pushed his plate away. Claire picked it up, dumped the remains into the garbage and put the dinnerware in the dishwasher with a little more clattering and zest than seemed necessary.

"Did you talk to anyone else?" Claire asked.

"No."

"What about Jim? Agnes said he called and invited us out to their summer place for Memorial Day weekend."

Mark tugged at his collar. "Oh yeah, he called yesterday. I didn't think we wanted to go."

"Did you tell him that?"

"No. I told him I would talk to you."

"And when were you going to talk to me?"

His jaw clenched in response to her tone. "Well, I guess I was going to talk to you when you were in a better mood."

"Well, I guess I would be in a better mood if I knew what was happening."

He eyed her warily. "Is this worth an argument?"

"It isn't about the trip to the Vineyard. You made a decision without asking me. Again. You know that infuriates me."

"I didn't make a decision. I said I would ask you. I just assumed you would rather spend time with our kids, especially when they need you."

"Mark, you make decisions all the time for me. I'm tired of it. I've gotten angry in the past when you do it. When are you going to learn?"

"I never make decisions without you. We always do what you want." When was she going to notice? He constantly compromised what he wanted in order to take care of his family.

"Then how did we end up here?" Claire's neck and cheeks turned red.

"What do you mean?" He fought an urge to run out of the condo, away from Claire, away from her anger, away from this fight they were having for the umpteenth time.

"I don't remember a talk about moving to Boston. I remember it as a statement. 'We. Are. Moving.' When did you ask what I thought or felt about it? Where was my input?"

"We talked about it. It was the best decision. Remember?"

"I didn't say I wouldn't come, or that I would have made another choice. I'm saying there was no mutual decision. You decided for both of us. Just like you decided we weren't going to spend Memorial Day with our friends."

"Your friends."

"My friends. Your friends. You made the decision and didn't even remember to tell me about the invitation."

His stomach tightened. He'd really forgotten. He thought maybe they could fly home for the three days. He thought Claire would like that. He'd moved here to keep the job that paid for things. So that was one more thing he'd done wrong. "What do you want to do?" He crossed the kitchen to the cabinet where they kept cold tablets, vitamins, and antacids.

Claire stared at him. "I want to talk."

"What are we doing right now?" He tossed two chalky antacid tablets into his mouth.

She folded her arms. "We've been blaming each other."

With a sigh of resignation, he said, "Tell me what you want? I'll do it."

"I want to consider going to the Vineyard. I don't see what good it will do to go home. Katie is not going to accept our help. I've offered. I suggested she move back to the ranch for a bit. She said she and Peter were working things out."

"Do you believe that?"

"No. But I also know there's little I can do. Katie has always been a hard learner. Besides, how can I fix her life when I can't even fix my own?"

Claire's shoulders dropped. He wanted to reach out and touch her but stopped himself. "Just tell me what you want me to do," he said again.

She shrugged. "I'm not sure I know. I think it would be good for us to go away for the weekend. Be with other adults. Distract ourselves. We might enjoy the East Coast if we did more than just exist here. If we have to be here for a while, let's see what people do to have fun."

"I'll call Jim and tell him we're interested," he offered, even as the thought of being with those people made him shudder and long for an escape to his own vineyard.

Chapter Thirty-Nine

Claire's fingers tightened around the steering wheel as the ferry docked. She hadn't driven onto a floating parking lot before. Mark decided to stay in town and ride with Jim on Friday and Agnes talked Claire into coming out on Wednesday. Agnes also talked Claire into packing her SUV with many of the weekend's needed supplies. Agnes kept producing piles of clean sheets, baskets of canned goods, and an assortment of mismatched beach towels.

"Pull forward," the ferryman called.

Claire waved at him and aimed the car toward the ramp. He pointed to follow the green Buick to the right side of the boat. It looked simple enough. She could do this.

Once she'd parked without denting anything, she got out, locked the car, and went up the nearest stairs. Some people inside were ordering coffee or drinks. Claire bought a diet soda and sat on the benches at the front of the ferry. Soon the horn blew, and the skipper cast off. The rain earlier in the day left the salt air cool and fresh. The breeze off the bow riffled through her hair and through her mind. She closed her eyes, let the sun and the breeze clear away the staleness that seemed to cling to her lately. Agnes, a new adventure, a good book, and a chair on the water's edge awaited on the opposite shore.

Once Mark agreed to go, the tension between them lessened. He enjoyed Jim and if he got to know Jeff, Mark would probably like him, too. Jeff would be at the party on Monday. A bubble of anxiety formed in her chest as she thought about Mark and Jeff becoming friends. Something she didn't want to deal with.

Last week at book group Jeff said he planned to bring his father. He'd hired an attendant from the facility who could stay with them. It'd be good for Jeff's dad to spend some time in a happy familiar place and it might stimulate memories of good times. She didn't think it would help his father as much as it might help Jeff come to peace with goodbyes and added forgiveness. Each day his father became frailer and more dependent.

Claire's own folks were in good health and their marriage still full of laughter, tenderness and respect. Her mother's energy sustained her at holidays when she prepared and cared for the gathering of family and Claire's father brought humor and debate to every event. She, unlike Mark, hadn't dealt with the loss of a parent or the invisible scars being fatherless left. She did though, feel the sting of never having been enough salve to heal his wounds.

"Mind if I sit here?"

Claire looked up at a young mother with two children, one in arms as the other clung tightly to her left leg.

"No." She moved her purse off the empty seat.

"Thanks." The mother put the little one on her knee while offering an awkward hand to the toddler who tried to climb into the other empty seat.

"Can I help?"

"Do you mind holding the baby a second?"

Claire took the infant. How familiar—how *good*—it felt, holding a baby again. The round-diapered bottom jetted her back to the warmth of Katie in her arms. The baby smiled and, as Claire made an instinctive cooing sound to the child, it broke into giggles.

"How old?" Claire asked the mother who reached for the little one.

"She's five months."

"I three," came a small voice from the other side. "I Brent."

"Hi, Brent. I'm Claire. Can you say Claire?"

The towhead looked puzzled and tried. "Care?"

"Close enough." She and the mother both smiled at the boy.

"Do you have a home on the island?" the young mother asked.

"No. I'm going out to visit a friend."

"Where are you from?"

"California. I mean I've been living in Boston for almost a year, but I'm really from California," Claire said as she made a face at the baby. "Do you have a place on the island?"

"Yes, we live there. I run the bakery in Chilmark. What part of the island are you going to?"

"I can never say it right. Menemsha?"

"Up island. Close enough. You'll be near to where I am. You should come in and let me treat you to a muffin."

"Thanks."

"Who are you staying with?"

"The Adams, Agnes and Jim."

"Oh, my yes. Agnes is a hoot, and don't you just love Big Jim?"

Claire smiled. Just like Paso Robles where you ran into friends of friends at the local Farmer's Market and felt like you belonged.

With entertaining the children, the forty-five-minute ride sailed by. Once land came into sight, everyone headed like marching ants to the cars in the cave. Claire followed. She got in her car, waited until others started their engines, and pulled out the hand-printed map Agnes had drawn.

Claire studied it and geared up for the next part of the adventure and was pleased to see the front of the ferry open. Cars pulled in single lines, exited, and crossed the wooden bridge to a small town. She struggled with the instructions the GPS spit out.

She hunted for the gray house with the red door on Lover's Lane, eyes occasionally flickering to follow the map. Most roads were no more than dirt drives and to ensure the privacy of the owners, rarely labeled. After two passes, she saw the small hand painted sign and took a chance it would lead to the house Agnes loved. Down a path lined with birch trees, in the middle of a pasture it sat, exactly as Agnes described—a remodeled barn painted gray, with a red door. Better yet, there stood Agnes waving her in. She indicated Claire should park under the front deck.

After exchanging hugs, they unloaded the contents of Claire's car into the large kitchen-dining room. Sun streamed through the skylight. All the modern appliances looked new or never used. A bay of windows framed a small round glass-top table. The room opened on to a large, open beamed, well-lived in sun room. Maple hardwood floors gleamed, and supported wicker furniture covered with blue striped pillows.

Beyond French doors, the knotted pine decking looked out onto vast fields and a path between parted, wintered reeds led to a pond. The deck wrapped around the house boasted several sitting areas. Claire ran her finger along the back of the teak bench while she took it all in.

"We have a little canoe on the pond there." Agnes pointed.

"I thought you had a boat."

"We do. But we moor it in Menemsha."

"Is that far?"

"Less than a mile. We walk or take bikes."

The thought of Agnes on a bike made Claire smile, but she quickly wiped it off.

"We have lots of parties here," Agnes said. "Come upstairs and I'll show you your room."

Claire followed and found four bedrooms and four baths. The west corner would be her and Mark's. Plantation shutters covered the wall of windows.

"Open these at night for the breeze."

"This is lovely." Claire fingered a white duvet on the king-sized bed. The walls awash in white with daffodil yellow accents. Her windows on the north side looked into the trees and on the west to the water. Halfway down the pasture to the shore a vine grew up a trellis.

"What is that?" Claire pointed to the twining plant.

"Blueberries. They grow well here. The ambitious guests pick them for morning muffins."

"You make muffins?"

"Get real, girl," Agnes drawled. "I said the ambitious guests pick them. They also make the muffins. I have a recipe. It's on the refrigerator. I enjoy the bakery in Chilmark for my breakfast."

"Oh, I met the woman who runs that."

Agnes' chin dipped. "Where did you meet Linda?"

"On the ferry with her kids, she said she knew you."

"Linda knows everybody and everything." Agnes's voice held a warning note.

"Well, her kids are cute."

"Yeah, just be careful around her. The bakery is the hub of this island. You'll discover how small a community it is out here."

"You forget, I'm from Paso Robles. I know all about small communities, gossip, and rumors." Besides, Claire wasn't a member of this one. "Well, you unpack and get a shower. I think we'll go into Edgartown for dinner."

"We aren't eating here?"

"Are you cooking?"

Claire chuckled. That's right, Agnes didn't cook, but knew all the good restaurants in Boston.

"I know a place we can get a good glass of wine, a perfect sunset and half a lobster," Agnes said.

The sunset couldn't be as grand as on the West Coast, but the lobster would be better. "Should I dress?" Claire asked.

"On the island, dress casual. Slacks and sweater will do. Oh yes, and mosquito repellent."

Claire laughed as Agnes headed toward the door. "Want to see our room?"

Claire followed as Agnes ushered her to a simple room with only a bed and two side tables with reading lamps. She expected something grand, like Agnes herself.

"Big Jim and I never agree on how to decorate. He likes wood beams and a gothic, manly bed. I want chintz and frills, preferably pink and lavender. So, we have a bed with his mother's quilt. Every Christmas we give each other the gift of doing the Vineyard bedroom. Every summer we can't agree on a thing. I find linens, he hates them. He sees a painting of starving kids with big eyes and it gives me nightmares. I'm telling you, for a man raised on culture, he has unbelievably bad taste."

Claire noticed the books on both pine bed stands. On one, she assumed Agnes's side, sat a dog-eared copy of *Summer Sisters*. There was a bookmark in a well-worn copy of *The Poems of Edgar Allen Poe* on the other stand. Surprising about Jim. She couldn't imagine the gentle man she knew liked the dark side of Poe. Yet she felt books defined people, especially night reading. She kept a book of Frost poems on her nightstand. When life had no answers, she could get lost in his descriptions. Mark kept a copy of the *Farm Journal*, a monthly publication. He read it every night and then replaced it when the new magazine arrived.

Agnes's cell phone ringing interrupted the tour.

"Hello," she yelled into the phone.

"Hello?" she repeated. "Damn phones don't work well out here," she said as she closed the phone and put it back in her pocket. "Everyone knows that. So, they'll call back on the main line."

Sure enough the phone on the night stand next to the alarm clock rang.

Agnes snatched up the receiver. "Hello," she said. "You know the cells aren't reliable out here."

Claire heard only one side of the conversation.

"Are you sure he's up for that?" A pause then, "I have Claire here, do you mind if she joins us?"

Who was Agnes negotiating with?

"Okay, give us an hour to get ready. We'll meet you there. I thought we would go to Venti, but I like George's. Okay. I understand." Then she hung up.

Agnes turned to Claire. "We have a date tonight."

"A date?"

"Not really. Jeff and the attendant are taking Jeff's father to dinner at a place called George's. It's a little hole in the wall place the old timers go. Good food, great chowder, and the wine list is respectable."

Excitement fluttered against her breastbone. Jeff would be at the party, but she hadn't realized he'd arrived early. She rethought the jeans she planned to wear to dinner. Perhaps the white belted slacks, and a scarf. The blue scarf that made her eyes pop.

"Jeff said his dad is having a good memory day. He seems to be younger here. Jeff thought George's would be good and not have a large crowd if we go early. Can you be ready in forty-five?"

"Sure."

"What you're wearing is just fine for George's."

"I thought I would put on slacks."

"Hell no, honey." Agnes drawled out the honey. "Just wash your face, run a comb through your hair and throw on some lipstick. I wish I could look as good as you with so little make up."

Agnes adjusted her stretch pants. "I'm going to throw on a clean shirt and paint my face."

Claire debated the slacks again, decided it might be too much, but did grab the scarf.

Chapter Forty

The tables in the restaurant were small and round. Agnes seemed to greet everyone at the bar as she "Honeyed" and "Dahlinged" her way past. Some earned a kiss on the cheek, others a pat on the behind. Claire tried to shrink behind her game-face smile. Jeff, sitting at a corner table against the window, waved them over, but Agnes was making her entrance.

In Agnes-time they finally arrived carrying two Long Island Iced Teas gathered along the way. Claire would have preferred wine, but the bartender handed them the drinks announcing they were compliments of someone. The "someone" got a loud, "Yee Haw," from Agnes.

Jeff stood and double kissed both women, then introduced his father, J.W. "Father, this is my friend, Claire. Remember I told you she was staying with Agnes for the weekend?"

"I don't believe we've met," J.W. said to Claire.

Claire had met him several times at the office, but didn't say so.

As the women took their seats, the elder Wentworth looked at his son. "I don't believe you told me how beautiful she is." He smiled at Claire. "Agnes." He turned to his old friend. "Marcia asked about you last week. You must make an effort to meet her for lunch."

Jeff hung his head and looked like he might correct his father. His mother, Marcia, died three years ago.

"Oh J.W., you ole fart, I had lunch with Marcia just the other day. We girls don't tell you everything." Agnes winked and patted his hand.

"So how do you know Junior?" he asked Claire.

"I met him at book group a few months ago and then helped out at the office on an unfair termination suit."

He looked puzzled. "I don't remember you in the office. Is Junior keeping you away from me?"

Claire flushed. She'd accidentally confused him. His memories were anchored in a past before her.

David, his caretaker, quickly changed the subject to sailboats.

"Agnes sails," J.W. said, looking at Claire. "Do you?"

"Only on the lake back home, not on open water. I love the ocean though and being on a boat."

"You'll have to join us." David nodded toward Jeff, Agnes, and Jeff's father.

"I'd love to." The young man impressed her. He did a good job re-directing J.W. and saving his dignity.

"Maurice," Jeff's father called for the waiter.

"Sir?" The waiter's shirt read Alan.

"We're ready to order. Ladies?"

Alan-Maurice took the order without making a note or an error. Dinner was served, and the conversation was about sails, lobster, locals, and the price of housing on the island.

J.W. sat between his son and David, who reminded him the names of folks who stopped by the table. J.W. would stand, shake their hand and ask, "How's the sailing?" It was obvious to those who knew him, he wasn't tracking on all eights, but they accepted him with the nonchalance and respect culture and old money buys.

When dinner came, J.W. hadn't remembered ordering his steak rare. "Maurice, I like my steak medium. Take it back." Alan did with a smile. Claire enjoyed the man and his dry sense of humor. He often forgot the punch line but either Agnes or Jeff finished the joke while J.W. took full credit.

He and Agnes seemed to share some tension, but Claire would get the full story and all the details later.

By the time Alan-Maurice set small dishes of crème brûlée in front of them, J.W. seemed confused. He looked between the spoon and the fork, as if unsure which to pick up. The glass of wine he ordered, David kept refilling with sparkling soda. When J.W. said something about the odd taste, David said, "Remember the new pills you're taking affect your taste buds."

The end of dinner came with coffee and a bill presented to Jeff.

J.W. snatched it up. "I'll get this."

"No, Dad, let me."

J.W. had already reached for his wallet and when he opened it, he fumbled with the few dollars in it. He looked at an array of plastic cards before pulling out a store discount card and handing it to the waiter.

Claire felt a tap on her knee. Jeff passed her his American Express. She took it from him and excused herself. She found the waiter and gave him the card. He smiled at her.

"Ole J.W. was one of my dad's favorite guests. J.W. would come in here and demand to sit at his table. If he had too much to drink, it was Dad's job to drive him home and hire a taxi for the women he picked up during the evening." Alan billed the evening to Jeff and handed Claire the receipt. "Tell, young Mr. Wentworth not to worry. We'll start a tab, and he can take care of it at the end of the season."

This was a community where people knew each other, and the past counted. They cared. Not unlike home. She returned to the table and passed the card back to Jeff. Their fingers touched. Then she caught his gaze. *Thank you.*

"Come on, J.W. Let's head back to the house," David said as he stood.

"How about one more drink?"

"You've had enough, and I need to sleep. Tonight, it's Perry Mason. We've got to get home so we can watch it."

"I love that show," Jeff's dad said.

David and J.W. left, and Agnes joined a group of people she met on the way back from the restroom, leaving Claire and Jeff alone.

"Your father is charming." Claire sipped the wine she'd finally been able to order with dinner.

"Tonight was a good night. He knew me. Sometimes he asks me where his son is and when will he visit."

"David is good with him."

"Yeah, when I talked to him about bringing Dad here, he was for it. David said it couldn't hurt and it might stir up some good times. Dad and Mom used to come out here every summer. He seems to miss her more out here though, than in Boston. Sometimes he knows she's gone and other times he acts as if she's coming on the next ferry."

"I'm proud of you taking this time to be with him."

He tilted his head closer. "I have you to thank."

"Me?"

"Remember when you told me to find a support group?"

"Sounds like something I would say." Claire had a vague memory of a late night in the office. What she remembered, a very sad Jeff, whom she talked to into the evening hours. She remembered his sadness, not giving advice.

"For the longest time, I couldn't let go of the anger. My father was an asshole."

She nodded slowly. "I do recall you saying something like that. Sure wouldn't get that from the two of you now." She smiled.

"I don't have a lot of intimate friends. I keep most people at a distance."

"What about Bunny?" Claire remembered the woman at the Thanksgiving dinner.

He grimaced. "Not dating her any more. She thought I should just put my dad in a home and forget about him. I wasn't opposed to that, but it didn't seem right."

"Hey, what are you two talking about?" Agnes dropped into her seat.

"Just a bit about Dad," Jeff said.

"That caretaker keeps him looking good." Agnes drained her drink.

"He was always handsome."

"I'm going to join the Reynolds for a night-cap." Agnes gathered her purse and jacket from the back of the chair. "You two want to come?"

Agnes had the car and Claire wasn't sure of the way home. She was along for the adventure.

"I want to take a little walk," Jeff said, "but you girls go on ahead, and maybe I'll join you later."

"Okay." Agnes pointed Claire to a group of people who looked like they spent the day at a spa. She realized how pale she was without her California tan.

"Would you rather walk with me?" Jeff asked.

"Do you mind?"

"No, I'd love it."

Their last walk had been interrupted by a phone call. Did he remember that? Did he want to repeat that walk—without the interruption? The flutters in her stomach...they didn't mean anything. Did they? Certainly not that she wanted to repeat that walk.

She kept her face blank as she and Jeff set a rendezvous point and time with Agnes for later.

They left the restaurant to see dusk, the last fleeting of twilight, lingering in the air. It hung suspended, waiting for the moon to take over. Part of the ocean ritual at home was to watch the sun set. The Pacific swallowed the sun along with the pinks, fuchsias, and oranges of the horizon. Mark explained away the magic, telling her the colors were because of the position of the earth, the dust in the sky or the clouds' reflections.

Tonight, there was no sun dipping into the Atlantic. The only color was a changing shade of gray as the day crept toward night and no Mark to explain away the magic of dusk. The shadows of trees danced across the path as she walked toward Edgartown until the lights in the stores took over. Jeff spoke softly about his father and reverently about Claire's help, sliding her hand into his.

"Enough about J.W." He pointed to a bench along the ocean's edge. "How are things with Katie?" They sat and he stretched out his legs.

"Fine, I think." She hesitated. "I'm not actually sure." Sadness as gray as the night sky fell around her. "We've had a difficult relationship. She pushes many of my buttons and I push hers. So, she tells me only part of what I need to know."

"Need to know or want to know?"

Jeff's question stopped her. "Need. I can't tell if she is really okay and has a handle on what's happening or if she's overwhelmed and in too deep. With my clients, I had a sixth sense, but not with Katie. With her, I just fear."

"My daughter and I are very close. She tells me everything. Or at least I think she does."

Jeff pulled Claire nearer, so their once joined hands rested against his waist. Claire's heart quickened.

"Katie and I actually doing better with some distance between us. We're closer now that we're farther apart, if that makes sense. She's telling me stuff she doesn't tell her father." She looked at Jeff's chiseled profile, back lit by the evening sky. "Mark is angry and wants her to leave Peter, assuming she would be safer here with us."

"She would be," Jeff interjected.

"Meaning?"

"You could protect her," he said.

Claire sighed and shook her head. "I don't know that. I could talk to her but unless she wants to end it, there's nothing I can do. I've offered. My best role at the moment is to keep communication open."

"Just be there for her?"

"Yeah, as powerless as that is."

Jeff stopped and put an arm around her. "You have your plate full and all I do is add to it with my father."

"We both have them full, but I hope you're finding some good moments with your dad."

"I am."

He leaned into her and his mouth found Claire's. She pulled back, looked into his eyes reflecting the rising moon, and kissed him, offering only an ounce of the passion she felt. His lips were as soft as she remembered, and again urgency grew in her.

He lowered his head to her neck, his breath sending a tremor down her spine. She cocked her head exposing her neck to his lips, letting him explore, licking and kissing her shoulder top, the lobe of her ear and down her cleavage. She placed her hand on the back of his head and let him guide his tongue between her breasts feeling his excitement against her leg. Not only did her body respond, all of her wanted more.

He stopped kissing, took her face in his hands, stared at her, then pulled her body close to his. They kissed again, letting their mouths part slightly. She tasted tannic from the red wine. As her nipples hardened, his hands traveled down her back. Then he whispered against her lips, "I need you."

Need. He said need. She wanted him, but what did she *need*?

"Stop," she whispered. What was she saying? Her body screamed for more. She took a shuddering breath. "Someone will see us."

"Let them," he said, still holding her.

"I need to be careful." Or did she? Could she let magic and desire win?

"I'll be careful," he said.

"I meant about people seeing us."

They let a tension-releasing half-laugh escape.

"You have to be careful. I have nothing to lose. But I do need you," he said.

"And I want you," she replied.

"Then let's make it happen."

They sat side-by-side a few moments, breathing in each other's perfumed longing, the half-moon their only witness. His hand massaged her upper thigh and brushed purposely against her breast before he placed his fingers on her cheek.

Jeff stood, took her hand, and helped her to her feet. "Shall we join the others?"

She nodded in agreement as she rose.

"Or we could blow them off and head to my place."

"Not tonight," she said.

"Perhaps another?"

"Yes." Finally, her voice agreed with her body.

They walked to the Reynolds's, holding hands that telegraphed a barrier crossed.

Jeff looked around the room at all the people drinking. He grew up alongside and with most of them. Agnes was drinking and joking like she was one of them. He, like most of the old line, knew they accepted Agnes because of Jim. They were all too polite to let her know that some of the conversation referenced events that were never fully explained to newcomers. Including his divorce from Anne.

Claire sat on the wing-back chair by the library. Two old men Jeff knew from the Yacht Club were talking to her, probably trying to categorize her. Except she defied all attempts to label or classify her. She was so much more than a *Californian*. Or a *social worker*. *A wife and mother*.

Agnes introduced her as her friend. That bought her entrance to the party. Tomorrow, however, the talk would be her arrival with him. He hadn't been thinking when he walked her to the party.

He sidled up next to Agnes, getting between her and Mrs. Larchmont, one of the eagle-eyed gossips who'd been eyeing Claire since they'd walked in. "Shouldn't you be protecting Claire from tomorrow's gossip?" he murmured into her ear.

Agnes faced him. "She's a big girl. Besides she already made *friends* with Linda on the ferry." Agnes made air quotes with the hand not holding her after dinner drink.

A sick feeling settled in Jeff's stomach. "Oh, crap."

"Fine, but you didn't help any by walking her here." Agnes drained her glass.

"We're just friends." Jeff held up his hands in a show of innocence.

"Of course you are." Agnes arched a brow.

Jeff chuckled as she sashayed over to Claire, hooked their elbows together. Agnes was a good soul who did fit in. She learned long ago where the boundaries of society were drawn. Most of the people in the room liked her, "for an outsider." Jeff liked her for her refreshing approach to life. She played her differences up, rather than try to fit in.

As Claire and Agnes left the party, Jeff let his eyes follow. Claire, in simple jeans, had a great figure. The blue in her eyes sparkled and her auburn hair bounced in unruly curls. It wasn't just her looks. He was attracted to her essence. Claire's spirit reminded him of fresh, intoxicating lilacs in bloom. Her mind and willingness to give of herself made him feel safe to risk. He had been shut down for so long, he forgot what caring for another more than himself felt like.

He missed her the moment she left.

Chapter Forty-One

The sun streaming in the east window woke Claire. Yawning, she inhaled the wisteria mixed with the subtle fragrance of the fabric-softened pillowcases. Her body felt alive to all five senses after dreaming Jeff held her through the night. His body spooned around hers with his exploring hand on her thigh. His breath in her ear matched the tempo of hers. Only a dream yet she wanted to slip back into it.

Last night on their walk he told her she was beautiful, and it wasn't a dream. She stretched and rubbed sleep from her eyes. She pulled the coverlet back over her and reveled in the singing of her body.

Hearing noises in the kitchen, she checked her watch for the time. Too early for Agnes. Before bed, Agnes announced they would sleep until ten and then walk to the bakery. She said something about riding a bike, but the thought of Agnes and her large upper half on a bike only made Claire laugh.

Turning over to snuggle deeper under the blanket, she smelled coffee. She sat up and listened closer to the unfamiliar sounds of a strange kitchen. Her nose never failed her, and she recognized good coffee and cinnamon. She grabbed her flowered robe, tied it tight and walked to the landing. The scent grew stronger, and a sweet warm fragrance came from the kitchen. Agnes said a cook would be joining them at the house, but Claire assumed it would be for the evening. Like a blood hound, she followed the aroma.

She entered the kitchen and at the table in the morning sun sat Jeff, drinking a cup of coffee and reading a newspaper, like he belonged.

"Good morning," he said.

"Good morning," she said as she pulled the neck of the robe closed. "What are you doing here? How did you get in? Did Agnes expect you?"

"Slow down. Agnes has a hidden key."

"Obviously not very hidden."

He smiled, exposing his dimples. "I thought you might want coffee and cake."

She tried to wrap her mind around the fact he was in the kitchen. "What time is it?"

Looking at his watch, he said, "A little after nine."

She heard Agnes upstairs. She was padding between her bedroom and bath. This wasn't a dream.

Jeff walked to the oven, opened it, and toothpick tested his cake. He then lifted his head toward the stairwell and yelled, "I know you're awake. Put on your face and come get

Jeff's special crumble cake. Better hurry. Looks like Claire might eat it all." He turned to Claire and winked.

At the mention of makeup, Claire realized she had none on, and her hair must be a mess. Her untamable curls went wild at night. Jeff poured a second cup and handed it to her.

"The cake will be out of the oven in less than ten. I picked up some fresh fruit at the Farmer's Market on the way over."

"Shouldn't you be doing this at your place? For your father?"

"Already did. He was up at five, part of the disease. He's up early and then sleeps on and off during the day."

"Oh," she said. Never at her wittiest before coffee.

"I believe you take milk." Jeff poured some into a pitcher then offered it to her. Their fingers touched and a jolt of excitement raced up her arm, straight into her heart.

Agnes rounded the corner into the kitchen.

"Morning," Jeff greeted her.

Agnes pulled her oversized insulated thermos from the cabinet and poured her own coffee.

"Damn you, Jeff. I told you not till ten." Agnes appeared annoyed. "How's a woman gonna get herself together before then?"

Jeff kissed her on the cheek. "You are still the prettiest thing I've ever seen," he said, mimicking her drawl.

"And you are a pain in the ass." Agnes turned to Claire. "See what I put up with out here?"

"You could have warned me," Claire chastised while trying to sort this whole thing. One didn't wake up with a potential lover in their kitchen making coffee—let alone cake. At least not in California.

Dreams were subconscious desires that didn't come true. Or maybe they did.

Mark woke early to pack for the trip with Jim. Claire had laid out slacks, matching short sleeve shirts, and a pair of sandals. Mark grimaced. He'd never worn sandals and wasn't about to start now.

He pulled a couple of clean pairs of jeans from the dresser drawer. After he examined the shirts, he rejected one plaid, two pastels, but kept the blue collared golf shirt. He pulled a duffle bag from the closet, folded everything including two old, faded favorite shirts. There was no room for the sandals. He only needed one pair of shoes and the gym sneakers would work.

He poured a thermos of coffee and waited for Jim. They planned to leave at six-thirty on the dot. Mark liked "on the dot" kind of people and indeed Jim knocked on the door five minutes early. His kind of man.

"Morning," Mark said as he opened the door. "I'm ready." He picked up the bag he'd placed at the door.

"I'm a little early. We have to stop on the way and pick up mustard." Jim sounded perturbed.

"I'm sure we have some."

"It won't be the right one," Jim huffed as he marched to the elevator. "Agnes drives me crazy with this stuff." He pushed the button and when the door whooshed open, he beckoned for Mark to hurry. "She has to have things just so. Give me yellow mustard on a bun and tell me it's a hot dog and I'm happy." He stabbed the button for the garage level where both men got out. "Agnes has to have Rainbow Buns, shipped from Texas and Piggly Wiggly all-beef dogs. It costs more to have them flown here, but that's what she had every Memorial Day as a child."

"We're having hot dogs?" This was the big party Claire demanded they attend? He watched Jim start the car and back out of the parking stall. It became obvious Jim really was in a hurry and Mark didn't understand why but decided to not question a man on a mission.

"No," Jim said as he turned onto the road. "We have a clam bake and lobster. Throw on some steaks with lots of good wine and beer. But Agnes has to have the dogs, too. They don't carry the mustard in the small store on the island, so I have to stop on the way. Women."

Mark thought the same thing. Women!

They stopped at a large market and Jim strode in to make his purchase.

The cellphone buzzing in Mark's pocket startled him. "Hello."

"Dad, it's Sean."

Mark had to swallow the uneasiness that gathered in his throat. "Everything okay?"

"Yeah, Katie's coming home. I guess she and Peter had a fight."

Mark scratched his head. He wasn't sure how much Sean had been told. "Tell us if she's okay."

"I will."

"We're going out to Martha's Vineyard, we might be out of cell service. I'll talk to you when I get back."

"Okay then, bye."

Jim exited the store as Mark pocketed his phone. He breathed a sigh of relief—Katie was safe.

"I hope we don't hit traffic on the way. We have to make the ferry, or we'll be spending the night in Woods Hole," Jim said.

Mark gripped the armrest as Jim made several turns onto the expressway. The men didn't talk until twenty-five miles out of Boston.

"Well, we're on our way, shouldn't be too bad now." Jim said, finally breaking the silence.

"Who all is coming?" Mark asked, trying to engage in small talk. He and Jim saw each other every morning at the gym but only exchanged five words each day. Some days, a simple head nod was enough.

"Agnes invites half the Vineyard. She also has the kids and their kids come. She pays the plane fare."

"You and Agnes have kids?" Mark couldn't remember either of them talking about children.

"Nah. These are her brother's kids. Duffy, her older brother, had two boys. He was much older than Agnes, so the kids are almost Agnes's age. Maybe ten years younger. Duff was killed in 'Nam, but Agnes stayed close to Rita, his wife. We've helped with some of the finances. Rita is solid. She works hard and makes it, but the extras just weren't in her budget."

"Is Rita coming also?"

"Not this year. The boys are bringing their wives and kids. There are three of them in their teens. They'll spend two weeks out there. Agnes will spoil them. All of them."

"Are they staying at the house?"

"Oh, no. Several years ago, we bought the land next to our place and built a duplex. They stay there and then we rent it out the rest of the season."

"You and Agnes never had kids?"

"Tried. Agnes had four miscarriages, then finally a daughter who lived just one day. The happiest and saddest day of my life."

Mark blinked. "I—I didn't know." Did it make him a terrible person that all he suddenly wanted to do was wrap all three of his healthy kids into a giant bear hug?

"Agnes had a nervous breakdown after that. It was right after Duff was shot down. She just wouldn't talk. Imagine that." Jim gave a forced-sounding chuckle. "Agnes not talking."

Mark flashed back to when Katie was born. He remembered a nurse handing him a wet semi-blue thing. She wasn't crying at first. The doctor said to pat her feet until she cried, then she opened her mouth and wailed. It was such a powerful feeling, watching a lump come to life. He couldn't imagine if she stopped crying. He remembered being happy when she woke in the night because he knew she was alive.

"How did you survive that?" Mark asked.

"You just do." Jim talked while automatically driving the interstate. "She eventually had to be admitted to Brigham

Women's Hospital. The doctors were able to get through to her there. We almost separated."

"You and Agnes?"

"Yep. She moved back to Texas for a year. She blamed me and that pissed me off."

"It wasn't your fault."

"I didn't say she made sense. She was mad at the world. The war killed her brother. God took her babies. She was mad as hell, and I was around for her to take it out on."

"What did you do?"

He shrugged. "I was pretty angry myself. Life wasn't fair, but you survive. You wake up the next day. You deal with it. That's how I did it. Agnes needed something to live for and Duffy's kids became that. Slowly, they healed her. She wanted to stay in Texas."

"Why didn't you?"

"I was invested in the family business here and couldn't just up and move. For a year we lived on separate ends of the continent."

"When did she change her mind and come back?"

He cocked his head. "It was strange. On the anniversary Margaret's death—that's what we named her—I wrote Agnes a letter. I told her how much that one day meant to me and how beautiful she was and how precious our little girl. I said a lot of other mushy stuff. The stuff that women like. How important they are. How beautiful. How I couldn't live without her."

Mark nodded. He couldn't imagine life without Claire or his kids.

"Agnes said the letter meant so much because I was the only one who knew our little Margaret. The one thing we shared no one else could."

"Wow. I guess that's true." No one could know what he'd shared with Claire. They were young when they met and had years of shared secrets.

"So, after months of marriage counseling, lots of tears, and a few big fights, we decided to bury the hatchet and learn to get along. There are days, like this and the damn mustard, I could just throw up my hands and call it quits. Why the hell do I need to get mustard? But then I remember...it's only a stop at a store. It's not like losing someone you love."

"I never would have guessed." Mark shook his head. Not seeing Jim struggle didn't mean he didn't. Did anyone know what happened to make them who they became?

"Agnes rarely talks about the past. She had a rough life. She just moves forward, driving us all a bit crazy with her enthusiasm."

"She does have spirit."

"She has a good heart."

Mark could see there was more to Agnes than he'd thought and maybe now he understood why Claire enjoyed her. He wondered if she knew the story. Claire used to tell him everything. Lately she wasn't saying anything.

Reaching the ferry, the car carrying the precious mustard and Mark, who looked forward to seeing his wife, maneuvered onto the platform.

Chapter Forty-Two

The two couples enjoyed a blissful two days before Memorial Day.

When Claire woke, only a dented pillow remained where Mark's head rested the night before. The sound of Agnes's loud drawl directing the hired help that swarmed the yard, setting tables, building a temporary dance floor and, of course, a bar.

Guilt nipped at Claire for sleeping in, but it never crossed her mind Agnes would be awake before eight.

Claire hurried through her shower, slipped into jeans, grabbed a tee, and descended into the chaos.

"How can I help?" she asked when she hit the porch.

"Grab yourself a cup of coffee and the broom and start sweeping those steps," Agnes ordered without a "please." Claire did as instructed and squelched the urge to salute.

"She has you working?" Claire turned to see Jeff sitting on a lawn-chair, out of Agnes's view.

"Yeah, and you better stay hidden or you'll be digging a hole to bury a pig or something."

Jeff laughed. "Give me that," he said, taking the broom from her. "Drink your coffee and let me."

"And expose yourself to Commander General?"

"I'll take my chances," he said as he swept. "Besides, you're spilling. You can't drink and sweep, I take it."

Claire looked down and saw she had dribbled. She bent and dabbed at the spots with her cotton tee.

"I always knew woman wore those oversized shirts for a reason."

"When my kids were little, I used it to wipe everything." She sipped from the mug. "My mother always carried a hand towel in her apron pocket, but I'm not sure I even own an apron."

"In my house, I don't remember my mother without a dress or jewelry. She always had a nicely pressed linen hankie tucked under her sleeve. She would use it to dab at whatever mess she encountered on me. Then fold it properly and returned it to her sleeve."

"You miss your mother?"

He cocked his head, looked into an unseen distance. "Some. She was detached, hard to know, always proper. She adored me. I do know that. I made her eyes dance. My father on the other hand, neither of us could ever please." Jeff shook his head. "Some days, he still tells me what I should do. This morning we re-battled the college issue. He woke, and he just realized I went to Stanford instead of Harvard."

"Is that why you're here?"

"That and to see you."

Claire felt the blush start. He moved closer to her then whispered, "Want to run away with me for a short sail?"

Of course, but what could she do about Mark? She couldn't say she'd gone shopping. Guilt owned her as she looked around for him. He could be anywhere.

She pulled away from Jeff. "I can't."

"Why not?"

"Mark is here."

"Come on, just disappear. Besides I don't see him." Jeff pushed his sunglasses up and checked out the crowd. "Seems he disappeared on you first," he said, smiling at her.

She shook her head. "I can't."

"You can," he said, with an edge to his voice. "You're saying you won't."

"You're right. I won't do that."

He nodded. "Okay. If you change your mind, just give me a wink and we'll sail. Great breeze for a put out to sea and with the crowd here, you won't be missed." Jeff handed her the broom and turned to leave.

Would Mark miss her? Maybe not.

Claire interpreted Jeff's slumped shoulders as he walked down the stairs as rejection. *Please, don't be mad.*

"Hey, Jeffery, when did you get here?" Jim yelled from across the drive. He and Mark climbed from Jim's Mercedes.

Jeff moved steps and a world away from Claire.

"A bit ago. I've been hiding from Agnes," Jeff called back.

"We all try to hide from her," Jim said, gathering bags from the trunk. "She caught me at the coffee pot this morning. Sent us"—he gestured to Mark—"out for fresh dill, and I was afraid I was going to have to go to the mainland for the damn stuff."

Mark waved at Claire. "Did you get to sleep in?"

"I've been up long enough to get coffee and orders."

Agnes trotted around the corner. "Why all the standing around? We have work to do. Jim, did you get the dill?"

"Of course, my sweet love." Jim jutted his chin to the bag he carried. "Of course."

"Hey, Claire, guess what I found?" Mark asked.

She stepped closer to Mark, hoping he hadn't seen how close she'd been standing to Jeff. "What?"

"A case of Gaslight Merlot."

"You're kidding."

"Is that a find?" Jeff asked.

"It's a small winery about fifteen miles from our place. They bottled a very good merlot a year ago, taking a few awards. I thought we could open a few for the party." He put down the box he'd been carrying and pulled out a bottle. "If it was noon, we could open one now."

"You all will wait until three o'clock before starting to drink." Agnes turned to Jeff. "Are you bringing J.W. over?"

Jeff shrugged. "He isn't having one of his better days. I'll see how he does later. Besides, I thought I might go for a short sail before the party."

"Don't I wish I could sail today," piped in Jim.

"Come with me."

"And have Agnes dismember me?"

"Anyone want to try for a sail?" Jeff looked right at Claire, but she cut her gaze away and no one else spoke. "Okay then, if no takers, I'll see you later."

Mark was too busy with his merlot find to notice Claire's eyes following Jeff down the drive. She turned back to Mark, picked up the broom and finished the last step. Life was on hold for a moment.

Jeff didn't return until the party was well under way. He arrived wind-burned, wearing Levi cut-offs, a red Black Dog tee shirt, deck shoes, and no socks. It was obvious he knew most of the people attending as he stopped often to kiss the ladies on the cheek and slap the guys on the back.

Claire saw him heading her way. Mark, who never liked big crowds, hadn't left her side. He made disparaging remarks about different couples.

Used to be, Claire found such comments intimate, a sign of their connection. Today, Mark just sounded judgmental.

Jeff stopped by the buffet table, piled his plate with food, and walked to Claire's table. Strange, he'd think of it as *her* table rather than the book group table. Of course, Jeff would sit with them. Glen, his wife, and their three boys sat next to Mark.

Jeff's mind raced back to the fax he'd received no more than a week ago. The document laid out the settlement Glen would be awarded. What a privilege he'd been given, helping this man and his family.

"Glen, good to see you and the family." Jeff clapped his friend's shoulder. Then with a nod toward Claire and Mark he continued, "And good to see that Agnes freed you two to enjoy the party."

Mark scoffed. "I thought Claire was a taskmaster when it came to throwing a party, but I have now worked for the Queen." He turned to Claire. "I'll never complain again."

"Careful what you say, I'm an attorney and you entered into an oral contract. I could get it typed up and have it notarized if you'd like, Claire," Jeff offered.

Her chuckle sounded forced. "I'm sure he'll still complain."

Claire's shoulders and neck tightened when Jeff joined their table. She didn't want Jeff to sit there and make jokes. She didn't want him to know Mark. She wanted Jeff to only know the parts of Mark she didn't like. The two of them commiserating over the misery women under pressure could dispense was not what she had in mind.

She turned and watched the dance floor where Agnes did the Texas two-step. Most of the guests didn't have a clue about the moves yet everyone gave it a go.

"Care to dance?" Big Jim asked.

"I can't dance," Claire automatically answered.

"As you can see, few here do." Jim took her hand and led her to the edge of the makeshift dance floor. Before she knew it, he marched her around the floor, spinning and dipping her until her feet hurt and she was breathless, having more fun than she'd expected. She'd forgotten how much she enjoyed dancing. She used to take classes with Val. When had she stopped? *Why* had she stopped?

"You dance fine," Jim said, waggling his brows at her. "You can dance, you just don't."

"And you lead real fine," she said as Jim dipped her once more before escorting her back to the table. She dropped into her seat, fanning herself and grinning. "Thank you for reminding me that a real man can dance."

She meant it as a compliment to Jim, but Mark scowled at her.

As night fell, everyone was dancing, drinking, and laughing. Claire danced with a variety of people, but not Mark.

The music was a mixture of rock and roll oldies and Country Western and while some people knew the rhythmic moves, others didn't. But no one seemed to care.

When the band played *Proud Mary*, Claire joined the floor without a partner for the first time. The song must have brought out the teenager in all. Everyone was on the dance floor.

Everyone except Mark, who had disappeared. Soon Jeff and his dancing feet moved in motion to the beat next to her. They weren't partners until the band played *Hey Jude*. Jeff pulled her into his arms for the slow dance.

She searched the crowd for Mark. They should dance together. At least once. But he had disappeared as successfully as Bear at bath time.

Claire allowed herself to relax into Jeff's embrace. Fingers crawled up her back. Darkness had fallen, so hopefully no one noticed. She allowed herself a five count to enjoy the sensations of his breath on her cheek.

Then she heard him whisper, "You should have come on the sail. It was a great day."

Her eyes flew open.

Mark and Jim were walking up from the pasture. They were talking, not looking toward the dancers. She pulled away, to what the nuns would have called "the proper distance," regained herself, looked into Jeff's eyes. She wetted her lips, spoke just above a whisper. "I will sail with you."

Chapter Forty-Three

The drive back to Boston Tuesday morning was long and quiet. Claire sat in the passenger seat, quietly fuming. Agnes had asked them to bring back some extra stuff and, naturally, Mark had to complain about it. In his opinion, which he shared with anyone who listened, Agnes over packed. He bragged he once traveled for six weeks in Europe with only a backpack. While loading the trunk, he had to broadcast that Agnes needed one suitcase for make-up alone and now he had to haul two over-stuffed Gucci bags back to Boston.

He still harped on it as they drove past the green trees along the MA-3. "I don't understand what a woman needs that requires four suitcases for a long weekend."

"She's there for the summer, Mark. It wasn't four suitcases just for her for one weekend. We're bringing back some linens and things she wants in the city. So drop it," Claire said, tired of his ranting. "Besides, it's no skin off our nose to bring them. We have plenty of room." She'd learned long ago there was a *right* way to pack a case. The right way was, of course, his way.

"Yeah, no skin off your nose because you don't have to haul them upstairs."

"I'll do it."

"No, you won't. They're too heavy. I could hardly lift them," he continued. Obviously, he wasn't going to drop it. "Jim agrees."

"I heard all about it, and you guys are lucky she didn't pack both of you in a trunk and ship you back UPS, the way you rode her."

Mark shot her a glance across the car. "Well, did you have fun?" he asked.

Still confused by the raw emotions charging inside her, Claire paused before answering. *Did she?* She had fun if having one of the sexiest men she knew kiss her counted. She had fun finding out she was still desired. She had fun if fun was walking a tightrope of undefined reality.

"I enjoyed myself," she finally said.

"I really like Jim. He's a good guy, but I'm not sure I have a lot in common with anyone else out there. And I'm not sure I like that guy you work for."

"Jeff?"

"Yeah, Jeff. I don't get him."

"He's a good guy, too. He's a good father to his daughter, and a good son to his father." She clamped her lips shut. What she didn't want to do was explain Jeff's good points to Mark. Better to change the subject.

"We're thirty miles out. We're making good time."

"Yeah, surprises me. I thought we would be in traffic all the way."

"Want to stop for a sandwich?"

"We could do that."

As Mark pulled off at the next promising exit, Claire's cell phone rang. She checked the number, making sure it wasn't Jeff, before answering. It was the number at the ranch house. "Hey, Sean."

"It's not Sean, it's me," she heard Katie say. *Why was she calling from the ranch?*

"Katie. Sorry, just saw the house number and assumed it was Sean. You visiting your brother?"

Mark had parked. He was already heading into the convenience store. She reached for her door handle.

"No. I'm moving home."

Claire slipped back against the leather seat.

"Okay." *Stay calm, this may not be good news.*

There was a long silence while Claire waited for Katie to say more. After checking the cell screen to be sure they were still connected, she said, "What's up?"

"I left Peter."

Claire wanted to sing the hallelujah song, but it caught in her throat.

"Are you okay?"

"I love him, Mom," she whimpered into the phone.

"I'm sure." Claire recognized the heartache of loving someone and discovering they aren't good for you. "You need to take care of yourself." Good advice Claire should follow. Correction, she planned to follow. "Is Sean with you?" He must be, but hopefully Katie would tell her more if she could keep her talking.

"He's at work, but will be home later. He knows I'm here."

"Did Peter hurt you?"

"No, I left before he could."

"That's good. It's hard, but it was a good move."

"I left with nothing."

"Dad and I have some money hidden in the bottom of Gram's hope chest in the back bedroom. I keep it there for an emergency and this is one. Get what you need."

"Thanks, Mom. I'll pay you back."

"Just be safe."

Claire looked up as Mark headed back to the car. He motioned for her to join him. She held up her finger signaling him to wait.

"Katie, bring Bear in the house with you. He's a good watch dog." *And a great comfort when you're hurting.* "You did a good and brave thing. I'm proud of you."

Katie sniffed. "Thanks, Mom." She hung up.

Mark got back into the car. "I thought you were following me." He handed her a sandwich and a bag of chips and put two bottles of water in the cup holders.

"That was Katie. She left Peter and moved home. I don't know a lot of what happened, but she's safe in her old room. Sean will be there later."

A gamut of emotions crossed Mark's face. Claire couldn't tell if he was relieved or pissed.

"That's where she belongs," he finally said. He started the car and pulled onto the highway. They continued back to Boston without any more conversation.

Claire played with her dry turkey sandwich. The emptiness that had overtaken her left her feeling homeless. Where was her touchstone? She'd thought it was the ranch, but that was Mark's. Who would she call if she left Mark? Would she go to her parent's? Or into Jeff's waiting arms?

Chapter Forty-Four

The following weeks, the excitement left by the party lessened with each passing day. Agnes planned to stay for the summer, and Claire hadn't heard from Jeff.

Claire lay in bed one morning, staring at the ceiling, thinking about Jeff, remembering the feel of his hands on her back, his lips on hers.

She'd thought he would call and tell her if Glen accepted the compromise. She wanted to work, but even more, she wanted to see him. Life boiled down to waking up, occasionally walking without Agnes, reading—even the book group disbanded for summer—and daily calls from Katie.

Mark's dark mood lifted once he found out Katie definitely moved back to the ranch. He and Claire talked about Katie but never the problems in their marriage. Oh, no. Mark spent his energy at work and saved just enough to listen to the progress their children made. His excitement, as always, was based on either his grapes and wines or the kids.

They got married because of the pregnancy. They bought the ranch for the kids' future. She took a job to pay for their educations. Now it looked like she was going to be one of those grandparents who helped raise a child, instead of it being her time to shine. She never thought money or jobs would be their focus after they turned fifty. It was supposed to be their time to enjoy the fruits of their labors. Instead here she was in Boston, three thousand miles away from what was important. Or what once was important.

The ringing phone pulled her to sit up. "Hello," she answered, wishing it were Jeff.

"Mom." Katie, earlier than usual. Claire's back stiffened against the headboard, afraid to hear any more bad news. "How are you doing?" Katie asked.

"I'm okay."

"Mom, Valerie called and suggested I get into some therapy. What do you think?"

Of course, she should but why call and ask permission? "It's a good idea."

"Well, I'm not sure. I don't see how someone else can help when I can talk to you anytime. Isn't that as good?"

Claire hesitated. She couldn't even get her own life on track. "No, dear, you need to see a professional. I'm your mother, so my advice is clouded."

Katie sighed. "Okay, I guess." Claire heard the voice of a woman so beaten down, she could no longer choose what was best. *Oh. How I wish I could have protected you.*

"Honey, trust Val. She'll find someone good for you."

"But I still can talk to you, can't I?" Katie's voice begged.

"Of course." Claire swallowed the sudden lump in her throat.

"Are you going to be home soon, Mom?"

Three months ago, the answer was an emphatic *yes*. Today she wasn't sure. "I think so."

Claire hung up, then stood and gazed out the window. The firefighting units flanked a freighter as it navigated the channel. If only she had a fire escort through life since this passage put her marriage at risk. She dreamed of an affair, which Mark wouldn't tolerate. Yet Mark appeared unwilling to change. His blinders only allowed him to move forward, no matter the cost.

Did he ever love me or was I just one more responsibility in his grinding path forward? They once had passion. They once had plans for the future. They once shared goals. All that seemed in the past though and now they were together only because it was too much work to change or leave.

In their very early years, an argument ended with promises to never let things build to that level, then making love. Passion saved them. Now, however, the fights were less and silence the punishment and she'd found passion elsewhere.

Was silence and being shut out more abusive than being hit? Some days, it felt like it might be. The deep inner pain she felt from not having a voice in their marriage brought tears to her eyes. Mark was always right, always judging, always decreeing from his place of righteousness. His habit of making all the decisions left her feeling like a child. And a burden.

While Jeff valued her, enjoyed her humor, and...he wanted her.

Her body shivered with the memory of the kiss.

Claire resolved to talk to Mark at dinner that night. Instead of leaving him a nasty note, she would suggest therapy. Again. She made a light pesto pasta with shrimp and waited. He should be home around seven.

At seven-fifteen, with no Mark yet, she twirled her hair around her little finger. Even as a small child when anxiety ruled, she would pull on her hair, sacrificing a curl to a school test. When she did her master's, she feared she might develop a bald spot. She stopped twisting when she heard the door open. This was going to be their chance.

"Do I smell pesto, garlic, and parmesan?" Mark called from the entrance.

"Yeah."

Mark inhaled his meal as Claire watched. He talked around forkfuls of pasta about his day, never once asking about hers. Every clink of his fork on the china set her teeth on edge.

She couldn't take it anymore and stood to clear the plates from the table. Standing at the sink, she took a deep breath. "Mark, I think we need therapy."

He looked at her.

"We're in trouble. We need counseling," she repeated.

"You know my opinion on therapy. It's a waste of money. Besides I don't have the time." His crossed leg jumped. "We don't need it."

"You think we're okay?" Did he realize he'd insulted her career, and he had the nerve to accuse her of doing it to rip women off? Just for the money?

"Claire, I don't see anything wrong except your negative mood."

The tightness in her jaw traveled down her neck to her shoulders. Instead of throwing down the dishcloth, she forced herself to speak calmly. "Mark, do you love me?"

"What the hell? That's a stupid question. I'm here."

So was she. Did that mean anything? "Did you ever love me?"

"Another stupid question, of course I did."

Did? He said did. So...was there anything left to even fight for? "Then why don't you say it?"

"You should know it."

"But I don't." Her shoulders dropped in defeat. He didn't get it. He would never get it.

"Then maybe you're the one who needs therapy."

"I definitely do. But I want you to come, too. I want us to work on this together." Why couldn't he see that? Or was it that he wouldn't see it? The despair she'd been cradling in her chest all day unfurled, like a spring shoot on a vine.

"I said, I don't have time. I'm tired and still have work to do." He stood and headed to the desk in the bedroom. She heard him shuffling papers. Drawing from years of experience, she knew—that was the end of the conversation.

She pulled on the curl and gave in to the desolation with a shuddering sob.

The following morning the high humidity threatened Claire's resolve to walk. Sweat dripped down her temples as she reached the coffee shop and purchased an iced tea for the ice more than for the tea. She picked up a newspaper and looked inside the shop for an open spot—preferably under an air conditioner vent. She sat at a table and pressed the cup against her face. The coolness felt as welcome as her hot coffee had been back in February.

"Hey."

She turned to see Jeff walking toward her carrying a tall coffee.

"Mind if I join you?" he asked.

"Please." She moved the paper off the table, making room for him. "Where've you been?" And why hadn't she heard word one from him?

"I'm still out at the island. I came in to run some errands and take Dad to the doctor."

"Oh, how's he doing?" she asked with a shortness in her voice. Sweat beaded on her upper lip.

"He's thriving, so I decided to stay out there. The ocean seems to calm him, and David and I got him on the boat the other day. He was like a kid."

Claire didn't want to talk about J.W., she wanted to hear about Jeff. "Is it good for *you*?" She softened.

"Actually, better than I thought it would be."

"When are you going back?"

"Tomorrow. I picked up some work I can take out with me."

Claire watched as he brought the cup to his lips. "I assume the case with Glen is settled."

Jeff's smile disappeared. "I thought you heard."

"And who would have told me?" Her voice cracked.

"Sorry, he had a second ruling," he said. He leaned back in his chair. "A lot of it is sealed so I can't tell you amounts, but they paid Glen a very nice compensation for the years he would have been promoted, future losses, and another sum for punitive." Jeff paused and looked out the window then back at her. "Glen has more than enough to support his family, and I talked to him the other day. He's opening his own firm."

Still miffed, she said, "I worked hard for you and it would have been nice if you—" here she slowed her speech and annunciated each word— "called...and...told...me."

He reached across the table and touched her arm. She pulled away and turned her head so he wouldn't see her tears.

Jeff stood, tugged his chair to hers and sat close enough so she felt his thigh touch hers. Her heart stopped.

"I'm really sorry. I thought Glen told you." He touched her back. She didn't pull away. "What can I do to make it up?"

Claire faced him, forced a small smile. "You really hurt me. I thought I meant something to you and haven't heard word one. What am I supposed to think?"

"That I'm an insensitive bum."

She looked into his eyes and saw sorrow, and she wanted to believe he was truly sorry.

"I don't use my cell out there, but I could have called. I should have called. I talk to the office and get email daily." He took her hand in both of his. "Come out to Agnes's for a week and let me make it up to you." He pulled her captured hand closer to his lap. "July and August in Boston are muggy, and most people leave." He smiled. "Are you planning to travel?"

"No, Mark wants to go home around harvest time, at the end of September."

"Then join us. I'm sure Agnes would love the company. I know she's invited you."

"You've seen Agnes?" she asked.

"A lot."

With all her day dreaming, she had made what happened bigger than it was, and to add insult to injury he saw Agnes. Maybe the humidity mildewed her memory cells.

"Agnes misses you and spends most of our time together talking about you." He pulled her hand to his heart. "I miss you."

"She did ask me to come out the other day. I should." Claire wanted to believe his liquid brown inviting eyes.

"Yes, you should." Still holding her hand, he said, "Maybe we could go for that sail." He winked, bringing her fingertips to his lips and brushing them with a soft kiss.

Claire's dreams were of the sails full of the breeze, the water smooth, and Jeff sitting in shorts, manning the tiller. She would sit next to him, his arm around her, drifting toward open water, away from land and problems.

"I'd like to come. I'll call Agnes."

He stood as if an alarm went off. "I need to get going. I promised to meet Dad and David at the eye doctor's and I'm late." He bent down and kissed her cheek. His hot breath on her hair suggested more. "Please come."

Claire looked around to see if anyone saw him kiss her. Then realized the innocence of the kiss, one he would give a sister, or friend. But it made her cheek burn.

She remained behind, considering if she wanted to walk back to the condo and Mark and his refusal to work on their marriage, or follow the man who said he was sorry for hurting her.

Claire picked up her phone to text Agnes: *If your invitation is still open, I would love to come and stay with you for a bit. Get back to me.* She'd let fate decide her future.

Before she arrived at the condo, she'd heard from Agnes: *Miss you, come for the summer.*

No longer doubting what to do, Claire smiled for the first time in sixteen hours.

By the time Mark arrived home Claire had one large suitcase packed and reservations for the eight-thirty ferry. She'd roasted a chicken. There would be enough for Mark to have leftovers, but she only ate crackers.

What if Mark came in and said he was sorry? Then would she stay?

No. She'd told Katie to seek professional help and to not go back to Peter unless he did the same. Claire would follow her own advice. Mark had to agree to marriage counseling.

"Did you have a good day?" she asked Mark as he settled at the dining table.

"No," he said, not looking at her. "And I don't want to talk about it." He ate without another word, moved to the recliner and turned on the television.

Any lingering doubts Claire harbored circled the drain and were washed away.

She followed him into the living room, turned off the television, and stood in front of Mark. "Did you think about the counseling anymore?"

"I said no." He pointed the remote at the set, but Claire blocked it. "Move," he said and then added, in a snarky tone, "Please."

"Okay," she said but didn't move. "Mark, I've been invited to spend some time with Agnes, and I'm going."

"Why?" he asked, not looking at her.

"I need some space. I want a place to think about how to help Katie. I want to decide if I want to find another job and honestly, I'm tired of fighting. I want to work on our marriage. You don't. I need to decide how I feel about that. If I'm willing to live with …"

He looked up at her, and for a brief second Claire felt a flicker of hope. Mark glanced down at her shaking knees then away. "Whatever."

Claire turned to leave and from behind she heard, "Don't threaten me," followed by the sound of the news broadcasting a disaster. But it was overseas, not the one on India Row in condo 18-C.

Chapter Forty-Five

Claire, depleted of energy and emotion, fell into the comfort of Agnes's arms. She asked no questions, poured a glass of wine, and led Claire to the lounge on the deck.

"Looks like you need some rest, Lovey." Agnes handed her the glass.

"More than you know," Claire said barely above a whisper.

"I'm going in and prepare a platter of cold meat and crackers. You sit and do nothing."

Do nothing. Could she do nothing?

Soft music floated out to the deck making the dusky sky surreal. More exhausted than she realized, Claire drifted in and out of sleep. Darkness owned her and the sky when she woke. She turned and saw Agnes sitting quietly reading a book in the deck chair next to her.

"I guess I fell asleep," Claire said.

Agnes looked over a pair of reading glasses. "For a couple of hours. Figured you needed it." Agnes poured herself and Claire another glass of pinot, passed it and suggested, "You might want to eat something."

"I'm not hungry, but thanks."

"My bet is you haven't been eating for a bit, and since this is your fourth glass of wine, food is a good idea," Agnes said.

Claire sat up and dizziness confirmed the wine consumption. "I don't drink that much."

"Food and aspirin will help." Agnes picked up a rye cracker with cheese on it and handed it along with a slice of deli-cut beef.

"You made this?" Claire asked as she took the napkin and tasted the beef.

"Of course not." Agnes removed her glasses and put them on the resting book. "I figured you wouldn't be up for going out, so I picked them up earlier."

What has she been told and from whom?

"You should sleep tonight and tomorrow we will start the day with a walk to the bakery. It is a bit further than we usually do, but a nice walk."

"Do you know why I'm here?" Claire set the glass down on the table.

"Figured the city got to you, and I'm a better deal?"

"Yes, and yes, but so much more." Claire's voice trailed off.

"None of my business," Agnes said picking up the glasses and book and reading by the light shining from the sunroom. "I'll listen when you're ready to talk, but no hurry."

"Thank you."

Agnes swatted at her arm. "Dang skeeters, I'm going in." She rose, leaving the food. "You getting bitten?"

"No, just a tad chilly, but not bitten."

"You're lying on an old quilt, wrap it around you and come in when ready."

Claire stayed on the lounge. Soon the lights in the room were turned off, and she looked to the sky for stars. There were none. While she slept, dark thunderclouds had rolled in. In the distance, lightning flashed, and she shook at the clap of warning thunder. She stayed for a long while, paralyzed by the angry and loud display of the heavens, puzzled that it was echoed by only emptiness within herself.

Early the next morning, Agnes knocked at her door. "Let's get some breakfast."

Claire lifted her head from the pillow. "What time is it?"

"Seven," Agnes announced.

"In the morning?" Claire didn't believe Agnes was up and dressed and ready to go.

"The good Danish is gone by eight, so move it."

Claire dressed and rushed to meet Agnes for a leisurely two-mile walk to the bakery. On the way, Claire talked about Katie but didn't mention Mark.

Linda, the woman Claire met on the ferry during her last visit, stood behind a display case full of cakes, cookies, and an assortment of sweet rolls. "Your usual?" Linda asked Agnes.

"Yes, and some butter please."

Linda turned to Claire. "Hi, you're the woman from the ferry, aren't you?"

"I'm surprised you remembered."

"I said my treat if you stopped in, so what can I get you?"

Agnes elbowed Claire pointing to a crumble-topped slice of apple pie. "Unless you would rather a wheat grass protein smoothie," she said.

"Both are good," Linda said with a smile. "But I'm known for my pie."

"I'll worry about health tomorrow, so give me a slice," Claire said.

"You girls find a table outside and I'll bring it to you, with, I assume, two large coffees." Linda pointed to a lattice covered patio out the back door. "We don't do those fancy blends, but there is cream and sugar on the tables."

Agnes found a table in the middle. She talked to couples on all four sides while they waited for a high-school aged girl to deliver their food. Agnes's plate held a large slice of cake with blueberries baked on top. She slathered on a knife full of butter and offered Claire a bite before digging in. The apples in Claire's pie were a bit on the tart side, but the honey sweetened crumble erased it.

People stopped by their table, extending invitations for Agnes to join them for parties, sailing, dinner, or drinks. She smiled but refused them all. Between bites of cake, she said, "Let's pick up something for dinner and stay in tonight."

"Sounds good to me. I brought a good book." A quiet evening was just what she needed.

They drank the last of their coffee and rose to leave. A few steps out the front door, Claire saw Jeff across the street. He waved. Agnes waved back.

Claire's body went heavy and warm. He headed their way.

"You ladies coming or going?" Jeff looked at Claire and not Agnes.

"We're heading back," Agnes answered.

"Can I buy you dinner tonight?" Jeff asked, still looking at Claire.

Agnes turned to Claire.

"I'm staying in tonight," Claire answered, then turned to Agnes, avoiding Jeff's eyes. "But if you want to go, don't let me hold you back."

"How about a rain check?" Agnes asked.

"I'm available any night, just let me know." He winked at Claire. "I owe you a nice meal and much more."

"Deal," Agnes said as they began the walk home. A half mile from the bakery, Agnes slowed their pace. "Why does he owe you a dinner?"

Claire bit her lip before she answered. "I think because of the work I did for him."

After their second night in, both Claire and Agnes were ready to join others. Usually Agnes ran into people who insisted they join their group for the evening. Claire regained her confidence and smile. On one or two occasions Jeff also joined the spontaneous party. One evening, they danced, but Claire kept her guard up, not willing to trust her emotions.

She called Mark once, but the connection was bad, so she sent him a short email saying she was fine.

He answered: Good. When are you coming home?

She replied: Not sure. You have Agnes's land line if you need to talk.

Later, as she and Agnes sat in pajamas on the deck, Claire shared her frustration about Mark, their marriage, their lives.

Once her bottled-up anxiety opened, it exploded and flowed like an uncorked magnum of champagne. At first, all over the place, then slowly foaming into a lather of hurt.

Over the next few days Claire slept, ate, and recovered. She waited for a phone call from Mark. A call that didn't come.

The tides, ruled by the moon, woke her desires.

She called Jeff and agreed to sail.

Mark's indifference drove her into Jeff's arms. Her life, as she knew it, like the sand beneath her feet, slipped away one grain at a time.

Mark's solution to any problem was *get over it and move on.*

When she said she was pregnant, he married her, but they never talked about it. When she asked, he just shrugged his shoulders and said, "Oh well, I planned on marrying you someday." That should have been her first clue.

At night Claire slept with the windows open, the salty smell of ocean air cleaned her mind and spoke to her dreams. Only an infrequent ghost of Mark appeared while Jeff danced her through the night.

The day of their sail, she woke early, wrapped herself in an oversized hooded sweater borrowed from Agnes and waited for Jeff at the end of the gravel road.

"Hope you have on something that can get wet," he said as he opened the door for her.

"Bathing suit under, but it is a bit cool still." She lifted the sweater showing him.

"It will warm up by the time we have coffee and are ready to shove off." He smiled.

Claire relaxed and smiled back, any lingering doubts disappearing as the sun burned away the marine layer fog. "Are we getting coffee at the bakery?"

"Not a good idea." He winked at her. "I picked up sandwiches and a large thermos of coffee to go."

"Good thinking," she said as she noticed a basket packed in the back seat.

They sat at the pier, drinking coffee, talking, teasing until the marina opened and staff arrived to load them aboard and help raise the sails.

"Do what I tell you," Jeff said as he pulled on ropes. "Once we are out a bit we can relax and let the wind do the work."

"Sure thing," she said, hoping she remembered what she learned when she sailed the catamaran on Huntington Lake.

Away from land and on open water, Jeff remained at the tiller and motioned Claire to join him. She moved aft, nestled next to him and they let the wind determine their course. She enjoyed the feel of his arm around her, the warmth of his legs alongside hers, the sparks his touch ignited deep inside her. It had been so long...

They touched, talked, laughed until the sun had faded and dipped towards the horizon, before finally heading back to the dock.

"Hungry?" he asked as he tied up.

"Famished." She was surprised to find it was true. She hadn't been so hungry in months. Maybe not since she'd left Paso Robles.

"I'll pick up mussels and steam them in a wine broth." He pushed her damp hair away from her eyes. He moved close and let his fingers move to the top of her neck.

She pulled him closer. This was where she wanted to be, held, cherished, desired and needed. She wanted to be naked, vulnerable, and exposed to him, and if she let him steam mussels, she would open up to him.

She felt his whispered breath against her ear. "Come home with me."

Yes! Did she scream that out loud?

A horn in the distance broke her resolve. Tightness stole across her chest. What was she doing? She was married.

She sighed. Why now did she have that sense of guilt? No one would find out.

She released him and looked up with an honesty she feared. "I want you, but ..."

"Please, Claire," Jeff said. "No but. I've wanted you from the day I saw you in the church basement." He didn't move his fingers from her hair. "You've changed my life, and I love every bit of you." He pulled her head against his chest.

"Thank you," she muffled into his damp cotton shirt.

"Thank me for what?"

"For wanting me." She turned her head and let her ear lay against his heart. "But I can't. Not yet."

"Because you love Mark?"

She lifted one shoulder. Honestly, she didn't know if she loved anyone at the moment, but she did know she would never forgive herself if she ended her marriage by having an affair. "No, it's because I need to understand the mistakes I made, or I'm doomed to repeat them."

"You think I'm a mistake? That my love isn't real?" His voice cracked.

"I'm asking you to give me some time to understand myself and clarify what I need."

Jeff dropped his hand to her back but didn't release her. "I know I love you," he said as he let go, stepped away and then put both hands on her shoulders. "I love you enough to wait and respect where you are."

She kissed the inner side of his elbow. "I promise to work fast on myself."

They stood there, each with their own sadness, while the sun disappeared, and along with it, her resolve.

Claire didn't want to let go of Jeff. In his arms, there was no loneliness or fear. He kept holding her while she listened to the lullaby of waves slapping boats against the dock. She pulled from Jeff's embrace when she heard a strange noise from the parking lot.

She shuddered when she saw Mark and Agnes coming her way.

Chapter Forty-Six

Daniel, carrying a case of wine, stood at Mark's office door. "I have the wines from the new supplier. Where do you want them?"

"Sorry, what?" Mark said. Since Claire left, he hadn't been able to concentrate.

Daniel placed the box on the floor next to Mark's desk. "You okay?"

"I'm fine, what is that?" Mark pointed to the wine.

"Wine from the new supplier." Daniel looked at his boss. "You asked me to get it so you could taste it yourself."

"They sent a whole case?" Mark examined the box on the floor.

"You only wanted to taste the chardonnay, but they sent two bottles each of all their whites." Daniel leaned down and pulled out a pair. "I wouldn't suggest trying them all in one night." He laughed.

"I've had a rough week and think I'll try the chardonnay and stop at that." More than a rough week. He'd had his life turned upside-down, and work wasn't enough. Why hadn't Claire come home?

Mark stopped for a take-out sandwich on his way back to the condo. He missed opening the door to the smells of dinner. This, however, was his new routine. He came home, put the sandwich of the day on a plate, grabbed a glass of wine, and sat in front of the television waiting for something—anything—to happen. The stack of dirty dishes reminded him Claire had been gone for eight days.

Tonight, on his way to the bedroom, he noticed the flashing message light on the answering machine. Probably some political call, so he ignored it. If the kids wanted him, they had his work and cell number. He didn't want to know it wasn't Claire. She would be complaining to Agnes because that's what she did with Valerie. She needed space and then she'd come back. He tried to not worry, but this time was longer than any before.

His cell phone vibrated in his pocket. He grabbed it and, seeing the screen display the ranch number said, "Hello, Sean."

"Dad," Sean began. "I've been trying to chase you down for hours. Where've you been?"

Perturbed, Mark answered, "I was at work."

"I tried there and left a message at home and on your cell."

"Well, you have me now. What's so important?"

"It's Paddy. He fell yesterday, and they took him by ambulance to the hospital last night. The doctors say he has a tumor on his brain stem. I need to get a hold of Mom and can't. She has to come home. Gram says he is going to die."

"Slow down." Mark tried to process what Sean said.

"Dad, it's serious. Gram called, and she needs Mom to get home. Mom isn't answering the phone. Where is she?"

"Your mother is out visiting a friend on the island. I'm not sure cell phones work out there. At least the connection is iffy."

"Can you get a hold of her?"

"Of course."

"Well, hurry."

Once again Mark begged his son, "Slow down, Sean, where is Paddy?"

"I told you, the hospital."

Mark inhaled deeply. "Which one?"

"St. Agnes. In the ICU."

"Where are you?" Mark asked

"I'm at the ranch and going over as soon as we get a hold of Mom."

"Is Alma at the hospital?"

"Yes, with Uncle Paul," Sean said.

"Okay, I'll get in touch with your mother, and we will catch the first plane out." He voiced his problem aloud. "I'm not sure if she can fly off the island or needs to come back to Boston first." Good at solving practical things, he already started a mental *To Do* list. "I'll keep my phone on unless I'm on a plane."

"Okay, Dad. I'll head over to Fresno."

"Good." Mark pulled an overnight case off the shelf. "See you soon, son."

Poor kid, this was his first life and death crisis. His kids, unlike him, had been lucky to avoid the catastrophe of a family member dying. Of course, Sean should go and be with his grandparents. That's what a large family did. They gathered together at times like this. Some families would hold hands, some would eat, and some would joke. The Flannigan clan would drink tea, eat butter cookies, and pray. He envisioned Alma with her beads wrapped around her fingers. That reminded him to look for the set she gave him when his mother died.

Katie only months old and he was going alone to the funeral. At the last-minute Alma announced Claire needed to go and she would watch the kids. As she sent them off to Wisconsin, she handed him a black rosary. Touched, even though his mother was Lutheran, and they weren't about to say a rosary at the wake. What moved him more was Alma insisting on the blessed beads and Claire. A son would need both.

He dialed Claire's cell and left a message she should call as soon as she could. He then called Agnes's number.

She answered on the second ring. "Howdy"

"Agnes, this is Mark. Let me talk to Claire."

"Something wrong?"

"Yes. Can I talk to Claire?"

"She isn't here ..." Agnes paused.

"What do you mean? She said she was coming to see you."

It was in the way Agnes said, "Well, she's here, she just isn't *here*," that made the hair on the back of Mark's neck prickle.

"I don't get it," he said.

"She's out," Agnes hesitated, "sailing and I assume dinner."

"She went to dinner alone?"

"I'll tell her to call when she gets in."

Mark felt anger rise. "Where the hell is she? Who is she with? Is she with Jeff?"

Agnes didn't reply.

"When you find her, tell her to listen to her phone messages."

"The cells don't always work out here."

Mark, irritated, said, "Well then tell her Paddy is dying, and she needs to get home."

"Mark, I'm so sorry." Agnes gulped. "I'll find her."

"Why don't you check Jeff's place? I'm sure he has a soft shoulder for her to cry on."

"Again, Mark, I'm sorry about Paddy. I will do my best to get Claire on the next plane out of here. I'll have her call you."

Mark hung up without saying any more. He didn't have time to deal with this. He needed to make plane reservations and get home to his kids and Claire's family. He pulled the rosary from his suitcase and stuck it in his pocket. It might help and couldn't hurt.

Mark, after rushing, settled into seat 26 D on the red eye flight out of Boston. He checked his phone for a message from Claire. Finding none, he turned it off. Sadness welled in him as he buckled in. Gravity pulled at him as the plane took off. He'd land tomorrow morning and have no idea how to explain why Claire was missing.

Chapter Forty-Seven

Claire, shocked to see Mark across the lot, pulled away from Jeff's arms.

She blinked and shook her head.

Only Agnes ran toward her, repeating Claire's name as she hurried.

But she'd seen Mark. With Agnes. Claire searched past Agnes and saw the back of a man walking away. Not Mark.

Shivering, Claire waved. "Down here on the beach."

Breathless, Agnes pulled Claire into a tight hug. "Oh, sugar, I'm so sorry. Mark called. You need to get home."

As she shared the details of Mark's call, Claire felt herself grow cold. Her father. A tumor? Dying? None of this made sense. "I don't understand."

"The next shuttle off the island isn't until tomorrow morning." Agnes gave her a look of love and sympathy.

"I'll arrange something," Jeff said as he led Claire to the car.

"I called Jim." Agnes stopped Jeff. "He fixed a private flight and booked her on the earliest morning flight out of Boston." Agnes looked at Jeff, then back at Claire. "I'm flying with you as far as Boston."

Claire, still reeling, didn't protest as Agnes took her numb hand from Jeff's arm and walked Claire to the waiting car. "Thanks," she whispered. It wasn't until they U-turned in the lot that she looked out the window. Jeff stood alone and waved as she left.

Agnes had brought her bags, so they drove directly to the airport. Once on the private Cessna, Claire tried to put together the fragmented pieces of information.

"I saw Mark with you back there. I know I did."

Agnes kept telling Claire, "No, Mark wasn't here. He called me."

Mark's message on her phone was short and curt. Did he assume she was with Jeff? She didn't have the time or the mental energy to process it all. She went into *get home* mode.

At the condo, she called Mark, but he didn't answer.

She did talk to Sean, who was with Alma at the hospital. Her mother sounded scared. Or was it Claire who was scared?

She spent the night doing laundry and cleaning. Mark had obviously lived on take out and coffee while she was gone.

The next morning, her flight was delayed on take-off which meant she might miss her connection. She worried all the way. It was easier to think about missing the plane in Dallas than to worry about meeting Mark in Fresno. She wasn't ready to see her dad hurting and couldn't contemplate him dying.

She made the flight to Fresno as they were about to close the door. Thankfully the seat next to her was empty so she wouldn't have to make small talk. As the Turbojet took off and Claire inhaled the forced cabin air, willing herself to relax, she leaned back and tried to recall the conversations.

I was standing with Jeff, on a beach. What exactly did Agnes say? Claire closed her eyes to remember. She had been so focused on Jeff she didn't see Agnes walking, no running, toward them. Her facial expression forewarned bad news.

"Claire," she yelled across the parking lot. How did Agnes know where to find her?

"Claire." She still heard her voice and saw her. She also saw Mark. She saw his face, the hurt, the betrayal. *I'm certain I did.*

"It's your father." Those were the words she used.

"Your father fell and has a tumor and might be dying." That's what Agnes said next, but Claire couldn't remember for sure. She said "might."

Claire shut her eyes, but it didn't help clear the cobwebs spun around the events. She lifted the shade on the small window and watched clouds puff under a bright blue sky. Did she say anything to Jeff, or just leave? Did he say anything? Agnes made calls from the land line and drove her to a small airport and flew, holding her hand, into Boston.

Mark wasn't answering his phone, but Sean did and told Claire "Everyone is meeting in Fresno."

Her brother Michael met her at the baggage claim after she landed.

He greeted her with a hug. "You made it."

She inhaled his strength, savored it, let it bolster her. "Tell me, what happened? Is Dad okay? Where's Mom?"

As they exited the airport into Fresno's dry heat, Claire took an involuntary gasp. She'd forgotten how the air could feel both welcoming after the artificial coolness of an air-conditioned building, but also angry, promising to make one miserable soon enough.

They headed toward the parking lot and Mike gave her a rehearsed review of events.

"Dad was out to dinner with Mom two nights ago and when they came home, he tripped on the front step. He couldn't get up, so a neighbor called 911. At first the docs thought he might have suffered a concussion, so they ordered an MRI and discovered a mass on his brain stem. He probably fell because it affected his balance."

"When are they going to operate?"

He shook his head. "There's no surgery, no treatment. The mass is fast growing and rapidly suppressing his whole system. He's already having trouble finding words. Soon the tumor will take over his ability to breathe."

Claire's eyelids felt dry and heavy. "I'm confused. He was healthy and in less than two days he's falling, losing his memory, unable to talk, and soon won't breathe?"

They stopped at Mike's Highlander. He took her by the shoulders and looked her in the eyes. "That summarizes it. He still can hear, and according to the doctor, this is our time to say what we need to."

"Can we help him breathe?"

"Sure. But Dad didn't want to be kept alive artificially. He always said, 'When the good Lord comes knocking, let me go,' and Mom said he meant it. So, there's a DNR on his chart already." Mike let go of her, put her bag in the back of the car, held the passenger door for her to climb in.

Tears gathered and a lump formed in her throat. "I'm not ready for that."

He gave her a sorrowful look as he started the car. "Sis, this isn't being put to a vote. He has a health care directive and Mom has power of attorney. I, personally, think she made the right choice, and you should respect it and be supportive."

Claire felt chastised by her older brother. Of course, she would support her mother.

Claire lowered the window and closed her eyes. She'd always relished the valley's warm jasmine-perfumed air on her face. Memories of nights on the back patio when, as a small child, she couldn't sleep, she would find her father and crawl in his lap while he smoked a pipe, soothed her. She would fall asleep breathing in the jasmine, orange blossoms, and cherry tobacco, while her father weaved a comforting story. Maybe this was a nightmare, and Dad would be on the patio waiting for her.

She searched the sky for a star. Sometimes, if the day was clear, she could pick out Venus. She would wish for a do-over. For what her family called a second chance.

Chapter Forty-Eight

Claire found her mother in the Intensive Care waiting room holding a paper cup. Alma sat tall and stiff with a vacant look in her eyes. Claire's heart raced, her knees threatened to buckle, and she had to swallow the scream that wanted to erupt.

"Mommy," she whispered.

Alma blinked, looked up, then offered a shaky smile. "My Claire. You made it."

"I came as soon as I could." She perched next to her mother and put an arm around her. She felt her mother tremble and she instinctively tightened her hold.

"My tea is cold," Alma said so softly Claire had to strain to hear her.

Claire took the cup. "Do you want me to get you another?"

Alma shook her head as if talking was too hard.

"Talk to me, Mom." Claire wasn't sure what to say or do. Her mother was the one who always passed out the comfort. Now their roles had changed, and Claire didn't know how to act.

It was Mike who showed up with hot tea a moment later. He handed the steaming liquid to his mother. "Is Dad hanging in? Anything new? Did the doctor show up? Did they increase his pain medication?"

Mike took charge and their mom responded. "There is no change, son. The doctor said if they increase the morphine, he will be less coherent." She pulled from Claire's arms and got up and walked to Mike.

"Talk to them, Mike. I don't want him in pain. Tell them to make him comfortable." Claire saw pleading in her mother's eyes. "Please."

"Sure, Mom, but he wanted to see Claire. She's here now so why don't we get her in there. Then I'll request more pain medication."

Claire swallowed. How would she stand seeing her strong, vibrant father in a hospital bed? She crossed her arms over her stomach. Mike took her elbow and led her to an intercom mounted outside on oversized door into the ICU.

"We have to ask permission for you to go in and they only allow one person at a time."

Claire nodded as if she understood.

The voice on the intercom, scratchy, starchy answered. "Yes?"

"Paddy Flannigan. Can we change visitors?"

The square box on the wall asked, "Relation?"

"Daughter."

Claire heard a buzz and Mike reached for the door. On the other side stood a nurse in blue scrubs. Lots of things—pens, a stethoscope, plastic gloves—hung from her pockets. Mike ushered Claire to her.

"You're Claire?"

"Yes."

"Your dad has been asking for you. We try to warn you what to expect when you see him. He's in and out of a deep sleep. Part of that is medication and part of it is the tumor. He may or may not recognize you." She paused, gave Claire and assessing look. "Paddy has been doing pretty well, considering. The pain has gotten worse over the last three hours, but he still can muster a smile in between our poking him. I will ask to have the other visitor leave when you get to the room."

Claire followed, listened, and tried to picture what awaited her. How bad could he be? The nurse, whose name Claire never learned, continued, "Your father has lots of tubes. He has two IVs, one in each arm. He has a catheter. He has several lines that are connected to monitors. They make noise." The nurse said all this in a monotone and then she turned to face Claire. Her eyes penetrated as her voice softened. "Don't worry about that. He can hear you and may even respond. If he is deep in sleep, we suggest you just hold his hand. Don't worry about the IV. He needs touch."

They reached a door protected only by a curtain. Metal holders slid across a rounded bar. The sound, like fingers on a blackboard, sent chills down Claire's spine. There was Paddy, lying motionless in a hospital gown. He looked gray.

Then she noticed Mark sitting alongside the bed, talking to Paddy. She took an involuntary step back and gave a small gasp.

Mark held her father's hand, talking softly. Claire couldn't make out the words.

Shock tingled down her spine. Not by the machines she had been warned about, but the sight of her husband. Why hadn't someone warned her? She blinked. Of course, Mark, Mr. Predictable, would be there. It shouldn't have been a surprise, but it was.

He looked over and saw her. She smiled. Mark picked up a wet cloth and wiped Paddy's forehead, then turned back to Claire. "He seems to like it."

It was that fast, a moment, just a bleep of the machine, and Claire realized how good Mark truly was. Memories flooded her, untapped moments of their life together, a foundation she'd forgotten. He passed Paddy's needled hand to her with tenderness, laying his own hand on hers for a brief moment, stroking his thumb down the back and along her middle finger.

"He's been asking for you." He leaned close to Paddy's ear and whispered, "She's here. Your Claire is here."

Claire took her father's hand on both of hers. She remembered Paddy insisting a priest marry her and Mark to make their union official. At the ceremony in her parents' living room, Paddy placed her hand in Mark's. That was so long ago, yet only yesterday. The history couldn't have been shared with anyone but him. It was Mark who knew the importance of family. It was Mark who had cared for her like he was now caring for her father. It would be Mark who in the future understood the power of now.

She then felt Paddy's fingers moving. Mark had left them alone.

Her father moaned and whimpered.

"Daddy, it's me."

"Claire?" His eyes barely flickered opened.

"Hush, Daddy, I'm here." She wiped his face with the cloth Mark left.

He repeated her name and closed his eyes again. She pulled his finger tips to her lips and whispered, "I love you, Daddy."

Chapter Forty-Nine

"Mrs. Flannigan." Paddy's primary physician turned and included the family sitting next to their mother. The doctor took Alma's hand in his. "Paddy isn't going to get better. All we can do is keep him comfortable. The only question is where." Alma stared, blank faced, at the doctor.

Mike put his arm around his mother.

Reality closed, like a panic room door, shutting out the hope Claire had clung to. She leaned against her brother, Paul.

"He broke two ribs when he fell," the doctor continued. "That's what is causing most of the pain. However, as the tumor grows, the headaches will increase. I want to keep him in the hospital for at least one more day." The doctor stood and hesitated before leaving. "You have lots of decisions to make and the hospital social worker will be in to explain them."

From the doorway, he turned back to the devastated family clinging to each other rather than a future. "Alma, kids," he said, "I am sorry."

The next day, day four as the family called it, after meeting with the social worker and discharge nurse, Alma seemed to rouse herself. She announced she would take Paddy home. "When I tried talking to him about surgery, he kept repeating one word, 'home,' so I've arranged for hospice."

"Mom, do you know how much work that is?" Paul asked.

"I have no clue, but I'll do it for Paddy." Alma jutted her chin in the familiar gesture that meant there would be no discussion. "Paul and Mike, you have jobs." She turned to her daughter. "Hopefully Claire can stay on and help."

"Of course," Claire said, turning to Mark. "I can stay, can't I?" He knew what being with her father for his final days would mean to her. To all of them.

Mark gazed at her a long moment before nodding. "I need to return, but there's no reason for you to come."

They assembled the mechanical hospital bed in the den looking out on the backyard Paddy designed and loved. The roses, trimmed perfectly, bloomed in a variety of colors. A healthy almond tree dropped nuts for the blue birds. Long ago Paddy gave up trying to harvest them.

At night, mother and daughter rotated sitting with Paddy. Claire came to treasure those private times when she played his favorite music, whispered his beloved prayers, spooned bits of butterscotch pudding into his mouth.

Like the days turning to night, he slipped further and further away. The moans increased, and the occasional smiles when she held his hand decreased.

Claire, like the rest of her family, knew he was always just one breath away from leaving. They sat vigil, taking turns holding his hand, rubbing his feet or reading old Irish poetry by Yeats or Seamus Heaney.

Claire was with him when he died on a Tuesday at the break of first light. She sat alone with the gurgling sounds of Paddy's inconsistent breaths. Words no longer necessary, she hoped her father felt her spirit as she could his. His sporadic gulps of air kept her attached. The distraction of the orange-red sun called her to the window on the east wall and away from his side.

She opened the curtains fully to a clear morning where the sun crawled into the sky over the Sierra Mountain Range. A new day was born.

"Look. It's going to be a golden day." She said aloud what Paddy used to say when he woke her in the morning for school.

A thick clear brogue answered, "Indeed, 'tis a glorious day."

Startled, she turned to the bed. Her father hadn't spoken, but he no longer struggled to breathe. There was a softness to Paddy she hadn't seen in days.

She waited a minute for the reflexive breath. When it didn't come, she called out for her mother. Claire turned back to the window and saw a bird flying toward the dawning sun.

Her eyes might have been playing a trick on her, but, she swore, the bird stopped mid-flight and did an Irish jig across the mountain tops. For a brief moment, she wanted to chase him like she had as a small child. A part of her left with him. But perhaps the best part of him stayed here with her.

Before long the whole family gathered in the room. It was a time to circle together. It was a time when the past was forgiven and the only thing that mattered was the union of the Flannigan clan, mother, father and children. This would be the last time they were this unit. As soon as they left the room, they would be leaderless.

Alma broke the silence. "Pray for us."

As if the family were in church on Sunday, they joined hands as Mom started, "Our Father who art in heaven."

Softly Claire joined the chorus. "Hallowed be thy name."

Praying together was the tradition. Their father taught them all the prayer. It was required to make their First Communion. Claire remembered being proud she was the first in her class to learn it. She ran home to show her father the Holy Card the nuns gave her. Her father kissed it and praised her. But, today, the prayer was a plea to claim their father and heal their loss.

Claire and the boys were the first to leave. They left their mother alone with their dad as they had so many other times. It was their private time and Claire's heart cried out for Mark.

She stepped away from her brothers to go outside. She inhaled at the fully risen sun and dialed Mark.

He answered immediately.

She looked east past the hills, wanting Mark to comfort her.

"He's gone." It was all she could say. All other words were suffocated in tears.

"I'll be there," Mark said.

Mark hung up, and looked around his office, not sure what do. It was his duty as her husband to be there, he knew that.

But he was hurt, he knew that too. She had been with another man. How could he look past that?

Claire spoiled what they had.

Of course she was devastated by the loss of Paddy, so was Mark. But he was gutted by her affair. The word even offended him. She cheated on him and now she expected him to behave as if it hadn't happened.

He needed to go. He sent emails, telling staff members of a death in the family, then headed to the condo, hardly seeing the other passengers on the T.

He kept blinking back tears, already missing Paddy, his joking, the teasing, their chiding of each other. Paddy accepted him long ago.

Mark remembered their talk the night Claire announced she was pregnant, and they would get married. It had been

Paddy who walked out into the night with him and asked, "Do you love her?"

Mark was shaken by the question long ago. Why had it come back now? It was as clear a question today as twenty-nine years ago.

Did he love her?

Back then, the answer was simple.

Of course, he loved her.

Today...it wasn't as easy.

Claire met Mark's plane, hoping they would talk before they reached the house. She hadn't told her mother about her indiscretion, the teapot no longer strong enough to withstand the pain. She needed to explain her pent-up anxiety to Mark, the man she'd viewed as dispensable. The man she now wanted to keep, to fight for even.

As she drove into the Fresno airport arrivals area Mark stood outside the baggage claim doors. The late afternoon heat baked the sidewalk, and he looked wrinkled and disheveled with drooping shoulders.

She remembered waiting for Jeff that last morning on the island and her sense of anticipation.

Bubbling and rebellion fought in her stomach as she maneuvered into the pick-up lane. She unlocked the door and Mark threw his suitcase in the back before climbing in.

Neither of them spoke as she drove them out of the airport.

"I'm glad you came," she finally said, breaking the silence. "Thank you."

Mark adjusted the seatbelt but didn't answer.

She swallowed and clutched the steering wheel. "Are you going to talk to me?"

"About what?"

"About …about us."

"There isn't much to say. Is there?" His tone was icier than the sidewalk outside the coffee shop last February.

"I think we—we have a lot to talk about. I want to tell you w—what's been happening to me."

Mark turned in the seat and looked at her. His blue eyes were cold as steel. His chin set. "Do you think you have an explanation that justifies adultery?"

Claire flinched. She hadn't committed adultery. She'd *thought* about an affair but hadn't. She drew a shaky breath. How could she explain this? She pulled the car into a fast food parking lot and tried to think where to begin.

She shifted to face him. "Mark, I've been lost for a while now."

"And the way to find yourself is to screw another man?"

"I *didn't*," she said.

"Don't make it worse by lying. You told me you were with Agnes. You weren't. You were with Jeff. Don't insult me anymore."

"Yes, I was with Jeff for the day, but we didn't have sex."

"You wanted to."

Claire inhaled sharply. Yes, she wanted to.

Now in the light of day, with her father dead, and Mark being the one who cared for him, she couldn't remember why. It was a lifetime ago.

"I lied to you. About why I was going to the island. I own that, and it was wrong, and I'm sorry."

He stared through the windshield at the brightly colored sign urging them to come in for burgers and fries. "Sorry isn't enough. I have never once even thought about cheating on you. How can a marriage survive when trust is broken?"

"Perhaps...maybe with counseling?"

He groaned. "That again? You think I want to go to some stranger and talk? It's simple. I vowed to be faithful, and I thought you did, too. Talking about it to some therapist, like yourself, isn't going to change the facts."

"There are things that led up to it," she said.

"So?"

"Well, a therapist can help us untangle this mess. There is so much more than the last year." She clasped her hands together, almost in supplication.

"You go. You go and figure out why I'm not enough for you," he said, his tone flat.

Claire's eyes blurred with tears. She turned her head away and let them flow.

Mark, hands folded across his chest, sat in silence.

Between sobs, she tried to tell him about her loneliness, her feelings of abandonment. Even as she said the words, she knew they sounded trite. None of it justified, even in her mind, hurting another.

"I made a mistake." She wanted him to take her in his arms and say it would be okay. They could work it out, but he didn't. She should have known. One thing about Mark. He was predictable, and she'd crossed the line.

When she had no more tears, no more words, no more emotions to spill, she started the car and pulled back into traffic. The silence between them crackled with tension.

"Look," he finally said, "we need to get through the funeral." He paused before adding, "After that, I'm going back to Boston." He didn't look at her when he said, "I don't want you to come. You've been miserable for a long time, Claire, and I can't seem to make you happy." He gazed out the front window. "Do what you need to do. I need space," he said as if he'd memorized it.

She wet her lips. "What about this week?"

"We will be civil to each other."

Claire wanted to yell. *Haven't we been doing that for too long?* She wiped her eyes. "Okay," then added, "maybe we can talk later?"

Mark didn't answer.

Lots of people were at the house by the time they arrived. Alma greeted Mark, and he gave her a long hug. He and his children went in the backyard. Alma sent out iced tea while Claire dashed inside to try and hide the signs of her tears.

Earlier Katie asked if something was wrong. Claire had lied and said, "No, just Paddy dying." She trusted Mark wouldn't tell the kids. They both kept the children from knowing about their fights. She suspected her mother had a clue, but Alma was so absorbed in the funeral arrangements, she didn't offer to bring the teapot down for a long talk.

That night, after eating the casseroles brought by church ladies, after the rosary, after the relatives all found places to sleep, Claire crawled into her childhood bed next to Mark. He slept on his back with one foot out from under the sheet. Claire opened the bedroom window to allow the night breeze in. She wanted Mark to hold her, but knew he wouldn't. Instead she curled, fetal-like, around her pillow.

Even the security of her old bed gave her little hope for the future.

Chapter Fifty

The day after the funeral, Mark asked Sean to drive him to the airport. Claire offered but Mark didn't want another scene. Claire didn't appreciate the time he took off to be with her, or the work he'd left on his desk. He needed his job and at least they valued him.

"You're awfully quiet, Dad," Sean said pulling on to the freeway.

"Lots on my mind."

"Are you okay?"

"Yeah, just been a long week and I have lots of work to catch up on."

"Do you think Mom will be okay?"

"She'll be fine," Mark said. He grimaced inwardly. Don't worry about Claire, she managed to get what she wanted. No matter who got hurt in the process.

"She said she wasn't going back to Boston. Does that mean she isn't going now? Will she be staying with Gram? Or do you think she'll come back to the ranch?" Sean asked, hardly taking a breath.

"Those are all questions only your mother has the answers to."

Mark turned toward the window at the dry, dusty, brown landscape along the freeway. The Central Valley begged for rain, but it wouldn't come for months. The dying grass stood in wait—as did everything in his life.

Claire, still in her cotton pajamas, took her coffee on the patio. The heat predictably miserable for early July. Things couldn't be any worse, and it was all her fault. Her loneliness, her longing, her unfulfilled heart. She couldn't blame it all on Mark. She was the one who cheated.

Her emotions lay against her heart a jumble, one on top of the other. Even as a trained therapist fixing your own problems was never easy and often dangerous. If only she could understand the emptiness, the longing to be loved. Was it just wantonness or need? What was wrong with her? Was she ever whole? She sat in her father's chair when a wave of unexpected sadness hit her. The evaporating morning dew triggered the reality he was gone. The abyss of hollowness expanded.

A crow on the clothesline taunted the neighbor's cat. Claire heard a chorus of the faceless righteousness. She knew right from wrong. She didn't want to be judged. She rose from the chair and found a rock in the garden and threw it at the bird. Anger mixed with guilt and a dash of sadness all fought to cover her fear of tomorrow.

Along with the bitter taste of the black coffee she swallowed was something she wouldn't recognize. Fear.

She was going to be okay. She had a job, her kids, and could take care of herself. It was time for her. She calmly listed all the things she thought of, all the things she would ask a client. She had logical answers to all. She would be okay. Perhaps the last man who honestly loved her was now buried.

Claire went in for a new cup when the first went cold. Alone in the kitchen, she decided to pull back the curtain and take a self-inventory. Instead of pouring another she brewed a large mug of tea. No need to bring down the pot. A brown cup was enough for early morning work, sans Mom. She added milk and sugar, went back to the patio and settled in her father's Adirondack, a safe place to do battle with ghosts.

There was an unidentified phantom lurking in the darkness of her soul, hiding behind the sadness, the guilt and the fear. Was she brave enough to call it forward? The phantom scared her, made her feel little and vulnerable. It needed a face, a name, a recognized life in order for her to battle it.

Claire breathed deeply, using the same technique learned long ago in yoga. She cleared her mind and let the feelings come. There were tears of sadness, gulps of guilt, and cries of anger.

Then the vapor grew. She looked at it. It was darkness. She saw the night sky without stars. They weren't there. Perhaps, she thought, they never were. All this time she waited for them to fall on her, to bring her joy and they may have never been there at all.

She spent so long waiting for the stars, she didn't see the beauty of the sky. A changing creature, at times brilliant with stars close enough to see falling to earth, other times the stars so far from earth you needed a telescope. They spent nights hidden by clouds, or let the full moon outshine them. The only thing for sure, the stars were there, always had been and always would be. Like Mark.

The back door opened, and Alma walked onto the patio. "You've been here a long time." She pulled an aluminum lawn chair alongside Claire. "Everything okay?"

Claire smiled. "It will be...I'm sure."

They sat drinking tea and waited until hunger spurred them to do something.

"I think there's some ham left from yesterday and I'm going in to make a sandwich," Claire said. "Should I make you one?"

"I'm not hungry," her mother said.

"You didn't eat enough yesterday to keep a mouse alive. At least let me make you some toast."

Claire's mother looked into her daughter's eyes and they both cried. No words were needed as waves of grief pulled them.

For two weeks, mother and daughter walked alongside each other, taking on one task a day. The hospital bed was returned the first day. Claire then started the process of bringing the couch and recliner back to the room. Her mother debated returning Dad's recliner to the same spot facing the television. She didn't really want that, but she couldn't let it be sold at the next church fund raiser. The compromise was to keep the chair and place it under Gram's old floor lamp. Claire found a stack of books for the side table and Alma placed her forgotten knitting on the other side.

The women talked of Paddy. The last of his cigars, hidden in the back of the closet, Claire gave to the priest when he came for a home visit. One night when sleep escaped her, she found herself sitting in the chair that still smelled of her father. She liked knowing his essence stayed even though most remnants of him were erased by the smell of cleaning products.

She should return to the ranch, but she'd already lost her father and didn't want to leave her mother.

On Sunday, Paul came by the house. Claire walked to her brother and wrapped her arms around him. "Mom and I have been cleaning parts of Dad away for the last two weeks and we've cried, yelled, and hung on to as much as our hearts will allow."

Paul wept on her shoulder. "I miss him and am afraid I'll forget him." Paul gulped.

"Never." Claire assured as she patted his back.

She went to the bedroom dresser and pulled out the green cable knit wool sweater Paul gave his Dad twelve Christmases ago. "Dad loved this and wore it all the time." She handed it to Paul. "It's too big but take and wear it whenever you need his hug."

Claire looked around at the bins labeled *Give-Away* to thrift store, trash, or church and realized they were done. The last of the jobs on Mom's list to do before Claire could head home.

Now what? Did she go to the ranch or back to Boston? Or could she stay there in that room while she decided which bin her marriage belonged in?

Chapter Fifty-One

Mark sat in his chair in a dark room in a dark mood. When the phone rang, he hoped it was Claire. He'd hung up on her two days earlier and now regretted it.

"Hello," he said, wanting to sound nonchalant and back in control.

"Oh, Mark, it's Agnes, is Claire there? I've tried her cell, and she isn't answering."

"She's not here."

"Okay, I'll keep trying her number." She hesitated before she continued, "How are you doing?"

The gall of the woman. She was part of the problem, the one who covered for Claire. Did betrayed sum it up or should he be devastated? "I'm fine," he finally said.

"Big Jim and I are worried about the two of you."

"No need to worry."

"If you want to talk, I'll listen," she said.

"Nothing much to talk about," he said after a long pause. "But thanks."

He disconnected. There weren't words to heal the rift Claire caused. She'd wanted to talk the other day when she called. He didn't. He couldn't. When she demanded he say something, he hung up.

Fury owned him, showing in everything he did. He'd stayed late last night to dictate a report and wanted it on his desk when he arrived. He yelled at his secretary this morning when it wasn't finished. Not his style but he slammed the door on her. He criticized Daniel at every opportunity. Mark's behavior separated by, before, or after Claire cheated on him.

Thoughts of Jeff made Mark want to roar. His hand fisted and his ears pounded. What kind of man had an affair with a married woman? What did Claire see in him?

For a week, he didn't sleep in the bed he'd once shared with Claire. Even though he washed the linens twice, the pillowcases still smelled of her. He preferred sleeping on the stiff sofa. Even the music he'd always loved didn't relax him.

Everything reminded him of what had been. He had worked for nothing. She'd thrown away all their plans for a future.

A continent away, Claire sat in the gazebo at the ranch waiting for Mark's call. She returned to her job in order to bring schedule and distraction back into her life. The other sixteen hours she couldn't function while she mourned her father and her marriage. Her kids pretended to not notice she was on the ranch and Dad still in Boston.

Katie settled into her old room and, consumed with her own needs, talked about Peter. She kept answering calls that ended in screams and tears, frightening Claire. She didn't have enough energy to help her daughter.

In a strange way, Claire felt she could identify more with Katie now. They both hurt. They talked only of dinner and dishes and recognized life went on around them without their participation.

"Mom, dinner," Katie called from the kitchen.

"I'm not hungry."

"I just heated the leftover spaghetti."

Claire came to the table and twirled red stained strands around her fork, lifting them to her mouth. It took too much energy to actually eat.

It was over the second glass of wine Claire heard a car coming up the gravel drive. Her thoughts flew first to Mark, but he would never drive that fast. Long ago they fought about the dust on her furniture. How she wished all their fights had been that silly. Furniture, unlike marriages, could always be dusted and given a new luster.

She and Katie turned from the table to look out the kitchen window, at the same time seeing a red Honda speeding toward the house.

"Shit," Katie said, "it's Peter."

"Peter?"

"Yeah, I wonder what he wants." Katie stood.

"So do I." Claire, well aware Katie hadn't talked to Peter in two days, had listened to only half the conversation when her daughter made it clear she didn't want to see him again. "Should I get rid of him?" Claire asked as she rose also.

"No. I'll see him."

Claire sighed. She would rather Katie stuck to her decisions and not be seduced by Peter. Instead she said, "I'm here if you need me," and returned to her seat.

"I'm okay." Katie wiped her mouth with the napkin and headed out the side door.

Claire sipped at the remains of the wine. There weren't remnants of an enjoyed meal, only pasta turning cold on the Fiesta plates. She began to clear the table. When she reached the sink, and started scraping the dishes into the disposal, Peter's voice stabbed the air.

She opened the curtain, her eyes resting on the couple. Obviously, they were fighting, as he towered over Katie and shook his fist close to her face.

Claire's neck tightened. Fear gripped her.

Katie stepped back. Peter pursued. He pushed Katie against the hood of the car.

Claire's feet were glued to the floor.

His fist raised and hit Katie a second time.

Claire moved toward the door, grabbed the phone, dialed 911, and looked around, desperately, for a weapon.

The fire extinguisher that Mark insisted be next to each entrance. Silly her, objecting because they didn't match her décor. Thank God, Mark won. She seized it and raced out the door.

A lifetime elapsed before Claire reached them.

"Back up, you son of a bitch!" she yelled so loud her throat hurt.

Peter turned to her. His face was red with rage. "This isn't your business, you crazy old lady."

"I've called the cops. Move," Claire said in clear, loud, modulated words to cover her shaking teeth.

"Make me." Peter took three giant steps in her direction, releasing Katie who slumped to the ground.

It happened as an instinct. Claire remembered learning how to discharge the canister. She aimed the hose at Peter and squeezed the trigger. A white plume hit him around the eyes.

He staggered back screaming, "You blinded me." Peter cursed as he covered his face.

"You touch my daughter again, I'll castrate you." If only she'd grabbed the knife.

She kept the hose aimed at him and inched over to Katie while sirens echoed in the silence of the night. Bear appeared from the shed, barking, and ran, teeth bared, toward Peter.

"Get him." Claire wanted to see the dog take Peter down. He deserved to be mauled. The police arrived about the time Bear reached Peter, who turned and ran down the drive.

Claire stretched for Katie and gathered her into her arms. She held her, rocking her like when she was little. Claire took her blouse to wipe Katie's face covered in blood and dirt. Katie turned into her mother's arms, letting the tears mix with the blood.

"What happened?" a police officer asked.

They had cuffs on Peter and another siren wailed in the distance.

"He hit her," is all Claire could manage.

"I called an ambulance," the officer said as he kneeled next to mother and daughter.

On the lawn, the other policeman used the water hose to rinse Peter.

The ambulance came, and the paramedic insisted Katie go to the hospital for stitches. For a few moments Claire feared the police might arrest her for being part of the fracas. They instead let her go.

An officer, whose badge read S. Mallano, gave her a card with a number for Victim Services. "Call this office and they'll help you with anything you need, from finding out court dates, to medical services."

"Will I have to press charges?" Katie asked from the back of the ambulance.

"The prosecutor makes that decision, not you." The officer tucked his pen into his pocket. "You get your stitches and concentrate on healing."

Before the emergency vehicles left, Claire picked up her cell phone and dialed Mark. He didn't answer. Claire kept hitting redial as she followed the ambulance into the hospital in the ranch truck. They took Katie to the nearest emergency room, twenty minutes from the ranch.

Jessie rode in on the tractor from the vineyard and offered to drive Claire, but she refused. She asked Jessie to stay at the house, by the phone, just in case.

Ignoring the distracted driving law, Claire hit star two on the cell phone then star five. Two was Mark's cell—five was the apartment. She prayed for him to pick up one of the phones. How had those numbers been assigned? She shook the random thought from her mind. How much easier to think about mundane things like programmed numbers rather than the seriousness of a battered daughter. What was she going to say to Mark? *Hey Mark, I failed to protect our daughter.*

The machine picked up. "Mark, it's Claire. Call me." She hesitated for a moment then added, "Katie's hurt. I'm on the cell." She left the same messages on his mobile.

Why was it taking so long to get there? A large delivery truck motored just ahead of her and this wasn't a good place to pass. *Breathe. Slow breathing. Calm. Katie is fine.* She debated calling Colleen and Sean but decided to wait until she was at the hospital and saw how Katie was.

As the hospital came into view, the unraveling started. She chewed on a fingernail she'd torn, biting it down to the quick.

Katie should already be entering the emergency bay, and Claire needed to find a parking spot. If she'd allowed Jessie to bring her, she wouldn't have to circle the crowded lot. She hit the top of the steering wheel in frustration. Her baby was hurting and she couldn't get to her fast enough.

There—she spied a space, the farthest from the entrance. She swung the truck into it then ran toward the electronic door that didn't open fast enough. She entered the emergency room covered in blood.

A nurse approached and asked where she was injured. Claire explained she was looking for her daughter and was led back to the exam room.

Katie lay on a bed. A nurse leaned over her, cleaning her wounds.

Claire walked to the opposite side. "Katie, you okay?" she asked as she touched her daughter's shoulder. Silly thing to ask, of course she wasn't okay. "I'm her mother," she said to the woman in scrubs.

The nurse looked at Katie, then to Claire. "If you're going to be here, don't get in the way."

"Is she going to be okay?" Claire repeated.

"I'll be okay," Katie said. Her voice, weak, the words garbled over swollen lips, and her eyes began to swell. There were fingerprints around her neck. It was worse than Claire realized.

"She's been pretty beat up. What happened?"

Claire nodded, unable to open her mouth.

"We need X-rays. It looks like she has a broken nose for sure." Never once, past the initial eye contact with Claire, did the nurse with blonde hair pulled efficiently back in a braid, take her eyes off her patient. "Dr. Barton called for an Obstetrics consult. We need to be sure the baby is safe."

Claire held onto Katie's hand. The other hand already had an IV.

"Katie, do you think you ever passed out?" the nurse asked.

Katie didn't respond. She just looked straight ahead and then to her mother.

"I don't think so," Claire answered.

"We'll watch her for any head injury," the nurse said, matter-of-factly. She had a checklist of things to do and she was doing them, in logical order, an order Claire wasn't familiar with. Claire wanted to have them tell her everything was fine, just a few cuts and bruises, not a head injury.

Two techs came in, pushing a machine. "We need you to step outside," one of them said.

"Why?"

"Dr. Swanson ordered a fetal heart monitor to check the baby. The doctor is on his way in." They were efficient and moved toward Katie, making it impossible for Claire to stay. She drew back to the door. She stood there as they pulled a curtain, the sound transporting her back to her father and his ICU room. Her mouth went dry and her throat closed.

"Okay, hon, we're going to change you into a gown," someone said.

Katie moaned. "Can't you give her anything for the pain," Claire called past the fabric divider.

"Sorry. Not yet. We need to make sure the baby's heart rate is safe." The words floated over the curtain rod.

Claire forgot about the baby. Of course, they would protect both lives. Katie would be okay, eventually. Now Claire worried about the baby. *The baby* she said over in her mind, *the baby*.

A woman in a blue suit came up beside her. "Mrs. Richert?"

"Yes."

"I'm MaryAnn Higgens, from Social Services. Why don't you come with me? I'll get you a cup of coffee or tea."

How ironic to have social workers greet her. It was her job to offer help and become the sympathetic ear. Claire stared at Ms. Higgens, who had to be half Claire's age. Nothing the caseworker offered could fix this mess.

Claire dismissed the social worker, choosing to wait alone with her fears.

She sat in a rose-colored chair in the waiting room, alternating between tapping her foot, chewing her fingernail, and checking her phone to see if Mark called. He would, eventually. He had to.

"Mrs. Richter?" a nurse finally called.

"That's me." Claire shot to her feet.

"The doctor just finished examining your daughter, and he wants to admit her."

Claire's head spun and she felt dizzy. *Now what?*

"We will be taking your daughter to the OB ward," the nurse said as she extended a hand to Claire who wobbled on her feet. "You okay?"

"Just stood up too fast," Claire said as she regained equilibrium.

"Katie asked you to come see her. Can you do that?"

"Of course." She nodded and followed the nurse back to the cubical to find Katie.

Claire forced a smile for her daughter. "I'm back," she said to the room.

Katie lay flat on the bed with needles and wires flowing out of her body.

"Mom, they say I've started labor." Katie's hand trembled as she reached for her mother. "Mommy, it's too soon, what if he isn't okay?"

Claire pulled calmness and courage from the pit of her being. "One step at a time." Mark's standard answer and the automatic response in the family when a crisis loomed. Where was he? Why hadn't he called?

Katie smiled tremulously back at her mother. "Okay. You eternal optimist, one step at a time."

The nurse with the kind smile and serious face looked at Claire. "It's early. We've given her medicine to stop the contractions. Katie isn't even feeling them. We would like to delay delivery as long as possible, every day he stays in, his chances improve." The nurse looked at Katie. "Hopefully we can go full term."

Soon an aide arrived with a gurney. Carefully the staff assisted Katie off the bed. Her bloodied clothes were collected in a plastic bag, labeled, and stored for the police to pick up.

Claire looked at her daughter and saw the wound above her eye sutured shut, the swelling pulled on the stitches.

The ward smelled of disinfectant and age. Mother and child were safe for this moment. Trained professionals abounded if Katie needed anything.

As the nurses took Katie's blood pressure and attached even more equipment to her already invaded body, Claire excused herself. She stepped into the small lobby down the hall where she could turn her phone back on and check for messages. Other waiting family members did the same. She overheard one gentleman tell about the birth of his daughter, another called for flowers to be delivered to his wife. Claire wasn't sure she wanted to share her story in such a public place.

Sean had left a message saying he and Colleen were on the way. The second message was from the officer who reminded her to take pictures of the injuries. A tear crept down her cheek. How do you get a picture of fear?

The third message was from Jeff, who had called a few times over the last month. Once to extend his condolences, another time to see if she planned to return to Boston, a third time begging her to return his calls and tell him how she was doing. She couldn't and wouldn't talk to him. She deleted his message and went to the fourth on the list of missed calls.

Mark. Claire checked the time. The silent digital wall clock flashed three-thirty. Not believing it, she checked her wristwatch for confirmation. Without knowing how the evening slipped into night, she redialed Mark. She rehearsed the preceding nine hours to be sure she could remember all that happened in the jumble of the past night. When he answered, she didn't wait for his hello before she relayed the details she remembered.

"How bad is Katie?" He had to break into her ramble.

"She's hurt and may lose the baby. She's in pain and they can't give her any drugs, or it might depress the baby's heart." Claire recited incidents in random order.

"Mark," she finally said, "Katie needs you." She hesitated before she said, "I need you."

After a long silence, Mark responded, "I'll be there."

Claire exhaled, blinked.

She turned her phone off, put it in her purse, and went back to her daughter.

Chapter Fifty-Two

Claire returned to Katie's room, greeted by a throng of buzzing nurses who hadn't bothered to pull the curtain around Katie's bed. Instead they were gathered around a machine spitting out a strip of paper.

Katie's face was now turning shades of red with hints of blue pooling under her swollen eyes. As Claire approached the bedside, she noticed Katie clenching her teeth and crying. The tears were lost in the valley between a broken nose and puffed cheek.

"What's going on?" Claire asked, but no one answered. They kept turning the three-inch strip of paper and marking it in measured intervals with a felt tip pen. Again, with her voice a bit louder, she cleared her throat and said, "I want to know what is happening."

An older, well rounded nurse turned toward her. "It looks like the drugs aren't stopping the labor and, as we have already told your daughter, the baby is showing signs of distress."

"What does that mean?"

The nurse took Katie's hand. At first Claire thought she was taking her pulse, but then she realized the woman was carefully holding the only part of Katie's arm that wasn't supporting a bruise, bandage, or needle.

"We don't have all the information yet. I am a nurse-midwife and I was asked by Dr. Swanson to take a look at Katie."

Claire dropped her shoulders, tilted her head back and then looked at the midwife inviting more explanation.

"We have given her one more drug. Hopefully that will stop the contractions and the baby's heart rate will stabilize. We really would like to get three more weeks for this guy to stay where he is. He's a little small to come into the world now …" She hesitated…"but if he is determined to come…" Her voice trailed off as Katie arched her back. The midwife now only paid attention to Katie.

Claire could see pain in her daughter's eyes, though maybe not the look of pain as much as pure fear.

"I'm all wet," Katie's words were slurred and fast.

The midwife pulled back the blanket as another nurse pulled the curtain fast around the now intimate group including Claire. She grabbed the bed's guard rail for support as her knees wobbled. The spot under Katie was pink with blood. She looked into the midwife's tension-creased face.

"Okay," she said to everyone, "looks like we aren't going to stop this." The woman's voice remained steady but her eyes telegraphed urgency to the nurse closest to the monitor. "What's the heart rate?"

The younger nurse didn't answer. She handed the strip to the midwife, and they both looked at each other. Claire instinctively knew she shouldn't demand an answer. It wasn't good. Everyone in the room went into choreographed motion.

"Call Swanson," the midwife barked at another aide in the room. Even as she spoke, the rest of the staff unhooked certain machines while others attached equipment that seemed to be hidden in drawers and closets.

The midwife, who had taken the role of director, efficiently, without intonation turned to Katie. "Okay, dear, your baby's heart rate has dropped. You are bleeding. We need to get him out now. We've called Dr. Swanson. He is close. By the time we get you to surgery and prepped, he will be here." Even as she explained, the bed traveled out of the room and down a hall toward two enormous doors that opened as the crew approached.

Claire followed. Halfway through, the nurse turned to Claire indicting she should stay beyond the secrecy of the doors.

"You dear, are going to have a baby," she said to Katie, then turned to Claire, "and you dear, are going to pray."

The entrance to surgery closed, engulfing Katie and leaving Claire alone in a too bright hallway. Her first instinct, call Mark.

She hurried to the lobby where the cell phone would work. She dialed, and it went to voice mail. He must be on the plane. She left a brief message.

Mark would come. Just like the stars of August, predictable and dependable.

After being on stand-by since noon, Mark took the last seat available on the eight o'clock flight. He climbed past an oversized young man who announced he was flying to UCLA for a basketball scholarship. On the other side, a mother picked up an infant who sat in Mark's assigned seat.

Mark didn't want to be lectured on UCLA's record, nor did he find the screaming baby cute. He should've waited for the morning flight, usually packed with business men quietly preparing for meetings at their final destination. He was tired. Drained. He had five and half hours, without delays to LAX and then a commuter flight to Paso Robles. He wanted home and wished he'd never left. Mark leaned his head against the seat as the jet gathered speed down the runway.

Memories flooded him.

Once in the air, he dug his earphones out of the carry-on case and put them on. Mark had perfected shutting out the world. He tuned his iPod to the classical selection.

He stirred mid-flight with the mother and child climbing over him to head for a walk up and down the aisle as she tried to comfort the baby. He woke, annoyed, and remembered all that happened in the last few weeks ending with his resolve to leave Claire.

He couldn't forgive her. She kissed another man. He didn't want to know how Jeff touched her or how she responded. Mark crossed his arms tight across his chest to calm his pounding heart. He tried to fall back asleep.

The picture of a red-haired pixie running after him in the fields flashed into his mind, like it was yesterday instead of eighteen years ago. She cried after him, wanting to be by his side. He couldn't imagine her, as Claire described, battered, bruised and defeated. He added Peter to his hate list.

When the weary mother returned with the still-not-sleeping child, Mark remembered the nights he walked Katie and Colleen, and wished the child had only loving hands touch her. He offered to hold her while the mother prepared a bottle. The soft diaper-padded bottom, a tactile reminder of Katie's baby waiting to be born. Until now it was an *it*. The future made him shudder.

Chapter Fifty-Three

Claire waited outside the doors of the operating room. Her body ached as she leaned against a wall. Her shoulder muscles carried the full weight of the day and throbbed as the adrenaline wore off. With a whoosh, the doors opened, and a neonatal basinet rolled past. The doctor, who was following the acrylic basket, stopped.

"It's a boy. He weighs only two kilograms. He is small but breathing with just the aid of oxygen. We had to resuscitate him, so he is on his way to the NICU." He shot off numbers and facts Claire didn't understand. The doctor kept talking, and Claire just took in the information as best she could. Her eyes were fixed on the tiny figure in the box. The baby, a boy, lay naked and exposed. His wrinkled red body, no bigger than a kitten, assaulted with miniature needles and tubes.

"How is Katie?"

One of the nurses who had been following the bassinet slowed. "Your daughter is okay. She has lost blood but will be fine, and we gave her morphine for pain." Then as the nurse turned to leave, she added, "I hope the guy who did this…" Her voice trailed off. She turned to Claire. "After we finish, your daughter will be taken from here to recovery. The head nurse will call you. The baby is going to be examined by one of the neonatologists. We'll know more soon. You may see him through the window in the nursery later."

The nurse extended her hand to Claire. She took it, finding it warm and friendly, betraying her tough in-charge attitude. "By the way, my name is Greta. If you have any other questions, I'm here for the next six hours. Dr. Swanson and I will be checking on both of them."

"Thank you," Claire said with words inadequate to convey her gratitude. Greta and her angels saved her daughter, saved her grandson and a *thank you* was all Claire could muster.

"She'll be all right. It might take some time, but your daughter is strong and with your support she will heal."

Claire didn't doubt Katie's wounds would heal but wasn't sure she would ever trust again. Claire crossed herself and offered a pleading prayer.

She walked to the lobby, which became a safe haven in this antiseptic building. Coffee brewed, a television softly relayed the news of the day and in the corner, a fish tank. Claire hadn't noticed it before, but now she sat and counted the bubbles from the air filter and thought of Baby Boy Richter absorbing the air bubbles from his nose tubes.

A missed call from Sean, who hadn't shown up at the hospital like he said or if he had might be lost in the labyrinth of hospital hallways. His number displayed on her cell's screen. She hit redial.

He answered on the third ring, "Hey, Mom, talk to me."

It felt good to hear his casual tone. "Sean. Where are you?"

"How about you tell me how my sister is, first."

"She just had an emergency C-Section. The baby was having trouble, so the doctors had to deliver him. Your sister is still in surgery. The baby is in intensive care."

Sean said nothing. Claire assumed he was processing it all. "You there?" she asked.

"Yes, I came by the hospital and found out Katie was taken to delivery. I couldn't find you, so I decided to meet Dad at the airport."

"Has he landed?" she asked.

"Any minute now."

"Okay, I'll try calling him."

"Mom?"

"Yeah?"

"You said he. Is it a boy and is he okay?"

Claire, embarrassed she hadn't told him, answered Sean. "A very little boy. He is okay." She concentrated on the bubbles again.

Mark's phone flashed a message before he deplaned. Claire. He hit *Call Back*.

"Claire," he said when she answered.

"Oh, Mark, hurry." He heard her cry.

"Just landed and Sean will pick me up at baggage." He hesitated, almost afraid to ask. "Anything new?" For a moment, there was silence then a gulping sob. "Listen, Claire, I need to find Sean."

Sean opened the door for him then brought him up to date on the latest with Katie as they pulled out of the airport. Mark slid his finger onto the button to lower the window, allowing the damp air on his face. A nice evening for August, but he knew the day had been hot. The sky barely dark enough to highlight stars. It was time for the Perseids. He watched for stars shooting across the sky.

In the hospital parking lot finally, Sean dropped him off. Mark stood at the entrance and took a deep breath. He wanted to see Katie but the thought of entering made him linger outside. It was like going into a foreign city where everyone else knew the language and where the secret hide-outs were. Once inside, the people spoke a strange language and often in abbreviation. He shook of the hesitation and approached the sliding doors then headed for the desk labeled *Information*.

"I'm looking for Katie Richert."

The woman behind the desk looked up at him. "Who?"

"Richert," he said, "Katie, maybe Kathleen." Of course, she would be under her given name. "Kathleen Richert, R-I-C-H-E-R-T"

"Let me see, Kathleen?"

"Yes. Katie."

The woman smiled wide, "Congratulations. She is in 505."

Mark shrugged his shoulders. And where was that? Fifth floor no doubt, but from past experience in hospitals he calculated it wouldn't be easy.

"Maternity, five north. Take the north tower elevator—off on five—turn left—follow the signs. You'll pass surgery, OBGYN and the NICU. Go through the double green doors and announce yourself at the desk."

"Thank you," Mark said while trying to memorize the directions, follow the signs—ask at the desk.

Five minutes later, he stood at the door to Katie's room. She sat in a wheelchair by the window looking so small and vulnerable, staring out beyond the slotted blinds and glass. What did she see? When he looked out, he saw hills, vineyards, the past and what was, but he also saw the future.

A month ago, he would've known what to do. He would have insisted Katie and the baby live with them. Claire and he would have nurtured them both. Life and energy would return on the farm. He would've moved back to the ranch and taken the risk of everything falling apart. Then why didn't he take the risk before? He shook the thought off. The answer was simple though. He didn't realize so much was at stake.

Katie turned. Her face lit up. "Hey, Dad."

He winced at her bruised face. "Katie." He swallowed, fighting to find his control. "I came as soon as I could." He wanted to reach out and touch her but didn't know where. "Your mother kept me informed. How's the baby doing?" He felt better asking questions, questions with answers.

Her eyes filled with tears. "The doctor said it's 'wait and see.' They've already reduced the oxygen. I might be able to hold him this evening."

"He isn't breathing, and they took him off oxygen?" He furrowed his brow. Were they giving up on the baby or was this just part of the foreign hospital language? He remembered Paddy on the respirator and the decision to remove him. It was just hours before Paddy's body followed his brain into death. Something seemed wrong in not chasing the life of a small child.

"Actually, all the tubes are still there, but they're seeing how many times he breathes on his own. When he doesn't, alarms go off."

"Okay. I didn't understand." Mark rocked from right foot to left and back again.

"Dad, can you help me back into bed? If you don't want to, could you call a nurse?"

Mark, glad to have something to do, moved alongside Katie and offered his arm. Her touch brought back memories of when she first learned to walk. She would only do it for him and only if he had an arm out for her.

"You okay?" he asked.

"I'm doing better," she said as she turned to the bed.

"Where's your mother?"

"She's been here for two days, so Colleen took her for some food and then home. She needs sleep."

"What about you?"

"I just got some medicine before you came in, so I'll fall asleep soon." She turned her head on the pillow. "That okay with you?"

"Sure. I'll sit here and watch you sleep."

"Thanks, Daddy."

Mark watched her eyes flutter close, or at least partially close. They were so swollen they couldn't shut all the way. Her face was a spectrum of colors ranging from bright red to deep purple. Rage grew in him. This didn't happen to good people. At least that's what he used to think. Claire, over the years, told him the women she worked with were no different than any of the women she knew.

Katie's body shivered and even asleep, tears fell. He reached over and pulled the extra blanket at the end of the bed up and around her, tucked it in and blotted the tears. He straightened to stand guard. Only he wasn't sure what to guard against, and Claire wasn't here to back him up.

Mark fell asleep with his head resting on the side of the bed. It wasn't until the nurse came in that he woke.

"I have some good news," the perky nurse announced. "Your baby has turned the corner and can breathe with minimum assistance." She went on to give oxygen percentages that Mark didn't understand, but he sensed optimism.

"He isn't out of the woods but …" She hesitated and shot a glance toward Mark. "If you like, we can go see him and maybe even hold him."

Katie smiled.

"By the way, have you named him yet?" The nurse assisted Katie to a sitting position.

"I want to name him Patrick. Patrick Karl." Katie looked at her father then back to the nurse. "After my two grandfathers."

"Two strong names," the nurse responded.

"Two strong men who need to watch over him. He'll have to grow into the names," Katie said.

Mark thought about his father and Paddy. They were both strong men in very different ways. His father Karl, so practical and basic, could pass determination down. Paddy, successful, playful, the dreamer who made magical things happen, would balance the hardness of Mark's father.

Before he had time to object, he followed the two of them down over-bright corridors, through doors marked *Do Not Enter*, to a small anteroom where he was given a blue paper gown and mask. He wore them with pride and followed Katie, still in the wheelchair, and the non-stop talking nurse to a Plexiglas box with all kinds of equipment attached. Inside laid the smallest baby he'd ever seen.

At one side was a woman looking at monitors, at charts, at the baby, and finally at Katie.

"Hi," she said, smiling wide, "I'm the Neonatologist, Dr. Margaret Pham." She extended a soft hand to Katie. "And you are?" she asked, as she hesitantly extended the same hand to Mark.

"This is my father. He just flew in from Boston. It is okay for him to be here." Katie shot a glance at him then the doctor. "Isn't it?"

"Of course." Dr. Pham proceeded to list, in clinical fashion, what the tubes were. "He's a fighter. His temperature is still unstable, but I expect that will take some time. He needs to learn to eat. In the meantime, we will keep the IV going and feed him through the little tube you see in his nose." Mark scanned the baby. Tears filled Mark's eyes and his heart pounded. This little guy—this precious and miraculous baby—was his grandson. Would he grow up with the iron will of his great-grandfather Karl? Or be a storyteller like Paddy? Maybe a farmer like his Grandpa Mark? Would he have Katie's red hair? One thing Mark knew already.

"His name is Patrick. And he's a fighter." Mark couldn't believe the words he was thinking just popped out of his mouth.

"Patrick," the doctor began, "has a lot of needs, but right now what you can give him is all your prayers and love. A lot of babies this premature do well, however some will not be as lucky. So, it is an hour by hour, then a day by day, fight."

"What can I do?" Katie's voice was soft and hesitant.

"Be here as much as possible. We don't have scientific proof, but it seems preemies do better when touched."

"I'll be here."

Mark put his hand on his daughter's shoulder. He would be here also.

"I have to check my other babies. One of my partners or I are always around. You'll get to know us all." She walked off toward another covey of parents with as much concern in their eyes.

Katie touched the top of the plastic crib holding her son. Mark walked next to her and put a hand on top of hers. He looked down and saw a tear drop on the basinet. Katie's. He went to wipe it away and saw a second. It wasn't until then he realized he was crying too. He brushed the dampness from his cheek. He wanted to be strong for his daughter. She took his hand and held it.

After several minutes or perhaps it was hours, for he no longer had a sense of time, he excused himself. Every fiber, every memory, every desire was for Claire. He hadn't been there to protect Katie.

Claire did.

Chapter Fifty-Four

Claire, dreaming of Father, Grams, and Leprechauns, woke with a start. She'd fallen asleep hours earlier, exhausted from her vigil at the hospital. The clock on Mark's side of the bed read a little after midnight. She must have been sleeping harder than she thought.

Shaking the dream from her mind, she called the hospital and talked to the nurse. Katie was doing fine and sleeping, the baby was stable. She should go back to bed. The nurse assured her they would call if anything changed. Claire wanted to ask the nurse if Mark stayed.

Claire had made wrong choices that would haunt her in the pre-dawn hours, choices with unwanted consequences.

Agnes once said, "What is, is." Claire missed the Southern belle. She didn't think she would, but she did, ole Agnes with her big breasts, oversized boots, and a heart as big as Texas itself. Claire checked the clock again and decided it was too early to call.

She couldn't fall back to sleep, so she walked to the kitchen and opened a bottle of Mark's wine. She sniffed the cork. She wasn't sure why since she knew the smell. Perhaps she was hunting for the essence of Mark, a part of him oozed from the grape itself. Full bodied, with a sweet fruity aftertaste. The open bottle in one hand, a glass in the other, she walked past the gazebo straight to the neatly plowed rows of the vineyard. This glass of wine needed to be drunk under the stars, paying homage to the richness of what was.

She and Mark used to wake when a baby cried in the night and walk them into the evening air. There was something calming and special about the smell of grapes, earth, and a gentle breeze. Many a night she fell asleep in the gazebo with a little cranky baby nuzzled against her neck.

The soil, still warm from the day, puffed around her bare feet while the light breeze lifted a wisp of curls from her cheek. The smell, the feel, everything spoke of Mark, of family, and of herself. She tried to see Jeff in this place. He didn't fit. She didn't fit in his life either. Changing a lifetime of West Coast orientation for the east was as foreign as drinking wine from a jelly glass.

A star shot across the sky.

"Star light. Star bright," she said aloud. "First star," she almost screamed, "Make my wish come true tonight."

Claire's power and peace, buried deep in her center, couldn't be put in words. She loved herself, and perhaps for the first time, realized happiness, security and dreams, existed always, waiting to shine. She swore she saw Paddy dancing on the Milky Way. He gathered a handful of stars and threw them over his head. "Catch them, darling." His voice sounded loud and clear.

She turned when Mark, calling her name, ran toward her.

"Wait, Claire," he called.

She turned to him. "Is Katie okay?" she yelled back.

"Katie and Patrick are fine," he said. When he reached her, he grabbed her hand, "I'm sorry I wasn't here when you and Katie needed me." He pulled her hand to his lips. Gathering her into his other arm, he whispered, "I'm so proud of you. You sacrificed your own safety to protect Katie." He kissed her lightly on the forehead.

Claire's body softened against him. "Mark," she whispered, "I'm sorry."

"Shh." He put a finger to her lips and pulled her tighter. "Later, we can talk later."

She saw another star, but no Paddy. She handed Mark the bottle of wine. He placed it on the post, letting the sliver of a moon backdrop it. He took the glass she was holding to his lips. "This is us. This blend, this adventure, this success or failure is us."

They drank from the glass, standing there under the stars. Watching some come to earth, others burning out before they came close, others shoot sideways, but each and every one of them beautiful. Each one announcing her wish had come true.

"This is the first time we aren't at the cabin for the meteor shower," she said.

"For the first time, I see their magic through your eyes," he said.

"Perhaps the real magic is they are predictable and return every August." She leaned closer and looked up at him. "Mark, do you love me?"

"If love means I am incomplete without you, then yes, I love you now and always have. Claire, you are the best part of me."

She melted against him, she felt his love, smelled it, absorbed it.

"Claire, do you love me?"

Her answer came swiftly. "Yes."

Epilogue

Ten Years Later...

Mark turned his face to the rising sun and drank in its warmth. He'd have to go in soon and Claire wouldn't be happy about all the mud on his shoes. He bent down and checked the water flowing from the pump as the stream stretched out through the rows of grapes.

His grapes, his vineyard, his winery. Who would have thought it possible that the wine he'd only made on a limited run would have taken over the market and allowed him and Claire to return to their beloved hills.

Last night she had teased him about the magical way it had all turned out and he assured her it was a logical progression. They'd laughed, and he pulled her against his chest for a long slow kiss. Thank God, she'd chosen him.

A few clouds gathered overhead, and he headed to his old truck. "Do I smell pecan rolls?" he asked when he entered the house and grabbed Claire around the waist, swinging her into his arms.

"The kids are coming home. It's their favorite." Claire kissed him on the cheek. "Two full pans now, with the three of them married and six grandchildren. How did that happen, Mark?"

"We need a bigger house," Mark commented as he did often. He could afford a much larger place now.

She reached up and touched the golden grapes at her throat. "I couldn't leave here. We did that once, and I was miserable."

"Are you sorry?"

She looked into his eyes and brushed the hair back from his graying temples. "I'm not sorry we moved. We both grew from it. I'm sorry we hurt each other, but it changed both of us for the better."

Tires crunching on gravel and a blaring horn announced the arrival of their offspring. Claire and Mark stepped out into the light shower and the vibrant hues of a rainbow arching across the sky.

She thought about pots of gold and leprechauns, he of prisms and reflecting lights.

Sean unwound from the car and held the door open for his wife, Megan. They each retrieved a child from their car seat before meeting his parents on the porch. "When do we leave for the lake?"

"As soon as the girls get here, and we have breakfast. We have plenty of time before the Perseid showers," Claire answered.

Mark caught her hand and brought it to his lips. "I think the more logical name is The Diamonds of August."

About the Author

Barbara Capell lives in Fresno, California. She has been married for fifty years and raised four children. Her lifelong commitment is to improve the lives and rights of the disabled.

When friends challenged her to write the stories she told, Ms. Capell's writing career began. She published her first essays after attending a writing course on Martha's Vineyard. Her collection of essays grows under the title of Pasta with a Side of Relatives.

Barbara's first nonfiction publication was in Physical Disability: Personal Perspectives. She wrote several articles for newsletters and magazines relating to raising a disabled child. She also has been published in Women's World. She has been given recognition at various writing conferences including, The Maui Conference, The William Saroyan Writer's Conference, and The Santa Barbara Conference.

Diamonds of August is her first novel.

Made in the USA
Coppell, TX
29 May 2020